Judith Lennox was born in Salisbury, Wiltshire, but spent most of her childhood in an isolated part of the Hampshire countryside, living in what had formerly been the gamekeeper's cottage of a large country house. After attending a variety of schools, she read English at Lancaster University, and has since worked as a civil servant, an abstracter of scientific reports, and as a pianist for a ballet school. She met her husband, Iain, at Lancaster. They have three sons and now live in Cambridgeshire. Her three most recent novels, *The Secret Years*, *The Winter House* and *Some Old Lover's Ghost*, are also published by Corgi Books.

Also by Judith Lennox

THE SECRET YEARS
THE WINTER HOUSE
SOME OLD LOVER'S GHOST

and published by Corgi Books

FOOTPRINTS ON THE SAND

Judith Lennox

CORGI BOOKS

FOOTPRINTS ON THE SAND
A CORGI BOOK : 0 552 14599 8

First publication in Great Britain

PRINTING HISTORY
Corgi edition published 1998

Set in 10/12pt Linotype Sabon by Kestrel Data, Exeter, Devon.

Corgi Books are published by Transworld Publishers Ltd,
61–63 Uxbridge Road, London W5 5SA,
in Australia by Transworld Publishers (Australia) Pty Ltd,
15–25 Helles Avenue, Moorebank, NSW 2170
and in New Zealand by Transworld Publishers (NZ) Ltd,
3 William Pickering Drive, Albany, Auckland.

Reproduced, printed and bound in Great Britain by
Cox & Wyman Ltd, Reading, Berks.

In memory of my mother

The Sandcastle

1920–1940

CHAPTER ONE

The first time she saw him, he was throwing a stick for a dog. The arc of his arm against a sky of gun-metal grey, the dog swimming through the icy sea to retrieve the stick; his red muffler a single bright light in all the monochrome. She noticed the way he bent and patted the mongrel, unbothered by the soaring droplets of water cast up from the shaken fur. When he threw the stick again, further out to sea, she closed her eyes and said to herself, *If he fetches it this time I shall train to be a stenographer*. When she looked up, she saw, just visible above the waves, the dog's muzzle, jaws clenching the stick, and she turned and walked back to the hotel.

It was April, a cold, cloudy April, and Poppy and her mother and sisters were holidaying in Deauville. Because of the war, the Vanburghs had not been abroad for over five years, since the summer of 1914. Yet Deauville was just as Poppy remembered it: the long, pale sands, the boardwalk, the casino and restaurant and shops. Had it not been for the young men in wheelchairs, scattered like so many bruised sunflowers to catch a non-existent sun, then Poppy, stupefied by boredom and restlessness, could have imagined herself immured still in her dull Edwardian childhood.

Breakfasts in the hotel were punctuated by Mama's

complaints about the food. 'The coffee . . . too dreadful . . . After all we have endured . . . The bread . . . such a frightful *colour* . . . and the rooms . . . so cold . . .' Each morning Poppy, thinking of the broken young men on the beach, wanted to say, *Yes, Mama, but at least you hadn't* sons! but each morning she remained silent and bit her lip, and let Rose and Iris soothe Mama's shattered nerves.

She had taken to walking alone after breakfast, bundling herself up in the fox fur that had been her birthday present the previous April, and striding fast along the sea front, the persistent wind whipping her yellow hair against her face as she tried to decide what to do with the rest of her life. In two weeks' time she would be twenty-one. Three years had passed since she had left school, three years that seemed to Poppy remarkable only for their lack of event. Even if she thought hard, she could remember little that had happened during those years. She was neither engaged nor married, and the succession of young men visiting the Vanburghs' London house had thinned noticeably as the war had progressed. She had no paid employment, and could think of none that particularly appealed to her. The annuity that her father had left her meant that she did not have to work for money, and when she mentally reviewed the jobs that girls of her age did – nurse, teacher, typist – she found it hard to imagine herself doing any of them. Yet she knew that she must do something. Her elder sisters showed her all too clearly what would become of her if she did nothing. Rose, at twenty-seven, was already slipping into old-maidish habits and turns of phrase, and Iris, at twenty-four, was dabbling in spiritualism.

The low, grey clouds that blurred the horizon, the

sting of rain that threaded through the wind, oppressed her. She loathed Deauville: it seemed to her as fixed and unchangeable and self-satisfied as home. Walking along the beach three times a day – before breakfast, after lunch, and at sunset – Poppy stabbed the heels of her shoes deep into the damp sand, as though by altering that small geography she could change the fixed routine of her life.

One cold Friday morning she saw him again. He was building a sandcastle. Because of the unseasonal weather, and the earliness of the hour, the beach was deserted except for the two of them, and the dog, cavorting on the shoreline. The castle flowered before him, an extraordinary edifice of turrets and draw-bridges and crenellations, encrusted with shells, beribboned with seaweed. It was the most beautiful sandcastle Poppy had ever seen. She marvelled that anyone should put such energy into something that was so inevitably temporary.

He was a big man, his fair hair a few shades darker than her own, his large hands delicate as they moulded shapes from the sand. His overcoat was long and heavy and collared with Persian lamb. The scarlet scarf flapped around his neck, and his head was covered with a wide-brimmed black hat that was slightly green with age. Certain that, absorbed in his task, he had not noticed her, she watched him press flat shells into ochre walls. His absorption in such a childish task fascinated her; she guessed that he was ten years or more older than she. She almost laughed at him, almost mocked him silently in her mind – but then a gleam of pink pierced the veil of grey cloud, the first sunshine in a fortnight, touching the miniature turrets, roofs and pinnacles with gold, giving the castle a fleeting, fairy-tale life. Poppy turned away, surprised that tears ached behind her eyes, yet as she began to walk back to the hotel a voice called after her. 'It needs flags, don't you think?' She glanced back and saw that he was standing upright, his hands in his pockets, looking at her. She had grown accustomed to men looking at her like that, so she put up the collar of her coat and walked haughtily on.

Yet, alone in the bedroom she shared with her elder sisters, Poppy found herself idly scribbling on the hotel notepaper. Flags, pennants, banners. And later, before dinner, she slid a cocktail stick from her glass into the palm of her glove. So silly, she told herself. Tomorrow the sandcastle would be gone, sucked away by the tides.

When she woke the following morning, she realized immediately that something had changed. The grey cloud had been dispersed by the sunlight that poured through the cracks in the shutters. A band of white light striped the polished floor. Poppy rose and dressed. Leaving the hotel, she felt the warmth on her bare arms and head as she ran along the sea front.

He was there, on the beach. It wasn't the same castle, but a new one, bigger and even more extravagant. She took the paper flags from her pocket. 'Here,' she said, and, as he looked up at her, he smiled.

'You must choose where to put them.'

She jabbed one cocktail stick into a turret, another at a corner of the battlements. Then she ran back to the hotel, to Mama's complaints and Rose and Iris's dullness.

They had come to Deauville ostensibly for Mama's health, in reality, Poppy guessed, because Mama treasured hopes of finding her three unwed daughters husbands among the other Britons holidaying there. Iris had once been engaged, but her young man had died in 1916, in the battle of the Somme.

'She has a photograph of Arthur, but it wasn't a good likeness, and now she can't really remember what he looked like,' Poppy explained to Ralph one day. Only he was not yet Ralph; he was still Mr Mulgrave.

They were walking along the sea front. He was always there when she went out for her early morning walk, and they had fallen quite naturally into the habit of conversation. In the warm spring sunlight he had abandoned his overcoat and scarf, and instead wore a jacket with patches on the elbows. Poppy said tentatively, 'And you, Mr Mulgrave? Did you . . . ?'

He was first bewildered, then amused. 'Fight for King and Country? Good God, no. What a perfectly appalling idea.'

'Oh,' she said, remembering posters (Your Country Needs You!), and white feathers, and certain newspaper articles. 'Were you a conscientious objector?'

He roared with laughter. 'The only thing worse than sitting in a trench and being shot at would be sitting in a prison cell being cold and hungry and miserable, for the sake of my *conscience*. I'm glad to say that I've never done anything for the sake of my conscience.'

They had stopped beside a small café. 'I've the most appalling headache,' he said. 'Shall we have coffee?'

Poppy knew that if she allowed Ralph Mulgrave to buy her coffee, she would be permitting the bounds of their friendship to progress from something that was acceptable to something that was not. She had not mentioned Mr Mulgrave to Mama; he was, she told herself, someone with whom she merely passed the time

13

of day. The café was small, dark, dingy, very French – not the sort of place Mama would permit her daughters to frequent. Mr Mulgrave held open the door; Poppy stepped inside.

Ralph ordered coffee for both of them, and a marc for himself. 'Hair of the dog,' he said, and Poppy smiled, uncomprehending. Then he said, 'I've been travelling for the past few years, actually. Mexico . . . Brazil . . . the Pacific . . .'

'How exciting!' she said, and then hated herself for sounding like a schoolgirl. 'I've always wanted to travel, but I've never been further than Deauville.'

'Hellish place,' he said. 'I hate the bloody north – gives me asthma.'

Poppy managed to hide her shock that he should swear in front of her.

'I did a spot of zinc mining in Brazil,' added Ralph. 'You can make a fortune, but it didn't suit my lungs. And I wrote a novel.'

'What was it called?'

'*Nymph in thy Orisons.*' He tipped sugar into his coffee.

Poppy's eyes widened. The Vanburghs' was neither a cultured nor a fashionable household, but even she had heard of *Nymph in thy Orisons*. She remembered Uncle Simon's outraged splutters as he had talked about the book.

'How clever you are!'

Ralph shrugged. 'It earned me some cash, but I'm not much of a writer, to tell the truth. I prefer to paint.'

'You're an artist?'

'I like to draw.' He fished in his pocket and took out a stub of pencil. Staring at her, Ralph began to sketch on the edge of the menu, his blue eyes darkening as he

14

concentrated. Suddenly nervous, Poppy felt obliged to fill in the gap.

'Rose wanted to be a landgirl, but Mama wouldn't let her, and Iris worked at the hospital for a while, but she found it very tiring. I thought I ought to do something, and when I left school I helped with rolling bandages, but I wasn't very good at it. They kept unrolling. And now I'm not sure *what* to do – I mean, girls aren't bus conductresses or tractor drivers any more, are they, and I suppose I could be a teacher or a nurse, but I'm probably not clever enough, and Mama wouldn't like it anyway. I should marry, but there don't seem to be many young men left, and—'

Her hand flew to her mouth, as if to halt the flow of words. He looked up at her and said calmly, 'Of course you'll marry. Beautiful girls can always find husbands.' Then he spun the menu round so that she could see the sketch that he had pencilled on one corner. Her heart-shaped face, framed by fair curls, her speedwell-blue eyes and unfashionably full mouth. It both shocked and excited her to see herself as he saw her.

'Oh!' she gasped. 'You *are* an artist!'

Ralph shook his head. 'I thought I might be once, but it didn't work out.' He tore off the corner of the menu, and presented it to her. 'Your portrait, Miss Vanburgh.'

On the rare occasions when Poppy was able to think clearly (when she was not envisaging his features, or recalling what he had said to her, word by word) it alarmed her to realize how easily she had drifted into the forbidden. The visit to the café became habitual; one day Ralph addressed her as Poppy, instead of Miss Vanburgh, and she, in turn, called him Ralph. He took her to another café, deeper in the backstreets of the town, crammed with friends who embraced him and welcomed her with kisses and compliments. He told her about himself: that he had run away from school at the age of sixteen, and had not returned to England since. He had travelled around Europe, sleeping in barns and ditches, and then had gone further afield, to Africa, and to the islands of the Pacific.

Ralph loathed England, and everything England stood for. He loathed the grey drizzle, the puritanical guilt of the English in taking pleasure, and their smug conviction of superiority. His ambition was to save enough money to buy a schooner and sail around the Mediterranean, trading in wine. He made friends easily – but Poppy knew that: when she walked through Deauville with Ralph, so many people waved and smiled. He was amusing, intelligent, perceptive and unconventional, and she knew also that she had fallen in love with him the very first time she had set eyes on him, throwing the stick for his dog. That everyone else seemed to love him both delighted and alarmed her: it confirmed the rightness of her affection, but made it possible that her passion, which seemed to her so unique, so particular, was not so.

She escaped from her mother and sisters one day after lunch, meeting Ralph at the road beyond the hotel. He had borrowed a motor-car, a gleaming open-top vehicle of cream and maroon, and he drove her along the coast to sample the gaudier delights of Trouville. He was taking her to visit a friend, he explained, a White Russian countess. Elena lived in a tall, thin, ramshackle house in the back streets of the town. Ralph introduced Poppy to Elena, who was dark and exotic and ageless, just as a White Russian countess should be. The party, which had already lasted a day and night, was not like any party she had been to before. Parties, in Poppy's experience, were restrained and rather awful affairs, in which one could earn lasting social ignominy by spilling one's glass of lemonade or saying the wrong thing, or dancing with the same partner too often. Here, she was given champagne, not lemonade. Here, she mistook the bathroom door, and found herself in a room where a couple embraced silently on a crimson brocade chaise-longue. Here, she danced all afternoon with Ralph, her head pressed against his shoulder, his big, gentle hands stroking her back.

Returning to Deauville she said, 'I won't be able to see you tomorrow, Ralph. It's my twenty-first birthday, so I'll have to spend the day with Mama and my sisters.'

He frowned, but said nothing, and she added, rather desperately, 'And in a few days' time, we're going home.'

'Do you want to go?'

'Of course not! But I must.'

'Must you?'

The champagne had begun to wear off, leaving her headachy and tired. She said tearfully, 'What else could I do?'

'You could stay here. With me.'

Her heart began to beat very fast. 'How?' she whispered.

'You just stay. You just don't go back. That's what I did.'

She wanted to say, *It's easy for you. You are a man*, but she did not, because they had turned the corner that led to the hotel, and there, on the pavement, like three avenging Fates, stood Mama and Rose and Iris.

Boxed in by traffic, there was no escape. Poppy had wild thoughts of hiding in the footwell, but Ralph restrained her. 'I shall introduce myself,' he said confidently, and threw his cigarette end out of the car as he drew to a halt beside Mrs Vanburgh and her daughters.

To Poppy it was a nightmare. Ralph was charm itself, his accent impeccable, and he did not swear once, but Mama, though civil, saw through him. Back at the hotel, the recriminations lasted for hours. Poppy told the truth sometimes (Ralph was of a respectable English family) and lied often (they had met each other once or twice, and they had just been on a short tour of Deauville), but her mother accurately sensed the worst. Questioned closely about Ralph's career, residence and prospects, Poppy found herself snufflingly admitting that he had no fixed abode, and had been, at various times, a tour guide, a commercial pilot, and a boat builder. *Labouring*, said Mrs Vanburgh, her lip curling in a condemnatory fashion, as Poppy managed to restrain herself from mentioning the time Ralph had danced with the wealthy ladies of Menton for money, or the winter he had kept himself from starvation by harvesting sugar beet.

Had it not been for Poppy's birthday the following day, then they would have entrained for Calais and the ferry that night. As it was, the birthday was a stiff, joyless affair, a weary round of breakfast and lunch and tea, and a duty call on two ladies Mama had known at school. Though everyone pretended that the shameful events of yesterday had not occurred, an air of disapproval lingered. Poppy had hoped for a note from Ralph – flowers, perhaps – but there was nothing. He knew it was her birthday, yet there was nothing.

Her jaw ached with the effort of smiling and, when she enquired at the hotel reception to be told yet again that there was no message, it was as though she had been stabbed to the heart.

By the time dinner was over, she knew that Mama had put him off, or his intentions had never been honourable, or she had been mistaken in believing that Ralph cared for her any more than he cared for the dozens of other women who were his friends. What should attractive, experienced Ralph Mulgrave see in silly, ignorant Poppy Vanburgh? Tomorrow they were to return to England. She could hardly recall her life there – it seemed like a dream – but she could imagine the emptiness of it. Tears stung her eyes, but she blinked them back. When dinner ended and Mama was stifling her yawns, and Iris and Rose were impatient to play bridge with the Colonel and his brother, Poppy rose from her seat.

'I'm going to look at the sea, Mama. I want to see the sunset for the last time.'

She walked outside before her mother could stop her. The breeze had picked up and she hugged her cold arms. The sun was a splash of gold and pink on the horizon, the colours caught by the rippling waves and the herringbone clouds. Poppy looked out at the water for a long time, mentally saying her farewells, and then she turned and saw him.

'Ralph. I thought you wouldn't come.'

'It's your birthday,' he said. 'I've brought you a present.' He handed her a scrap of paper.

She thought it was another sketch, but instead, unfolding it, she saw an official-looking form, printed in French. In her confusion she could not understand a word of it.

'It's a special marriage licence,' he said. 'I've been to Paris and back today for that.'

Speechless, she stared at him, her mouth open.

'They'll marry us tomorrow afternoon. And then we can go south. I have the most marvellous idea. Water-coolers. There must be a fortune to be made in water-coolers.'

'*Ralph*,' she whispered. 'I can't—'

'You can.' He laid his palms against her cheeks, raising her face towards his. 'I told you, dearest Poppy. You just walk out. You take a change of clothes and your passport and you walk out.'

'Mama will never give her permission—'

'You don't need your mother's permission. You are twenty-one.' Ralph pressed his lips against her forehead. 'It's up to you, Poppy. If you like, you can tell me to go, and I'll push off and you'll never see me again. Or you can come with me. Please come with me. I'll take you to the loveliest places on earth. You'll never be cold again, you'll never be bored again, and you'll never be lonely again. Please say that you'll come with me.'

The piece of paper shook in her hands like a leaf. Poppy whispered, 'Oh, *Ralph*,' and then she ran back into the hotel.

Poppy lost her virginity that night in a hotel somewhere between Deauville and Paris. They were married the next day, and then they travelled south. In rooms where the shutters were closed to keep out the burning southern sun, they made love, their bodies never quite sated, their delight in each other expressed not by words but by caresses and embraces.

Ralph kept his promises: Poppy saw the Provençal

hills and the exquisite beaches of the Côte d'Azur, and she was never bored, and never lonely. The birth of their daughter, Faith, not quite nine months later, in December, sealed their happiness. By then they were living in Italy, in a big Umbrian farmhouse. Poppy's annuity, and royalties from *Nymph in thy Orisons* supported them during lean months. Ralph was perfecting the water-cooler which would fund the schooner he intended to buy. Poppy imagined sailing through azure seas, her baby in a Moses basket on the deck, shaded by a parasol from the sun. In the early mornings, lying in bed, the sun gleaming in white strips through the shutters, Ralph's arms surrounded Poppy as he described to her the route their schooner would sail round the Mediterranean. 'Naples, Sardinia . . . and then Zante – Zante's the most beautiful island you've ever seen, Poppy.' She could see it in her mind's eye, the white sand and turquoise waves.

Friends of Ralph's called frequently, staying sometimes a few days, often for several months. Ralph was generous with his time, his company, his hospitality, and the house always resounded with argument and conversation and music. In April, when they moved to Greece, Ralph's friends came with them, a straggling caravanserai to share their stormy voyage across the Adriatic, to laugh and chatter as they rode mules through the stony hills of the isthmus. By then Poppy, who had rarely been allowed to trespass in the kitchen of her London home, had learned to make paellas and frittatas, roasts and *bourguignons*. She liked cooking, but loathed housework, so they lived in a well-fed, amicable mess.

A year later she gave birth to Jake. Jake was an active, tiring baby not much given to sleeping.

They had moved back to Italy, to Naples. The water-cooler had not proved a success, so they had had to delay the purchase of the schooner. Meanwhile they shared a tenement block with two potters. The big, dark rooms smelt of clay and paint. Ralph was to handle the financial side of the potters' business. Ralph's friends, whom Poppy had nicknamed the Lodgers, followed the Mulgraves to Naples. By now, Poppy had learned that Ralph, a man of extremes, had no acquaintances – he either loved wholeheartedly, or he took an immediate and irreversible dislike. To those he loved he was unstintingly generous. He had the knack of making each friend feel that they were the most important person in his life. He loved, Poppy realized, as a child did – uncritically, unreservedly. She recognized her own burgeoning jealousy of the Lodgers' demands on Ralph to be unreasonable, a shameful smallness of the heart. They, after all, only cherished what she herself loved.

Nicole was born in 1923, a painful and difficult confinement during which Poppy, for the first time since her marriage, cried for her mother. Poppy was unwell after the birth, so Ralph fed and bathed the newborn baby. He adored Nicole, whom he immediately perceived to be the prettiest and the brightest of the three.

When Poppy had recovered, the Mulgraves travelled to France, where Ralph rented a bar, the potters having absconded with the profits of Ralph's previous venture. Horribly short of money, they could afford neither a cook nor a nursemaid. Poppy learned how to make stews out of scrag end of lamb and boiling fowl, while the children ran wild. Sometimes she was so tired she fell asleep over the stove. She began to resent the

Lodgers, who drank the profits of the bar. When she complained to Ralph, he said, bewildered, 'But they are my *friends*, Poppy.' They quarrelled bitterly.

They were saved by Genya de Bainville, an old friend of Ralph's who, hearing of their arrival in the neighbourhood, and visiting the bar one day, noticed Poppy's grey face and Ralph's sulkiness. Genya invited all the Mulgraves to her château. La Rouilly was near Royan, on the Atlantic coast, and Genya was a Polish émigrée who had married a wealthy Frenchman. The remains of beauty could still be seen in Genya's high-cheekboned face, but the heat had baked her delicate complexion, so that it was cracked and crazed like the fields and vineyards of her estate. The years which had robbed Genya of her looks had also stolen from her much of her fortune. Parts of La Rouilly were semi-derelict, and, though Genya was in her sixties, she helped with the grape harvest, just as the Mulgraves did.

La Rouilly was four-square, its many windows enclosed by peeling green shutters, its lawns yellowed and dry, the gardens a half-hearted tangle of diseased begonias and roses which put out a great deal of leaf and very few flowers. Behind the château was a rank green lake, and behind that acres of woodland. Vineyards swathed the gently rolling hills. Poppy adored La Rouilly. She could have lived there for ever, helping Genya's ancient maid, Sarah, cook in the vast kitchen, coaxing fruit and flowers from the crumbling earth. The children and the Lodgers could easily be accommodated in La Rouilly's many rooms, and Genya, like Ralph, enjoyed company.

But as autumn came Ralph grew restless, new enthusiasms demanding his time and money, and they became nomads again, pursuing Ralph's dreams of the perfect country, the best-situated house, the scheme that would make the Mulgrave family's fortune. One year they travelled to Tahiti and to Goa; another year they sailed to Shanghai. In Shanghai, they all caught dengue fever, and it was thought for a while that Nicole would not recover. After that, Poppy insisted they remain within Europe.

Each summer, when things did not work out as Ralph had hoped, they returned to La Rouilly, to enjoy Genya's hospitality and to help with the *vendange*. Poppy measured the passing of the years by the heights of her children's heads against the twisted branches of the vines. In 1932 Jake, aged ten, caught up with Faith, to Faith's outrage and fury.

And in 1932, they met Guy.

Ralph brought Guy Neville back to La Rouilly one evening in August. Poppy was plucking chickens in the kitchen. She heard Ralph call from the back door.

'Where's the bloody key to the cellar, Poppy?'

She shouted, 'I think Nicole has it. She may have buried it.' She heard Ralph swear, so she added, 'She's with Felix. In the music room.'

Felix, who was a composer and a regular visitor to La Rouilly, was one of Poppy's favourite Lodgers.

'Dear God . . .' Ralph raised his voice again. 'I've brought someone.'

A young man emerged out of the gloom to stand in the kitchen doorway. He said hesitantly, 'Sorry to barge in on you like this, Mrs Mulgrave. I brought you these.'

'These' were a bunch of poppies and oxeye daisies. 'Just wild flowers,' he added apologetically.

'They're beautiful.' Poppy took the bunch from him and smiled. 'I'll find a vase. And you are . . . ?'

'Guy Neville.' He held out his hand.

He was tall and thin, and his silky dark hair was tinged with copper. She guessed him to be nineteen, twenty perhaps. He had the most extraordinary eyes: an intense bluish-green, with impossibly deep lids that crinkled up when he smiled. His accent was educated, middle-class English, the accent of Poppy's childhood, and she felt an unexpected pang of nostalgia. Quickly she mentally calculated whether dinner would stretch to another guest, decided it would, and wiped her bloody hands on her apron.

'I'm Poppy Mulgrave. You must excuse me. I do so loathe this job. The feathers are bad enough, but . . .' She made a face.

'I'll gut them, if you like. It's not nearly as bad as dissecting a lung.' He picked up a knife and set to.

'Are you a doctor?'

'A medical student. I finished my first year in July, so I thought I'd travel a bit.'

The door opened and Faith came in. 'Nicole is crying because Pa made her dig up the key. But I'm glad, because it's better than that awful caterwauling.'

Faith, at eleven and a half, was small and scrawny and Poppy's principal comfort. Faith had a vein of common sense that, Poppy feared, both her brother and her sister lacked. Just now, she was wearing a long lace petticoat that swept the ground and an old jersey of Poppy's with holes in the elbows. She glanced across the kitchen and whispered: 'One of Pa's waifs and strays?'

'I think so,' Poppy whispered back. 'He's very good at gutting poultry, though.'

Faith circled the table, the better to see Guy. 'Hello.'

Guy looked up. 'Hello.'

She watched him for a moment, and then said, 'There always seems to be far more of that stuff' – she indicated the mass of offal – 'than one would reasonably think, doesn't there?'

He grinned. 'I suppose so.'

She explained, 'Felix is teaching Nicole to sing and Jake to play the piano, but he says that it's pointless doing anything with me because I'm tone deaf.'

'Me too,' said Guy amiably. 'If I hit the right note it's just luck.'

Back at Poppy's side, Faith muttered, 'He looks awfully hungry, don't you think?'

Poppy glanced at Guy. He looked, she thought, half starved. As though he hadn't had a decent meal for weeks. 'The chicken will take ages to cook – they're rather old and scraggy. Find some bread and cheese, won't you, darling?'

Because there were ten other guests staying at La Rouilly, each one demanding Ralph's time and attention, Faith decided to adopt Guy. He intrigued her. He had gutted the chickens with such careful precision – a Mulgrave would have stabbed wildly and violently, achieving much the same result, but with far more mess. At dinner, he argued with Ralph, but with a politeness and restraint never seen before at La Rouilly. He did not slam his wineglass on the table to make his point, or storm off in a huff when Ralph told him that his opinions were idiotic. Every time Poppy stood up, Guy sprang up too, helping her to collect dirty plates, opening the door for her.

The drinking and conversation drifted to a halt in the

early hours of the morning. Poppy had gone to bed hours ago, and Ralph had fallen asleep in his chair. Guy glanced at his watch and said, 'I hadn't realized . . . how rude of me. I must go.'

He retrieved his knapsack from the kitchen, and stumbled out into the dark. Faith followed him. On the gravel forecourt he paused, looking blearily around him.

'Are you all right?'

'Lost my bearings rather. Can't remember the way back to the village.'

'Don't you want to stay the night?'

'I couldn't impose—'

'You could have one of the attic bedrooms, but really, they're not very pleasant – bits fall off the ceiling. It would probably be much nicer sleeping in the barn.'

'May I? If it's not too much trouble—'

'No trouble at all,' said Faith politely. 'I'll get you a blanket.'

After she had fetched the blanket and a pillow, she showed him the barn. 'You just hump up some straw and curl up in the blanket. Nicole and I sometimes sleep out here when it's very hot. It's best to be high up because of the rats.'

He was emptying the contents of his knapsack onto the straw. She watched him. 'Everything's *folded*.'

'Habit. Boarding school, you see.'

She plumped up the pillow for him, and took a stub of candle from her pocket. 'You can have this if you want to read.'

'Thanks, but I've a torch. I wouldn't want to burn the place down, and I just might, the amount I've drunk.'

Faith brought Guy breakfast the next morning: two white peaches and a bread roll, wrapped in a grubby tea cloth, and a mug of black coffee. He was asleep, all but his head and one outstretched arm wrapped in the blanket. She looked at him for a moment, thinking how still he was, how different from Jake, who always snored and snuffled in his sleep, and then, softly, she said his name. He groaned, and opened one blue-green eye. Focusing, he said, 'I have the most appalling headache.'

'Pa's guests often do, I'm afraid. I've brought you something to eat.'

He sat up. 'I'm not all that hungry.'

Sitting in the straw beside him, she wrapped his hands round the coffee. 'Drink this, then. I made it.'

Guy glanced at his watch. 'Eleven o'clock – good God—' He groaned again, screwing up his eyes.

'Only Genya and me are up. At least, I'm not sure where Jake is. He's my brother,' she explained. 'We haven't seen him since . . .' she scowled '. . . Tuesday.'

It was Sunday. Guy said, 'Are your parents worried?'

Faith shrugged. 'Jake goes away for weeks, sometimes. Ma fusses a bit. Drink your coffee, Guy,' she added kindly, 'and then you'll feel better.'

He drank; she fed him little bits of bread roll. After a while he said, 'I must go.'

'Why?'

'I don't want to outstay my welcome.'

Faith looked at him, fascinated. She could not recall any of the Lodgers ever saying such a thing. 'Pa won't mind, you know. In fact, he'll be furious if you leave today, because it's his birthday. We're to go and look at a boat that he wants to buy, and then we're having a picnic on the beach. We always have a picnic on the beach on his birthday. He'll expect you to be there.'

'Really?'

'Really,' she said firmly. 'Where did Ralph meet you, Guy?'

He looked rueful. 'I was trying to hitch-hike to Calais. Some bastard – sorry, some blighter – in Bordeaux stole my wallet and my passport. I'll have to go to the consulate, I suppose.'

She studied him again. His dark eyelashes were longer than hers, which seemed unfair. 'Where do you live?'

'In England. In London.'

'What's your house like?'

'Just an ordinary red-brick London villa. You know the sort of thing.'

She didn't, but she nodded. 'And your family?'

'There's just my father and me.'

'You haven't a mother?'

'She died when I was quite little.'

'Won't your father be lonely, all by himself?'

He grimaced. 'He says not. He told me to go – he believes that travel broadens the mind.'

'Then Mulgraves must have immensely broad minds,' she said, 'because we're always travelling.'

He glanced at her. 'What do you do about school? Do you have a governess?'

'Ma tries every now and then, but they always seem to leave. The last one didn't like spiders, so you can imagine what she thought of La Rouilly. Sometimes Jake goes to the village school, but he gets into fights. Felix has taught us music, and one of the Lodgers taught us to shoot and to ride. Pa says that those are the most important things.'

Over the next few days, Guy said every now and then, 'I really ought to leave . . .' but Faith reassured him, and La Rouilly worked its magic, and after a while he, like the rest of them, seemed to slip into a different rhythm, rising late, eating long, lazy meals, arguing and drinking with Ralph until the early hours of the morning, passing the day in the company of Poppy or Felix or the children.

Rowing on the slimy, frog-infested lake behind the château, Jake pestered Guy for stories about school.

'A cold bath every morning? When you weren't even dirty? Why?'

'Next to godliness, I suppose,' said Guy, sculling the oars.

All three Mulgraves looked at him blankly. 'If you're well washed, you're close to God,' explained Guy. He shrugged. 'Ridiculous, of course.'

'Tell us about the breakfasts,' said Nicole.

'Porridge and kippers. Porridge is a sort of pudding made from oatmeal, and kippers are smoked fish with lots of little bones.'

'It sounds disgusting.'

'It was perfectly foul. But you had to eat it.'

'Why?'

'It was a rule.'

'Like Mulgrave Rules,' said Faith.

He asked curiously, 'What are Mulgrave Rules?'

Faith glanced at her brother and sister. 'Keep out of Pa's way when he's in a temper,' she recited. 'Try to persuade Pa to let Ma choose the house.'

'If the natives are hostile,' supplied Jake, 'then speak in a foreign language to confuse them.'

'And if they are really horrible and throw stones at you, then never, ever let them see that you mind,' finished Nicole. 'Stick together whatever the cost.' She stared at Guy. 'Was your school always in the same place?'

'After I was twelve, yes.'

Faith took the oars from Guy. 'We've never lived in the same place for more than a year, you see, Guy. Apart from La Rouilly, of course, but that's only for a few months at a time. We envy you terribly. You're so lucky.'

'School was quite dull, actually. Not enviable at all.'

Faith fixed her mournful grey-green eyes on him. 'But your things would always be in the same place. You'd have your own plates and chairs, not other people's. You could have nice things and they wouldn't get lost, and they wouldn't have to be left behind because they couldn't be fitted into a suitcase. And having your dinner at the same time each day.' Her voice was awed. 'And socks without holes.'

'I hadn't thought of it like that.'

Faith began to row across the lake, her skinny arms pulling at the oars, the boat lurching as they became entangled in duckweed. 'So lucky,' she said again.

He came back to La Rouilly the following summer. Faith was sunbathing on the roof when she caught sight of him, a little matchstick man at first, and then unmistakably Guy, walking down the long winding path to La Rouilly. He visited again the next summer, and the summer after that. Faith always thought of Guy as her responsibility. She, alone among the Mulgraves, sensed a vulnerability in Guy, a darker side to his easy-going nature, a willingness to take the troubles of the world upon his shoulders. If she came across him looking bleak, then she suggested diversions, or simply mocked him until he cheered up. The best moment of the whole year, she thought privately, the moment she would have liked to set in amber, was the moment that Guy Neville returned to La Rouilly.

Each summer, they swam in the lake, where the water was a thick, limpid green. Each summer they picnicked on wild strawberries picked from the borders of the fields, washed down with the château's sharp white wine. Each summer the entire family, Lodgers and estate workers as well, lined up on La Rouilly's front steps when Guy took a photograph with his box Brownie.

In the summer of 1935 they hunted for truffles in the forest. Nicole thwacked the undergrowth with a stick in a desultory fashion.

'What do they look like?'

'Like dirty stones.'

'We need a truffle hound.'

'Jake has Genya's pig.'

'I loathe truffles anyway. And it's too hot to walk.' Nicole collapsed to the forest floor, flinging her bare legs out in front of her, her back resting against a tree trunk. 'Let's play charades.'

'Not enough people.' Faith peered through the dark canopy of the forest. 'I can't see Jake or Guy.'

'Or the pig.' Nicole giggled. 'Associations, then.'

Associations was a fearfully complicated game of Ralph's. Faith perched on a branch above Nicole. 'Much too hot. I've a headache already.'

'Favourite things, then.'

'If you like. Only don't ask me about music, because I can never remember.'

Nicole looked up at Faith. 'You must tell the truth, remember.'

'Cross my heart and hope to die.'

'Favourite beach, then.'

'Zante.'

'I preferred Capri. Favourite house.'

'La Rouilly, of course.'

'Of course.'

'My turn. Favourite book.'

'*Wuthering Heights*. Absolutely most favourite hero – Heathcliff, naturally.'

'He would be impossible to live with,' said Faith. 'He would fuss if his toast was burnt, or if there wasn't enough sugar in his coffee.'

'And you, Faith?'

'And me, what?'

'Your absolutely most favourite hero.'

Faith sat on the branch, swinging her legs. Every now and then a ray of sunlight pushed through the tapestry of branches, blinding her.

Nicole called up, 'The truth, mind!'

'It's a silly game.' She jumped down, scattering Nicole with leaf-mould.

'That's not fair.' Nicole was aggrieved. 'You promised. You must at least tell me what he looks like. Is he dark or fair?'

'Dark.'

'His eyes . . . are they blue or brown?'

She thought, *They are a dark bluish-green, the colour of the Mediterranean sea when it's in shade*. She felt inexplicably miserable, and began to walk away from Nicole, kicking a path through the ranks of wild garlic. Nicole's voice followed her – 'It's not fair! So mean, Faith!' – as she ran down the slope, out of earshot.

The undergrowth became more luxuriant as she descended the bank. The thick froth of hemlock and bramble reached her waist, and goosegrass clung to her skirt, so she hoicked it up, tucking it into her navy-blue knickers. Tall green stems brushed against her thighs. The trees made a dark roof overhead, pierced by strands of golden light. As she walked into the bowl of the valley, the heat weighed her down. The trees thinned, and sunshine illuminated the tangle of brambles and shrubs. She saw that the flowers and foliage were dotted with Holly Blue butterflies, their tiny wings a pale purplish-blue edged with a narrow border of black. As Faith approached, they rose in the air like fragile scraps of blue silk blown by the wind, shimmering in the sun.

The adder was invisible, coiled among the crumbling leaf-mould and dog's mercury. The earth seemed for a moment to squirm beneath her foot, and then something stabbed her ankle. She saw the snake slither away, and she looked down at the two small puncture marks it had left in her skin. It was strange, Faith thought, how things could change in a moment from being pleasant and ordinary to being quite frightening. She imagined the poison seeping through her veins, tainting her blood, chilling her heart. She looked quickly around, and could at first see no-one. The forest seemed cold, unpopulated, threatening. Then, on the high bank ahead, she saw a shadow move, and, calling out, she began to clamber up the slope.

'Faith?'

She heard Guy's voice, and she looked up. 'An adder's bitten me, Guy.'

He said quickly, 'Don't move. Keep still,' and he ran down the bank, hacking through the undergrowth, hitting the nettles and brambles aside with a stick. When he reached her, he knelt on the ground and pulled off her sandal and put his mouth to her ankle and sucked, pausing every now and then to spit out venom. After a while Faith began to feel cold and shivery inside, so Guy, standing up, peeled off his jacket and wrapped it round her. Then he scooped her up in his arms.

Her foot felt as though someone had bashed it with a mallet. Overhead, glimpsed through the dark branches of the trees, the sun was a hard, bright drumskin that throbbed in rhythm with her aching foot. Carrying her, Guy pushed fast through the forest, knocking the low-slung branches aside with his shoulders. When they emerged from the shelter of the trees, the sun bore down with full force. Heat and drought had reduced the lawn to a square of baked earth; the grass was a stubble of dried, brownish raffia. The sky itself glared. There was a shout as Poppy, weeding the vegetable patch, caught sight of them and began to run across the lawn.

For the next couple of days, Faith sat on the battered sofa in the kitchen, her swollen foot propped on a heap of cushions. An endless stream of visitors diverted her. 'Felix has sung to me,' she explained to Guy, 'and Luc and Philippe have played poker with me, and all the children have come to see the marks the adder's teeth made. Really, I'm not used to it, Guy – it's usually Nicole and Jake who get all the attention, because they are better-looking and more talented and altogether more adorable.'

In Faith, the Mulgrave features had concentrated into something not conventionally beautiful. Faith despaired of her high, bony forehead, her pale hair that

35

neither curled nor lay straight, her onyx-green eyes that, no matter how she felt, always looked desolate.

Guy ruffled her hair. 'You won't have time for me.'

She looked up at him. 'Oh, I'll always have time for you, Guy. You saved my life. That means that I'll always be indebted to you. I'm yours for ever now, aren't I?'

In the autumn, they travelled to Spain. Three of Ralph's friends had bought a farmhouse where they intended to make their fortunes growing saffron. 'Worth its weight in gold, Poppy,' explained Ralph. The Mulgraves had lived in Spain before, in Barcelona and Seville, so Poppy anticipated blue seas and lemon trees and fountains in marbled courtyards.

The saffron farm shocked her. Clinging to the edge of a village on a vast, featureless plain, the house, which they would share with Ralph's friends, was sprawling and tumbledown. Small windows looked out onto land so arid that Poppy found it hard to believe that anything could grow there. The only colours were red and ochre and brown. The village was peopled by skinny donkeys and downtrodden peasants whose way of life, Poppy thought, must have altered little since the time of the Black Death. When it rained, the dust turned to mud so deep it came up to Nicole's knees. There was mud everywhere; even the peasants' shacks seemed to be made of mud. The house had neither running water nor a stove. Water had to be fetched from the village well, food cooked on an open fire. The saffron farmers, all male, seemed to have lived on unleavened bread and olives – the house was littered with crusts and pips. Showing Poppy the primitive kitchen, one of Ralph's friends said, 'I'm so glad you've come. You'll be able to cook us proper meals.' Poppy, looking at the kitchen, wanted to weep.

At the end of a week, she drew Ralph aside and told him that it was impossible. He looked at her, uncomprehending. The house, she explained. The village. The cold, poverty-stricken countryside. They must leave, they must return to civilization.

Ralph was bewildered. The house was fine, the company was good. Why on earth should they leave?

Poppy argued, Ralph became truculent. Their voices rose, echoing against the smoky ceiling of the house. Ralph remained obdurate – they'd make a fortune if only she would be patient, and besides, he had invested the income from both his royalties and Poppy's annuity in bulbs and equipment. They could not possibly leave. When Poppy, losing her temper, hurled a plate at his head, Ralph escaped to his saffron fields, to drown his feelings in a bottle of sour red wine.

When she was alone, Poppy's anger dissipated into misery, and she collapsed on a chair and wept. Over the next few weeks, she tried to make the house habitable. But it defeated her constantly. Ralph's friends left a trail of muddy footprints through every room; the kitchen fire, infected by the damp and cold of the plain, died at the most inopportune moments. Sheets and towels once washed grew mould before they dried. The lack of any adult female company depressed her.

As the winter passed at last, and a feeble spring approached, she began to feel unwell. Because she had not fallen pregnant in the twelve years since Nicole's birth, Poppy did not realize that she was expecting a fourth child until she was several months gone. She put her nausea and lethargy down to the damp house, the hateful countryside. But, visiting a doctor in Madrid, she was told that she was pregnant, and the child would be born in September. Poppy heaved a sigh of relief: her baby would be born at La Rouilly with dear, reliable old Dr Lepage in attendance.

If parts of her life with Ralph had not worked out quite as she had expected (yet what had she expected, leaving for Paris with him, that long-ago evening in Deauville?), she had always delighted in her babies, and to have a fourth child would be a luxury. Her first three children had been born in such quick succession that, by the time Nicole had come along, she had been almost too exhausted to enjoy her. Poppy knitted tiny cardigans, and sewed nightdresses, and dreamed of France and leaning out of her *bateau-lit* and seeing her son in a cradle beside her. She was sure that she was expecting a boy.

She gave birth to a son, but in Spain, not France. Her child was born two months early, in the bedroom that she shared with Ralph. There was no doctor for fifty miles, so a black-shawled woman from the village helped with the delivery. Poppy did not possess a cradle, but in the event she did not need one, because her baby lived only for a few hours. She lay in bed with her son nestled in the crook of her arm, willing him to live. He was too weak to suckle from her breast. The midwife insisted on fetching a priest, who christened the child Philip, after Poppy's favourite uncle. When the small movement of the child's lungs finally stilled, Ralph sobbed as he took the infant from Poppy's arms.

A week later, Ralph suggested that they leave early for France. Poppy refused. She had said little since Philip's birth and death; now she voiced a small but definite no. When Ralph explained to her that the soil had proved unsuitable for saffron, and that the house was too remote for many of his friends to visit, and that he had just thought of a marvellous scheme to recover the money they had lost, still she shook her head. Throughout the day, she sat in the shade of the porch, her eyes fixed on the shrivelled remains of the plants in the field, and on the distant churchyard.

In mid-July, when civil war broke out in Madrid, Ralph again urged her to leave. Once more, Poppy shook her head. It was only when one of Ralph's friends explained to her that the chaos that was enveloping Spain was a threat to the Mulgraves' remaining children that she finally agreed that Faith should pack.

They left Spain two days later, travelling overland to Barcelona, and from Barcelona to Nice on a boat packed with refugees and soldiers and nuns. Sitting on the deck, watching the Spanish coast slide away, it seemed to Poppy as though her heart was being torn from her ribcage.

At La Rouilly, she tried to explain to Genya how she felt. 'I had to leave him behind, in that awful place, on his own. So dreadful, to have to leave him there on his own!' Poppy broke off, blinking rapidly. 'Such a horrible place. I thought I would go mad there. So desolate and vile and everyone seemed so poor. And I've read in the newspapers that they are burning the churches and killing the priests. And I keep thinking . . . I keep thinking, Genya, what if they desecrate the graves? What if—?' Poppy's hand clutched Genya's fragile wrist. She looked as though she might be sick.

Genya hugged her. Poppy's entire body shook as she

wept. After a while, Genya poured a glass of brandy, and enfolded it between Poppy's shaking fingers.

'Drink, dear Poppy – it will make you feel better. I have a cousin in Madrid. If you tell me the name of the village in which you lived, Manya may be able to check that everything is all right.'

Poppy stared at her. 'Oh, Genya. Would you?'

'It may take a while. Where does Ralph plan to go this autumn?'

She shrugged. 'I don't know. You know what he's like – I don't know until the day he tells me to pack.' Her voice was bitter. 'The riviera, perhaps. Ralph likes the riviera in winter.'

'Then I'll write poste restante to Nice when I have news.'

Poppy rose, and went to the window. She said slowly, 'Do you know, Genya, a few mornings ago I opened the shutters, and I couldn't for a moment remember which country I was in. It all begins to look the same after a while. Trees with yellowing leaves, and fields where nothing much seems to grow, and dreary, peeling little buildings. It all begins to look the same.'

She did not, though, tell Genya how angry she felt with Ralph: she could not voice that to anyone. It was like a living thing, a consuming passion, stronger even than grief, nurtured in any quiet moments. Although a part of her knew that she was unfair in blaming Ralph for Philip's death – her body had cast the child out too soon, after all – her anger persisted. *If* he had not taken her to that awful place; *if* he had not insisted on staying there in spite of her pleas to leave. She did what she had never done before: she turned away from him in bed, telling him that she had not yet recovered from the premature birth. It pleased her to see the hurt on Ralph's face when she rejected his embraces.

They stayed that winter in Marseilles, in an apartment in the back streets of the city. Ralph was pursuing his latest venture, selling rugs imported from Morocco. Poppy travelled each month to Nice, calling at the post office. The letter arrived in February. Genya wrote, 'My cousin Manya was able to visit the village where you lived just after Christmas. The church and the graveyard are untouched, Poppy. Manya put flowers on the grave as I asked her to.'

Standing alone on the sea front, looking out to the shingly beach, Poppy wept. After a while she realized that the grey waves, the overcast sky, reminded her of that long-ago holiday in Deauville in 1920. She knew – had known for some weeks – that Ralph, hurt by her coldness, had begun a flirtation with a Lodger called Louise. Louise, a very silly girl, bestowed on Ralph an uncritical admiration that was a balm to his wounded pride. Poppy knew that she now had a choice: she could punish Ralph further and in doing so give him to Louise or Louise's successor, and let her marriage fall apart; or she could reclaim him, and show him that, although things had changed, she still loved him. She thought of her children, and she recalled a man building a sandcastle on a beach: a fragile edifice, but one whose beauty had made her cry. Blowing her nose, wiping away her tears, Poppy headed for the railway station.

At home, she showed Genya's letter to Ralph. He said nothing, but stood by the window, his back to her. But she saw that the single piece of paper trembled in his hands, so she went and put her arms round his bent shoulders and kissed the back of his neck. She noticed

41

that he had put on weight, and that his hair was now more silver than fair. Though she was thirteen years younger than Ralph, she felt just then much older. They stood for a long time holding each other and then they went to bed and made love.

Yet some of the changes in her were permanent. When Ralph, showing her a scrap of paper on which he had scribbled figures, said, 'We'll have enough for the schooner in six months' time, Poppy, I believe. The rug business is going well – people here will pay ten times what they charge for these things in North Africa,' she smiled, but said nothing, knowing that none of his previous ventures had lasted more than a year. For the first time she set up a bank account in her own name and put the interest from her annuity into it instead of giving it to Ralph. The apartment in which they were staying was small and poky. Poppy sensed the approach of harder times.

And she had begun to long for dull English summers, and box hedges fringed grey with frost, and a pale, early morning sun gleaming through bare oaks and beeches. Losing her son, she had also lost her ability to share Ralph's belief in a rosy future. She saw the pitfalls, the dangers, of their way of life. At the age of thirty-eight, she had begun at last, she thought, to grow up.

When, in the summer of 1937, the first week of August came and went and Guy had not yet arrived at La Rouilly, Faith took to haunting the château's vast attics, where she could be alone with the heat and the flies, and from where she could see, through small, dusty windows, the path that wound through the woodland from the road.

The attics were full of treasures. Hideous lampshades and impossibly dull, mould-encrusted books, and an entire trunkful of rusting swords. And boxes and boxes of clothes. Faith unfolded them carefully, reverently. Tissue paper whispered like butterfly wings. Buttons glinted, ribbons gleamed. The names embroidered on the labels – Poiret, Vionnet, Doucet – seemed like poetry. In the dim light of the attics, she exchanged her faded cottons for chiffon the colour of gossamer and cool waterfalls of silk. In a gold-framed mirror she studied her reflection. The past year had altered her. She had grown taller. Cheekbones had given shape to her face; newly acquired breasts and hips made the dresses hang properly.

Yet growing up seemed also to have peeled a layer from the surface of her heart. Though she had always anticipated Guy Neville's arrival at La Rouilly with pleasure, his lateness this summer made her edgy and uncertain. Nervous of ridicule, she confided her misery to no-one. Though they all waited for Guy – though Poppy tutted and glanced at the calendar, and Ralph and Jake argued noisily – Faith found herself unable to voice the fear that had gripped her: that Guy would not come to La Rouilly again. That he had forgotten them. That he had found better things to do.

A year ago she would have grumbled with Nicole; a year ago she would have soothed Jake's temper. Now she could not. She was caught in a cobweb as dense as any spun from the rafters of the attic, a web of tedium and irritation and longing. She wondered whether she was in love with Guy, and thought that if she was, then love was not as wonderful as novels led you to believe. She lost the desire to take part in the pleasures and distractions that La Rouilly provided. Without Guy, she did not want to row on the lake, or to picnic in the forest. She found it hard to fill the days. Thus the attics, which were her kingdom, and empty of reminders.

She saw him first through the fingertip-width of cobweb she had rubbed from a window pane. A small, dark figure, hunchbacked from his rucksack, walking down the winding path that led from the road to the château. In an instant she forgot all the boredom, all the waiting, and, calling his name, ran downstairs.

On Ralph's fifty-second birthday, they picnicked on the beach at Royan. From a conical pyre of driftwood, smoke drifted lazily out to sea. The sun, dipping towards the horizon, washed the waves with a gleaming, satiny fire.

They talked about Spain. Faith, watching the sunset, half listened to the conversation.

'The Republicans will win,' declared Jake.

Felix shook his head. 'Not a hope, my dear boy.'

'But they *have* to—'

'With Stalin's help—' began Guy.

'Stalin has been half-hearted.' Felix was dismissive. 'He's afraid that if he's seen to support the Republic, then Germany will have an excuse to attack Russia.'

The last fishing-boats, sailing into harbour, were silhouetted against a golden sky. Faith watched Guy drain the last drop of wine from his glass. Ralph uncorked another bottle. 'Nothing to do with us, anyway. The whole bloody mess is nothing to do with anyone but the Spanish.'

'Not so, Ralph. If we let Franco win then sooner or later we'll all be dragged in.'

'To a civil war? Nonsense. Absolute bloody

nonsense. The sun has turned your brain, Felix.' Ralph refilled Felix's glass.

One of the Lodgers, a French poet, said, 'Spain is the last romantic war, don't you think? I'd join the International Brigades myself if it wasn't for my liver.'

'*Romantic?*' roared Ralph. 'Since when was war romantic? Hideous bloody business.'

'Ralph, dear.' Poppy patted his hand.

The oyster nets, and the masts of the fishing-boats, were like black lace against the shifting silk of the sea. Felix threw another piece of driftwood on the fire, and coughed.

'I have to tell you, Ralph – and you, dear Poppy – that I shall sail for America at the end of September. My visa has come through at last.' Felix placed a hand on Ralph's arm, and said gently, 'You must understand, Ralph. It'll be safer.'

'Good God, man – what are you talking about?'

'I am Jewish, Ralph.'

Faith, sitting on the sand, only just caught the quiet words. There was a patient, almost pitying expression in Felix's eyes. Recently, Faith had sometimes seen Poppy look at Ralph like that.

'Ralph, who is to say what may happen to France in a year or two? Where will you go when you leave La Rouilly in the autumn? Spain is in turmoil, and Italy has its own brand of fascism.' Felix shook his head. 'I cannot stay.'

There was a silence. The sun touched the horizon, spilling bronze shadows over the tranquil sea. Ralph said truculently, 'All my friends are abandoning me. Richard Deschamps is working as a *banker*, for God's sake, and Michael and Ruth have gone back to England because they want to send their sprogs to some hellish prison camp of a school. Lulu wrote to me to say that she's nursing her sick mother. *Lulu*. Mopping fevered brows! And I haven't seen Jules since he fell in love with that boy in Tunis. As for you, Felix, you are a money-grabbing little Jew who'll probably become a millionaire writing music for appalling Hollywood films.'

Felix was not offended. 'What a pleasant prospect. I shall send you a photograph, Ralph, of my chauffeur and my Daimler.'

Faith saw that Guy had risen, and was walking away from the circle on the beach, towards the dunes. She followed him, placing her bare feet in the indentations in the sand that his steps had made. She caught up with him as he climbed to the summit of a dune. The setting sun made inky shadows in the hollow below.

He smiled at her. 'That's a beautiful dress, Faith.'

Guy rarely noticed what she wore. She felt a surge of pleasure. 'It's my Holly Blue dress, Guy. You know, after the butterfly – it's the same colour, you see.' The silk crêpe de Chine was a pale violet-blue, and the sleeves of the dress were decorated with narrow black velvet ribbon. 'It belonged to Genya, but she doesn't fit in it any more, so she's given it to me. It's made by the House of Paquin.'

Guy looked blank. She hooked her hand round his arm. 'You are an ignoramus, Guy. Madame Paquin is a very famous couturier.'

He touched the filmy fabric. 'It suits you.'

Her delight doubled. 'Do you think so?'

He frowned, and looked out to sea, and said, 'I'd meant to tell Ralph that I'll have to leave in a day or two, but it doesn't seem the right time, because of Felix.'

46

Her happiness was extinguished, a fragile candle flame snuffed between forefinger and thumb.

'You've only been here a few days, Guy.'

He took his cigarettes out of his pocket. 'I'm worried about my father. He won't admit it, but I think he's ill.' Guy struck a match, but the breeze blew it out. 'Damn.' He glanced at her, grinned, and grabbed her hand. 'Run for it.'

They tumbled down the steep slope of the dune, landing in a sprawling, laughing heap in the hollow of sand. Guy flung his jacket over the spiky marram grass. 'Here, Faith.'

She sat down beside him. The dunes cut them off from the party on the beach. Sand squeezed between her toes. Guy offered her a cigarette. Faith had practised smoking with Jake: she held her untidy curtain of hair out of the way while Guy struck a match.

She said, after a while, 'Tell me about London. I always think it sounds so marvellous.' Poppy had described afternoon teas at Fortnum & Mason, and shopping in Liberty and the Army & Navy store.

'Hackney's pretty hideous, to tell the truth. A lot of hardship – fathers out of work, kids without shoes. Most people are uninsured, which means they have to pay for a doctor. And the places they live – vile basements and rooms that are damp and infested with cockroaches.' She could hear the anger in his voice. 'So they need good doctors, you see.'

'And your father's a good doctor?'

'One of the best. Only—' Guy stubbed his cigarette out in the sand.

'What, Guy?'

'Only I'd meant to be a surgeon.' He shrugged. 'But

47

Dad needs help, and the practice doesn't pay well, so it all seems rather impossible.' He scowled. 'It doesn't matter. It's doing good that's the important thing, isn't it? Making people's lives better . . . giving them a chance. Not letting them die of curable diseases just because they happen to be poor.'

He lay back on the sand, his arms cushioning his head. Faith shivered. The sun had almost set, and it was growing colder. The Holly Blue dress was flimsy.

'Here. Lean on me.' Guy curled his arm round her, drawing her to him. 'I'll keep you warm.'

She laid her head on his chest. He had held her before, when she was a child, when, perhaps, she had fallen and he had comforted her, but now his touch seemed different. Stranger, more wonderful. She heard him say, 'And you, Faith – what do you want to do?'

She looked up at the sky. The first stars were showing. She smiled. 'I'd quite like to be one of those ladies who works in a casino.'

'A croupier?'

'Mmm. Then I could wear an extraordinary dress with sequins and ostrich feathers. Or I'd like to be in a film, but Pa says I have a voice like gravel in a bucket. Or I could be a hairdresser for poodles.'

'Do they have such things?'

'They have beauty parlours for poodles in Nice, Guy. Dogs always like me, and I'm sure I could get the hang of the curlers.'

She knew that he was laughing because his ribs, beneath her head, shook. He said, 'You are entirely adorable, Faith, and I'm going to miss you terribly.'

Her heart pounded. 'Oh,' she said lightly, 'I expect that you'll forget me as soon as you set foot in England. All those smart places and sophisticated women. You'll fall in love with one of them in no time at all. Just look at Jake – he's in love with a different woman each month. The last one was twenty-five and had a coat made out of fox tails.'

He laughed. 'Jake is destined to be a Lothario, I'm afraid.' His hand threaded through her hair, winding her curls round his fingers. 'Anyway, I haven't enough money even to consider marriage.'

'Nicole believes that there's one perfect man waiting for her. She's sure that she'll know as soon as she meets him that he's The One. Do you think she's right, Guy?'

'Nicole is a romantic,' he said dismissively, adding, 'but I suppose I do believe that one should wait until one's found one's ideal. That marriage should be for life . . . and that there should be intensity . . . a meeting of minds.'

She lay still. The moment seemed to pivot, to hang in the balance, about to fall one way or the other.

Guy said, 'In any case, I don't intend to fall in love with anyone for a very long time. I've more important things to do.'

She knew, though, that falling in love was not a thing that you chose: it chose you. She shut her eyes, glad of the darkness. Mulgrave Rules, she said to herself. Never let them see that you mind.

CHAPTER TWO

The day after Guy Neville left La Rouilly, Faith went into Jake's bedroom at mid-morning, and found the note on his pillow. It said, 'Have gone to Spain to join the International Brigades. Tell Ma not to fuss. Will send a postcard.'

Ralph shouted and swore and rushed off to the Spanish border in search of his son. Within a week, he returned alone to La Rouilly, still cursing. Nicole retreated to the walled garden with a heap of novels and a bag of chocolates, but Faith weathered the storm and tried to comfort Poppy.

'I'm sure Jake will be all right. He's very good at looking after himself. Don't you remember that time he fell off the roof and we all thought he was dead, and he had just one tiny bruise?'

Poppy smiled, but felt terrible inside. The thought of her only surviving son with a rifle in his hand, being shot at, was quite dreadful. He's not yet *sixteen*, she thought. Just a child.

Ralph's hurt and outrage persisted. 'The boy's never had an ounce of sense. All these years I've tried to knock some into him, and look what he does. Just ups and leaves.'

Poppy said reasonably, 'You did the same, Ralph. You left home when you were sixteen.'

'It isn't the same at all. I was at some God-awful school, in that God-awful dreary country. And I didn't leave home with the sole intention of getting myself killed fighting someone else's war.'

Poppy shivered. Ralph stomped off to the bar in the village, to get very drunk. Upstairs in Jake's room, Poppy tried not to weep as she went through cupboards and drawers. Picking out warm jerseys and vests (Spain could be so cold in winter), she wrote a long letter and parcelled it and the clothes up and sent them to Jake via the Red Cross.

Some of what Ralph had said remained with her, though. For the first time, she feared for her children. Not only for Jake, but for Faith and Nicole too. She knew that, though the temptations for girls were different, they nevertheless existed. She found herself regretting not having given her children a formal education. Faith was intelligent and sensible, but there was a diffidence about her, a lack of direction that might lead her to drift through life, never finding quite the right thing. As for Nicole – though she was only fourteen, village boys already lurked around the gateway to La Rouilly, hoping for a glimpse of her. Just now, Nicole would have paid more attention to a wounded bird or a lost kitten, but that would not always be so.

They travelled south in the autumn, settling eventually in Menton. There, Poppy withdrew money from her bank account and went to visit the Mother Superior at the convent. Home again, she drew the girls aside, took a deep breath, and told them that they were to start school the following week. 'The nuns all seem very kind, and they showed me the lovely work that the girls do – embroidery and drawing and dressmaking –

and they play games and there is a choir and I'm sure you'll make lots of friends . . .' Her voice trailed off when she saw her daughters' faces.

Nicole named her price: the King Charles spaniel she had seen imprisoned in a local pet shop. Faith refused. 'It wouldn't do at all, Ma. I'm nearly seventeen, far too old for school. Anyway, I've found a job in a lingerie shop. It's marvellous because I have to wear silk stockings so that when gentlemen come into the shop they'll see how lovely they look and buy them for their wives and mistresses.'

Poppy said faintly, 'But *arithmetic* . . . and *geography* . . .'

Faith was unimpressed. 'I have to work out change at the shop, which is very good for my arithmetic, and we've travelled a lot, haven't we? So much better than looking in an atlas.'

Poppy gave in. On Monday, Nicole, wearing a dark brown uniform about which Ralph was unfailingly rude, started at the convent. Poppy seemed to spend most of the day holding her breath, but Nicole returned home at four o'clock, smugly pleased with herself.

'The other girls are not too awful, and Soeur Hélène says that my voice must be trained.'

Faith, who had the afternoon off, made vomiting noises, but Poppy breathed a huge sigh of relief. Then she went back to the table and finished her letter to Jake. She wrote every other day, never receiving a reply, not knowing whether her son was alive or dead.

Guy Neville abandoned his ambition of becoming a surgeon on the day his father died. After the funeral – his father's patients huddled beneath thin coats in the rain, standing a respectful distance from the graveside – he went back to his home in Malt Street. The house was echoing and empty. He had given the maid, a permanently flustered girl called Biddy, the afternoon off. He made himself a sandwich and began to go through his father's account books. The task, after a while, appalled him, and he poured himself a whisky, and sat down beside a fire he could not be bothered to light. There were three photographs on the mantel-piece: his mother, his father, and the last snapshot of the Mulgraves that he had taken at La Rouilly. He drank the Scotch slowly, and just ached with the absence of them all.

Guy held the regular morning surgery the following day, in the room at the back of the house. He did not finish until one o'clock, and then he paused just long enough to drink the soup that Biddy had made before going out on his rounds. The rain was incessant; he could not remember when he had last seen sunshine. It was February, always a busy time of year. He diagnosed bronchitis, diphtheria and scabies, and sent what he suspected was a case of early tuberculosis to the isolation hospital. When he had finished his rounds, he attempted the account books again. Going to bed at midnight, he slept soundly for the first night since his father's death.

His work absorbed him utterly. He had little time for grief or for minding that he had put aside his ambitions. One day, he was called to a house in Rickett Lane, one of the poorest areas of Hackney. He knew the family, the Robertsons, well. Joe Robertson suffered from chronic asthma, and drifted in and out of work in consequence. His wife, a stout woman, was a loving if foul-mouthed mother to her five children, and as good a housekeeper as the damp, infested little house allowed.

This time, the patient was Frank, the couple's six-year-old son. After Guy had taken the child's pulse and examined his abdomen, he turned to Mrs Robertson.

'I think I'll try and get him into St Anne's. It's probably nothing serious, but just to be on the safe side.'

St Anne's, in Islington, was the nearest big teaching hospital. Mrs Robertson wrapped Frank up in a threadbare blanket, and Guy drove them both to the hospital. In the outpatients department the duty doctor examined Frank, and then drew Guy aside. 'I don't think we need admit him. Just a stomach upset, I suspect.'

'I think it may be appendicitis.'

'Do you?' The sneer was perceptible. 'I wouldn't leap to that conclusion, Dr Neville.'

Guy struggled to keep his temper. 'And if I'm right?'

'We only perform routine appendectomies on our private patients. The boy would have to go to the local authority hospital.'

The local authority hospital took the less interesting cases that St Anne's did not want. In the middle of a slum district, it attracted few highly educated or experienced staff.

Guy said, 'Frank's been delicate since birth. I'd be much happier if he was looked after here.'

'We don't run St Anne's to please you, doctor.'

The patronizing tone set Guy's teeth on edge. He went back into the cubicle, and, later in the day as Frank's temperature continued to rise, had him admitted to the local hospital where he was subsequently operated on for appendicitis.

Ten days later the Robertsons' eldest daughter delivered a note to the Malt Street surgery, asking Guy to call. Frank had been discharged from hospital the previous day. 'He doesn't look right, doctor,' Mrs Robertson whispered anxiously as they climbed the stairs to the bedroom Frank shared with his younger brother.

What Guy discovered appalled him. A high fever and an inflamed wound suggested post-operative infection. He drove pell-mell to St Anne's, the child in a cocoon of grubby blankets beside him. In the outpatients department, he saw the supercilious houseman to whom he had previously spoken, and pushed past him, Frank in his arms. Then he glimpsed a consultant emerging from a cubicle. You could always pick out the consultants: they were smooth-faced and expensively suited, and invariably surrounded by a cluster of terrified junior doctors and cringing nurses in goffered caps.

Guy, forcing his way through the entourage, tapped on a Savile Row besuited shoulder.

'Excuse me, sir, but I've a patient you need to look at. A week or so ago I tried to have a child admitted to St Anne's with suspected appendicitis. Your buffoon of a houseman diagnosed it as a stomach-ache, and told me that anyway they don't operate on poor kids here. So he was sent to some butcher at the local authority hospital. And they've sent him home with an infected wound.'

The sister, who wore a particularly intimidating cap, said, 'Really, doctor, you mustn't take up Dr Stephens's time—' but the consultant interrupted her.

'Not at all, sister. Bring the boy in here.' A curtain was pulled aside.

'We'll do what we can,' said Dr Stephens, as he examined Frank. 'Believe me, we'll do what we can.'

A week later, a card arrived in the post. It invited Guy to have supper the following Friday with a Dr Selwyn Stephens and Miss Eleanor Stephens. There was a note scribbled on the foot of the card. 'You will be pleased to hear, Dr Neville, that Frank Robertson is recovering well. Sister tells me that he is teaching his wide vocabulary to the other incumbents of the children's ward.'

As his only acquaintance with Selwyn Stephens had been brief and not altogether cordial, Guy was inclined to make an excuse, anticipating a dull evening in the company of bores. But he recognized the invitation as a generous gesture, a peace offering, and forced himself to write a note of acceptance.

The evening was every bit as tiresome as he had feared. Dressing, he discovered that his dinner jacket had been nibbled by moths, and that Biddy had burnt the collar of his starched shirt. Gloomily he hurled on the unfamiliar and uncomfortable garments, only to discover that his car would not start. Dashing through icy rain to the station, he just missed a train and had to wait ten minutes for the next. The carriages were crowded; Guy travelled with a stranger's umbrella jabbing his toe, his face pressed against someone's rancid overcoat. And though he ran the distance between the station and the Stephenses' Bloomsbury house, he was still twenty minutes late.

He disliked his fellow guests on sight. There were three doctors, one middle-aged, with a protruding stomach and smooth hands, the other two junior doctors from St Anne's. There was also a writer whose ridiculous name, Piers Peacock, Guy recalled from the cover of a novel he had found discarded on a train; he had attempted to read it and had found himself so irritated and bored that he had cast the book out of the window and stared at the passing landscape instead. The two wives were little echoes of their husbands, without an independent thought between them.

And then there was Eleanor, Selwyn Stephens's daughter. Dark-eyed, dark-haired, statuesque in a dress of blue satin, Guy noticed immediately her vitality, her energy. It seemed to blaze from her. She seemed an entirely different species from the pale, worn women whom he saw every day in his surgery. Eleanor Stephens supervised the serving of the food and directed the conversation with unobtrusive efficiency. Just to look at her was a pleasure, a consolation in an evening of otherwise unrelieved dullness.

They had reached the cheese when Dr Humphreys said, 'I've just helped my nephew buy a practice in Kensington, Selwyn. Qualified a few years ago, if you remember – good place to start out,' and Guy heard himself say: 'It might have been more use to humanity, though, if you'd bought him a practice in Poplar or in Bethnal Green.'

There was a silence. Everyone stared at Guy. He stared defiantly back.

'What an extraordinary thing to say.'

Guy met Dr Humphreys's gaze. 'Is it? There are three times as many medical practices in Kensington as in Hackney.'

Miss Stephens spoke. 'Is that so? Why?'

'Because Kensington,' said Guy bluntly, 'pays better than Hackney.'

Dr Humphreys blotted his lips with his napkin. 'We all have to live, Dr Neville.'

The cutlery was silver, the tableware bone china. Guy said angrily, 'We live exceedingly well. And in consequence, our poorer patients are forced to depend on charity.'

'Patients should be grateful to doctors such as Selwyn who give their services to the hospital free.'

Guy's precarious hold on his temper was slipping away. 'No-one should have to rely on some Lord or Lady Bountiful for their well-being – or their children's well-being—'

'I say—'

Selwyn Stephens interrupted. 'My daughter works for the charity board of St Anne's. Are you disparaging such voluntary work, Dr Neville?'

Guy felt himself redden. 'No. No, of course not, sir.' He tried to explain. 'It's just that charity shouldn't be necessary. Good health should be everyone's by right.'

The novelist smiled patronizingly. 'Are you a socialist, Dr Neville?'

Guy ignored him. 'The system we have at the moment – if we can call such a patchwork mess a system – is inequitable.' It was a subject that preoccupied Guy constantly. 'Patients put up with treatable diseases for want of money to pay the doctor. Every day I see women with advanced hypothyroidism, for instance – and prolapsed wombs and varicose ulcers—'

'Not at the dinner table, old boy,' murmured the Cambridge doctor. 'The ladies . . .'

Guy subsided. 'I beg your pardon,' he muttered.

'And what's your solution, Dr Neville?' Piers Peacock lit a cigar. 'Who do you believe should pay for those unfortunates' ill health?'

'I suppose I think that we all should.'

'I was brought up to believe that I'm not my brother's keeper.'

The smug smile that accompanied the words reignited Guy's fury. 'And *I* was brought up not to walk by on the other side of the road!'

'And to give the widow's mite, if that's all we have left,' Eleanor Stephens put in unexpectedly. 'More cheese, anyone? No? Then shall we take coffee in the drawing-room?'

Guy escaped to the bathroom, where he flung open the window and took deep breaths of icy air. Glancing at his reflection in the mirror, he knew that he had made a fool of himself. He had lived alone too long, and he had lost what social skills he had once possessed.

It took an effort of will to return to the drawing-room. While Miss Stephens played a Beethoven piano sonata, Guy sat in a corner of the room and let the music wash over him, calming him. At midnight, he judged it permissible to leave, so he made polite farewells, took his hat and coat from the maid, and stepped out into the night. It had stopped raining, but the roads and pavements were sheened with water, like black silk. Before he reached the corner of the square, he heard footsteps running along the pavement towards him, and he turned and saw Miss Stephens.

'Your umbrella, Dr Neville!' She held it out to him. Her cheeks were flushed pink from the run.

He took the umbrella from her and thanked her, and said, 'I'm glad of the opportunity to speak to you alone. I must apologize for my behaviour tonight. It was unforgivable.'

She laughed. 'Not at all. It's I who should be

apologizing to you. I hadn't realized they were such a collection of pompous bores.'

'I thought—'

'That they were my bosom friends?' Miss Stephens shook her head. 'Father loathes Edmund Humphreys, but he has to keep on good terms with him because of his work. And we owed him an invitation. And I supposed that Piers Peacock would have been interesting – you'd think that someone who writes mystery stories would be interesting, wouldn't you? – but I'm afraid that he wasn't at all. Thank goodness you were there, Dr Neville, or I should probably have fallen asleep over my pudding.'

He was curious. 'I probably shouldn't ask, but why on earth *did* you invite me?'

She smiled mischievously. 'Father told me about your . . . *encounter* at St Anne's. I thought it was amusing.' The smile disappeared. 'Apart from the poor little boy, of course. But I was curious to meet you. Most young doctors are terrified of Father. I can't think why – he's such a sweetie.'

Guy made an effort. 'Then again, I'm sorry that some of the things I said were out of order.'

'Were they? Which ones? Didn't you mean what you said, Dr Neville?'

He answered her honestly. 'I meant every word of it.'

'Good,' she said. 'Because I respected you. One should be true to oneself.' She held out her hand. 'Goodnight, Dr Neville. I hope that we may meet again.'

Eleanor Stephens had lived all her life in the Holland Square house. Since she was nine, the large building had been occupied only by herself, her father and the live-in maid. After her mother's death, her father had suggested they engage a housekeeper, but Eleanor had persuaded him not to. She had told him that she could not bear to see another woman take her mother's place, which was true, but only part of the reason. She had wanted to run the house herself. She had known even then that she could do it. She liked to organize things. The family home was just a bigger version of the dolls' house in her bedroom. She enjoyed discussing the dinner menu each morning with the cook, and she remembered how her mother had run her finger along the shelves to check the maids' work. She did not let her household duties affect her school work, and left school at seventeen with a respectable school certificate. She knew that she was not academic, though, and did not consider going to university.

For the first few years after leaving school Eleanor was happy at home. She played the piano in an amateur trio, and attended a watercolour class. She started up a tradition of little supper parties to which she would invite medical students and junior doctors from St Anne's Hospital. She was kind to the more bashful doctors, helping to bring them out, and gently deflating to the flirtatious ones. It became an honour amongst the lower ranks at St Anne's to be invited to one of Miss Stephens's supper parties. She began by helping on flag days at St Anne's, but was soon offered a place on the charity's committee.

Yet, turning twenty-four at the beginning of the previous year, she had felt unsettled. Her birthday celebration – a five-course dinner served to a dozen guests – went smoothly. The compliments ('Dear Eleanor, such a wonderful hostess. You are so lucky, Selwyn') were automatic. The same compliments had been expressed for the past seven years. It was not that she thought them insincere, just that, looking ahead, their repetition had acquired a horrible predictability.

But it was when she met Hilary Taylor in Fortnum's food hall one afternoon that she had begun to question her future. She had known Hilary at school. 'How lovely to see you, darling,' she had said, and had kissed Hilary on the cheek. At school, Hilary had been rather looked down on because she had tended to spots, and because her mother had taken in lodgers. Hilary's complexion, Eleanor noticed, was now velvety and unblemished. 'Are you baking?' she asked. There was a jar of cherries in Hilary's basket.

Hilary let out a peal of laughter. 'Good lord, no! I wouldn't know how. I eat them when I have a deadline – they keep me awake. I don't know whether it's the sugar or the Maraschino.'

Over tea and scones, Hilary had explained to Eleanor that she was now the editor of a smart magazine called *Chantilly*. Eleanor enquired about the diamond ring on Hilary's third finger. 'Jules is a racing driver,' explained Hilary. 'I don't know whether I'll marry him, because he wants me to go back to Argentina with him, and I do so adore my job.'

Hilary had then asked Eleanor what she was doing. Eleanor had said, just as she always did, 'Oh, the usual. My hospital work. Looking after Father,' but for the first time she had felt dull – frumpy even – instead of touchingly noble.

There had been a short silence, and then Hilary had said sympathetically, 'Poor old you. You did rather get landed with the domestic bit, didn't you?'

Hilary's words had bitten, leaving a scar. Looking in the mirror that night, Eleanor had seen her expensive tweeds, her sensibly cropped curls, and had recalled Hilary's sleek, shoulder-length bob and quirkily stylish clothes. She had seen also that within a few short years she had evolved from being clever, tragic Eleanor, who had coped so superbly after her mother's death, to being dear Eleanor who always did things so well. In the not too distant future, she might become poor Eleanor, who had been robbed of opportunity by circumstance.

She thought she should travel and that summer toured southern France and northern Italy, and found the experience interesting but unsatisfying. She thought of getting a job, but could not think of anything that she would enjoy more than Holland Square and the hospital. She knew that she had no particular talents, and was seized by a dreadful suspicion that this was all life had to offer, and that her energy, her sense of purpose, might dissipate in coffee mornings and supper parties and endless indecisive committees. Then she thought of marriage.

She had been to the theatre and to parties with men, of course, but none of her relationships had lasted more than a few months. The junior doctors that she invited to her supper parties seemed so young, so lacking in fire. She joined a bridge club and, to her father's amusement, the Left Book Club. She lost her virginity and found it a disappointing experience. She supposed that women married so that they might have children, yet, visiting a friend in a maternity home, she found the newborn child, with its crumpled face and peeling skin, repellent. Presumably, she told herself, one would feel differently about one's own.

She was perceptive enough to realize that some men were daunted by her air of efficiency. She tried to be silly and frivolous, but found it unbearable. She understood also that every man she met she compared with her father, and found wanting.

The bright sunlight hurt Guy's eyes as he emerged from the vestibule of the hospital. He blinked, and heard a voice say, 'Would you buy a daisy for St Anne's, sir?' Turning, he saw Eleanor Stephens standing on the steps, a collecting box in her hand. When she recognized him, she smiled.

'I'm so sorry, I didn't realize it was you, Dr Neville. It's our flag day, you see.' She was carrying a tray of white paper flowers. 'We ask people to buy a daisy to help St Anne's.'

Guy delved into his pocket for change, and she pinned the flower to his lapel. 'There,' she said. 'That's my last one. I must go home now, Father will be expecting his supper.' She glanced at Guy. 'Where do you live? Can we walk home together?'

'Malt Street. Hackney. Not in your direction, I'm afraid, Miss Stephens.'

'It's such a lovely day, though . . . and I need to stretch my legs. Perhaps I could telephone for a cab from your house, Dr Neville.'

He smiled. 'I'd be grateful for the company.'

The worst of the evening rush hour was over, and the streets had begun to empty. After they had walked in silence for a while, Miss Stephens said, 'A bad day, Dr Neville?'

'A woman with pregnancy complications. They put off calling a doctor because of the cost. St Anne's doesn't hold out much hope. Such a waste. And there are other children, of course. God knows what will happen to them.'

She murmured sympathy, and they walked on. A few streaks of cotton wool cloud were the only blemishes in a sapphire sky. Guy realized that the silence had gone on too long, that he was being unsociable. The old Guy Neville, the Guy Neville who had once talked and laughed into the early hours of the morning at La Rouilly, seemed lately to have deserted him.

They turned the corner into Malt Street. She followed him into the house. It was only once he was inside that he saw the place as others must see it: the heap of coats in the hallway, the dusty banisters. The house was cold and unwelcoming, a caricature of a bachelor's home.

He remembered the Stephenses' ordered, glittering rooms, and apologized. 'I'm not much good at housekeeping.'

'Haven't you a maid, Dr Neville?'

'I have, but she's a bit haphazard at the best of times.'

'I know that it's difficult to find good servants these days, but my grandmother lives in Derbyshire and has always been able to find me a sensible village girl. I could have a word with her, if you like.'

Guy thought privately that a sensible village girl would only reduce poor Biddy to hysterics. He suspected that the parlour was still festooned with the remains of breakfast, so he led Eleanor into the front room that he used as a study. There, he groaned. The desk was heaped with bills and record books. The previous night he had made another half-hearted attempt to sort through them, but had fallen asleep after ten minutes.

'I'll move these out of the way,' he muttered.

'Can't I help, Dr Neville?' Eleanor glanced at the

bills and invoices. 'I'm very good at this sort of thing. I do all my father's secretarial work. Why don't you let me see what I can do?'

'Because that would be imposing on you, Miss Stephens.'

'I don't mind at all . . . and if you were to open the window to let in some fresh air . . . and make a cup of tea. Oh dear. I'm organizing you, aren't I? Father always tells me that I organize even the tinkers who come to the door.'

'I've been trying to force myself to go through this lot ever since Dad died, but there hasn't been time. I'm setting up a mother and baby clinic, you see – so much ill health could be avoided if preventative measures were properly applied—and if the patients won't come to the surgery, then we must visit them. I've been thinking of engaging a nurse to weigh the babies, and to do the routine checks—' He broke off, focusing on her. 'I'm sorry. One of my obsessions.'

'It sounds a marvellous idea, Dr Neville. But you need to keep up with all this, or everything will get into a muddle.'

He smiled crookedly. 'It's just that I loathe paperwork, I'm afraid.'

'*I* don't.' She sat down at the table. Guy flung open the window, and went to the kitchen to fetch tea for Eleanor and Scotch and water for himself.

When he returned, she was frowning. 'Some are marked "n/c". What does that mean?'

He peered over her shoulder. 'Nominal charge,' he explained. 'People who are too proud to accept charity, but can't afford the full cost of the visit and prescription. You see, we have a few good payers – Colonel Walker, for instance, and Mrs Crawford – so we charge them six guineas a quarter, which means that we can bill the poorer patients for just five shillings or so, even though they've had a dozen visits.'

'You mean,' said Miss Stephens slowly, 'that your Colonel Walker and your Mrs Crawford *subsidize* your poorer patients?'

'I suppose so. I hadn't thought of it like that. I suppose it smacks of socialism. Mrs Crawford would be horrified. She thinks all socialists are in league with the devil.'

Eleanor looked down at the papers again. Her hair was so dark it was almost black, and it had a healthy gloss. It gleamed, Guy thought, like tar . . . or treacle. No, that wasn't right. He hadn't the knack of the poetic simile. One did not want to touch tar or treacle.

He added, 'And of course I had to buy the practice after my father's death. Things are rather grim at present.'

She looked up. 'Poor Dr Neville.' Her brown eyes were sympathetic.

'If you're to become my accountant, Miss Stephens, then you should call me Guy.'

She smiled. 'On two conditions.'

'What?'

'The first, naturally, is that you call me Eleanor. The second is that you pour me a Scotch and water. Tea really isn't strong enough to deal with this muddle.'

Eleanor called at the Malt Street house twice a week to sort out Guy's accounts. After she had transcribed all his scraps of paper into a sensible bound notebook, he took her to a concert to thank her. In the interim, he made an effort with the house, engaging a window cleaner and coaxing Biddy to scrub floors and do a little tidying. He realized after a while that, without his intending it, they had fallen into a routine. Eleanor would work through Friday afternoon to bring the practice's accounts up to date, and then they would have tea together or go to a pub. Once she had streamlined his accounts, Eleanor applied her considerable energies to other causes, finding a grocer who would deliver to the house, a handyman to mend the window frames and paint the front door, and a reliable laundry. Returning from his rounds one Friday evening, Guy found Eleanor on her hands and knees in the glory hole under the stairs.

'I was looking for a duster, Guy, because I thought I should make a start on the dispensary files. But the cabinet's very grubby, and I couldn't find any cloths in the kitchen or the airing-cupboard, so I looked in here.' Eleanor shuffled backwards, and stood up. With her sleeves rolled up and her smart dress enveloped in a dusty apron, she looked to Guy younger, more vulnerable.

'Such an extraordinary collection of things! An old wireless, and candelabra, and boxes full of periodicals, and the most lovely little chair that I'm sure is Regency.'

He said, 'You have a cobweb on your forehead,' and swept it away with the tip of his finger. Her skin was cool and fine-grained. 'I shall cook you supper, Eleanor – your reward for tackling this. I don't believe anyone's ventured into that cupboard in decades. Will scrambled eggs be all right?'

They ate in the dining-room, surrounded by heavy, dark furniture that had been Guy's mother's wedding present. Eleanor inspected the family photographs in their silver frames. 'Is this your mother? She's very beautiful. You have her eyes, Guy. And this must be your father.' She put the photograph down and moved on to the next. 'And who are these? Cousins, perhaps?'

He shook his head. 'They're my friends, the Mulgraves.'

'Where was it taken? The house looks very grand.'

'In France. That lady—' he pointed out Genya – 'owns the château.' He smiled, remembering. 'They are the most extraordinary people, Eleanor. I should love to introduce the Mulgraves to you – you would adore them, I know you would. So original and different. They keep to no-one's rules but their own. The children are quite fearless.' Yet even as he spoke, he thought that was not true of Faith; and that she, unlike Jake and Nicole, preceded her recklessness with a sharp intake of breath.

He told her how Ralph had found him stranded near Bordeaux and had invited him to La Rouilly, and how, somehow, he had ended up staying there a month. 'And Poppy, Ralph's wife, is the most magnificent woman – never gets into a flap, always copes with anything. And the children all speak half a dozen languages, but I'm not sure they've ever had a day's schooling in their lives.'

'That may make things rather difficult for them in the future,' suggested Eleanor.

'You don't notice, somehow. Faith – she's the eldest – seems to me quite perfect as she is.'

'How old is she?'

He had to think for a moment. 'Seventeen, I suppose.'

'Is she pretty? She's half hidden in this snapshot.'

Guy had never considered whether Faith was pretty or not. 'I really have no idea.' He laughed. 'She dresses in the most extraordinary clothes. Things her mother and Genya have cast off. Edwardian tea gowns and feather boas.'

Eleanor said, 'You sound as though you are in love with her, Guy.'

He glanced at her, surprised. 'Of course I'm not. Faith is like a sister to me. I don't have much of a family of my own – I suppose the Mulgraves have been a sort of adopted family.'

'Don't be cross, Guy. After all, we are adults. It's not as though either of us won't have had close friendships before.'

There was something so untouched, so clean and well scrubbed about Eleanor Stephens that it had not occurred to Guy to consider whether or not she had had lovers. Now, the image of her in bed with another man, her body smooth and firm and voluptuous, entered his mind.

Eleanor laughed. 'Father always says that doctors should marry young so that they have someone to make their breakfast before they have an early duty, and someone to warm their bed when they come home late at night. Oh dear—' She broke off, reddening. 'I didn't mean – I know that you don't think of me in that way—'

She was visibly mortified. That she should be flustered was touchingly at odds with her usual self-possessed efficiency. Depressed by the death of his father, and absorbed in his work, Guy found it hard to remember when he had last felt attracted to a woman. Yet Eleanor's obvious health and vitality was an immediate and compelling contrast to the worn, sickly women he saw each day in his surgery, and his sudden desire for her took him by surprise.

He said, 'And how do you think I think of you?'

She shook her head, biting her lip. He saw how others might see her as just sensible, competent Eleanor, and thus diminish her, and he said softly, 'Actually, I think of you as a very attractive woman. Actually, I think of you as someone I should very much like to kiss.' And he did so.

It was midnight when Eleanor returned to the Holland Square house. As she came into the hall, her father called, 'A nightcap?' and she followed him into the drawing-room.

He poured out the brandies; she curled up at the foot of his favourite chair by the fire. Sitting down, he said: 'And how is your fiery Dr Neville, my dear?'

She said, 'Guy's very well, but he isn't *my* Dr Neville.' Yet she smiled to herself.

'Isn't he? You've been seeing a lot of each other recently, Eleanor.'

Her face, remembering Guy's kisses, was hot. She looked up at her father. 'Do you mind, Daddy? Do you like him?' Eleanor realized that she was waiting, her breath held, for his verdict.

Her father considered. 'Dr Neville has a good reputation in the profession, I believe. Of course, he's young yet. But yes, I do approve of him. A certain amount of idealism is necessary in the young. I've always held that without it a doctor could not endure the first few years of his training. One hopes that he'll become more pragmatic in time, however.' He paused, and then asked tentatively, 'Are you fond of him, my dear?'

'We are . . . we are good friends.' Yet when she thought of Guy her heart pounded, and something in the core of her body tightened with excitement. It occurred to Eleanor that she must be in love with Guy

71

Neville. She had never succumbed to romantic love before; she had assumed it to be a fiction.

'He doesn't appear to be well off,' warned her father. 'Be careful, my dear – one can't buy a house or support a family on ideals.'

'Guy has a perfectly nice house.'

'In Hackney?' Selwyn Stephens's tone was disbelieving.

'With a little decoration . . . The front rooms are pleasantly airy, and with some touches of colour and fabric they could be delightful.'

'Poor Dr Neville may not want his house altered, Eleanor.' He patted her shoulder. 'Be careful, my dear – I sometimes think you have a rather ruthless streak.' His voice was kind. 'Seriously, though – *Hackney* . . . Very different from Bloomsbury, my dear. And the life of a struggling GP's wife . . . it wouldn't be what you're used to, Eleanor.'

She thought, *But I don't want what I am used to! It wearies me, it bores me, it no longer has any challenge. And I could do so much for Guy. With my help, he need not remain a struggling GP, and he need not remain in Malt Street.* But she only said, 'We're just friends, Father.'

'Of course. But should your interest become serious, then I would naturally be willing to help. As you know, I'm not a rich man, but I could perhaps offer Dr Neville a partnership.' Selwyn Stephens smiled. 'Should he relax his principles sufficiently to accept it, that is.'

She seized her father's hand. 'Oh, you are so good to me! But I've no intention of marrying Guy. After all – who would look after you?'

'I would manage. I wouldn't want you to give up what you truly want for my sake.'

Eleanor closed her eyes. Into her sleepy head drifted Guy's voice. *Faith seems to me quite perfect.* Eleanor, before her father reminded her that she was tired, and should go to bed, had just enough time to reflect that Faith sounded the sort of girl that men rather than women admired, and that she was glad that Faith Mulgrave lived far away, in France.

The Mulgraves heard nothing from Jake for over a year. They spent the winter of 1938 to 1939 in Marseilles. Faith liked Marseilles. She found two Fortuny dresses, rolled up in tubes like sausages, in a street market, and found also a job in a café near the docks. Working, she could see the forest of masts bobbing on the water. There was a sail maker to one side of the café, a chandler to another. There was always something going on outside – a brawl or an argument between lovers, and once, in front of the café, a man was stabbed, and Faith had to hold a tablecloth over the wound to staunch it while the *patron* ran for the doctor.

She served breakfasts and lunches, and worked behind the bar. There was a piano player and, in the evenings, dancing. The clientele was a mixture of sailors and businessmen. One of the businessmen, whose name was Gilles, wore smart suits and had a coppery skin and sleek black hair and a small moustache. He drove a large grey car with maroon leather seats and always insisted that Faith, and no-one else, serve his coffee. Nicole, who sang in the café in the evenings, was impressed by Gilles. 'I expect he sells opium, or is a white slave trader. Just think, Faith, you could be in his harem.'

Gilles let Faith read his morning newspaper.

'I need to know what's happening,' she explained to him. 'There might be a war, and as we haven't really got a proper home we'd have to think where best to go.'

'If there's a war, beautiful Faith, then you must come to North Africa with me. I have an enchanting villa in Algiers. My servants would attend you, and you'd never have to wait at table again.'

Gilles always said that, and Faith always smiled and said 'No thank you' very politely, while laughing privately at a vision of herself in harem pants and a yashmak.

Ralph and Poppy went to Nice for a week, to stay with friends. The postman gave Faith a letter, forwarded by Genya, as she left the apartment one morning. She read the letter walking through the maze of alleyways to the café. It was in French, from someone called Luis, and it told her that Jake was ill in a refugee camp near Perpignan.

Gilles was already in the café when she arrived. Faith gave him coffee and borrowed his newspaper and read the column about Spain and planned. Pouring Gilles his second cup of coffee she said: 'Do you think I might borrow your car, Gilles?'

She noticed that he blenched, but, always a gentleman, quickly hid his discomfiture. 'Of course. May one enquire why?'

'My brother's in a refugee camp in Argelès. Apparently he hasn't any papers so the guards don't believe that he's English. I thought they might believe me if I arrive in your splendid car, wearing a fur coat.'

'Money always impresses,' agreed Gilles. He took a bundle of keys out of his pocket. 'Of course you may

74

borrow my car, *ma chère* Faith.' He glanced at her. 'You do know how to drive, I assume?'

She had driven Genya's old Citroën van around the fields of La Rouilly, and expected that Gilles's car worked on much the same principle. She kissed him on both cheeks, and went to find the café's owner to plead for two days' leave of absence. At home, she changed into the Holly Blue dress and Poppy's old fox fur and a pair of diamond earrings, and applied layers of lipstick and powder. Glancing at herself in the mirror, she thought that she looked at least twenty-five, and terribly wealthy.

Gilles's car was not as easy as she had expected. Faith scraped it once or twice negotiating the narrow streets that led out of Marseilles, but fortunately the paint did not seem too badly marked. It was easier driving west along the coast towards Argelès. The car's soft top protected her from the worst of the wind and sleet, and she was able to relax sufficiently to plan what she would do when she reached the camp.

In the late January of 1939, as General Franco's army advanced through Catalonia, Jake had marched with a column of tens of thousands of other refugees from Barcelona to the French border. His progress was slow because he had contracted influenza, so that, as he shuffled along the stony roads, his cough tormented him even more than the aeroplanes of the Condor Legion which took pot-shots at them as they walked. Though the weather was uniformly unpleasant, a mixture of icy rain, sleet and snow – a fitting backdrop, Jake thought, to the death of the Republic – his body lurched between extremes of temperature. Sometimes a chill seemed to spread out from the region of his heart, at others an aching heat made rivulets of sweat trickle down his face. He supposed that he had a fever, and he would have very much liked to curl up in a ditch and lie there until both the coughing and the sweating stopped, but he kept on walking simply because all his friends kept walking, having discovered in this confused, confusing war that loyalty to the friends who had fought alongside him was the only sentiment he need not feel ambivalent about. When he flagged, when he paused for a few moments at the side of the road and the whole of battered, tortured Spain seemed to stumble by – women holding babies, children clutching a doll's head or a punctured ball, mementoes of a once happy childhood – then Luis remained with him. So for Luis's sake Jake got up, walked on, forced himself to continue to place one foot in front of the other.

At the border they cheered, scenting safety. Around him Jake saw many who stooped and picked up a fistful of Spanish soil to carry with them into France. At first the French let through only the women and children and the wounded; a few days later the men were allowed to follow them. In the camp at Argelès, which was nothing more than an area of sand dune enclosed by barbed wire, Jake dreamed. He dreamed of the boy who had refused to fight any more, and who had been taken aside by men in leather coats and shot in the back of the head; he dreamed of the children he had seen sprawled in the mud, slain by the aeroplanes of the Condor Legion; he dreamed of the prisoner who had been buried alive in a ditch at the side of the road: payment for old scores, Jake assumed. Between these nightmares he had different visions. He was at La Rouilly, picnicking in the wood behind the château. All the others were there: his parents, Faith, Nicole, Guy, Felix. The sun was shining and Jake was aware of a feeling of almost unbearable longing.

At Argelès there was no shelter and, at first, no food or water. Luis dug a hole in the sand, and Jake curled up inside like a hibernating animal, his greatcoat wrapped around him. In the long, cold, dull hours, they talked about the future. Luis had friends in Paris who ran a left-wing newspaper; he would go there when he was able. Jake must come too – the Parisian girls were beautiful, added Luis, with a curving gesture of the hands. Jake coughed and tried to smile. Luis, worried about him, told the armed French guard that Jake was English, but the guard did not believe him. Jake had no proof of nationality, no passport, no papers, and, when the fever was at its height, he rambled in several different languages. Most of the other foreign nationals had left Spain in October, when the International Brigades had been disbanded. Luis managed to smuggle out a letter to Faith, addressing it to La Rouilly. Jake, who did not at that moment know where his family was living, felt sometimes terribly lonely.

He was having the horrible dream about the man being buried alive when the guard came for him. Because of the dream, he struggled a bit, until Luis told him to calm down, and that his sister was waiting for him. He couldn't take that in for a while; he couldn't imagine Faith amid the squalor and cold of Argelès, and he was unable to stop himself letting out a sob of relief. Then he flung his arms round Luis, whispered 'I'll see you in Paris', and followed the guard across the dunes.

He didn't recognize Faith at first. She was wearing

her old blue dress and Ma's fur coat and looked, he grudgingly admitted to himself, rather stunning in an outlandish way. The guards certainly seemed to think so: they were offering her cigarettes and coffee and making up to her quite sickeningly. She was laughing and simpering in a most un-Faithlike fashion, and then she turned and saw him and her expression altered. 'Oh, *Jake*,' she said, and ran to him and embraced him. He only realized that she was weeping when her tears made his neck wet.

Because Jake looked so awful, Faith did not at first ask questions, but talked to him, sensing that he needed the distraction of her voice to stop him breaking down. 'I said that I was the daughter of an English duke, and that you were my brother. I had to bribe them, you know – it's a good thing there was some money in the car.'

When he saw the car, Jake's eyes widened, and he said, 'Good God, a *Phantom*,' so she explained about Gilles.

'Are you his mistress?'

'Of course not.' Faith rummaged in the glove compartment and found Gilles's flask of brandy. 'He's just a customer in the café where I work. He's awfully nice. I think he's a smuggler.'

She fed Jake brandy and little bits of chocolate, and wrapped rugs around him so that he did not feel cold. They drove for a while, and she saw him visibly relax, as though putting Spain and the camp behind him. After a while she said: 'Why did you go, Jake?'

He shrugged. 'Because of what Felix said. About the Republicans losing.' He laughed. 'I thought I was

78

fighting for freedom. I didn't exactly stem the rising tide of fascism, did I?'

Faith glanced at him. He had changed a great deal since he had left La Rouilly eighteen months before. Even if one discounted the hollow cheeks, the dirt and the stubble, she sensed that the alterations were deep and permanent. 'You always were sickeningly over-ambitious, Jake,' she said. But she squeezed his hand as she spoke. 'What was it like?'

Gobs of sleet slid slowly down the windscreen. Jake said, 'It rained a great deal, and I had a hole in my boot that gave me a septic blister, and I had diarrhoea most of the time, and I got lost rather a lot. I seemed to spend most of the time marching to places, and then as soon as I got there I'd have to march somewhere else. And it was cold and exhausting and my rifle kept jamming.' He took a battered tobacco pouch from his pocket and gave it to Faith. 'Roll me one, won't you? My hands are shaking too much.'

He was coughing, but she rolled him a cigarette anyway. Jake smoked for a while, and then he said: 'I was never quite sure what I was supposed to be doing. I'd thought it would be . . . obvious. Straightforward. Good and evil, all that. But it wasn't.' He began to cough again. When he had recovered he said, 'I mean, it was, of course, in a way, and it's just bloody awful that the fascists seem to have won. But I saw the most frightful things done by people that were supposed to be on the same side as me, and it made me think—' He blinked, and for a long time just looked out of the window, not speaking.

After a while she said gently, 'What will you do now, Jake?'

'Get rid of this damned cough.' His expression altered, replaced suddenly by the familiar charming smile. 'And then I'll go to Paris. A friend of mine knows someone who owns a newspaper there. You should come too, Faith.'

CHAPTER THREE

In Paris, Jake shared an apartment in the rue des Sts-Pères on the Left Bank with Luis and an English painter called Rufus Foxwell. Rufus was scathing about the newspaper that Luis and Jake worked for. '*L'Espoir*? *Le Désespoir*, more like.' Jake was inclined to agree with Rufus: what passion he had once had for politics had perished in the embers of the Spanish Civil War, and besides, working for *L'Espoir* seemed largely to consist of standing in the rain, trying to foist the wretched thing on uninterested passers-by. After a month he left the newspaper and started work in a bar, where the pay was better, and you were at least dry.

Jake adored Paris. He adored the wide roads, the pale, graceful buildings, and the early morning sunlight on the Seine. After the heavy warmth of the Gironde, the Parisian air seemed like fine wine. The women were every bit as beautiful and elegant as Luis had suggested, with slim, silk-clad legs, and chic little hats over burnished curls. He fell in love on his very first day in Paris, but in less than a week had transferred his affections to another. He learned how with a look, a smile, to convey his interest. He pursued the objects of his desire with tenacity: that they were married, or religious, or promised to a *poilu* immured in fortifications on the Marne only added to the excitement. He became adept at writing neat little notes – notes that combined just the right amount of finality and regret – when he had made his conquest and grown bored.

On the day that France declared war on Germany, Jake and Luis and Rufus Foxwell drank brandy into the early hours. A week later, Rufus brought Anni back to the apartment. Anni was German, and she had once been Rufus's lover. She was short and buxom and had cropped dark hair and coal-black eyes. She wore slacks and striped knitted jerseys, and looked, Jake thought, like a dumpy, sharp-tempered schoolboy. Jake, who had invited his latest girlfriend, a long-legged blonde called Marie-Joseph, to dinner, found Anni rather dislikable. She had decided and uncomfortable opinions about everything, and no compunction about making her views clear to everyone else. As they ate the beef in red wine that Luis had cooked, conversation naturally turned to the war. Georges, who edited the newspaper, was convinced that it would be over within a few months. Then Anni, in her accented, throaty voice, said: 'Where will you go, Luis? After all, you're a Spanish Communist, so you'll be no safer in Paris than I.'

Everyone stared at her. Rufus said, 'What do you mean, Anni?'

She lit her cigarette before replying. 'I mean, when the Nazis occupy Paris, of course.'

Someone laughed. Jake said, 'The Nazis will never occupy Paris. That's ridiculous.'

'Is it?' Her dark, unreadable eyes focused on him. Jake felt as though he was being judged, and found wanting.

'Perhaps you're being rather pessimistic, darling.' Rufus refilled everyone's glass. 'Germany tried and failed to take Paris in the last war. Why should things be different now?'

Anni shrugged. 'Because people are different. Because the situation is different. Everything changes.'

'Countries don't change.'

She looked at Jake coldly. 'Nine years ago I lived with my family in a nice apartment in Berlin. My father was the leader of a trade union. There was always food on the table, and I was to study art at college.' Anni raised her palms and spread out her fingers. 'And now my father is dead, and I can no longer live in Berlin, and my family owns nothing.'

'That was Germany,' said Jake angrily. 'And this is France. It's not the same at all.' Anni had put into his mind a sudden horrible vision of a Paris with swastikas and jackboots, and, even worse, a La Rouilly that was no longer the paradise that the Mulgraves had always known.

Jake turned away, and concentrated on Marie-Joseph for the remainder of the evening. Yet his annoyance lingered, and when, early the following morning, Marie-Joseph tried to coax him into letting her stay, he shook his head, explaining abruptly that he had to meet his sister, who was travelling to Paris by the night train.

Faith thought the *wagon-lit* was wonderful. There was a fold-down bed, and a tiny washbasin in a cupboard and a little blind to cover the window. She shared the sleeping compartment with one other occupant, an elderly nun who wore corsets that creaked, and prayed, Faith told Jake when she met him at the Gare d'Austerlitz, for hours.

'I thought she'd fallen asleep on her knees. I was

83

going to nudge her with my toe, but then she said a last Hail Mary and leapt into bed.'

Jake took Faith back to the apartment in the rue Sts-Pères. 'The others are out just now,' he explained, 'but they'll be back later. I've cleared a room for you.'

The room was tiny, about six foot square, but the single small window looked down to a tangle of cafés and market stalls. Faith beamed. 'Oh, Jake! It's wonderful.'

He glanced at his watch. 'I have to go to work. Will you be all right? You can unpack, or make yourself something to eat, whatever you like.'

He left, and she wandered around the apartment. There didn't seem to be much point in unpacking as there was nowhere other than the suitcase to put her clothes. In the kitchen a tower of crockery teetered precariously in the sink and every saucepan was encrusted with something unrecognizable or filled with grey water. One of the cups on the table brimmed with cigarette stubs. In the adjacent studio huge canvases were stacked against the wall. Faith inspected them. She was halfway through when a voice from behind her said, 'Those aren't my best. I'm going to paint over the lot of them.'

A man was standing in the doorway. He was a little older than Jake, she guessed, shorter and wirier, with untidy reddish-brown hair and very dark eyes. He wore baggy, paint-stained corduroy trousers and a jacket with patched elbows and missing buttons.

'I like this one.' Faith pointed to a canvas.

He came in, and looked down. 'A bit derivative. Owes rather too much to Marc Chagall.' He held out his hand. 'Rufus Foxwell. You must be Faith.'

'Jake had to go to work,' she explained. 'He said it

would be all right if I stayed here till he came back.'

'I'm afraid that it's not all right at all,' said Rufus, and smiled. 'You can't possibly spend your first morning in Paris cooped up in a dump like this. Fetch your jacket, Miss Mulgrave. You and I are going out on the town.'

He took her first to a café for croissants and coffee, and then for a ride on a boat along the Seine. In the afternoon, after a long, lazy lunch, they went to the Louvre, where they talked endlessly and laughed a great deal. Strolling through the Tuileries, Rufus draped his arm round her shoulders. Back at the apartment, Faith napped in her room while Rufus painted in his studio. By the time she woke up Jake had come home. He introduced her to Luis, who was cooking: tempting aromas of garlic and tomatoes overlaid the smells of paint and linseed oil.

After they had eaten, people began to drift into the apartment. A rather empty-headed blonde called Marie-Joseph, whom Faith took to be Jake's latest lover (Jake still had awful taste in women), a tall, thin man called Georges, a German girl in slacks, and then she began to lose track of names and faces. The rooms became thick with cigarette smoke and argument. Someone sang, but complained that there was no piano, so half a dozen men ran down the street, wheeled a piano from a nearby bar, and heaved it upstairs, to the complaints of most of the other residents of the apartment block. Faith danced with countless different partners, and someone planted a loud smacking kiss on her cheek. An artist offered to paint her, and a woman gave her the address of the *costumier* for whom she worked. 'I'll find you something nice from the bargain rail, *chérie*.' It all reminded

Faith of the evenings at La Rouilly, when they were younger.

Her head aching slightly, she escaped to the kitchen to make coffee. A great many empty bottles had accumulated beside the dirty crockery. Searching for clean cups, she heard the door close behind her and, looking round, she saw Rufus. He murmured, 'Fancy old Jake keeping you hidden away for so long. Damnably inconsiderate of him, I think. And that's the most gorgeous dress.'

'Do you like it?' A find from La Rouilly's attics, folds of cobweb-grey lace dating, she guessed, from the first decade of the century.

'*La Belle Dame sans Merci*,' muttered Rufus. 'Alone and palely loitering . . .'

She let him kiss her for a while, and then she pulled away and said: 'Rufus. I like you immensely, but—'

'This is too sudden?' He grinned. 'I thought you were a free spirit, like Jake. But I'm willing to wait, if that's what you want, Faith. Till tomorrow, at least.'

The palms of his hands were flat against the wall, enclosing her. 'It's not that,' she said.

'Damn. Then I'm just not your type?'

She laughed. 'I don't know what my type is.'

'Or is there someone else?' He seemed to see the change in her expression. 'Ah. Jake didn't mention . . .'

'No.' She shook her head, thinking of Guy.

He said, 'I shall persevere, you know. I don't give up easily,' and then the door opened, and Jake said cheerfully, 'Keep your hands off my sister, Foxwell, or I'll throttle you.'

Rufus leapt back. 'No offence meant.'

'None taken.'

Faith was searching through a cupboard. 'I can't find any coffee cups.'

'There are jam jars in the cupboard under the sink. Rufus uses them for turps sometimes, don't you, Rufe, but don't let that worry you.'

They drank the coffee perched on the edge of the kitchen table, looking out to where stars were reflected on the smooth black surface of the Seine. Jake said, 'Enjoying yourself?' and Faith nodded.

'You'll stay a few weeks, won't you? There's masses of people I want you to meet.'

'I'll stay a while.' She hooked her hand through his arm. 'Jake. Do you think we should go to England?'

'England? What on earth for? I thought you liked Paris.'

'I adore it. I meant that we should all go to England. Because of the war.'

Jake said, 'You sound like that awful Anni.' He tipped the dregs of his coffee into the sink.

'Don't be cross, Jake. The English Lodgers have gone home, you know.'

His back was to her. After a while he said, 'Home? Where is home for us, Faith?'

'La Rouilly, I suppose. But we are English. We have English passports.' She touched his taut shoulder. 'If something bad should happen . . . *if*, Jake . . . you will come back to us, won't you?'

'You'll never persuade Pa to go to England.'

'It won't be easy, I know. But I think that Ma would like to.'

He said curiously, 'Do you want to go because of Guy?'

She had not seen Guy for over two years. She shook

her head. 'Not really. He's probably forgotten me by now.'

'Nonsense. Guy isn't the forgetting sort.'

She found it hard to imagine England, harder still to imagine herself there, in a land where it was always wet or foggy or cold. Yet that very isolation, that sea-bound fastness, might keep them safe. She said again, 'You will come home, won't you, Jake?'

He humoured her. 'Of course I will. I promise, Faith.'

At Christmas Jake travelled down to his family in Marseilles, argued with Ralph, and then returned early to Paris. Coming back to the rue Ste-Pères apartment, he found it deserted except for Anni, who was sitting at the table eating pickled cabbage out of a jar with her fingers.

Jake dumped his knapsack on the floor. 'What are you doing here?'

She went on eating the cabbage. 'So charming, Jake. As it happens, Rufus has let me borrow his studio. I have rats, and they eat my things. Rufus didn't think there would be anyone here over New Year.' She eyed Jake. 'It seems that he was mistaken. I apologize, and I shall go.'

He knew that he was being boorish, so he made an effort. 'You don't have to go. I came back early.'

'The family festivities were not to your liking?'

'Something like that.' He looked at the cabbage with distaste. 'Haven't you a spoon?'

She gestured to the kitchen. 'I don't believe in doing other people's washing-up.'

The sink was piled even higher than usual. Jake groaned, searched in his pockets for matches, and, after a short battle, lit the geyser. Then he began to sort through the crockery. Cursing the absent Luis, who was spending New Year in Le Touquet with some rich friends of Rufus's, he began irritably to wash up. He was aware, as he worked, of Anni, sitting at the table behind him. After a while, she said: 'I need to work, you understand. You need not worry that I'll intrude upon your *amours*.'

Something in her tone of voice made his irritation boil over into anger. He snapped, 'It's none of your business what I do.'

'Of course it isn't. That's what I said.' She got up and sauntered into Rufus's studio. Jake vented his temper in cleaning the kitchen, until the floors and tabletop gleamed with unnatural brightness and there wasn't a single dirty plate in the apartment. Then he took his address book out of his knapsack and began to go through a long list of names. Marie-Joseph had long since been succeeded by Suzanne, by Martine, by Pepita, but all of them, he discovered after trudging round Paris that New Year's Eve, had prior engagements. He began to feel distinctly sorry for himself, and almost to regret having precipitately left Marseilles. Returning to the apartment, he discovered a bouquet of flowers left outside the front door, addressed to Mademoiselle Anni Schwartz. He could hear the gramophone indoors; he supposed she hadn't heard the doorbell.

He gathered up the bouquet, went inside, and knocked at the door of the studio. 'You're the Cream in my Coffee' was playing very loudly. Anni was sitting at the table, her head bent over a square of paper. She looked up and said, 'Jake. I didn't know you cared,' and he glanced at the flowers and flushed.

'Not me – they were outside – the gramophone—'

'I know, *Liebchen*, I know.' She turned down the volume so that the song just whispered in the background. Then she ruffled his hair and took the flowers from him. She had a way of effortlessly making him feel foolish. 'Chrysanthemums – ugh.' She glanced at the card. 'And they're from Christian.' She made a face. 'Christian is very, very dull. I'll give them to the concierge. Why does one so often receive flowers from men one does not want to receive them from?'

He caught sight of the woodcut on the table. 'This is lovely,' he said. He had not meant to stay, and he certainly had not meant to compliment her, but he could not help himself. The small print was of a graceful château, surrounded by woodland. He asked, 'Where is it?'

'It's nowhere in particular. A little bit of each of my favourite places put together.'

'It reminds me of somewhere.' Yet Anni's picture was of a much older building than La Rouilly, a château with turrets and pinnacles and formal gardens. He tried to explain. 'It looks . . . peaceful.'

'Then I've done good work today. But you, Jake, I didn't think I'd see you again until tomorrow. Have your lady friends deserted you?'

He said sullenly, 'They've all got things fixed up.'

'Poor Jake. And is your heart broken?'

'Of course it is. I adore them.'

She began to clear away her cutting tools. 'I rather thought you despised them.'

'What a ridiculous thing to say.'

She wiped ink from the table with a cloth. She was wearing paint-stained slacks and a threadbare old shirt and looked, Jake thought, even more dreadful than usual. He heard her say, 'You court beautiful women believing that they are unattainable, but when they return your admiration you no longer want them. You only want what you cannot have.'

'Dear God,' he said. 'I thought you were an artist, not a psychoanalyst.'

She smiled. 'And now, poor Jake, all your sweethearts are managing quite well without you. There is only one thing to do, I'm afraid. We shall have to celebrate the New Year together.'

He thought at first that she was still laughing at him. But when she began to search through a cardboard box, withdrawing eventually a slightly cleaner shirt, and she turned to him and said, 'Don't you think you should go, Jake, while I change my clothes?' he realized that she was serious, and he went red and mumbled something and left the room.

They went to smoky basement cafés in seedy backstreets, rooms filled with jazz music, sweet with the scent of hashish. He made a hundred new friends, and could not remember any of their names. At midnight, he drew her aside and kissed her. Her lips were cool against his, and afterwards he found himself watching her, searching for her as she threaded through the crowds, laughing, and embracing her friends. What had once seemed to him objectionable or repulsive – her short, cropped hair, her small, strong body – had become intriguing.

At dawn, they walked back to the apartment. He was rather drunk, and at that stage of tiredness when everything seems tinged with unreality. There was a bottle of champagne in his pocket – he could not remember where he had taken it from – and his mouth was stale with tobacco smoke. Anni walked beside him, her hands dug deep into the pockets of her jacket, unaffected by fatigue, her stride as quick and bouncy as ever. In Rufus's apartment Jake opened the champagne while Anni found glasses and put on a record. 'To 1940,' he said. 'To love and fame and fortune,' he began to add, but she placed her finger against his mouth, silencing him.

'Don't think of the future,' she said, as she unbuttoned his shirt.

She seduced him, something that had not happened to him since he lost his virginity at sixteen. She did things to him that no woman had done before. But it was not *that* – the caresses, the kisses, the geography of love – that took his breath away, leaving him tight-chested and exhausted, as though he had run for miles through a dark, winding forest. What was different was that for the first time in his life he had lost himself; a small part of him no longer stood back, mocking him, watching her, assessing, finding something wanting. When at last he fell back onto the pillow, he did not know whether they had made love for a few moments or for a day. He had lost the ability to divide time into hours, minutes, seconds. There was just Anni: her skin against his, her scent filling his lungs, her heart echoing the beat of his.

He was woken by a door slamming in the apartment below. He was alone. He got up, still naked, and wandered from one room to the next. She was not there and, had it not been for the small ribbon of red left by her fingernails on the skin across his shoulder blades, he would have wondered whether he had imagined the events of the night.

* * *

The Mulgraves spent the winter travelling. It seemed to Faith that they moved faster and faster, in an ever-constricting spiral. The snow and frost of an icy season bit into them, driving from Menton to Antibes, Antibes to St-Jean-de-Luz. They remained nowhere for more than a few weeks at a time. Arriving at each new hotel, lodging-house or rented flat, Ralph looked and said, 'Yes, this is the place,' but in a month, sometimes less, his satisfaction evaporated, and he herded them back into the car, heaping them with suitcases and birdcages and boxes of books.

Ralph had spent the money destined for the schooner on an ageing and enormous Citroën which broke down at monotonously inconvenient moments. Poppy endured the breakdowns and the cold and the ever smaller and pokier houses with her mouth set in a line of grim endurance. Nicole, sitting on the back seat of the car with Minette, her King Charles spaniel, and her kittens, her rabbit and a cageful of canaries, shivered in the mangy mink she had bought from a market in Toulon. At each new town Faith found a job in a shop or restaurant, and saved her wages. Half in francs, half in pounds sterling, just in case.

One night, travelling through northern Italy, Poppy, in the front passenger seat, dozed. Nicole stared out of the window. Snowflakes like bronze coins sparkled in the beams from the headlamps. Ralph, driving, glanced at the map. 'Nearly there.'

Nearly where? Faith thought. Which house? Which country? She had forgotten the names of the friends with whom they were to stay.

'The Lovatts always winter in Italy,' said Ralph confidently.

In the early hours of the morning, he drew to a halt

outside a house tucked into the hillside. The building was in darkness. Faith could see only the gates, and the cypresses heavy with snow. Ralph shook Poppy to wake her, and began to unload cases from the boot. Nicole climbed out of the car. A padlock tied the gates of the house together. The snow fell at an oblique angle. Nicole, her coat pulled tightly about her, squeezed through the gap between the gatepost and the hedge. Faith followed her.

Their boots crunched the snow as they walked up the drive. There were no other indentations in the smooth, white carpet, no lamp in the doorway, no motor-car parked on the forecourt. Every now and then the moon would show its face between the clouds, and illuminate the shuttered windows, the closed doors. The sisters circled the house, treading a path through the garden. The snow hid the flowers in the parterres and distorted the statues, transforming nymphs into grotesques.

After a while, Nicole said, 'There's no-one here, is there, Faith?' She was shivering.

'They must have stayed in England this winter.'

'It's too still. Too quiet. I hate this place.'

Faith did not reply. She was aware, looking at the shuttered house, of a feeling of utter desolation. It was as though, she thought, they had been spun out to the edge of a vortex, and could not return to the centre, but lingered on the periphery, excluded. As though they occupied a limbo set aside for vagrants.

Nicole was throwing snowballs at a statue. The savage movement of her arm broke the frozen immobility of the landscape. Clumps of snow tumbled in a powdery haze to the ground. 'I can't bear,' she said angrily, 'when things just stay the same.'

* * *

Jake noticed neither the cold weather nor the increasingly gloomy news. When, all too rarely, he was with Anni, he could think of nothing but her; when she was not there, he was consumed by wondering where she was, who she was with, what she was doing. Just as certain foods were now restricted in Paris, so Anni seemed to ration herself. Sometimes Jake did not see her for weeks at a time, and he would be aware of a burgeoning, almost murderous anger, and then she would knock at his door or appear at the bar, and all his resentment would melt away. Sometimes he would try to break away from her, chagrined by her absences, her obstinacy, her opinionatedness. His attempts at separation, however, would last only to her next telephone call, her next letter.

Once she asked him back to the room she rented near the Père-Lachaise cemetery. There was a press in one corner of the room, and a table heaped with inks and wood-cutting tools, and a mattress, and not much else. They made love on the mattress, and afterwards lit cigarettes and lay still, drowsy with pleasure, hardly able to move, watching the smoke rings float to the ceiling. She said, 'Perhaps we should marry,' in a voice so muted, so casual, that he thought he had mistaken her words.

'Pardon?'

'I said, perhaps we should marry.'

He laughed. 'Mr and Mrs Mulgrave, walking down the aisle. Can you imagine? What would you wear, Anni? White satin or your painter's smock with ink stains on it?'

She did not reply. He could not see her face, only her springy dark hair, cradled in the crook of his arm. His words echoed in the small, dingy room.

At the beginning of May, after the surrender of Norway to Germany, Rufus went back to London, leaving his apartment to Jake and Luis. On 15 May, Holland capitulated; the German army pushed relentlessly south. Jake, noticing the haunted look in Luis's eyes, dragged him out to a bar, where they drank a great deal of brandy. Jake tried to cheer him up, but Luis just looked at him with mournful brown eyes and said little. A few days later Jake came back to the apartment after work, and discovered a note signed by Luis. 'Am heading for Mexico by way of North Africa. Remember me. *No pasaran!*' Jake crumpled up the note, and hurled it out of the window. The German army had reached the English Channel. To Jake, the apartment seemed overlarge, empty, echoing.

Jake tried to persuade Anni to move in with him now that Rufus and Luis were gone. But she smiled and shook her head and said, 'Oh no, Jake. I don't think that would be a good idea. You're too untidy and I have to be alone to work.'

He had a sense of things coming to an end, slipping through his fingers. He wanted to hold on to all that he had found: to Paris, and to his strange, seesawing happiness with Anni. Yet by the end of May, when he received Faith's letter, a great many of his friends had already left the city. He glanced at the note, then stuffed it into his pocket. He could not go home, as Faith had asked him to, because he had not seen Anni for a fortnight. Jake knew that Anni, unlike Luis and Rufus, had not left France, because he had several times walked to her apartment and peered through the window and seen the clothes, the neatly stacked cups and saucers, the inks and cutters and press. Fleeing the country, she might have abandoned her scruffy shirts and chipped cups, but he knew that she would not have left behind the tools of her trade.

Now he read the newspapers, and now the wireless was on constantly in the bar and in the apartment. As German tanks swept remorselessly south, as the French army of the Meuse fragmented at the onslaught, and as remnants of the British Expeditionary Force waited for rescue on the beaches of Dunkirk, refugees from the north trailed dispiritedly into Paris. Some of the sights he saw seemed to Jake surreal: a Dutch farmer and his cattle resting at Les Invalides, the cows cropping the grass, and, outside the city, the endless rivers of rattling, dusty motor-cars, crowded with grandmothers and children, a mattress on the roof of each vehicle. German planes circled overhead, dropping their bombs on the suburbs. Jake, remembering Spain, considered possibilities, weighed choices.

Yet the cafés were still thronged with women in pretty dresses and impatient men calling for beer, and students still browsed among the bookstalls on the Left Bank. Posters pasted to the walls exhorted the citizens of Paris. *Chantons quand même! Citoyens! Aux armes!*

On 10 June Paris seemed to Jake like a ghost town. The Champs-Elysées were silent; the rich, with their cars, had left the city. Only the curious, the fatalistic, and a scattering of Americans, immune to fear because of their nationality, remained. The sun burned, a hard bronze disc in the sky. Jake did not go to work, but walked from bar to bar, café to café, revisiting all the places he remembered from New Year's Eve, looking for Anni.

Just after lunch, he was rewarded. A Senegalese saxophonist drawled, 'Anni? Saw her a couple of hours ago, *mon brave*. She was heading for the Gare d'Austerlitz.'

Jake ran along the bank of the Seine towards the station. His shirt stuck to his back with sweat. As he neared the Gare d'Austerlitz, the vast crowds that surrounded the building slowed him. Though he pushed and shoved, though he was younger and stronger and taller than most, he could make little headway. He was swimming against a great tide of humanity, seized by a terrible feeling of impotence, an awful fear that he would never see her again. He had to force himself to think rationally. Skirting round to the back of the station, shoving his way through the press of people, he found eventually a gate leading into the goods yard. Clambering up, he hauled himself over the gate, careful of the spikes along the top. Then, weaving through the crates and trunks and packing-cases, he made for the passenger platforms.

The people on the platform seemed to Jake to be crushed into a solid mass. The children did not cry, but their faces were wrinkled and old. Their abjectness shook him from his own anguish, but then he thought, *Anni*, and began to push through the crowds again. He was shocked by the sight of people passing babies over the heads of the crowd to the safety of a side room so that they would not be crushed. Trains seemed to be scattered anyhow around the station, passengers' limbs and faces pressed against the glass. The heat was unbearable. He saw an old woman faint, a draining of colour from her face, a closing of her eyes, yet she remained upright, kept on her feet by the press of the crowd to either side of her. As Jake tried to reach the train, he searched constantly for Anni, his gaze darting from one dark-haired woman to another.

And then he saw her. She was sitting in the window seat of one of the carriages, just a few yards away from him. The engine let out a burst of steam, and Jake made a last terrible effort, waving his hands above his head and shouting her name, shoving the whole weight of his body forward, not caring whom he pushed aside. Slowly, she turned towards him, and her eyes, behind the partition of glass, focused.

She pushed down the window. 'Jake!' she called. 'What are you doing here?'

He shouted, 'I came to find you!' and he tried to inch forward again, reaching out to her. 'I had to see you. Where are you going?'

'I'm going to Nice. I'm meeting Christian there.'

Jake remembered the chrysanthemums that Anni had received on New Year's Eve. They had been sent to her by someone called Christian.

'We're going to be married.'

He was stilled suddenly, as much by her words as by the crowds that pressed against him.

She called, 'You must look after your family, Jake. Don't worry about me.'

He found his voice at last. 'You said that he was dull – you can't *marry* him—'

'Christian has a farm in Kenya. I'll be safe there.'

Jake lunged forward, his hand outstretched. He felt that if only he could touch her, then she would remember what they had meant to each other, and give up this foolish idea of marrying the unknown, tedious Christian. The guard's whistle shrieked as he shouted, 'You should marry *me*.'

She smiled. 'I thought we discussed that already, *Liebchen.*'

Jake's outstretched fingers slipped to his side. He

remembered lying in bed with Anni; and he remembered that she had said, *Perhaps we should marry*. He remembered also that he had laughed.

As the pistons on the carriages began slowly to move she called out, 'And besides, if I went to Britain, I would be interned.' The train started to pull away from the platform; desperately, he threw himself towards her.

'*Anni.*'

'You must go home, Jake,' she shouted back to him. 'You must save your family. The Nazis will intern all Britons. You must—'

But the rest of her words were swallowed up in the scream of the engines, and the collective howl of those left behind on the platform as the train swung down the rails.

He stood quite still, unable to believe that she had gone, that he had lost her. At length Jake pushed back through the crowds, looking for an exit. It took him over an hour to make his way through the crowds to the apartment. There he drank a large glass of brandy and veered between cursing Anni and wanting to weep. Then he turned on the wireless and heard that the German army was approaching Pontoise, only thirty kilometres from Paris. Reaching into his jacket pocket for his cigarettes, he rediscovered Faith's note. After he had read it again, he screwed the stopper back on the brandy bottle, sluiced his face with water, and threw some things into a knapsack. Then he left the apartment, not bothering to lock the door after him.

Walking south, he reckoned his chances. The scenes at the Gare d'Austerlitz had told him that he hadn't a hope in hell of leaving the city by train. The wireless had said that the main roads from Paris were blocked with cars and vans, many of which had run out of petrol. He walked on, thinking, and then he saw a row of bicycles propped against a wall outside a church. He chose the newest and sturdiest bicycle, climbed on it and cycled out of the city. Mulgrave Rules, Jake reminded himself, as his legs began to ache, and sweat poured down his face. Stick together whatever happens.

Even La Rouilly had changed. The Lodgers, like Felix, like Guy, had scattered to their own corners of the earth, and there persisted an undercurrent of tension, the ozone-scent as the storm crackles on the horizon. Yet Ralph's conviction that he and his family would remain in France was, until the June of 1940, unshaken. When the wireless announced that the German army was outside Paris, Ralph swore and drank a great deal, and rose the following morning filled with a new resolve. Paris might fall, Tours might fall, Bordeaux might fall, but La Rouilly would not. Ransacking the garden sheds for spades and shovels, Ralph organized the digging of tank traps. With the help of the girls and Reynaud the handyman, he dug deep pits in the woodland around La Rouilly, covering the pits with staves. Genya, Sarah and Poppy, on Ralph's orders, hauled sides of ham and bags of dried beans and rice into the cellar. Ralph inspected the shelves of provisions, the bottles of wine, with approval. 'We can hole up here for weeks. We'll show the bastards.'

The following evening, he ordered Faith and Nicole to follow him up to the attic. All three climbed onto the roof of the château. Ralph carried with him three nailed crosspieces of wood. From the roof they could see to the distant silvery line of the Gironde, and to the shifting, mirrored sea. Ralph shaded his eyes with his hand.

'We'll position the guns here' – he pointed first to a chimney, then to the jutting corners of the parapet – 'here, and here.' He placed the crosspieces on the positions he had indicated. 'We can use these to aim.'

Nicole and Faith exchanged glances. 'What are we to shoot, Pa?'

'Who, not what. The Hun, of course.'

Faith tugged Ralph's sleeve. 'When Jake comes home, we'll go to England, won't we, Pa?'

'England? Never!' Ralph ducked into the skylight. 'I'm going to the kitchen to help Genya make pipe bombs.'

Faith sat down, her back against a chimney stack, feeling suddenly hopeless. Nicole sat beside her. Faith heard Nicole say, 'If it happens – if they come here, Faith – do you think any of this will make any difference?'

Just then, it seemed to Faith entirely possible that they would stay, and that in weeks – days – she might watch armoured cars drive through the woods that surrounded La Rouilly, their heavy wheels crushing the wild flowers, scarring the lawn. Her dread lay like a stone in her stomach. Mutely, she shook her head.

'I won't hide in the cellar,' declared Nicole. 'I hate the cellar. It's too dark, and there are bats.'

Faith said, 'Ma wants to go to England. I asked her.'

They sat in silence for a while, their knees hunched up to their chins, watching the last flare of sunset ebb from the sky. Eventually Faith added miserably: 'We must persuade him.'

'How?' Nicole scowled. 'Pa won't listen to you.'

'And he won't listen to Ma.'

'And Jake isn't here.'

'Jake'll come home soon.'

'He is a rat, to stay away so long. A damnable rat. He should talk to Pa.'

'Pa never listens to Jake, you know that, Nicole. Anyway, I've written to him. He'll be home any day. He promised.'

The sky had darkened. The first bright star had appeared over the horizon. They looked at each other, and they both whispered together, '*Genya*.'

By Tuesday night Jake had travelled as far as Etampes, only forty kilometres south of Paris. The roads were thick with all sorts of vehicles: cars and lorries, farmers' hay carts, even an ancient horse-drawn carriage. It all reminded Jake horribly of his flight from Spain. The queues of traffic, punctuated frequently by abandoned vehicles, impeded even the bicycle. The anger and misery of the refugees was palpable, and he was tormented constantly by the fear that he had left Paris too late. *If something bad should happen, you will come back to us, won't you?* Faith's voice haunted him. He imagined his parents and sisters in a camp like the one at Argelès, interned as enemy aliens.

He slept overnight in a ditch with a thousand other vagrants. The following morning he rose early and took the first track he could find leading away from the main road. He cycled past a herd of bullocks and through channels of wheat and beneath huge, lichened beech trees, stopping at length in the shade and studying the map again.

Hauling the bicycle over high hedges and across ditches was exhausting, but Jake was rewarded eventually by the sight of a narrow, winding back road, empty of traffic. He cycled at speed until the fingers of dusk that spread across the road prevented him from seeing where he was going. Then he lugged the bike behind a hedge, curled up in the undergrowth and was asleep within minutes.

He was woken early the next morning by a cow licking his face. He breakfasted on tinned peaches and the last inch of water in his flask, and then he set off again. Towards midday, when the sun was burning his scalp, he flagged down a farmer on his hay cart, and offered to exchange the remains of his brandy for a lift to the next village. The farmer spat on the ground, and said nothing, but took the brandy and allowed Jake to haul himself and the bicycle onto the hay. He slept deeply, and woke with a sunburnt nose in a village near Pithiviers. The village was populated by soldiers and by abandoned dogs, both wandering the streets in a similarly aimless fashion. All the shops and the café had run out of food, but Jake bought strawberries from an old woman working in her allotment. When he asked her why she too was not fleeing the German army, she shrugged and said, 'The sun burns my crops and the drought shrivels my seedlings. What difference will the Germans make to that?' Then she filled Jake's water bottle for him, and wished him *bonne chance*, and went back to her weeding.

Outside the village, he was caught up once more in the stream of refugees. As they moved slowly along, he heard in the distance a sound that chilled him. For a moment he was back on the road from Barcelona, trying to escape the aeroplanes of the Condor Legion. Swinging round, he saw the half-dozen tiny silver marks against the forget-me-not-blue sky. He had to shade his hand over his eyes and squint to make out the shape of the aeroplanes, their nationality. His heart began to hammer as he recognized the German Stukas. He looked around for a place to hide, and caught sight of a ditch to the far side of the road. Shouting a warning, he flung his bicycle into the ditch. He knew that without the bicycle he hadn't a hope of reaching La Rouilly in time. Then, hearing screams of panic, he hauled children out of cars and dumped them unceremoniously in the ditch, and piggybacked a fragile old man to the shelter of a tree. He felt the impact of the bombs through the baked earth before he heard their explosion. Curled in the ditch, his hands covering his head, Jake's fear was overlaid by an anger so intense it exhausted him. When the bombardment had finished, when the Stukas had had their sport, he climbed out of the ditch and looked around. Once he would have wept at such sights: the tangled metal of the cars, the craters in the cornfields, the splintered limbs and sprawled bodies. Now, as the exodus began again, the refugees white-faced and stumbling with shock, his anger and grief were superseded by a dread that he would not reach La Rouilly in time. He despised himself for having waited for Anni, who had not loved him enough. He left the main road once more, venting both his fury and his anxiety in the speed of his pedalling.

Travelling along winding back roads, he saw no-one until mid-afternoon. Then, as he freewheeled down a hill, he caught sight of a motor-car stationary in the middle of the road. A very smart motor-car: an Alfa, he thought, one of those natty little sports jobs more suited to the circuit at Le Mans than to French back roads. As he drew closer, he saw the woman sitting on the verge. She, like the car, was expensive and glossy;

her head was sheltered from the sun by a wide-brimmed straw hat, and she was smoking a cigarette in a holder. She was thirtyish, he guessed, and she wore a beautifully cut suit, silk stockings and dark glasses. When he braked, her face tilted towards him. 'I have a puncture,' she said, as though he were a mechanic that she had called out from a garage.

'Where are you heading?'

'To a château near Blois.'

Jake thought quickly. 'I'll repair your puncture if you give me a lift to Blois.'

She shrugged. 'Very well.'

She just sat there while he sweated and panted over the puncture. The wheel nuts were stiff, and he had to use all his strength to budge them. When it was done, and he had wiped his oily hands on the grass and emptied the contents of his water flask over his head, he squeezed his bicycle into the narrow back seat.

'Just about fits. Come on.'

She drove fast and skilfully, the Alfa taking the narrow, curving lanes with a speed that almost took Jake's breath away. He could feel the miles slipping away behind him, and his optimism began to return. After a while, discomfited by her silence, he said: 'If we're to be travelling companions, perhaps I should introduce myself. My name's Jake Mulgrave.'

'The Comtesse de Chevillard. But you may call me Hélène.' She extended a white-gloved hand. 'There's brandy in the glove compartment, Jake.'

They both drank as they travelled. Her driving became faster, more reckless. The sky dimmed, and the trees cast long purple shadows across the road. In the darkness, unable to read the map, he lost track of their route. It felt as though they were the last people alive, speeding along the lanes of rural France, beneath a moon that was huge and pale in an inky sky. The brandy added to Jake's sense of unreality, his feeling that the world as he had known it had changed for ever. When he saw the lids of Hélène's eyes slide slowly shut, he grabbed the steering wheel from her and said, 'You're tired. We should stop for a while.'

She whispered, 'Yes,' and he glanced at his watch. It was almost ten o'clock.

He said, 'Let me drive while you look out for somewhere.'

They exchanged seats; Jake drove, and after a while she said, 'Here. Turn here.' They headed through wrought-iron gates, down a narrow, tree-lined avenue. At length he saw, outlined by moonlight, a large house. The fairy-tale turrets and pinnacles reminded him of the château in Anni's engraving, and he felt a stab of pain and anger at her leaving of him.

He brought the Alfa to a halt on the gravel courtyard in front of the house. Hélène climbed out of the car and walked to the door. The steps were strewn with a haphazard tangle of clothes and household goods – spoons, jewellery, children's toys – as though someone had held a rummage sale in the porch. Jake tried the handle, and the door slid open. Striking a match, he peered into the vestibule. Picture frames, their canvases torn away, lay splintered on the carpet. Pale squares on the walls showed where they had once hung.

He muttered, 'Looters.'

She clutched his elbow. 'They may still be here.'

'I don't think so.' Like her, he whispered. 'There may be food. I'm starving.'

He went back to the car and took a torch from the boot. Back in the silent house, he searched for a kitchen or pantry. The house was littered with evidence of its despoliation. The clatter of Hélène's high-heeled shoes seemed unnaturally loud. He heard her say, 'They haven't even *taken* things. They've just broken them – just ripped them apart.' He saw fragments of Venetian glass and an Aubusson rug slashed by someone's knife, and he was unmoved, remembering the column of refugees, the bombers.

The kitchen and pantries had been stripped. There was something obscene about the empty shelves, the gaping cupboards. But he found a crate of vegetables beneath a rubbish bin, and there was, miraculously, coal in the stove. He turned to ask her whether she could cook, and then knew it would be pointless, and set about peeling potatoes and scrubbing carrots himself. She wandered into the moonlit garden. When the vegetables were boiled, he discovered that Hélène had put a small posy of flowers in the centre of the large wooden table, and had laid it for two with silver cutlery and Murano glass that the looters had somehow overlooked. 'There must be a cellar,' he said. Searching the house, he found a locked door, but no key. There was an axe in the outhouse: hacking at the door, Jake thought he was no better than those who had previously defiled this beautiful house. But the wine was good; he needed the wine.

After they had eaten, they went upstairs. The bedrooms were opulent, the four-posters draped with silks and velvets. Jake pulled off his boots before collapsing on the bed. After a while, when the day's events had begun to shift uneasily into dreams (the strawberries the old woman offered him were small, beating hearts; the flesh of the fallen refugees at the roadside peeled away as he turned their faces to the sun), he was jerked suddenly into wakefulness by the sound of the door opening. He sat up, staring into the darkness, his heart pounding. Then he heard Hélène say, 'I couldn't sleep. I keep thinking they might come back. Do you mind if I share your bed?'

She was wearing a silk camisole and knickers. She pulled apart the sheets and slipped between them. They fell asleep, her body curled against his, but at dawn Jake woke, and touched his lips against her satiny shoulder. Making love to Hélène, his desire was intensified by a need to revenge himself for Anni's desertion of him. Afterwards they rose and dressed and drove on. When they parted at Blois at midday, they shook hands and said polite farewells.

The fast progress he had made the previous day dissipated that afternoon. It began to rain, heavy drops that turned the dust to mud. On an unmetalled road, the bicycle punctured, and it seemed to take an age, crouched on the verge, rain streaming down his face, to repair it. Passing through a village whose streets swarmed with refugees, he saw, pinned to the board outside the Hôtel de Ville, a series of notices. 'Madame Lebrun, staying next door to the church, is looking for her sons Edouard (4 years) and Paul (6 years), lost here on 11 June.' And 'Madame Tabouis, poste restante, Bordeaux, seeks news of her daughter, Marianne, aged eight, lost ten kilometres from Tours on 12 June.' There were photographs pinned next to the advertisements. Jake looked for a moment at the small, smiling faces, then climbed on his bicycle and cycled on.

He spent the night in a barn halfway between Tours and Poitiers. The farmer's wife fed him and half a dozen others soup and home-made bread. Every muscle in his body ached, and he shivered in his damp clothing. As she collected the empty bowls the farmer's wife told them that Paris had fallen to the German army. Then she handed each of them an enamel mug of fine champagne. '*Liberté*,' she said, and drank.

The wireless in the kitchen at La Rouilly was tuned to the BBC. The Mulgraves, Genya and Sarah listened to the news, and then to the small, distant voice of the Queen of England, as she sent a message of hope and affection to France. Afterwards, the chords of the Marseillaise and 'God Save the King' echoed round the room.

Genya's voice broke the ensuing silence. Placing her small, wrinkled hand over Ralph's massive paw, she said gently, 'You must go, my dear Ralph. You must all go to England. You'll be safe there.'

'Can't bear the bloody place—' Ralph began, but Genya squeezed his fingers, silencing him.

'France will survive. La Rouilly will survive. Your family, if you remain, may not. When all this horror is over, you will come back, dear Ralph, and everything will be just the same.'

Nicole knelt at Ralph's side. 'I don't want to stay here, Pa.'

He barked, 'Why? Are you frightened? Of all of you, I thought that you, Nicole, were the least likely—'

She interrupted calmly, 'Of course I'm not frightened, but I'm afraid that everything will become dull and tiresome, and you know how I hate that.'

There were tears in his eyes. He said gruffly, 'And the boy? Can't leave without the boy.'

'Jake will come home,' said Faith. 'He promised me.'

Slowly, Ralph turned to Genya. 'And you, dear Genya?'

Genya smiled. 'I am far too old for such a journey. I have travelled from Poland to La Rouilly, and at La Rouilly Sarah and I will remain. It's our home. You, Ralph, have no home. Perhaps now you must find one.'

Poppy whispered, '*Please*, Ralph.'

Ralph rubbed the back of his hand across his eyes. When, almost imperceptibly, he nodded, it seemed to Faith that the house itself let out a small, quiet sigh of relief.

Poppy said, 'Then we must pack.'

Nicole hugged Ralph. 'Darling Pa.'

'There's petrol in the car.'

'We'll take one of the shotguns. Nicole, fetch a gun and a box of cartridges—'

'And Minette . . .' Nicole knelt beside her dog. 'And Snip and Snap . . . and the rabbits . . . and my goldfish—'

'You can take the dog – could be useful against the Hun. As for the rabbits, they might come in handy if we run out of food.'

'*Pa!*'

'I shall look after the rabbits and the kittens and the goldfish,' said Genya hastily. 'You mustn't worry, *ma chère*. Now, go and fetch the shotgun for your father.'

'Poppy, first aid stuff. Bandages and disinfectant, in case we are wounded. Faith – torches and candles, as many as Genya can spare.' Ralph turned to Genya. His voice softened. 'Dearest Genya, come with us. You will come with us, won't you?'

She shook her head. 'No, Ralph.'

'But *Poland* . . . Look what the blackguards have done to Poland.'

'I know, Ralph. And that's why I shall stay. I shall burn La Rouilly to the ground, waving a Polish flag in the embers, rather than let them take it. And I will die happy if I know that you are safe.'

Faith saved what could be fitted into her battered old rucksack. The cobweb-grey evening dress, a Vionnet cape, the two pleated Fortuny gowns, a black crêpe, and, of course, the Holly Blue dress. She folded it carefully, a talisman against an uncertain future, wrapping it in tissue paper.

She did not sleep at all that night. Countless times she rose and went to the window, looking for Jake. In the early hours of the morning, when it was still dark, she dressed, and found Ralph alone in the front room, poring over a map. Tugging his sleeve, she said, '*Jake*,' and he growled, 'He'll find us,' but she saw the agony in his eyes. Tears began to slide down her cheeks; she rubbed them angrily away with her fingers. Ralph said, 'I thought Bordeaux, but I've telephoned Sophie and she tells me that the place is so chock-a-block with refugees you can't move.'

'The government has moved there from Tours.'

'And the Gironde is mined, and they're bombing the railway station.' Ralph sounded furious. 'So I've decided that we should drive north. Everyone else will be going in the opposite direction. We'll make for La Rochelle. We'll find a boat there. I know dozens of people in La Rochelle. And besides . . .'

His words trailed off. She knew, though, the hope that he dared not voice. *And besides, we may meet Jake on his way south.*

When, an hour later, they left La Rouilly, the sun had not yet risen. The stars that peppered the sky were reflected in the dark, limpid waters of the lake. The two sisters knelt on the back seat of the Citroën, looking back, not even blinking, trying to sear Genya, waving from the courtyard, and the house, pale in the pre-dawn light, into their memories so that they could keep them both there in all the fathomless months to come.

Jake's journey had acquired a dreamlike quality: one of those nightmares where you run as fast as you can only to find yourself frozen to one spot. He knew that somewhere not far behind him the German army was sweeping south, and that he had to find his family before the Nazis found him and interned him as an enemy alien. Fleeting, terrible scenes fixed themselves in his memory as he travelled. A priest pushing an ancient woman in a wheelbarrow; lost infants wandering at the roadside, crying for their mothers. A cluster of British soldiers, separated from their regiment, sitting beneath a copse, listening to a gramophone. He had called out to them to find out where he was, and they had shrugged and shouted cheerfully back, 'Haven't a fucking clue, mate.'

He had run out of food, and his belly ached with hunger. Every muscle hurt. Turning the pedals was the act of an automaton. He had given up cursing himself for not leaving Paris earlier; he had not the strength for either regret or anger. Sometimes he did not bother to look for shelter as the Stukas circled overhead, but cycled on as the bombs fell around him.

At midday he slid off the saddle and fell asleep at the side of the road. He was woken by a movement, a scraping of metal and rubber. His lids jerked open, and he focused on the man stooping beside his bicycle.

'That's *mine*,' said Jake angrily.

A boot struck him in the stomach. He retched, but sprang to his feet, fury and fear giving him speed.

Weaving through the column of refugees he managed to grab the back mudguard. The wheels shook and slowed; Jake hurled himself at the thief. They both crashed to the ground. Jake was younger, stronger, fitter: seizing a clump of filthy, matted hair, he struck the other man's head repeatedly against the hard, sun-baked surface of the road.

The grip on his arms loosened, and the man lay still. Jake's first emotion was one of relief that the bicycle had not been damaged in the struggle. He cycled away. There was a daub of blood on his shirt. He expected someone to stop him, to call him to account. A hundred people must have seen him batter that man. He might even have killed him. And the bicycle wasn't really his anyway.

But no-one called out. Dulled eyes glanced at him and then turned away. He realized then that everything had changed, that nothing was ever going to be the same again.

Faith drove the car. Every now and then the column of refugees spilled over both sides of the road, and then Ralph leaned out of the side window and fired the shotgun into the air, and the men and women and children shuffled back to the right side of the road, and the Mulgraves drove on.

When Faith reached the fork in the road that swung off to La Rochelle she braked and looked at Ralph. He shook his head, and said, 'No. We can turn off further north.' She felt as though the last little bit of hope was squeezed like sand in the palm of her hand, trickling slowly away. Every fair-haired young man she glimpsed on the road made her heart pound first with optimism, and then with despair.

In the middle of the afternoon, they approached the crossroads that branched off to the coast. Faith knew that if they were to drive further north, they risked reaching the port after the last ship had sailed, or worse, meeting the invading German army.

Ralph stared at the long, straight rise of the road ahead of them. He said, 'We'll stop and eat. Half an hour. And then we'll drive to La Rochelle.'

The hill seemed endless. He had retreated inside himself, so that he was no longer aware of the burning sun, or his hunger and thirst, or his cramping limbs. He had forgotten Anni. In his mind's eye, as he cycled uphill, Jake recalled scenes from his childhood. He remembered jellyfish, translucent and beribboned with long, trailing tentacles, bobbing in blue water. He remembered a farmhouse in Tuscany, playing hide-and-seek in the cool darkness of the barns and wine cellars. And he remembered the woods behind La Rouilly, picnicking with Faith and Nicole and Guy. He wondered whether Guy knew that Faith loved him. He thought it would be nice to be like Faith, always loving the same person.

He reached the top of the hill at last, and slid his feet from the pedals, leaning his wheezing lungs against the handlebars, looking down. The sky was dotted with stars, though it was afternoon. When Jake blinked, the stars vanished. And when he looked down again, he saw that the road was empty except for a solitary car, parked on the verge.

He thought at first that he was imagining them. That, exhausted and dehydrated as he was, his memory had kept hold of the ghosts of the past and had transplanted them to the present. For there, at the foot of the hill, were his family. They were picnicking.

Poppy was handing round sandwiches, Ralph was uncorking a bottle of wine. Minette rested her head on Nicole's lap, waiting for scraps. Jake closed his eyes, but when he opened them again his family were still there.

He thought, *and who but the Mulgraves would picnic while the world ended?* As he climbed back onto the saddle and freewheeled down the hill, he found that he was laughing.

Unfamiliar Shores

July 1940 – December 1941

Chapter Four

London was vast, grey and dusty. By day, sunlight glittered on the roof tiles, and the barrage balloons dotting the sky were gold and sapphire and silver as they twisted slowly in the heat haze. At night, in the blackout, the only pinpoints of brightness were the stars. When Faith looked out of the windows of her room, it seemed to her that the snarl of roads and buildings went on for ever.

Rufus Foxwell had suggested Faith and Jake share the house he rented in Mahonia Road in Islington. The house was part of a dilapidated Georgian terrace that had once, long ago, been elegant. Rufus had also recommended to Jake a pub in need of barmen, and had put Faith in touch with an acquaintance looking for a paid companion. Rufus had resolved their most pressing problems: a place to live, money so that they could buy food to eat. The nightmares remained. The recollection of their first night in England haunted Faith. When they docked in a tiny fishing village on the south coast after a day and a night at sea, Ralph had insisted they continue to London. But the nearest railway station had been several miles away, and after they had walked for an hour or two it had grown dark, and they had realized that they were lost, and Poppy had wept with exhaustion. She had just sat on her suitcase, and cried into her pocket handkerchief. They had slept in a field that night, curled up in the corn, marooned on the borders of an unfamiliar land. Silently, looking up at the stars, Faith too had wept: for France, for all that they had lost.

In the morning they had discovered a bus stop only a few hundred yards away. The bus had taken them to the railway station at Woodleigh. Faith's savings had paid for their tickets to London. They had arrived at Aunt Iris's house filthy, exhausted, and with a total of eleven shillings and sixpence between them. Aunt Iris had been helpful, but understandably distant. She and Poppy had neither spoken nor written to each other for twenty years. Iris had offered Ralph, Poppy and Nicole her holiday cottage in Norfolk. Faith and Jake had remained in London, with Rufus.

They had been quickly absorbed into Rufus's easy-going, shifting circle of friends. Many were in uniform, and would appear for an evening, drink and smoke and dance a great deal, and be gone the next morning. The city was emptying, the stations crowded with service-men and evacuees. The air of waiting, of edgy anticipation, the rumours of invasion, the sirens that warned of air raids that never materialized, all echoed Faith's mood. She had thought that in England she would feel safe, but she found that she did not. Instead, she was confused, anchorless, out of place. Though they had always travelled, there had been a continuity in their wanderings. Ralph's whims, Ralph's vision had guided them. Predictable only in his unpredictability, he had nevertheless been the still centre of their ever-orbiting universe. Now, confined against his wishes in a country he loathed, he seemed diminished, vanquished. The Mulgrave family had been split in two.

Fleeing France, they had lost both their home and their money, but they had lost also a way of life that could not be transposed to England.

For the first few weeks, the evenings in the pub, the impromptu parties and noisy, tearful leave-takings as Rufus's friends left for the forces, and the days spent walking her employer's dogs or searching for the needlework that she constantly mislaid, occupied Faith. Then, with a sudden rush of impatience, she overcame the curious reluctance that had seized her since her arrival in London. In the public library, she searched through the directories. Running her finger down the column, she found Guy's name. *Dr G. Neville, 7 Malt Street.* She wrote down his telephone number. Her heart pounded. She had not seen Guy for three years. If she telephoned, might she, in a dreadful fraction of a second, recognize in his voice consternation or reluctance or forced geniality? Worse, might she say her name and hear him pause, struggling momentarily to place it?

The district of London in which Guy lived was a mixture of tiny houses crushed together like dog kennels and larger villas, their red brick blackened by soot, the laurels and privets in the gardens dulled by a felting of dust. Guy's house was one of the red-brick villas. It had a twisty front path and little turrets and painted bargeboards. At the gate Faith paused.

'D'you think . . . ?' She glanced up at Jake. *Do you think he will remember us?*

Jake said, 'Come on, idiot,' and grabbed her hand, pulling her into the garden.

In the space between the chiming of the doorbell and the patter of footsteps in the hall, Faith twisted the lace cuff of her blouse into a grubby knot. The door opened, and then, suddenly, Guy was standing in the doorway. She saw his shock first, and then, to her immense relief and joy, the delight in his eyes.

'Faith! Good God! How marvellous!'

The sense of dislocation ebbed away as Guy's heart beat next to hers, as his arms squeezed the breath from her lungs, as he said her name over and over again.

He took them into the house. She seemed to see everything very clearly: the coloured glass in the front door, the shiny-leaved plants in brass jardinières.

Then, from another room, a woman's voice called, 'Won't you introduce me, Guy?' and, glancing into an adjacent room, seeing the young, dark-haired woman sitting on a sofa, she started to say, *Guy, you never told us you had a sister.*

But he spoke first.

'Eleanor, I want you to meet my dear friends, Faith and Jake Mulgrave. Faith – Jake – this is Eleanor, my wife.'

This is Eleanor, my wife. Memories tumbled, jagged and painful, through her head. *I don't intend to fall in love . . . I've more important things to do.* She recognized her own foolishness and naivety in assuming Guy would remain true to such a casual vow. He had probably forgotten his words before he had even left the beach. Whereas she, poor fool, had kept them scratched on her heart.

She looked at him, and saw that he had changed. His untidy dark hair had been clipped short, and his clothes were different – neater, better fitting. When he crossed the room to shake Jake's hand, Faith saw that his stride was uneven.

She herself seemed to have stilled, standing in the doorway, as though time itself had ceased to march on in the minutes since he had said, *Faith – this is Eleanor, my wife*. She had forgotten what one was supposed to do, what one was supposed to say. Only the shock and anger on Jake's face jerked her out of her silent immobility. She said brightly, 'I had no idea you were married, Guy. Congratulations. And living in such a splendid house.' She was unsure whether her capacity for dissembling pleased her or disgusted her.

'Eleanor has redecorated,' said Guy. 'When I came back from France I hardly recognized the place.'

Eleanor Neville said, 'Won't you sit down, Miss Mulgrave? Mr Mulgrave? Would you like tea?'

'Tea would be lovely.' She stared at Jake. *Never let them see that you mind*.

He took his cue, and smiled charmingly. 'It's very kind of you, Mrs Neville, but we don't want to be any trouble.'

'Nonsense. We're delighted that you've come to see us. We don't have many visitors, do we, darling? We're becoming a regular old married couple.' Eleanor laughed.

'When were you in France, Guy?'

'A couple of months ago. I was a medical officer with the BEF.'

'Poor Guy was wounded.' Eleanor touched Guy's hand. 'We've been nursing him back to health.'

'Nothing heroic – broke my ankle jumping into a ditch. The damned thing hasn't set right, unfortunately.'

'*Guy.*'

'Sorry, darling. It has grounded me rather, you see.'

Eleanor left the room. There was a silence. Guy

smiled. 'And you? It's so marvellous to see you both again. I never thought you'd come to England. Ralph always told me that he detested England.'

'He does.' She had stopped shaking; she was even able to twist her features into a smile. 'Nicole and I bullied him.'

'So did Genya.'

'We gave him no choice.'

'*We* had no choice,' said Jake. 'We'd have been interned.'

'Hideous. Just imagine, stuck in some damnable prison camp. So dull and dreary.' She could not quite believe that the empty, rattling words came from her. Eleanor Neville had returned with the tea things, and she took the cup that Eleanor handed her, and found that she had somehow without noticing dropped in half a dozen cubes of sugar. Tea slopped into the saucer. 'So sorry. I must have used up all your ration . . .'

'Eleanor has a secret cache of sugar.'

'Just a few things put by,' said Eleanor lightly. 'You were saying, Miss Mulgrave?'

She walked to the window and breathed in the heavy, sickly scent of the lilies. 'Jake cycled and I drove and we all sailed from La Rochelle. It was the most terrific fun, actually. But Pa thinks England is absolutely hellish, and he's in a foul temper, so Jake and I have stayed in London.'

'Where are Ralph and Poppy living?'

'In a cottage in Norfolk. Pa loathes it. The people in the village think that he's odd because he wears his black coat and his hat – you remember his old hat, Guy – even on a warm day. But Pa doesn't think it's ever really warm, you see.' Her voice was too loud and she knew that she was talking too much, yet she could not stop herself. 'Nicole – she's our younger sister, Mrs Neville – is living there too, but she intends to leave soon because she's going to be a famous singer.'

'Will Ralph and Poppy remain in Norfolk?'

'I don't believe they have a great deal of choice just now. We've nowhere else, and we lost all our money – not that we had much in the first place – when we left France.'

'The Germans seized all assets belonging to Britons,' explained Jake.

'So we're paupers. Not a novel experience for Mulgraves, I must say.'

'What will you do?'

She looked at Guy properly for the first time since he had said, *This is Eleanor, my wife.* It was unfair, she thought, that though she was no longer dear to him he had not diminished, he had not become worthless to her.

'I have a job, Guy. I look after an old lady. Rufus found her for me.'

'Rufus?'

'Rufus Foxwell. He's an artist, but he's joined the merchant navy. We knew him in Paris. Mrs Childerley is a friend of his, and she's very old and needs someone to talk to and to walk her dogs, so Rufus thought of me. And Jake works in a pub called the Grasshopper, don't you, Jake?'

'I'll join up, though.'

'Which branch of the services appeals to you, Mr Mulgrave?'

'The army, I suppose. I fought in Spain, you see.' He grinned. 'Better the devil you know.'

'Jake was an officer,' said Faith. Her head was beginning to ache. She thought that once she finished drinking the disgusting, sugary tea, it would be all right to leave. 'And you, Guy?'

'I've been discharged from the army because of this wretched ankle. It's probably for the best. I've a feeling that my services will be needed in London soon.'

'Do you think that the Germans will bomb London?'

'It's inevitable, don't you agree?' He turned to Eleanor, placed his hand on hers, and said gently, 'You and Oliver will be safe in the countryside.'

'Who's Oliver?' Faith expected Guy to say, *My dog*, or *My father-in-law*.

'Oliver is my son.'

She heard Jake start to talk, filling in the gap, discussing the war in the Atlantic, and she pressed her knuckles together until they hurt, so that she was soon able to say:

'How old is Oliver, Mrs Neville?'

'He's six months old. He was born on New Year's Day. Guy and I were married on New Year's Day last year, so Oliver was a wonderful first anniversary present for us.'

Guy said, 'Would you like to see him, Faith? I'll take you to the nursery.'

'You'll wake him, Guy. You know how lightly he sleeps.'

Guy touched Eleanor's shoulder. 'I promise that we'll be as quiet as mice. And if he should wake, then I'll rock him back to sleep.' He smiled. 'Oliver is the only person in the entire world, Faith, who appreciates my singing.'

Faith followed Guy upstairs to the nursery. The nightlight showed her the cot to one side of the room. Pink-cheeked, Oliver slept on his back, the blankets kicked aside, his arms flung above his head. She whispered, 'He's golden-haired, Guy!' and Guy smiled and whispered back: 'We think he's a changeling. He's so much better-looking and cleverer than either of us.' He bent and kissed his son's forehead.

She felt tears sting her eyes as she looked down at the sleeping baby. She thought that for her the future was as dark and confusing as the vast city that surrounded them. But she said, 'He's beautiful, Guy. You must be so proud of him.'

Jake was waiting for her in the hallway. Guy made her write down their address on a scrap of paper. Her writing was peculiar, uneven and jagged. They left the house. As Faith walked along the pavement, tears began to trail down her face.

Jake swore. 'Have my sleeve.'

Faith rubbed her face against his outstretched arm and drew in a great, bubbling breath. She heard Jake say furiously, 'How *could* he? How could he marry *her*?'

'Why not? Why shouldn't Guy marry whomever he likes?'

'Because of you, of course.'

'Don't be silly, Jake.' Her voice was harsh. 'Guy was never mine. It wasn't ever like that. And besides' – she recalled the house – 'think of that lovely room. The curtains matched the cushions. And those beautiful flowers. I couldn't do that.' Jake, catching up with her, hooked her arm through his, and they walked very fast through the dark, unfamiliar streets.

Guy said, 'What did you think? They're delightful, aren't they?'

They were in the kitchen; Eleanor was putting away the tea things. She said, 'Jake is quite charming. Rather rough and ready, of course, but charming nevertheless. I shall ask him to one of my little suppers.'

'And Faith?'

Eleanor's back was turned as she polished tea-spoons. 'I found Miss Mulgrave rather wearing, I'm afraid.'

'She seemed restless, didn't she?'

'And those clothes!' Eleanor laughed.

Guy could not now remember what Faith had been wearing. Something long and floating, he thought.

'The hem of her skirt was down at the back,' said Eleanor. 'And she had no stockings or gloves. And rope-soled sandals . . . oh dear. I'm afraid that I thought she lacked her brother's natural gentility.'

'You're being rather harsh, aren't you, Eleanor? They probably had to flee France with nothing but the clothes they stood up in.'

She folded the tea towel, and laid it to dry on the stove. 'Of course. And I don't mean to be unkind. I'm sure that Miss Mulgrave's recent experiences and up-bringing account for her rather colourful language, as well. One must make allowances for a gypsy way of life.'

Standing on tiptoe, she kissed him on the cheek. When he put his arm round her, he thought how different she felt from Faith. So much more substantial, so much more real.

He heard from upstairs a familiar sound. 'Oliver's crying.'

Eleanor listened. The thin wail was just audible. 'It's too bad!' she said crossly, pulling away. 'It's only an hour and a half since he was fed! The book says that he should go for four hours between feeds at his age.'

'Babies don't always keep to the book, darling.' Guy

kissed her forehead, still creased into a frown. 'I'll go, if you like. Perhaps he's too warm.'

'It's so vexing that we have not been able to find a competent nanny.'

Old Mrs Stephens's supply of hard-working country girls had deserted to better wages in the factories and the services. Guy said mildly, 'We should have kept Biddy, perhaps.'

'Biddy was incompetent, Guy, and hysterical.'

He left the kitchen, welcoming the cool, dark silence of the hallway. Upstairs in the nursery he gathered his furious son into his arms. His ankle ached, and he felt tired, though it was only nine o'clock. He had reopened the surgery at the beginning of the month. Though his list of patients had shrunk – many of the mothers and children had been evacuated, and the young men had gone into the services – he was still busy.

The crying calmed a little, so Guy eased himself into the wicker chair in the corner of the room, Oliver cradled against his chest. Closing his eyes, Guy breathed in the sweet, powdery scent of the baby's skin. During the past eighteen months, events had followed one another with such bewildering haste that he had had little time to absorb their implications. His engagement to Eleanor had been brief, the small wedding hastily planned, as war had by then seemed inevitable. He blamed himself for what difficulties their marriage had run into. His refusal of Selwyn Stephens's offer of a partnership in his exclusive practice had, he knew, upset Eleanor. He had explained to her that he had become a doctor to help those who needed it most, and he thought that she had eventually understood.

Oddly, it had been a trivial thing that had led to their first real quarrel. He had been called to a dying man, and, after he had done what he could to ease his patient's passing, he had sat and drunk tea with the widow while they waited for the other relatives to arrive. By the time he had returned to Malt Street it had been almost ten o'clock. Entering the house, he had been surprised by the number of coats on the hatstand in the hall, equally mystified by the voices issuing from the dining-room. It had taken him a few moments to recall what he had completely forgotten: the dinner party that Eleanor had arranged.

She was the familiar, competent Eleanor until the last of the guests had gone. Then, closing the door, she had turned to him with a cold anger in her eyes that had shocked him. 'I planned it for you,' she had said. 'Three months – *three months* it took me, Guy, to persuade John Taylor-Quest to accept my invitation. He could have been such a help to you with your career! And where were you? Drinking tea with some wretched charwoman! How could you, Guy?'

Her coldness, her fury, had infected him. He remembered saying, 'I don't need help with my career, Eleanor. And Mrs Tuttle needed me far more than John Taylor-whatever did.'

She had not spoken to him for two days. She had turned away from him in bed, leaving him aching for her smooth, firm flesh. Then he had noticed how white and peaky she had looked at the breakfast table, and, questioning her, he had realized what Eleanor herself had not guessed: that she was pregnant. He had understood that her mood was due to her condition, and he had bought her armfuls of flowers, and they had made up. The following January, Oliver had been born. Guy had received his call-up papers not long afterwards, and had left for France in March, returning injured to England just two months later.

Oliver had fallen asleep. Guy did not yet put him back into his cot, but sat for a while, enjoying the warmth and proximity of the sleeping infant. His delight in his child was complete, but he knew that Oliver was not an easy baby, and that Eleanor was often exhausted and overstrained. Though he would miss them both, he thought that if the threatened bombardment began, and Eleanor and Oliver left as planned for old Mrs Stephens's house in Derbyshire, the country air would be good for both of them.

Guy remembered Faith's expression as she had stooped and looked down at the baby. He thought how delightful it had been to see her again – it was as though a missing piece of jigsaw had fallen into place. Such a relief, too, to know that the Mulgraves had not been engulfed by the tidal wave that had swept through France. He put down the feverish surface glitter that he had noticed in her to reaction to the Mulgraves' nightmarish flight from France. *It was the most terrific fun*, she had said, but Guy, who had glimpsed in Faith's eyes the fear that still lingered behind the bravado, did not believe that for one minute.

Nicole did not intend to stay long in Norfolk. She was going to become a famous singer, and she was going to fall in love. She enjoyed her long walks with Minette across the silvery marshes, and she liked to glimpse the sea in the distance, grey-green, the waves sometimes tipped with light. She was disappointed that the beach was fenced off with barbed wire, because of the expected invasion. Aunt Iris's holiday cottage, Heronsmead, was tiny, with two rooms and an outside lavatory downstairs and two bedrooms upstairs. The garden was disproportionately large, a tangle of nettle and briar on which Poppy had immediately set to with a scythe. Nicole tried to cheer up Ralph, but he was resolute in refusing to be cheered up.

'Frightful bloody place, and the natives are all halfwits. I shall cut my throat, I tell you, Nicole, if I have to stay here much longer.'

As the summer progressed, the numbers of planes shot down during the Battle of Britain were given like cricket scores in the local newspaper. On the back of the same paper, Nicole found the advertisement for a talent contest in Cromer. She cycled there on Aunt Iris's ancient bicycle, with Minette sitting in the basket attached to the handlebars. There were twelve other contestants, mostly dancers and singers, plus a juggler and a man with a ventriloquist's dummy. Because the piano was out of tune, Nicole sang an unaccompanied folk song called 'Once I Had a Sweetheart'. One of the Lodgers had taught it to her ages ago, and she particularly liked the last verse.

'I'll set sail of silver and steer towards the sun, And my false love will weep for me after I'm gone.'

When she had finished, the small audience applauded vigorously. The mayor presented to Nicole the first prize, a book about Clark Gable and a bar of chocolate. She divided the chocolate between Minette and the other contestants, and the man with the ventriloquist's dummy said, 'I say, are you going in for the show in Cambridge? You should do, you know – you really are awfully good.' So she borrowed a pencil and scribbled details on the back of the chocolate wrapper. She had absolutely no money at all, but she managed to charm Mr Phypers, who owned the grocery store, into lending her enough for the train fare. The contest, an altogether grander affair than the one in Cromer, was held in a small theatre on the Newmarket Road. Backstage, the other girls crowded into the lavatory, applying lipstick and powder. Nicole ran a comb through her hair, kissed Minette, and gave her music to the pianist.

She sang 'What is life to me without thee' from Gluck's *Orfeo*. Felix had taught it to her, and as she sang about love and loss she remembered La Rouilly and the vineyards and the woods with the wild garlic and adders. She won, as she had known she would. On the journey home, crushed into a carriage with what seemed like a hundred other passengers, she worked out how she would spend her five pounds prize money. Two shillings and sixpence to Mr Phypers for the train fare. A pound to Pa, to cheer him up. Ten shillings on dress material and thread. The rest was for her train fare to Bristol, so that she could audition for the BBC, as the judge of the talent contest had suggested she should.

Faith dusted every one of the hundreds of books in her employer's library, cut the back lawn and hedge with a pair of blunt shears, and washed all three of Mrs Childerley's old, cantankerous dogs. The heat persisted, stilling every blade of grass. She found herself wishing for an event so dramatic, so all-encompassing, that it would fill the echoing silences in her head. Some of Rufus's friends claimed to be in love with her, so she let them kiss her and dance with her. Dancing, she would sometimes forget what had happened, but then the music would end, and the misery and humiliation would return. Like the city, her admirers seemed strange and unfamiliar, but she tried hard to fall in love with them, seeing them off at the station when they left London to join their barracks or their ship.

Late one August night, Rufus returned to Mahonia Road, dumped his kitbag, and collapsed on the sofa. In the morning, Faith brought him a cup of tea. Unshaven and still in his merchant navy uniform, he yawned and rubbed his eyes.

She sat beside him as he drank. It was Saturday, so she did not have to go to work. When he had finished, he kissed her scratchily on the cheek, and said, 'I must have a bath. Any chance of toast, darling Faith?'

After she had assembled a stack of toast, she tapped on the bathroom door. 'It's ready. Are you decent?'

'Not really, but you can avert your eyes. Come and talk to me.'

The bathwater was opaque with grime and soap. She said, 'We're supposed to fill the bath up to that little black line, Rufus, not up to our necks.' She handed him the plate and perched on the lavatory seat, her knees bunched up to her chin.

He was smoking a cigarette, flicking the ash into the water. 'Share with me, Faith – for reasons of economy, of course.'

She shook her head. His eye sockets were hollow, and the stubble on his chin gave him a rakish, piratical look. He slid down into the water, resting the back of his head on the curved lip of the bath, closing his eyes. Only his tangled hair and his kneecaps were visible.

'How much leave have you got?'

He surfaced. 'Three days. But tomorrow I must go and see my mother. Where's Jake?'

'Asleep.'

'Wake him up. We're going out on the town.' There

was a tidal wave of water as Rufus climbed out of the bath.

They toured the streets, gathering friends as a magnet gathers iron filings. At midday they picnicked on Hampstead Heath, eating bread and cheese and apples. Later, they went from one pub to another, ending up in the Café Royal. A man, fiftyish and rotund, squeezed onto their table.

Rufus waved a careless hand. 'Bruno, let me introduce you to Jake and Faith Mulgrave. Mulgraves – this is Bruno Gage. He writes frightfully acerbic reviews.' Rufus screwed up his eyes. 'Didn't you mention that your father had written something, Jake?'

Bruno Gage glanced at Jake. 'Mulgrave? There was a writer called Mulgrave . . . *Nymph in thy Orisons?*'

Jake stubbed out his cigarette. 'Pa's sole literary adventure.'

'Do you know it, darling Linda?' Bruno looked up at the woman who had joined them. She shook her smooth, blond head. 'A *succès de scandale*, I recall. I read it at school. In its time it was thought to be stunningly wicked. Rather tame now, of course. I hid my copy in my tuck box, under the fruit cake.'

'How marvellous, to have a famous father.'

'I've always thought it complete nonsense, actually,' said Jake. 'I gave up halfway through.'

'You must introduce me. I should adore to meet Ralph Mulgrave.' Bruno glanced at his watch. 'And now you shall all come home with me. I have emptied my cellar. I'm having a party.'

'Bruno has invited simply hundreds of people,' said Linda. Her pale eyes were focused on Jake.

'It's my *Après nous le déluge* party,' explained Bruno. 'We're to drink all my champagne and eat all my marvellous tinned salmon, so that the Germans, when they invade, shan't have a thing.'

They left the café. Bruno Gage lived in an elegant, four-storeyed terraced Knightsbridge townhouse. When he flung open the French windows, the scent of jasmine and rose drifted from the garden into the drawing-room. The gunfire of the champagne corks made one of the girls first cry out, and then scream with relief. 'I thought it was . . . I thought it was . . .' she began, and could not finish her sentence.

'If they invade tonight, I intend to be too drunk to care,' said someone.

Another voice said, 'If they invade tonight, I shan't have to be a bridesmaid at my cousin's wedding, and wear that frightful frock.' There was a roar of laughter.

Someone put a record on the gramophone. 'You made me love you, I didn't want to do it' . . . Rufus took Faith in his arms, and they quickstepped onto the lawn. When he held her close and she shut her eyes, Faith thought, *I have almost forgotten*. Over the past weeks it had seemed as though Guy was etched onto her heart, an etching that she must try desperately to erase or to replace, extinguishing his image by covering it with another's. Some of her misery had been super-seded by anger: her recognition that she had not meant as much to Guy as he had to her was deeply humiliat-ing.

The party became noisier, wilder. Faith, searching for the bathroom, stumbled over a girl being sick into a Chinese vase, and a couple embracing on the landing. When she came back, Rufus said, 'Shall we go?' and Faith nodded. She had drunk rather a lot: walking home, they sang the choruses of the songs, and Rufus told a great many very bad jokes. The jokes seemed immensely funny, and she no longer cared that she could not sing in tune. Rufus's arm was around her waist, supporting her when she stumbled. Because it was almost dark, she did not, lurching round the corner of Mahonia Road, at first recognize the man standing outside the front door of her house. Then, hearing the laughter and shrieks, he turned towards them.

She whispered, '*Guy*.'

Rufus, slightly unsteady, squinted. Faith fell against him. Guy crossed the road.

He said, 'I was in the area, so I thought I'd drop by.' She saw the curl of his lip as he glanced first at her and then at Rufus. 'But you're obviously otherwise engaged.'

Then he turned on his heel and walked away. She gave a little gasp and pressed her knuckles against her mouth.

Rufus muttered, 'Friendly type.'

She turned to Rufus. 'Shall we go in?'

Rufus fitted the key into the lock. Faith ran upstairs. If she had time to think, her resolution would fail her. In her bedroom, she unbuttoned her dress and let it slide to the floor. Rufus slid his hands around her stomach, and kissed the back of her neck. She was glad that the light from the single bulb was poor; her camisole was old and had greyed in the wash. His lips touched the hollow of her spine. He paused only once, when they were in bed, looking up at her with opaque dark eyes. 'You have done this before, haven't you, Faith?'

'Of course I have.'

She had expected ecstasy or horror, but she found neither. It was all, she thought, rather insignificant; a small invasion of one body by another. When it was over she was relieved; she had crossed a bridge, she had left one life, which she had grown out of, behind.

At the party, Jake danced with several of the girls, kissed one or two, and drank a great many glasses of Bruno Gage's excellent champagne. Searching for the bathroom, he stumbled round the house, opening doors, looking through windows. The rooms had a gold and lacquer splendour that reminded him of something, though he could not immediately place the fleeting memory. Not La Rouilly: this frenzied chinoiserie bore no resemblance to La Rouilly's faded grandeur. Jake tried not to think what must have happened to La Rouilly, marooned on the strip of Occupied Zone that ran the length of the western coast of France.

From behind him, a voice said, 'Admiring the decor? Rather busy, don't you think? I find it gives me a headache after a while.'

He spun round. The blonde woman from the Café Royal stood in the doorway. Jake said, confused, 'I thought that you and Bruno . . . ?'

'Were man and wife?' She smiled. 'What a simply frightful idea.' She came into the room, closing the door behind her. 'My name's Linda Forrester.' She held out her hand.

She was, he thought, a very beautiful woman: tall and pale-haired and very slender, with shoulders that sloped like a ballerina's.

'I can't help thinking that Bruno has been rather precipitate,' she said. 'I mean, German soldiers clumping through the garden – it really doesn't seem very likely. You just can't imagine it, can you?'

He looked down at the garden, with its lawn, striped

in two shades of green, its neat shrubs and colourful annuals. He managed to focus the elusive memory, and realized that this house reminded him of the château in which he had spent the night on his last, desperate journey through France. He remembered the broken windows, the pale patches on the walls where paintings had once hung.

He said, 'I can imagine it very easily.' He glanced round the room. 'Rich pickings, after all. A Cézanne and a . . . a Dufy, isn't it? I'd say this house would be high on the list.'

Her sudden anger was visible only in her pale blue eyes; she was, he guessed, the sort of woman who would take care neither to frown nor to smile, in case of wrinkles.

'You're trying to frighten me.'

Jake shrugged. 'Not at all. Just giving you my opinion.'

She was silent for a moment, and then she said, 'Though it's a good excuse, isn't it, for all this?'

Looking out of the window again, he saw what she meant by 'all this'. The party-goers had spilled out into the garden, hokey-cokeying round the flower beds. In the shade of a beech tree, a couple embraced. Their long shadows were dark in the dusk.

He realized that she was not, as he had assumed, stupid, and that the beautiful blandness of her features was a mask for intelligence and, perhaps, ruthlessness.

'The war is shuffling us up, like a pack of cards,' she said. 'Making different pairs.'

The invitation was unmistakable. He took her hand in his, and traced the structure of the long, slender bones with his fingertip, stopping when he reached the ring on her third finger. 'Your husband . . . ?'

'Harold's in North Africa.'

His fingers continued the length of her bare arm, and then came to rest, caressing the hollow of her neck. She shivered, and then she said lightly: 'It's the tedium that's so unbearable, isn't it? I've always loathed waiting for things.'

It's the tedium that's so unbearable . . . In his mind's eye, Jake saw the long exodus of women and children enduring the cold of Spain, the heat of France, and he felt a sudden and intense revulsion. His hand dropped suddenly to his side, and he took his cigarettes out of his pocket, and lit one, and said, 'Actually, I usually find that what one can have easily is hardly worth the bother of taking.'

As he left the room, he heard her say, 'It's a funny thing, Jake – the handsomest men often don't come up to scratch. Like a beautiful rose, I suppose, that has no scent.'

When Faith awoke the next morning, Rufus was silhouetted against the window. 'I've a train to catch at eight,' he explained. He paused, one sock on, one sock off.

'What?'

'You lied to me last night, didn't you? I was the first, wasn't I?'

'Does it matter? Someone had to be.'

She saw his expression alter. 'I didn't mean that, Rufus,' she said quickly. 'Please don't be cross.'

He sat down on the edge of the bed. He took his cigarettes out of his pocket, offered one to her, and lit both. 'You are in love with someone else,' he said flatly.

'No. Not any more.' Faith tried to explain. 'He's married. He has a baby son.'

'That doesn't prevent—' Rufus broke off, shaking his head. 'I'm just not sure that I appreciate being quite so . . . interchangeable.'

There was a silence. Tears bit the corners of her eyes. Rufus said, 'Was it that chap who was waiting here last night?'

She did not reply.

'Tell me. I think you owe me that.'

She said dully, 'He's called Guy Neville. I've known him for years, since I was eleven. He used to visit us in France.'

'You love him?'

She said baldly, 'I've always loved him. I can't remember a time when I haven't loved him.' She saw the pain on Rufus's face, but added, 'I think I fell in love with Guy the first time I saw him. He was gutting a chicken – imagine, falling in love with a man who was gutting a chicken!'

She pressed her fingers against her eyes, stemming the tears. After a while, he drew her to him, cradling her face in the hollow of his shoulder. He said, 'I was once in love with a girl who worked on my uncle's farm. It was the way she talked to the pigs when she was mucking them out. I wanted her to talk to me like that.'

She laughed unsteadily. 'Guy saved my life once, you see, Rufus. I was bitten by an adder, and he sucked the poison out. It's not that I've particularly thought of *marrying* him . . . just that I assumed he'd always be there. For me, I mean.' She said nothing for a while, but forced herself to think back. 'And now I see how stupid I've been. I only ever saw Guy for a few weeks each year. I was just a child. And it was just a – a holiday for him. But for me it was—'

'What?'

'The best part of the year,' she said simply. 'The most real part. But most of Guy's life went on the rest of the time, didn't it, without me. I didn't really know anything about him. I'd never met his family. I'd never seen where he lived. I'd never even been to England.'

Rufus shrugged. 'Those things don't necessarily matter.'

'Oh, they do, Rufus. It's a question of belonging, isn't it?' Her voice was harsh. After a while, she added, 'And when I saw him, well, he looked so happy. He has such a lovely, tidy house, and a dear little baby boy, and his wife is beautiful and clever and kind. And I just thought, why on earth did I ever think Guy would love *me*?'

He stood up and began to throw things into a kitbag. 'Do you hate me?'

He looked round at her. 'I don't think so. What would be the point?'

She winced. Rufus went back to his packing. Buckling his kitbag, he said, 'There'll be more important things to worry about soon, anyway. All this . . . all this *nonsense* about who loves whom and who sleeps with whom will seem so feeble. Only just now it doesn't seem so, and actually, Faith, I think I'll go.' He smiled crookedly. 'It's against my principles to mind about things like this, so you must have rather got under my skin. When we next meet I promise you that I'll be perfectly civilized.'

He left the house. She did not think she had ever felt so ashamed of herself. After a while she got up, bathed, dressed, and went out, unable to bear the silence of the rooms. Though it was not yet eight o'clock, it was already warm. Walking, she continued to put one foot in front of the other, to cross roads and to turn corners, because that, she assumed, was what one had to do. But it seemed to her as though one direction was just as good as another, and that if she walked into the river, or onto a busy road, it would not matter very much. She, who had travelled half the globe, had lost her sense of direction.

After a while, she saw the vast Victorian edifice of Liverpool Street station. She dug her hand in her pocket and counted her change. On the train she wept, her tears blurring red-brick suburbs and golden fields alike. She walked the few miles from the station to Heronsmead, arriving at mid-afternoon. She did not go to the front door, but went round to the garden at the back of the house. She saw them before they saw her: Ralph sitting in a deckchair, a sunhat tilted over his nose, reading; Poppy on her knees, weeding a flower bed. The sun was high in the sky, the grass burnt to straw, and some of her shame and sadness slipped away as she waved and called out to her family.

The train left Bristol at five o'clock, but then crawled through suburbs and countryside, pausing in sidings, shunting aimlessly backwards and forwards along rusty sections of track. When, finally, it stopped at a station, Nicole could see by the clock that it was almost half past six. She had a window seat; she rubbed at the sooty glass with her fingers. She could not see the name of the station – the signs had been removed in advance of the threatened invasion – and the guard's announcement was drowned by the noise of engines and passengers. Most of the soldiers who had travelled in the carriage with Nicole since Bristol tumbled out, and half a dozen passengers in civilian clothes climbed in. A man said, 'Is this seat taken?' and Nicole smiled and gathered up Minette, who had sprawled over the cushion.

'Minette hasn't a ticket, and is quite happy to share with me.'

He sat down. He was wearing a pinstripe suit and a hat, and he carried a rolled-up umbrella and a briefcase. An English gentleman, thought Nicole approvingly. She asked, 'Do you know where we are?'

'Oxford. Dreaming spires and all that, you see.'

'Oh.' She looked out of the window again. 'It's a bit like Florence, isn't it, only different colours.'

He smiled. 'I suppose so.'

'I mean – golds and greens instead of pinks and terracottas.'

'Yes.' He seemed to think for a while. 'Yes – I believe you're right.'

'All cities have a different colour, don't you think? Just like names.'

'Names?'

'My name – Nicole – is scarlet and black, and my brother's name, Jake, is a fiery purple, and my sister's name, Faith, is a rather nice pinky-brown.'

'My name's David,' he said. 'What colour is that?'

She looked at him. His eyes were expressive and intelligent, and there was a touch of grey in the dark hair at his temples. 'Royal blue,' she said with certainty.

'Really? I have a royal-blue tie that I'm rather fond of and I wear on high days and holidays. Most of the time, unfortunately, my work demands subdued stripes.'

'What do you do?'

144

He said vaguely, 'Oh, this and that. Office stuff, very dull. What about you?'

'I'm a singer. I've just been auditioning for a programme on the wireless.'

'Really? How splendid. How did it go?'

She thought back. She had been nervous at first, unaccustomed to the microphone, but once she had begun to sing she had felt better. 'It went very well.'

'You sound very confident.'

The train got up speed, so that the countryside was a blur of green and brown. She explained, 'Anything I really want I always get, you see. It's just a question of wanting it enough.'

He looked amused. 'And you don't worry about . . . tempting fate?'

Nicole shook her head. 'Not in the least.' She looked at him again. 'What's your favourite song?'

He considered. 'I adore Handel. And Mozart, of course. If I had to pick a favourite, which I would find very difficult, I suppose it would be "Dove sono i bei momenti" from *The Marriage of Figaro*.'

Very softly, she murmured the opening bars. The train plunged into a tunnel. When they emerged and it became light again, she said, 'Would you like a plum? They're very nice – I picked them this morning.'

'If you've any to spare, a plum would be delightful.'

'We're supposed to make them into jam, but there isn't enough sugar and I think they're better like this.' She took a brown paper bag out of her music case and offered it to him. The train had slowed again, and the surrounding countryside had become clear, a patchwork of greyish-brown villages among fields of ochre stubble. The pistons of the carriages creaked in a laboured rhythm. He said, 'How far are you travelling?' and she said, 'To Holt, in Norfolk,' and then, in a jumble of dog and plums and hat and umbrella, he flung himself at her, dragging her from her seat to the floor.

She did not immediately realize what was happening. She knew only that the noise was awful, and she was lying on the floor, and he was crouched over her, shadowing her face with his body. His hand gripped her arm, preventing her from standing up. When she winced at the *crack-crack* of the bullets, he said sharply, 'It's all right, it's going to be all right,' and then, as the train shuddered and screamed to a halt, she lurched forward, hitting her head against the door. The engine squealed, and she heard the enemy aeroplane whine as it soared back up into the sky.

Everything became still and quiet. The silence was broken by a sob, then a muttered swear word, and an 'I say – mind the broken glass'. Nicole opened her eyes.

He said, 'I'm so sorry – I must have frightened you, but I saw the plane . . . Are you all right?'

She nodded, too breathless to speak.

'Then I'll see if there's anything I can do. Just wait there, won't you? I'll be back in a tick.'

She dusted the broken glass from the seat, and sat, hugging Minette to her chest. Gingerly, she felt the back of her head and discovered an egg-shaped lump. Across the aisle, a woman was weeping. The bullet holes in the roof of the carriage looked, Nicole thought, like a dot-to-dot puzzle.

After ten minutes or so, David came back. 'There are a few casualties, but there are a couple of nurses on the train, and they're coping with them. The water tank's holed, and some of the carriages are badly damaged. They'll send another train, but it'll take hours, I suspect. It might be quicker to make our own way.'

She flung open the carriage door. They were in the countryside: she could see no houses, only a criss-cross of fields and hedgerows and woodland. The evening sun gleamed on the corn stubble and on the dried mud paths. He jumped out first, and then reached up to help her.

'Shall I take your case?'

Nicole shook her head. 'It's not heavy, and Minette can walk.' She set down the dog, who yelped and ran along the perimeter of the field. 'Do you know where we are?'

'Bedfordshire, somewhere,' he said, looking around. 'If we can find a village, perhaps there'll be a bus. And you should telephone your people. They'll be worried about you.'

'Oh no,' she said cheerfully. 'Well, Ma might worry, but Pa knows I'll always turn up. Anyway, we haven't a telephone.'

They saw the needlepoint of a church spire on the horizon. They began to trudge towards it across the dusty field. Though it was evening, it was still warm, so Nicole slipped off her jacket and put it in her case. When they reached the village, David paused outside a public house.

'Would you like a brandy? Medicinal purposes – might calm your nerves a bit – pretty terrifying for you back there.'

'That sort of thing doesn't really frighten me,' she said. 'But I should love a brandy.'

Because the bar room was low and dark and crowded they sat in the tiny back garden. David discovered that there was a bus to Bedford in half an hour; from Bedford there should be a train to Cambridge, where Nicole could catch her connection to Holt. He asked curiously: 'If being shot at on a train doesn't frighten you, what on earth does?'

Nicole considered. 'Oh, being on my own. I hate to be on my own. And I detest being underground – caves and things. And' – she wrinkled up her nose – 'I hate to be bored.'

He held out his hand. 'I've just realized – I haven't introduced myself properly. You know nothing about me other than that I have a royal-blue name. I'm called David Kemp.'

'Nicole Mulgrave,' she said, and shook his hand.

Although Eleanor had quickly become competent at looking after Oliver, she had not found in him the joy that she had expected would automatically accompany motherhood. As she recovered from the birth, she had realized that her principal emotion during the long hours she spent with her son was one of boredom. The repetitive nature of caring for a young baby – the endless cycle of feed, change, bathe, the dull walks with the pram, the dreary games with rattle and teddy bear – she found tedious. Motherhood was both unbelievably time-consuming and achingly dull. Her mind remained unsatisfied while her body was exhausted. If she began to read a book, Oliver's cries would interrupt her before she completed a page or two. Playing the piano seemed to agitate him. Visits to her father, her friends, were ruined by the company of a wakeful, restless baby. She could not remember when she had last attended a concert. If Guy was able to find a free evening, if Eleanor herself was able to persuade a local girl to babysit, then like as not her arrangements would fall through at the last minute – babysitters were unreliable, and Oliver had a knack of running a temperature just before they were due to leave the house, so that Guy would worry about measles or chickenpox or any one of the thousands of childhood ailments, each of which Oliver seemed determined to work his way through.

In March, Guy had left for France, leaving Eleanor to lonely evenings and nights interrupted by a baby who seemed unable to settle to any sort of routine. A friend offered to look after Oliver one afternoon while Eleanor went to a Women's Voluntary Service meeting. She realized, listening to the discussions about canteens and emergency clothing supplies and rest centres, just how much she had missed this sort of thing – her committees, that sense of being part of the world that belonging to an organization gave you. Pregnancy sickness had forced her to resign from her hospital work.

Travelling back to Malt Street by bus, she was fired with enthusiasm. The local WVS branch was headed by a woman called Doreen Tillotson, who had sat on the St Anne's charity committee with Eleanor. Eleanor knew Mrs Tillotson to be an indecisive and inefficient leader. Eleanor also knew that she herself could do considerably better than poor Doreen. In the course of the two-hour discussion she pinpointed half a dozen changes that needed to be made, from little things like making sure they had enough teaspoons (one always ran out of teaspoons) to bigger issues such as fund-raising and recruitment. She drew up a plan of action that very night, listing in order of importance the changes that must be made.

But Guy returned injured from France, and any

babysitter Eleanor attempted to engage was put off by Oliver's tears and temper. In desperation she brought Oliver with her to a WVS meeting. Though he slept in his Moses basket on the bus, he began to grizzle as soon as she put down the basket in a corner of the room. After five minutes, his grizzles developed to full-throated howling. Eleanor tried rocking him to sleep, but he still cried, so after a while she put the basket in one of the upstairs rooms, shutting the door firmly. The howls filtered downstairs, but Eleanor ignored the other ladies' reproachful glances.

When his broken ankle had recovered sufficiently for him to manage on his own, Guy suggested that Eleanor and Oliver go to Derbyshire, to stay with her grandmother. Mrs Stephens looked after the baby while Eleanor rested. In Derbyshire, Eleanor rediscovered what it was like to sleep for an uninterrupted eight hours. She went out for long cycle rides, and realized guiltily, dropping pleasantly exhausted into bed one night, that she had not seen Oliver the entire day, and had not missed him a bit. She did miss London, though. She was a town girl, and she longed for the shops, the theatres, the concert halls, the conversation.

Grandmother adored Oliver and spoiled him horribly, so that when Eleanor returned to London with him he cried throughout the long train journey. Reunited with Guy at the railway station, her first impulse was to tell him how awful Oliver had been. But she saw suddenly the dangers of that. As the Battle of Britain began, as fighter aeroplanes painted their delicate, deadly lacework in the ultramarine sky, Guy proposed what Eleanor had already anticipated: that she and Oliver leave London. Eleanor prevaricated; she would make her decision when the bombardment began, not before. The crease of worry between Guy's brows deepened, but he accepted her decision.

Then the Mulgraves visited. Eleanor noticed how Faith looked at Guy. What Guy was unaware of, Eleanor perceived instantly. Faith Mulgrave was in love with Guy. Meeting Faith, with her raffish clothing and her ungoverned manner – forgivable, even somewhat attractive, in a man like Jake, but necessarily repellent in a woman – Eleanor had to hide the depth of her antipathy. Eleanor was sufficiently perceptive to understand that she and Faith might both appeal to different aspects of Guy's character. She knew then that she must not be absent from London long enough for Guy to realize that Faith Mulgrave was no longer the enchanting child of his memory, but a grown woman, a woman lacking the morals and self-restraint that might keep her from loving another woman's husband.

CHAPTER FIVE

Nicole, meeting David Kemp outside the Cumberland Hotel, stood on tiptoe and kissed him on the cheek. Tentatively he presented her with a bunch of flowers. 'I thought . . . congratulation or consolation.'

'Congratulations,' she said, and buried her nose in the velvety petals. 'I've been chosen to sing with the Geoff Dexter Band.'

'You'll be famous,' he said. 'People will be envious when I tell them that I've eaten plums with the famous singer, Miss Nicole Mulgrave.'

They went inside the hotel. After they had ordered tea, she said, 'I'm to sing at my first concert in a fortnight's time. I was allowed to choose two dresses from Harrods. They are absolutely divine, David.'

'Where are you staying?'

'With my sister, Faith, in Islington. She's decided to become an ambulance driver. She has to take a driving test next week.'

'Tell me about your family.'

She told him about Ralph and Poppy and Jake and Genya and the Lodgers, and about La Rouilly, and about the countries she had visited as a child. When the tea arrived, she poured and he said, 'It sounds so exotic and adventurous. I've always envied people with big families. My father died soon after I was born, so there was only my mother and I. And we've always lived in the same house, of course.'

'Where is your house, David?'

'It's in Wiltshire, not far from Salisbury.'

'Is it a nice house?'

He smiled. 'Compton Deverall is cold and draughty and terribly inconvenient. But I adore it.'

She was going to ask him more when she heard the air-raid siren. She glanced at him. 'A false alarm?'

'Probably. There's a shelter in the basement.' Some of the other diners were leaving the room.

'Sugar?' she said calmly, remaining in her seat, passing him the bowl.

She heard a distant, dull *crump*, and stirred her tea and ate a sandwich. Another bomb fell, and then another. The dining-room was almost empty. She said, 'What on earth is in these sandwiches—' and then there was a crash, and her teaspoon shivered in the saucer.

David said, 'Fish paste, I'm afraid.' He touched her hand. 'It's still some distance away but, Nicole, I do think that we should go to the shelter.'

She followed him downstairs. She loathed basements: the lack of light and the way the ceiling pressed down on one. She said after a while, 'David, I can't bear this. Would you mind if we go?'

He glanced down at her and looked suddenly penitent. 'I'd forgotten. You don't like to be underground, do you? I'll tell you what – my house isn't far away, and the dining-room table is immensely strong. So if you don't mind taking your chance in the street—'

Outside, in the autumn sunshine, Nicole's fear evaporated. When she looked up, she could see the V-shaped formations of aeroplanes in the sky, like so many migrating geese, each silver aeroplane trailing a puff of thistledown. She saw the white plume that rose from a stricken building. The cloud unfolded, billowing like an unfurling sail, and then became vast, tinged with red. It looked, she thought, quite beautiful.

'The East End's getting the worst of it.' David took her hand, hurrying her. 'Come on.'

In a tall terraced house in Devonshire Place, he led her into the dining-room. Nicole's gaze was drawn to the photograph on the sideboard.

'She's lovely.' The portrait was of a dark, pensive-looking woman. 'Who is she?'

He said, 'She was called Susan. She died of TB. We were engaged to be married.'

'Oh, David' – she went to him – 'how dreadful for you.' There were tears in her eyes.

'It was a long time ago.'

When the all-clear sounded at a quarter past six, they went into the kitchen, where he made omelettes and salad. 'My mother sends eggs and vegetables up from home,' he explained. 'I feel rather guilty about it. Rather spoiled.'

She crunched salad. 'This is delicious, David. Don't feel guilty. I never do.'

He was washing a punnet of late raspberries for pudding when the siren sounded again.

'We'd better eat them under the table.'

'We must have champagne, David. Have you champagne? Champagne goes so well with raspberries.'

The explosion of the champagne cork echoed the crack of the falling bombs. Nicole drank her first glass quickly. 'They're coming closer.'

David explained, 'They dropped the incendiaries this afternoon to light up the target area. I'm afraid it's going to be a bad night.'

She held out her glass. 'Then pour me another drink, darling David.'

He frowned. 'I'm not quite sure—'

'What?'

'You are very young, Nicole.'

She said indignantly, 'I'm seventeen!'

'Seventeen . . . good God.' He shook his head. 'I'm thirty-two.'

'My father is thirteen years older than my mother,' said Nicole, 'and they've always been the best of friends. And besides' – and she began to giggle – 'how on earth can you worry about me drinking a few glasses of champagne just now?' She had to shout to be heard above the noise of the bombardment. Looking at her, he, too, began to laugh.

Walking home from the hospital the next day, Guy thought that it had been a sort of baptism. The sense of disbelief that had lasted since the declaration of war a year ago – since Munich, perhaps – had been destroyed. A new realism must accompany the shattered landscape that confronted everyone this fine September morning.

He had been home once in the night, to check that Eleanor and Oliver were safely in the Anderson shelter. The rest of the time he had helped to deal with casualties of the Blitz. Now, in spite of a night without sleep, he felt strangely exhilarated. There seemed to be a pleasure just in being alive. He was glad that it was Sunday and he had no surgery. He must talk to Eleanor, make arrangements, phone the station for train times to Derby, and then he could rest.

He dreaded their leaving – the thought of returning to a lonely bachelor existence appalled him – but he knew that he had no choice. Turning the corner into

Malt Street, Guy saw that the houses were undamaged, and there was just a light covering of brick dust blown in by the breeze, dulling the leaves and grass. The shattered houses of Stepney and Whitechapel were still vivid in his mind, though, along with the memory of what falling roofs and walls could do to fragile human bodies.

At home, he found Eleanor in the kitchen. He kissed the back of her neck, delighting as always in her gleaming hair and taut skin, her wholeness.

'How's Oliver?'

'Asleep, thank goodness. He cried the whole night in the shelter.'

'I'll phone the station and check the times of the Derby train. Will you be able to get everything ready today, darling?'

She was grating cheese for a sauce. She said, 'All Oliver's clothes are washed and ironed. And I'll only need night things.'

'Night things? You'll need to take warm clothes, Eleanor. I've a horrible feeling this may go on into the winter.'

Without turning to look at him, she said calmly, 'Guy, I shall take Oliver to Grandmother's house, and then I shall come home.'

He sat down opposite her, and rubbed the balls of his thumbs across his eyes. His lids were gritty with brick dust. 'Eleanor,' he said, 'I want you to go to Derbyshire with Oliver. And I want you to stay there.'

'No, Guy.' She wrapped the leftover cheese in a piece of greaseproof paper and put it aside. 'I'm going to come back here to help you.'

He took her hand, and tried to explain. 'I don't want

you to go, Eleanor – I shall miss you terribly. But I want you to be safe.'

'There is the Anderson shelter,' she said. 'I'll make it cosy with a thermos and books and blankets. It'll be quite delightful, you'll see.'

'But *Oliver* . . .'

'Oliver will be fine in Derbyshire. I've written to Grandmother, and she's longing to have him to herself.'

He stared at her. 'You've arranged all this?'

'Of course.' She squeezed his hand and drew away, stooping to gather potatoes out of a sack.

'Without consulting me?'

'I didn't want to bother you, Guy. You've enough to worry about.'

'Oliver is my *son* . . . I can't believe that you have gone ahead and made such an arrangement behind my back.'

'Don't be ridiculous, Guy.' Eleanor's voice remained light and unconcerned. 'You make it sound . . . conspiratorial. I've merely arranged things for the best for all of us.'

'It's hardly the best for Oliver!' He was unable to disguise his growing anger.

'Of course it is.' She put the potatoes in the sink and ran the tap. 'He'll be safe, which is the important thing.'

'A child needs his mother.'

'Nonsense, Guy. An eight-month-old baby can't tell one person from another. As long as he's warm and fed and dry Oliver doesn't care who's looking after him.'

'I really don't think that's true, Eleanor – I really think that you are mistaken—'

'Besides, we both managed quite well without our mothers, didn't we?'

Guy had been at preparatory school when his mother had died. His housemaster had drawn him aside and broken the news to him. In recognition of his bereaved state, he had been allowed to eat his lunch in the infirmary – he remembered that he had been given ice cream, as though that might console him in his grief.

He said angrily, 'I don't want Oliver to *manage* – I want him to be happy!'

'Are you suggesting that I do not, Guy?'

She turned to him. For the first time he saw the steel in her eyes. Eleanor put down her vegetable knife, and wiped her hands on a tea cloth.

'It'll be the best solution for all of us,' she repeated. 'Oliver will be safe and well looked after, and I'll be able to continue to help you and to make a real contribution to the WVS.' She smiled, but her eyes were still hard. 'Come, Guy – don't you remember the muddle you were in before you met me? And you're going to be busier than ever, I suspect. I don't think you'd be able to manage without me.'

He almost said, *I managed perfectly well before I met you*, but he bit the words back, realizing how they would sound. He ran his hands through his filthy hair and closed his eyes. Into his darkened vision came the memory of Faith as he had last seen her. Walking home at night from the hospital, he had realized that he was within a few streets of the house in which Faith and Jake were staying. He had decided to visit them, regretting that he had not had time to call on them before. And then he had seen Faith in the street, laughing, obviously the worse for wear, all over her seedy-looking escort. It had been obvious to him that they were lovers. He could not recall what he had said to her, only his sense of shock, his awareness of the sudden shattering of an illusion.

Guy's anger intensified, and then suddenly ebbed away. He was overcome by a drowning exhaustion that all the long night's work had not induced in him. After a while he said wearily, 'If this is what you feel you must do, Eleanor, then I suppose I have no option but to agree.'

'Good,' said Eleanor briskly. 'I knew you'd understand that it's the only sensible solution. Now, Guy, why don't you go and wash? You're making the kitchen floor grubby. I shall run you a nice, hot bath, and then I'll bring you some toast and tea, and you must have a long rest. It'll all work out perfectly, you'll see.'

A friend had suggested ambulance work to Faith. 'You haven't passed any exams and you can't type. Driving seems to be the only thing you can do.' Faith had been piqued at having her accomplishments so casually dismissed, but the suggestion nevertheless appealed to her. She could drive ambulances at night and continue to look after Mrs Childerley, of whom she had grown fond, by day.

She passed the driving test on her second attempt – the test car was huge, ancient and temperamental, like the old Citroën Ralph had been forced to abandon in France, and thus reasonably familiar. She was issued with a cotton coat and blouse and a tin hat, and taught first aid. The ambulances were private cars painted grey, with runners for the stretchers. The drivers worked in pairs, and were assigned to a different district each night.

At first, it all seemed impossibly confusing. Faith's chief anxiety was that she would lose her way in the dark; many of the roads were closed because of bomb damage or unexploded bombs, so her hastily acquired knowledge of London was almost useless. If she stopped and asked for directions, people would often, confused by the noise and destruction, send her the wrong way. At the bomb-sites, the doctors and nurses dealt with the casualties, seeing to their immediate injuries. Then Faith and Bunty, her partner, would stretcher them into the ambulance and drive them to hospital. She was supposed to label her casualties with their name and a brief description of their injuries, but somehow there never seemed to be time, or she would mislay her pencil, or be unable, in the dark and the dust, to see clearly enough to write. At the hospital they would leave the casualties in the emergency room and reclaim the stretchers and blankets. Then they would drive back to the ambulance station, and wait to be called out again.

There seemed to be so many opportunities to make mistakes. She would forget to collect her blankets, and the supervisor would make a tremendous fuss about issuing new ones. She would veer to avoid a crater in the road, and the unfortunates in the back would groan and complain. She once turned up at the wrong place entirely, and it was fully ten minutes before she realized that she was in Green Street, and not Green Road. Between call-outs, waiting in the basement beside the telephones, she and Bunty drank endless cups of tea.

'It's hauling the stretchers into the van that's the worst thing,' complained Bunty, as she poured more water into the kettle. 'Doesn't half do my back in.'

'I thought I'd end up in *Dover*, last night, I got so

muddled.' Faith looked at Bunty. 'And I worry about—' She stopped.

'What?'

'If it's awful. We've only had' – she counted on her fingers – 'ten casualties so far. And none have been badly hurt. I'm afraid I might be sick, or just useless.'

'I've an aunt faints at the sight of blood,' agreed Bunty.

Faith had to confront her worst fears the following night. It was a heavy raid; arriving back at the basement after each call-out, they did not have time to boil the kettle before the telephone rang again. At three o'clock in the morning the smoke and brick dust were too thick to see through the windscreen. Bunty leaned out of the passenger window, calling directions.

'Slow down . . . left a bit, road's a mess . . . slower . . . Better stop here, there's something in the road.'

They climbed out of the van. Bunty walked ahead, to where the dimmed lights of their headlamps picked out the obstacle lying on the tarmac. Then she whispered, 'Oh, *God*,' and Faith looked down.

The child must have been flung into the air by the force of the blast; the small body had split open on impact with the road. Faith heard Bunty start to cry, a peculiar tearless gulping. She herself did not, oddly, weep or scream or do any of the things that she had dreaded. She just fetched a blanket from the ambulance and wrapped the dead infant in it, and laid him gently on one of the stretchers. Then she lit a cigarette and placed it between Bunty's shaking fingers. A warden yelled 'Put out that light!' but she ignored him, unable to believe that in such an inferno the pinpoint of a cigarette would be visible from the sky.

The following night, she felt a strange relief, as

though she had passed a test. At first, the warble of the air-raid siren and the low thrum of the bombers had nauseated her. The whine of every falling bomb had provoked a heart-fluttering panic that she had been able to suppress only because her fear of making a fool of herself was greater. But her terror had eased with surprising rapidity: you simply could not sustain that intensity of fear for long. It became manageable, something that could be lived with. The noise and chaos of the air raids was all-absorbing: the warble of the siren, the clatter of incendiaries as they struck the road; the crash of collapsing walls and chimneys. The fires that seemed to engulf the whole of London; the smoke that blotted out the sky. She had wanted drama, she had wanted distraction; she had found both a thousand times over.

She fell into a routine, coming home at six o'clock in the morning, sleeping until one o'clock, staying with Mrs Childerley until it was time to leave for the ambulance station at six in the evening. She earned three pounds a week from her ambulance driving, and two pounds and ten shillings from Mrs Childerley, and felt, at the end of the first week, rich. Though the bombs frightened her, she did not think she would have felt any less frightened in a shelter. When, at the end of the first fortnight, she had a day off, she went to Heronsmead, and worried about Ralph's persisting discontent and Poppy's pallor. She suggested that Ralph visit her in London; Poppy, she thought, looked relieved.

Back in London, the telephone at the ambulance station rang continually. Fires struck out the stars, smothering them with a wash of burnt sienna. They were assigned to a new district. Faith drove through unfamiliar streets while Bunty read the map and yelled out directions. They had to slow as they reached an area of tangled railings and broken brick walls that jutted from the rubble like jagged teeth. Flames soared; dust rose in terracotta clouds. Objects had been flung anyhow around the blitzed area, giving it the look of a surrealist painting. A lamp-post was draped with a woman's frock; a chair perched on top of a dustbin; a potted aspidistra had somehow wedged itself into a bicycle basket. The front of a block of flats had peeled off in its entirety, revealing shabby wallpaper and battered furniture. It felt intrusive to look into the pathetic interiors of strangers' homes; Faith turned away.

They parked some distance from the bomb-site, clambering over the heap of rubble to reach the casualties. The stretcher was heavy, and grit tore the palms of Faith's hands. Dust choked her. She had to rub her eyes to distinguish the figures working in the ruins: the doctors and nurses, bending over their patients; the men of the heavy rescue squad, prising apart bricks and concrete in their search for survivors; the firemen attempting to dowse the flames. One of the nurses called out, 'Here, you girls!' and beckoned to Faith and Bunty.

A workman from the heavy rescue squad was levering up a slab of wall. The nurse explained, 'They've almost got her out. She's in a bad way, though. You'd better take her first and come back for the others.'

The woman buried beneath the bricks looked like a shapeless bundle of rags. A doctor crouched beside her. Both were reddish-brown with brick dust.

The doctor said suddenly, 'No. No – we've lost her,' and stood up.

Faith recognized his voice immediately. She knew that it was already too late to turn aside, to try to hide. She watched as Guy wiped the dust from his eyes. Then, slowly, he focused on her.

He said, 'Well, well, fancy that. Faith Mulgrave. So you've managed to find enough room in your crowded social life to do a little war work.' And before she could think of a reply he had walked away and had become lost again in the smoke and the dust.

Ralph came to stay at the Mahonia Road house at the beginning of November. Poppy remained in Norfolk: afraid of the bombs, Ralph explained with disgust. Rufus, home on leave for a few days, showed Ralph around London on the nights that Faith was working. On her evening off, they were invited to dinner. 'Linda Forrester's place,' explained Rufus, knotting his tie. 'I suppose, as a discarded lover, I should be tactful and decline the invitation, but Linda has a cupboardful of tinned salmon.'

Faith remembered Linda Forrester as the elegant, icy blonde at Bruno Gage's party. 'She's married, isn't she, Rufus?'

Rufus ran a comb through his hair, but it still stood up in untidy spikes. 'Harold's twenty years older than Linda. Married him for his money, of course. The day after Harold left for Africa, she held a party to celebrate. I expect she'll hold another little get-together when she hears that he's died for King and Country. I can almost – *almost*, mind – feel sorry for the poor sod. Only he's such a pompous ass I can't quite manage it.'

At Linda Forrester's luxurious apartment in Queen Square, they ate salmon and peas washed down with Chablis, followed by blancmange and peaches. Linda wore a sinuous sheath of white crêpe, with a dusting of tiny silver beads at the neck. Ralph sat to one side of her, Bruno Gage to the other.

'Too clever, Ralph, writing a book.' Linda offered Ralph the dish of peaches. 'I get bored just writing a letter.'

Bruno topped up Ralph's glass. 'Tell me, Ralph, did "Nymph" draw on your own experiences? Was the girl in the book . . . I've forgotten her name—'

'Maria,' supplied Ralph.

'Was the girl in the book an old flame?'

'We're longing to hear.'

Ralph said, 'I met her in Brazil, actually.'

' "Mexicali Rose . . ." ' sang someone.

'*Brazil*, silly.'

' "Roses of Picardy" is more your era, isn't it, Ralph?'

Ralph seemed, Faith thought, to have come alive. The morose, hunched Pa of the past few months had gone, erased by wine and company. But he had aged; the experience of being uprooted from his accustomed way of life had added a decade to his appearance. Ralph was now fifty-five, and though he had always seemed both strong and ageless, and had shaken off the vicissitudes of life with ease, Faith could see how much the past six months had changed him. His fair hair was now completely white, pouches of flesh gathered under his eyes, and she sensed for the first time his vulnerability.

There was a ripple of laughter. Ralph had been regaling them with tales of his youth.

'A *gigolo*, Ralph – I'm shocked.'

'One imagines you with a monocle and a cigarette holder. A regular lounge lizard.'

Ralph leaned back in his chair. 'Did I tell you about the time my friend Bunny and I dressed up as toffs and managed to wangle our way into the Crillon?'

'*Do* tell, Ralph.'

'We're all ears.'

'Frightfully daring.'

Faith could bear it no longer. She touched Ralph's hand. 'We should go, Pa. It's late.'

'You haven't had your coffee, Miss Mulgrave.'

'*Coffee*, Linda?' drawled Bruno. 'Did you sell your body, or your soul?'

Ralph eyed his daughter blearily. 'Don't be so dull, Faith. I haven't had such a good time since I came to this godforsaken island.'

She thought, *But they're using you, Pa, and they're laughing at you*, and she walked out of the room. She did not leave the house, however, but remained in the adjacent corridor. The ceilings were high and corniced, the walls an elegant cream, panelled to waist height in dark wood. Blackout material covered the window; she could not see out. She lit a cigarette, and took pleasure in flicking the ash onto the carpet. After a while she heard footsteps, and she turned and saw Linda Forrester.

'I thought you'd like some coffee, Miss Mulgrave.' She handed Faith a cup and saucer. 'You mustn't mind them. They are rather drunk, I'm afraid. And Ralph is a sweetie. Such an original, and very amusing. He's promised to come to my birthday party next month. You must come too, Miss Mulgrave.'

'I work most nights. I drive an ambulance.'

'How extraordinary. And your brother – Jake – how is Jake?'

'Jake's fine,' she said. 'He's waiting for his posting.'

'Perhaps I'll send him an invitation too.'

Linda's face, Faith thought, resembled a mask. A pale, perfect mask. 'If you wish.'

Linda smiled. 'You must come back to the drawing-room, Miss Mulgrave. We're to play bezique.'

She heard, as Linda opened the door, Ralph's voice.

'Ridiculous war. I lived in Berlin for a year, y'know, before the first one. Charming people, the Germans. Just because some madmen have been let loose, there's no need to tar the lot of them with the same brush.'

'Pa.' Faith touched his shoulder.

He glared up at her. 'Felix, for instance. Felix is one of the best, isn't he?'

'Of course he is, Pa.'

'As for the Italians . . . we had a villa on the Ligurian coast. Delightful place. Do you remember, Faith? Everyone was so welcoming. Do you remember Signora Cavalli? Marvellous woman . . .'

She said gently, 'Pa, it's your turn to deal. Everyone's waiting,' and, resigning herself to an evening of irritation and boredom, sat down beside him. She knew that this company was just an imperfect substitute for what Ralph had had before. And that he needed friends, any friends, even those who treasured him for what amusement he could give them rather than for his generous heart, his innocence.

They left the flat at five o'clock in the morning. Rufus had gone home hours before, but Faith had remained behind with Ralph. Someone gave them a lift part of the way, and they walked the rest, Ralph stumbling on the kerb in the darkness, swearing loudly. At last, the sky began to lighten. Every now and then Ralph paused in the road, gazing at the bomb damage.

'Extraordinary,' he muttered. Huge metal girders twisted among the fallen bricks like Brobdingnagian ivy tendrils. Ducks swam on emergency water tanks that had been made from the basements of fallen buildings. The tatters of wallpaper clinging to the ruined walls were reflected in rainwashed, shifting patterns. Among the ruins a forest of rosebay willow-herb flourished, and now, in October, the purple flowers had turned to downy seed cases, each drift of tiny parachutes like a puff of smoke.

After a while Ralph said suddenly, 'Didn't you tell me you'd seen Guy, Faith?'

'Once or twice,' she said noncommittally.

'Dear old Guy.' Ralph was sentimental. 'I shall buy him a drink. Hackney, isn't it, Faith? It won't take us long. You can show me the way.'

She realized with sudden horror that he intended to set off for Hackney at that moment, to roam drunkenly around London until he reached Malt Street. Faith looked at her father. He wore his familiar old great-coat, red scarf and black hat, but now she noticed that the greatcoat was stained and threadbare, that the scarf had frayed, and that a cobweb trailed from the brim of the hat like a length of grey lace. Her mind, momen-tarily paralysed, was filled only by a frozen vision of Ralph, in his disintegrating coat and cobweb-strewn hat, knocking on Guy's front door, and being shown – swearing and the worse for drink – into the Nevilles' immaculate house.

Panicking, she said, 'We can't call on Guy now, Pa. He'll still be asleep.'

'Surprise him,' suggested Ralph gleefully.

She remembered Guy at the bomb-site: the contempt, the censoriousness in his eyes. *So you've managed to find enough room in your crowded social life to do a little war work.*

'Pa, we can't—'

Ralph roared, 'Don't be so *dull*, Faith! You were always the dullest of my children! Guy will be delighted to see us, of course he will!'

She took a deep breath. She saw that she was going to have to tell him the truth. 'Pa, Guy and I have fallen out with each other. I really don't think he wants to see me.'

'Guy isn't the sort of fellow to bear a grudge. And neither should you, Faith. Come on.'

In desperation, she prevaricated.

'Then we'll invite him to lunch, Pa. On Sunday. That's a better idea, isn't it?'

To her relief, he nodded.

When, two days later, Faith returned from Mrs Childerley's house, there was a note from Guy on the doormat. 'Eleanor and I are delighted to accept your kind invitation. We look forward to seeing you on Sunday.' The cold formality of the note made her clench her teeth.

She resolved that everything should be perfect. Remembering Eleanor Neville's elegance and gentility, she set out to emulate it. She was haunted by nightmares: Ralph would take one of his irrational dislikes to Eleanor and be unremittingly rude to her; or some of Rufus's more disreputable friends would choose Sunday lunchtime to visit.

Returning from work to Mahonia Road after her Saturday night shift, Faith did not sleep, but began to scrub floors, peel vegetables and polish cutlery. She plumped up the cushions, so that they looked almost like the ones in Eleanor Neville's drawing-room, except they did not match; and she found an old bedspread to cover the scratched dining-room table. She spent half an hour washing the brick dust out of her hair, twisting it into a reasonably tidy knot on the back of her head, and another half-hour trying on her entire collection of dresses, settling eventually on a black crêpe that one of the Lodgers, who had been in mourning, had discarded at La Rouilly. Ralph, appearing blearily in his dressing-gown at half past eleven, looked at her and muttered, 'Good God, Faith, you look like a missionary,' and poured himself a drink. While he shuffled upstairs to dress, she hid the whisky bottle in the bookcase, and placed a bowl of flowers on the dining-table. She had been able to find only old man's beard and brambles, but she thought they looked pretty. Then she put the cat, which was lapping the milk for the blancmange, outdoors, and rushed around the house, searching vainly for four matching plates and pudding bowls. By one o'clock, when Guy and Eleanor were expected, she felt dazed with exhaustion.

Yet the worst of her fears proved unfounded. Ralph embraced Guy and was polite to Eleanor. Faith handed everyone a glass of sherry, and went back to the kitchen to attend to the cooking. She had made stuffed savoury crêpes, a dish that could easily be adapted to shortages in the shops.

The lunch passed without mishap. Ralph and Guy reminisced about La Rouilly; Eleanor told Faith about her WVS work. Every now and then Ralph would try to include Faith and Guy in the same conversation; Faith ignored him. After they had dined, she longed for Guy and Eleanor to go; she longed to collapse on the sofa and sleep. But when Eleanor offered to help with the washing-up, Ralph said, 'Not at all. Faith and Guy shall wash up. Guy was always a good washer-up, I recall. It's a fine day, and you and I shall go for a walk, Eleanor.'

She realized, with a rush of irritation, that Ralph was trying clumsily to mend things between herself and Guy. After Ralph and Eleanor had left the house, there was a long, awkward silence. Eventually Faith said stiffly, 'You don't have to help, Guy, there's not much to do.'

But he followed her into the kitchen. She saw the expression on his face as he took in the scale of the disaster: the pots and pans piled precariously in the sink, the vegetable peelings in the colander and bowl, the fragments of batter clinging to the ceiling where she had tossed a pancake too vigorously. She began to heave dirty saucepans out of the sink, so that she could fill the basin with clean water. Some of the water spilled onto the floor, mingling with the onion skins and splashes of batter.

'Eleanor cleans up as she goes along,' said Guy coldly.

She stared at him. 'I hadn't realized that you could be so . . . *censorius*, Guy.'

'Censorius?'

'Yes. And judgemental. Ever since you saw Rufus and me—'

'Rufus . . . is that his name?' Grabbing the broom, turning his back to her, Guy began, with inappropriate force, to sweep the floor.

She pulled the broom out of his hands, and hissed, '*Leave* it, I said! I'll do everything!' The heap of peelings and dust scattered over the tiles.

'As you wish.'

Angrily, inaccurately, Faith swept the scraps into the dustpan. She tried to explain. 'Rufus is my friend, Guy.'

'Yes. Well. That was obvious.'

His sneer was audible. Her temper snapped; she heard herself yell 'What the hell is it to do with you?' and he shrugged, and said: 'Nothing, of course. If you choose to go to bed with half the men in London, then I have no right to comment.'

She gasped, and looked up at him, momentarily unable to speak. The dustpan slipped from her hand, and she rose shakily to her feet, and leaned against the edge of the sink, looking out of the window, but seeing nothing.

There was a long silence. At last she heard him mutter, 'Sorry. I'm sorry, Faith. I shouldn't have said that.'

Slowly, she turned to face him. She whispered, 'I slept with Rufus once. It was a mistake. A bad mistake.' Her voice trembled. 'Don't you ever make mistakes, Guy?'

'Of course I do.' He took his cigarettes from his pocket, and offered her the packet: she shook her head. She heard the hiss of the match as he lit his cigarette. One by one she slid the dirty plates into the sink. She felt drained, exhausted, overcome by a wave of almost intolerable fatigue. Tears smudged her sight, and her head ached, but she continued blindly to try to sort out the mess. She heard Guy say: 'The thing is, I just don't want you to get hurt.'

She paused, biting her lip, her hands plunged in the grimy water.

'Your friend . . . Rufus . . . he was in merchant navy uniform.'

'He's gone back to sea.' She turned back to him, wiping her soapy hands on her skirt.

'You must miss him.' She knew that he was making an effort at conciliation. 'You must worry about him.'

'I do miss him, and I do worry about him.' Her gaze met Guy's, and she added firmly, 'As one would worry about a friend.' Filling the kettle with water, she placed it on the stove.

His back was to her; he was looking out of the window. He said suddenly, 'Don't you get lonely here, Faith? Or frightened?'

She shook her head. 'Not really. I'm too tired to be frightened.' She began to fling open cupboard doors.

'What are you looking for?'

'The teapot.'

'You put it in the larder just a moment ago.'

She went to the larder and there it was, among the canisters of flour and gravy browning. She had no recollection at all of placing it there. She went back to the stove, but fumbled opening the tea caddy. Small black flecks scattered over the floor. She heard Guy say, with a weariness that matched her own, 'Oh, for God's sake, Faith, sit down, and let me do it.'

'I can manage, thank you.' Only she was not sure that she could; her mind seemed stewed with exhaustion.

He held out a chair and pushed her into it. After he had made the tea, he began to plunge dishes into the dirty water. 'The little mop is on the hook by the door,' she said, but her voice sounded blurred. She watched him for a while, intending to get up and help, but she did not seem able to move, and after a while she let her head slip forward onto her folded arms, and she slept.

* * *

As they turned the corner of the street, Eleanor said to Guy: 'Serving pancakes as a main course! How extraordinary!'

'It's quite common in France.'

'Really?' Eleanor was disbelieving. 'And that bowl of weeds on the table . . . and Miss Mulgrave's *coiffure* . . . She would be so much improved by a neat bob. I must give her the name of my hairdresser.'

Appalled by the idea of Faith with a neat bob, Guy said, 'Don't you think that would be rather . . . uncivil?'

'Oh, you know that I'd be tactful, Guy. Really, it would be a kindness to the poor girl. We'll have to return the invitation, I suppose, so I can mention Angela to her then.'

They walked for a while in silence. Their journey took longer than they might have expected because of the frequent diversions caused by bomb-damage. When they reached Malt Street, Eleanor looked up at the missing roof tiles, the broken windows that had been replaced by squares of hardboard, and tutted.

'If this gets any worse, then we'll go and live with my father.'

Guy unlocked the door. As always, he half expected to hear Oliver's cry, and as always, the knowledge that he would neither hear nor see Oliver for weeks, maybe months, to come, was raw and painful.

'Such a mess!' said Eleanor. A pyramid of brick dust had trickled from a crack in the wall to the stair carpet.

He said, 'If you'd gone with Oliver to Derbyshire, as I suggested, then you wouldn't have to put up with this.'

'Oh, Guy, let's not go through all that again.' Eleanor's voice was patient, falsely cheerful, as though she was humouring a sullen child. She hung up her coat and hat. 'Everything's working out for the best, as I told you it would. I had a letter from Grandmother only this morning – I'll show it you – she says that Oliver is perfectly well and happy. He has a new tooth.'

Guy wondered how changed Oliver would be when he saw him again. Babies altered so quickly. The pain of missing Oliver was like a physical wound. In his study, the door open, Guy closed his eyes, his back to Eleanor, and only after a while listened to what she was saying.

'. . . the Holland Square house is so much more solidly built. And it's further away from the East End, of course.'

He realized that she was still trying to persuade him to decamp to her father's house. He said firmly, 'We can't possibly leave Malt Street, Eleanor. Think of my patients.'

'The surgery could remain here, Guy. There's a bus, after all, and you have a bicycle. It would be easy for you to travel back to Malt Street for your surgery.'

He forbore to point out that bus journeys were these days long-drawn-out and unpredictable ventures. Instead he said, 'It wouldn't work, Eleanor. What of emergencies? I have to be here in case I'm needed quickly.'

She was picking out the dead flowers from the vase on the mantelpiece. 'There are telephones, Guy.'

He snorted. 'How many of my patients have a telephone?'

'I meant that there are public telephone boxes.'

'Some of my patients don't feel at ease using a telephone. Many of the old ladies have never used one in their lives.'

She said briskly, 'Then it's about time they learned,' and continued to extract dead roses, placing them neatly on a square of old newspaper.

'Don't be ridiculous, Eleanor!' Guy's voice was sharp. 'There's no question of us moving to Holland Square. You must understand that I won't consider it.'

She continued to do the flowers; he watched her for a while, and then he went to her and said, 'Don't be angry, Eleanor, please.' He put his hand on her shoulder. 'I do see that things must be difficult for you. And I know that you worry about your father.' He bent his head, and kissed the back of her neck. He could not remember when they had last made love: his night shifts and Eleanor's WVS work meant that they rarely shared a bed for an entire night.

'*Guy,*' she said, but he continued to kiss her. Her skin was firm and clean, her hair soft and springy. One-handedly he reached out and pulled down the blind.

She said, 'The neighbours . . . and if there's a raid . . .'

'If there's a raid, then we'll be safer here than upstairs.' He began to unbutton the front of her blouse.

'No, Guy.' She pulled away from him, and began to tidy her hair with her hands. 'I have to make out the rotas for the tea vans. They're late already.'

She left the room. He pulled the blind back up, and looked out of the window, through the criss-cross of white strips that covered the panes. A small voice echoed in his head. *Don't you ever make mistakes, Guy?* He pushed the words ruthlessly away, sat down in an armchair, closed his eyes and dozed off.

* * *

Nicole had only a very vague idea of what David Kemp did: he had made it clear that he could not talk much about his work and, really, she was not all that interested. That he travelled a lot she knew; that he knew a great many important people she suspected. She knew also that he was unfailingly kind, gentle and generous. He coped with any situation – from a tardy waiter to falling bombs – with unshakeable calmness and quiet confidence. She had never met anyone like him before. Nicole realized after a while that each part of David's day was mapped out, that he kept in touch with friends and relations with self-imposed regularity, that his life was governed by an order that he took for granted.

Travelling, she wrote to him, sometimes several times a week, long, carelessly scrawled, ill-spelt letters. Twice a month she sang in London with the Geoff Dexter Band; the concert was broadcast on the wireless. She had also begun to tour the country, taking part in concerts put on for the troops. Some of it she loved: the dark, crowded train journeys across an anonymous England; tramping across a field, wearing an evening dress and gumboots, to some distant air or army base. Most of all she loved the way that the applause, half-hearted as she approached the stage, altered in character, becoming tumultuous by the time she sang her last song.

She discovered how to make her audience love her. She became adept at choosing her songs to fit her listeners, their mood. She would start her act with something rousing, then drop down the tempo a little, becoming seductive. Towards the end of her set, she would bring tears to her audience's eyes with a wistful, plaintive little number, finishing, of course, with a song that was stirring and patriotic. She could be childlike, reminding the older men of their distant daughters, and she could be a temptress. She made each person feel that she was singing only to them.

Though she adored singing, Nicole disliked some aspects of the way of life that touring enforced on her. The dreary little lodging-houses; the disapproving land-ladies. Though she was not acquisitive, she had always loved beautiful things. Drabness and ugliness unsettled her. She hated having to share a bathroom with strangers. A ring of hairs and scum round a bathtub made her feel physically ill.

In November, entertaining the troops stationed in army camps near York, Nicole was quartered in grim lodgings in the back streets of the city. Her room was small, its ceiling high, and the walls were painted a dark greyish-green, giving it a cavernous appearance. Because of the pressure on lodgings, the rest of the concert party were scattered throughout the city, which meant that in the evenings, after the performance, Nicole was on her own. She was not used to being alone: there had always been Ralph and Poppy, Jake and Faith, and the endless procession of Lodgers. The silence, the emptiness of the room, unsettled her. She did not know how to fill the hours. And she could hardly bear to sleep in the bed. The blankets were stained, the sheets almost transparent in the middle where a hundred other unknown bodies had twisted and turned on them. She realized for the first time that though her way of life – the way of life of the Mulgrave family – had been unconventional, it had never been squalid. Poppy had seen to that.

They were to stay three weeks in York, a prospect which, by the end of the first week, appalled her.

Nicole slept wrapped in her coat each night, so as to avoid contact with the awful bed. She could not eat the food her landlady served her. The plates were chipped and scratched, and were sometimes, at dinner-time, adorned with solidified yellow blobs that were the remains of the morning's breakfast egg. She knew that she was being ungrateful and over-fastidious, that men were dying daily that she should eat, but she could not: the boiled cabbage, the gristly meat stuck in her throat. She began to feel very tired and sometimes rather faint. She missed her family and friends dreadfully.

After ten days, she returned to her lodgings one evening to find a telegram waiting for her. It was from David Kemp, telling her that he had business in the north of England, and that he would call on her on the nineteenth. She realized, with a leap of joy and relief, that it was the nineteenth tomorrow.

He was waiting for her outside her lodging-house when she came home the following evening. She ran to him, and hugged him. He offered to take her for dinner, and she suggested they walk for a while first. As they walked, she told him amusing little anecdotes about the other members of the concert party. He listened and laughed, but after a while he said: 'What is it, Nicole? What's wrong?'

'Nothing's wrong,' she said. 'Nothing's wrong at all.'

He did not believe her. Slowly, he coaxed the truth out of her, and she found herself admitting to him her loneliness, the inedible stews, her awful room, the bed. 'And the eiderdown, David! Awful pink roses, like cabbages. One expects pink worms to slide out at any moment!' She laughed, trying to make a joke of it.

He looked down at her, concerned. 'You look tired, Nicole. It's not right. You shouldn't be living like this.'

'I had to take the eiderdown off the bed. Only then I was so cold I couldn't sleep. So now I sleep with my coat on, like a lady tramp.' Nicole laughed again. Then she said, 'Tell me about your home, David. Tell me about Compton Deverall.'

They were walking through narrow medieval alleyways towards the city walls. In spite of the blackout, the brilliance of the moon and stars lit up the dark streets.

She heard him say, 'The house is surrounded by woodland. It's Jacobean, mostly, though my father was always convinced that one or two of the inner walls and chimneys are much older – medieval, perhaps. There are a great many long, narrow windows with mullioned panes – they glitter when the sun shines. The Kemp who built it, centuries ago, was an admirer of Hardwick Hall, you see. Compton Deverall's much smaller, of course.'

Nicole had never heard of Hardwick Hall, but she made suitably impressed noises.

David added, 'When I was a little boy, I tried to see how many windows there were, but I always lost count after seventy or so. There's a priest's hole – my family were Roman Catholic until Charles II's time – and a ghost, of course.'

'A ghost! So romantic, David!'

He grinned. 'The old place is somewhat less romantic now, I'm afraid – we've half a girls' boarding school billeted on us. And dozens of windows are a nightmare in the blackout. But my mother's coping admirably, though she escapes to her garden as often as possible.'

Nicole had always loved old houses, beautiful gardens, woods and forests. She thought of the lodging-house, with its dingy dining-room tablecloths stained with brown sauce, and she shuddered.

They had reached the city walls. She began to climb the steps, but he called out, halting her.

'It's not safe. You might slip and fall.'

'Not me, David,' she said confidently. 'I'm very sure-footed. You can follow me, can't you?'

He said, 'Oh, Nicole, I'd follow you anywhere. You know that by now, don't you?' and she turned and looked down at him.

'David. I didn't realize—'

'That I love you? I've loved you since the moment I first set eyes on you. I never thought I'd say that to anyone – such a cliché, and I'm not a romantic man – but it happens to be true.'

He sounded, she thought, terribly sad. She ran down the steps. 'Why didn't you tell me before?'

He sighed. 'Because I am thirty-two and you are seventeen. Because I am old and plain and you are the most beautiful woman I have ever seen. Because I am dull and you – you are like quicksilver.'

'Shh.' She put her fingers over his mouth, silencing him. Then she took his hand and guided him up the steps until they reached the summit of the wall. There, she touched her lips against his. After a while, he began to kiss her properly. She opened her eyes only once, to see the golden sickle moon, flat on its back in a lamp-black sky, and the stars sprinkled all around. She thought that she could not have chosen a more romantic place for her first kiss.

Then he asked her to marry him. Nicole saw how blind she had been not to have realized before that David was The One. Fate had placed them together on the train, and, later, in the Blitz, had brought them closer to each other. She considered what her life could be like if she married David Kemp. She imagined living in a lovely house amid beautiful woodland. In her mind's eye she saw Compton Deverall as an English version of La Rouilly. She would be able to ride horses, and to keep as many dogs as she chose. She imagined parties and long, wonderful evenings with friends, talking and laughing. She would become part of an old, established English family, and in doing so she would never feel lonely again. She saw that, in David Kemp, she had found a sanctuary.

After she had accepted his proposal, he held her in his arms for a long time, stroking her silky, fair hair. Then they kissed again. He said, 'I wish I could take you home this very weekend. You'll adore Mother, and she'll adore you, but the house may give you second thoughts.'

Nicole was sure that it would not. She drew away from him, and began to dance along the narrow path that led along the wall, laughing at his entreaties to be careful.

Meeting Nicole, David Kemp had felt reborn. The lonely, empty years since his fiancée's death had fallen away, and he had begun to live again. He had not thought, after Susan, to find love again – he had resigned himself to remaining a bachelor – but since that eventful train journey across the English country-side, he had discovered that he had been mistaken.

That Nicole should also love him seemed to him a miracle. He had no photograph of her, but her image was engraved in his heart. Her long, silver-fair hair, her blue-green eyes, her graceful, fragile limbs. She had come into his life, a piece of thistledown, the stuff of

182

magic, and she had changed him for ever. Her impulsiveness, her brightness, enchanted him. He did not fall in love easily, but having done so he loved deeply. He knew that in Nicole he had found someone unique, someone precious. He resolved to take her away from the exhausting, demanding life she now led as soon as possible.

He longed to take her to Compton Deverall. He had been born in the house; it had belonged to his family for centuries. David's father had died at the battle of Mons in 1914, and since then he and his mother had lived alone at Compton Deverall apart from a rapidly decreasing complement of servants. He had no brothers or sisters. After schooling at Marlborough College, and reading PPE at Oxford, he had worked at the Treasury. Since the summer of 1940, when, after the fall of France and the Dunkirk evacuation, Neville Chamberlain's leadership had given way to Winston Churchill's, David had been assigned to Hugh Dalton's Ministry of Economic Supply. The job involved long hours, much travelling, and a mountain of paperwork, but it took advantage of his strengths: a talent for detail and the ability to pick the essential fact from a quagmire of irrelevance.

Given a weekend's leave, David managed to obtain enough petrol to drive to Wiltshire. He and Nicole left London for Compton Deverall early one cold November morning. Driving, he frequently glanced aside at her, as if to reassure himself of his good fortune.

He did not need to look at a map, or to worry about the lack of signposts, which had been removed to baffle the expected invaders. He knew the journey off by heart; he was intimate with the way the landscape changed as they left London behind. His spirits rose as he saw the great dark bruise of Salisbury Plain looming against the chill blue sky, and the swell of the downland, the white chalk pressing like bones through the grass. His family had grazed sheep on the downland for centuries, and he, as a boy holidaying from school, had chased Chalk Hill Blues there, and discovered rare orchids in their secret places on the meadow borders. Always, coming home, he was aware of a sense of peace. Through the dark years that had followed Susan's death, he had been comforted by the sense of continuity and permanence that his home and his family had given to him. Now, he longed to add Nicole's beauty, her luminous spirit, to all that he loved.

At midday, they turned off the main road and drove through the avenue of tall beech trees that led to the house. It was, David thought, the sort of day he would have chosen for Nicole's first sight of Compton Deverall. The last of the falling leaves were like flakes of bronze, and through the lacework of branches he glimpsed the house's ornate Elizabethan chimneys among a glitter of roof tile.

He heard Nicole gasp. '*David*. It's *beautiful*.'

He smiled, and braked. 'Isn't it?'

'It's like . . . Oh, one expects Good Queen Bess to step out of the front door in her farthingale and ruff . . . Or Sir Walter Raleigh to fling his cloak over one of the puddles.'

'There are rather a lot of puddles, I'm afraid. It looks very romantic, but it isn't really – just a lot of hard work.'

Nicole was climbing out of the car. '*I* think it's romantic. *I* think it'll be like living in a story book. I think I'm going to be wonderfully happy here.' She bent over the car door, and kissed the top of his head. 'And I'm going to make you wonderfully happy too, David.'

Later that evening, after he had said goodnight to Nicole, David found his mother in the kitchen.

'Cocoa?' asked Laura Kemp, holding up a tin.

'Please.' He perched against the Aga. 'Well? You like her, don't you?'

'She's delightful.' Laura smiled at her son. 'She makes the house seem brighter.' She measured out cocoa and sugar. 'It's only . . .' she said, and paused.

'What?'

She put aside the spoon, and turned and faced him. 'Nicole is very young, David.' She added hastily, 'Not that it matters necessarily. Only, if it weren't wartime, then I would suggest a long engagement.'

Nicole wanted the wedding to take place before Christmas. David frowned. 'Are you afraid that she'll change her mind?'

Laura Kemp shook her head. 'No, I don't think so. She seems so fond of you. But is she ready for – for all this?' Her gesture took in the cavernous kitchen, the huge old Aga, the ice already forming on the inside of the windows.

'She adores the place. She told me so.'

'David.' Mrs Kemp touched his arm. 'I'm very happy for you. You must realize that.'

He smiled at her. 'I know, Mother.' He dug his hands in his pockets, and walked to the stove and looked down at the milk pan.

'Will Nicole's parents insist that she waits until she is twenty-one?'

He laughed. 'I doubt it. It sounds as though she can wind her father round her little finger.'

'Have you met him?'

'Not yet. I've only been introduced to her elder sister, who's charming. Mr and Mrs Mulgrave live in Norfolk. I know that it would have been better form to speak to her father before asking Nicole to marry me, but I just couldn't wait.'

'What does Mr Mulgrave do?'

'A jack of all trades, by the sound of it. Not quite out of the top drawer – though her mother was a Vanburgh. But you know I've never given a damn about that sort of thing.'

'The only advantage,' said his mother firmly, 'in marrying a girl from one's own class is that she would know the ropes. Where do you intend to live after the wedding, David?'

'I'm going to bring Nicole down here. I want to get her away from London.' He frowned. 'I'm away a great deal, you see, Mother, so I'd feel happier if I knew that she was safe here with you.'

'Of course. I only wish that you could stay with us too, darling. I do so worry about you.' She glanced at him anxiously. 'Is London very grim just now?'

'Pretty awful. Though we pen-pushers have very splendid bomb shelters, so you mustn't worry about me.'

She said, 'Will there be an invasion?'

His mother never, ever voiced her worries to him. He realized that this was as close as she would come to telling him that she was afraid. He went to her, and hugged her.

'I don't think so. There was a risk in September, but I'm more optimistic now. It's just a question of sticking it out. Making sure there's enough food in the larder. Keeping one's spirits up.'

'How long do you think it will go on?'

'A long time,' he said simply. 'And I'm afraid that it's going to get worse before it gets better. But you'll be fine here, and so will Nicole.' He glanced at his mother. 'And our evacuees.'

Three classes of a girls' boarding school now inhabited Compton Deverall's attics. Laura Kemp smiled ruefully.

'They have such *appetites*, David. And sometimes, the *noise* . . .'

He laughed. 'You've always adored the place for its peace and quiet, haven't you, Mother?' His expression became serious again. 'So, do I have your blessing?'

'The milk's boiling over,' said Laura Kemp gently. 'And yes, David, of course you have my blessing.'

CHAPTER SIX

Nicole married David Kemp in December. The ceremony took place in the tiny twelfth-century church a mile from Compton Deverall. Nicole looked enchanting in a Victorian lace wedding dress that had once belonged to David's grandmother. Ralph, Poppy, Faith and Jake attended the ceremony. As they left the church, a few flakes of snow fell from the iron-grey sky. It was good luck, someone said, for snow to fall on your wedding day.

Faith spent Christmas at Heronsmead, where she slept a great deal, and noticed that Poppy was very tired and that Ralph was bad-tempered and drinking too much. Back in London, she received an invitation to supper from the Nevilles. Guy and Eleanor were now living in Eleanor's father's house in Holland Square in Bloomsbury. The food, in spite of rationing, was delicious, and the rooms were elegant and restful. Faith was thankful that she and Guy seemed to have slipped into a more easy-going acquaintance. She did not think she could have borne anything else. Her exhaustion, and the nightmarish strangeness of the London streets, would have made passion on her part, or anger on his, intolerable.

Even when she had a night off, her sleep was broken by the endless wail of the air-raid siren, and the thunder of bombs and falling masonry. Her weariness became an almost tangible thing, something to be gathered up and taken with her wherever she went. If she had a spare half-hour, she slept. She slept sitting on a bench in the park, while Mrs Childerley's dogs peed incontinently on the grass, she slept waiting at the ambulance station for the telephone to ring, a cup of tea beside her, playing cards cradled in her hands. Momentarily, she slept queuing at the butcher's for bacon ('like a horse in a stable', she wrote to Jake, who was stationed in the north of England), and, if she went to the cinema, she slept from the newsreel to the credits. She continued to work with reasonable competence, but in a sort of stupor. Her muscles ached all the time. To think was a tortuous process, like swimming through jelly, like the beginnings of a migraine.

In February she received a letter from Nicole. 'I'm expecting a sprog, Faith. Too ghastly, and it makes me sick *all the time*.' The air raids continued sporadically through the early part of the year. Faith welcomed bad weather and, like the rest of London, feared clear skies and full moons – 'bombers' moons'. The Mahonia Road house was like a decaying dowager, less and less able to withstand the ravages of the long, interrupted nights. There was not one unbroken window; she no longer had the energy or the will to replace broken or missing glass with hardboard, so the cold wind and sleety rain whistled through the house unimpeded. Strange, snaking cracks, like vine tendrils, crept along the old walls. The staircase seemed to have slipped sideways, detached from both wall and banisters. One of the bedroom ceilings had collapsed, and rain, seeping through missing roof tiles, made a grey porridge of the fallen plaster. It seemed to Faith that the house suited the London of 1941, its surreal, dreamlike quality matching the quiet, bomb-damaged streets.

Yet the dull food, the interrupted water supplies, had become unimportant. What mattered was waking up in the morning and knowing that those you loved were safe. What mattered were visits from Rufus and Ralph, letters from Poppy and Nicole and Jake, the chatter of the girls in the ambulance station, and the occasional wave from Guy across the chaos of a bomb-site.

Late one night, driving back from the hospital to the ambulance station, weaving the complicated route dictated by the yellow 'Diversion' boards, Bunty grabbed Faith's arm as they swung round a corner. 'Half a mo. I'm nearly home. Give me a tick and I'll check my mum's all right.'

'Won't she be in the shelter?'

'Can't stand it. Too crowded, she says. And the Anderson's full of water, so she goes under the stairs. See you in a sec.'

Bunty slipped out of the cab. Faith watched her running down the street, her small, stocky body illuminated by the reddish glow of the sky. Faith opened the door, climbed out, and fumbled in her pocket for her cigarettes. The raid had been heavy, and the night air was thick with brick dust. She was striking the match when the bomb fell. There was a whoosh of air, as though she had been sucked up by a very large straw, then an explosion of light, followed by a noise of such stupefying clamour that she was robbed of all capacity for thought. When she opened her eyes, she found that she was lying on her front in a puddle, squashed up against someone's garden wall. The air was a dusty soup; she struggled to take it into her lungs. Her cigarette was still in one hand, the match in the other. She sat up cautiously. When she blinked, she could see the imprint of the flash of light on her inner eyelid. All sounds – the thunder of falling masonry, the roar of the bombers, the screams of the injured – seemed curiously muffled.

She stood up. She thought, *Bunty*, and swung round, looking for the street her friend had run down. But the landscape was now unrecognizable, the pattern of road and house completely altered from what it had been only a few moments earlier. Faith walked back to the ambulance. Ragged shards of glass now bordered every window. She tried to reconstruct her memory of the scene before the blast. She remembered sitting in the cab, watching Bunty run along the pavement, and she began to trace her friend's path along the blasted road, clambering over heaps of broken masonry, skirting the vast crater that the bomb had made. She called out Bunty's name, but her voice sounded distant, smothered by the thick, clotted air. Flames soared to one side of the street, illuminating the ruins so that she had no need of her torch. Her mind was dazed, unable to connect this scene to the one of only ten minutes before.

She caught sight of a scrap of cloth beneath a pile of bricks, and recognized it as the plaid coat that Bunty had been wearing that night. Kneeling in the debris, she clawed at the fallen stones with her hands. The mortar tore her fingers, but she did not notice the pain. The ruins of the house toppled above her, the jagged walls like ripped paper against the blanched face of the moon. She dug desperately into the rubble, throwing aside bricks, broken roof tiles, fragments of cloth and carpet. She seemed to have been digging for hours when someone touched her shoulder and said: 'Leave her, miss. It's not safe here.'

She brushed him aside, and continued to claw at the rubble. Bunty's *shoe*, she thought, catching sight of a leather ankle boot. Bunty had always taken great care of her shoes. She rubbed at the dusty, scuffed surface with the sleeve of her coat.

The man shook her shoulder again. Looking up, she saw his helmet, his ARP overalls. 'I said, you've got to come away now, miss. This lot could fall any time.'

She said furiously, 'I've got to get her out.'

'Friend of yours?'

She did not reply. He leaned forward, felt Bunty's wrist where it was outflung from the debris, and said gently, 'There's nothing you can do for her now, love. And your friend wouldn't have wanted you to hurt yourself on her account, would she? Here's the Heavy Rescue boys. They'll get her out, I promise you.'

She let herself be helped to her feet, and led away from the damaged building. Her mind was oddly blank, unable to trace a continuous thought. She had watched Bunty run down the road to her mother's house – *I'll check my mum's all right . . . See you in a sec* – and then the bomb had fallen. It was not possible that in those few moments Bunty had died. She had seen death before, a hundred times now, but not until tonight the death of someone she had known well. A woman placed a mug of tea between her bloodied fingers, and she stared at the cup, watching the liquid jiggle in rhythm with her shaking hands. She continued to watch as the men moved aside the broken rafters and floorboards. She only believed that Bunty was dead when they lifted her body from the rubble, and she saw the way her limbs sprawled, and how her head hung at a dreadful angle.

After Bunty's death, everything changed. Faith's confidence in the future evaporated. She knew that she could not rely on waking up after she had fallen asleep; neither could she know when, like a thief in the night, death would take her friends or family. Her ability to sleep at any time, anywhere, deserted her. When she did sleep, she had nightmares. Though she had never been superstitious, she became so now, muttering charms as she shut the front door behind her when she left the house in the evening, carrying out the same routine each morning before she went to bed, alarmed and fearful of retribution if she diverted from an order that seemed so far to have protected her. She feared that her luck, which she had always taken for granted, would desert her. She took to wearing a bracelet which Ralph had bought her years ago in Italy, and when she mislaid it one night she was convinced that she would not live to see the dawn. When the first light came, gleaming over the ruins of London, she laughed at her fears, but the dread persisted, gnawing at her heart.

On 19 March, the night of the heaviest raid so far, something frightening happened. She was waiting at the ambulance station in the early hours of the morning, when the telephone rang to tell her where to pick up casualties. The next moment, or so it seemed, it was dawn, and she was standing on the doorstep of the Mahonia Road house, fitting her key into the lock. She had no idea at all of how the intervening hours had passed. All memory of them had been erased. When she went into the house, she discovered a loaf and the breadknife on the kitchen table, so she assumed that she must have come home in the middle of the night for something to eat, as she occasionally did. When she returned to work that evening, no-one questioned her, no-one looked at her oddly, so she supposed that she had carried out her work competently. But the disturbing gap remained, and, try as she might, could not be filled.

The same thing happened a week later. A missing couple of hours again, cut from the night, as though someone had taken a pair of scissors to her life. She had been able to pass off her first blackout as a fluke, an aberration: she could not do that the second time. It occurred to her that she was going mad, that there was something wrong inside her head. She remembered one of the Lodgers who, after behaving increasingly oddly even for a Lodger, had ended up locked in the asylum at Basle. She had visited once with Ralph: now, in her lowest moments, she saw herself in a long ward whose windows were barred with iron. She knew that she should consult a doctor, but was afraid to do so. She took to glancing at her watch every ten minutes or so, as though to convince herself that the frightening absence had not happened again, as though to fix herself in time.

Minden Hall, where Jake was stationed, was a square, Victorian lump of a house perched sullenly on the edge of an inhospitable northern moorland. Nissen huts surrounded the Hall, crouching on the grass like squat, dark toads. The huts were invariably cold, the lawns spongy with rainwater. Jake's first day at Minden Hall seemed to last for a week, his first week a month. The year and a half that he had spent fighting in Spain had been dull, cold, wet, and yes, ultimately futile. But Minden Hall, and the endless shuffling of papers that seemed to be his lot, brought futility to an art form.

Most of the men who shared Jake's Nissen hut seemed not to question the grey skies or the numbing dullness of the work. But Jake's boredom was mixed with fury, and an inability to accept that this must be what the war meant to him. He remembered Linda Forrester saying to him, *It's the tedium that's so unbearable*, and though he had despised her then, perceiving her as frivolous and selfish, now he found himself reluctantly agreeing with her.

After a fortnight, he went to his commanding officer to ask for a transfer. To Captain Crawford he pointed out that he was thoroughly wasted filling in forms. Captain Crawford reminded Jake that he had not passed his medical with flying colours, that the episode of bronchitis in early 1939 had left some permanent damage to his lungs. Jake vowed that he was perfectly fit now, and reminded Captain Crawford that he had fought in the International Brigades. Captain Crawford, not looking at Jake, said, 'Some rum types fought in Spain, Mulgrave. And no schooling. Looks bad, don't you know.' Jake, uncomprehending, was dismissed.

That evening, in the pub, he repeated the entire conversation to a colleague called Crabbe. Crabbe eyed him through a cloud of blue pipe smoke.

'Not the right sort, you see, Mulgrave. Not quite British enough. They can't place you.'

'Place me?' repeated Jake, bewildered.

'Class, my dear fellow. You are neither fish nor flesh nor good red herring. You have distinctly *foreign* traits . . . You've lived abroad . . . and fought for the Reds.' Crabbe inaccurately mimicked Captain Crawford's plummy accent. 'Not quite the thing, old boy. Suspect loyalties and all that.'

Faced with the unending dullness of his work, Jake decided to sample what entertainment Minden Hall had to offer. There was no shortage of willing girls, and if they showed signs of lingering – looking in jewellers' windows, perhaps, or talking about romantic wartime weddings – then Jake quickly put an end to the affair. He became adept at choosing only the girls who wanted the same as he – pleasure without involvement, the fleeting elation of sex without risk of emotional pain. Bored and lonely, he discovered how to make himself popular. He never refused a dare or a bet. He bribed one of the ATS girls to filch from the laundry a pair of their commanding officer's vast bloomers, and affixed them to the flagpole on the front lawn, where they flapped triumphantly in the breeze. Extremely drunk one night, he climbed the drainpipe attached to the side of Minden Hall, and decorated the roof with paper chains. An audience gathered on the lawn below, cheering him on. He received a severe dressing down for that, and a sprained ankle when he fell the last few yards on the way down.

Yet in spite of the popularity that he had manipulated for himself, he nevertheless felt excluded, on the outside, never really a part of things, consigned to the fringes rather than belonging. He could not fit into this bleak, grey country. He was able to feel little for an England that permitted him so inactive a role in its struggle for survival. His love affair with Anni seemed now a long time ago, inextricably bound up with a nervous, pre-war Paris, and the heat and despair of June 1940. Looking back, he was never quite certain who was to blame – Anni, for not having loved him enough, or himself, for not having had the courage to make the leap of trust. Of one thing only was he sure: that whatever he truly cared about crumbled to dust of its own accord, or was destroyed by him. What passion he had once felt for politics had died along with Republican Spain. If he had ever had a home, then it had been La Rouilly, and yet he, along with so many others, had deserted a dying France. He would never see Anni, whom he had loved, again.

The loyalties that had once been his had been cast off for ever in his desperate flight from Europe. He had arrived on these island shores naked of both possessions and belief. He and his family had, by the skin of their teeth, survived. Though his letters to his parents and to his sisters were intermittent, though he saw them infrequently, and took their affection and constancy for granted, Jake knew that his sole remaining allegiance was to his family. Ralph had never hid his contempt of country, patriotism, or politics. Jake was beginning to realize how much he had in common with his father.

The gleam of wintry sunlight through Compton Deverall's old mullioned windows, the wisps of mist on the lawns, delighted Nicole. It was all so entrancingly different, so magical, so *foreign*. On fine days, she took long walks through the beech woods; when it rained, she explored the house, emerging from rooms unused for decades clutching newly discovered treasures, cobwebs in her hair. Young and beautiful and charming, she received invitations from the local families of importance. In turn, she invited her hosts back to Compton Deverall. In a winter made cheerless by shortages and bad news, the evenings that the young

Mrs Kemp presided over became a delightful beacon in an ocean of gloom. While Laura Kemp conjured delicious meals out of the rations, Nicole amused her guests with games of charades and sardines, as well as other games of Ralph's devising, hitherto known only to Mulgraves. Laura, who preferred digging the garden to entertaining, happily acknowledged Nicole as the superior hostess, and left the parties to her daughter-in-law.

Because there was a home farm, with pigs and hens and turkeys, and because of the huge, walled kitchen garden, tended by Laura, they were never hungry. Each weekend, people drifted from London to Wiltshire, enticed by the prospect of good food and an uninterrupted night's sleep. Nicole welcomed equally to the house David's friends and her own, from her days with the BBC and ENSA. Dust cloths were shaken from furniture in rooms in little-used corridors, floors polished, beds made up. Racks of dinner plates, in storage for years, were washed and set upon dressers. One weekend thirty people dined at the huge old oak table.

Like Ralph, Nicole made friends easily. Queuing in shops, or waiting for a bus, she would talk to people. Strangers would rapidly become acquaintances; acquaintances would, in a day or two, become dear friends. Because of the proximity of Salisbury Plain, many of the weekend guests at Compton Deverall were soldiers and airmen. The old panelled walls of the house echoed with half a dozen languages. Free French, Dutch and Belgian airmen ate Laura Kemp's food, and danced with Laura Kemp's beautiful daughter-in-law. When Nicole greeted a Polish flyer with a few words of his native language, taught to her years before by

Genya, he knelt and kissed the hem of her skirt.

David had to return to London in mid-January; Nicole did not realize that she was pregnant until the following month. Horribly sick, she put down her illness at first to having eaten something that disagreed with her. Laura Kemp, who had different suspicions, insisted on calling the doctor. When she was told that she was expecting a baby, Nicole's first reaction was one of disbelief. Though she knew in theory that married people tended to have babies, she had not imagined it happening to her. She wrote to David telling him the good news, and kept her reservations to herself.

On good days, Nicole's nausea wore off by lunchtime; on bad days, she would eat little and escape at discreet intervals to the lavatory. When the sickness was at its worst she would circle the house, Minette at her heels, trying to count the windows. The numbers never came out the same. Laura Kemp suggested she rest, but Nicole loathed resting. She liked people, company, adventure. She liked riding over the downs with Thierry Duquesnay, a Free French airman, and only ceased doing so when the doctor scolded her severely, and told her that if she continued to ride she would lose her baby. To her annoyance, she found that she was too breathless to sing. She still loved to dance, though, to tango and foxtrot to the ancient wind-up gramophone in the Great Hall, with the faded escutcheons and emblems of the Kemps looking down at her from the ceiling. One of the airmen brought her new records to supplement the scratched seventy-eights in David's collection. A Canadian taught her how to jive, and with Thierry she waltzed like a bird round the perimeter of the hall.

Since the last raid, there had been no running water in the Mahonia Road house, yet the walls were moist, dripping. Touching them, Faith was half convinced that when she drew her hand away her fingertips would be red with blood. At night, the damaged fabric of the house creaked and groaned. It was as though it had suffered some fatal, internal wound, and its outward symptoms worsened as the days passed. Indoors, she moved from room to room, sleeping in whichever seemed most comfortable. Through fallen ceiling plaster and missing roof tiles, she was able to see the stars, white pinpoints in a navy-blue sky. When it was cold, she gathered broken window frames and pieces of stair rail, and made a fire of them. Because the chimney was damaged, the room filled with smoke, but it dispersed quickly through the unglazed windows. When the gas and electricity were cut off, Faith lit candles and ate out of tins. She did not mind; she was used to living hand to mouth. It was not that which frightened her.

It terrified her that she continued to suffer from blackouts. Sometimes she would be free of them for a week or more, but then she would with no warning lose an hour, or maybe two, erased from memory, leaving no shadow. As no-one had told her otherwise, she was forced to assume that she continued to drive, to load the wounded into the ambulance, to take them to hospital, just as she always did. Afraid of the consequences, she mentioned the blackouts to no-one. She doubted that her superiors would want to employ an ambulance driver who sometimes lost her memory. In the public library she studied medical textbooks, and read of growths in the brain and divided personalities.

With a shudder she recalled the story of Jekyll and Hyde, and wondered how that other, unknown Faith Mulgrave differed from her.

The fear that she was going mad negated all her other fears. She no longer flinched at the rumble of the enemy aircraft overhead, and her stomach no longer squeezed at the distant thunder of the first falling bombs. She acquired a reputation for bravery, even foolhardiness. If another pair of hands was needed to hold a lantern in a crumbling building as a doctor worked to save the life of a child, then Faith offered hers. Driving at breakneck speed to bomb-sites, swerving round craters as incendiaries rained scarlet from the sky, she was unafraid of the sudden snuffing-out of life, but haunted by the fear that her mind might slowly decay.

On the night of 19 April, the raid was heavy. The pounding of the falling bombs seemed to make the earth itself shake. Sent to fetch casualties from a bomb-site in Poplar, she was aware of a strange exhilaration as the noise, and the bright, piercing colour of the flames, filled her senses, freeing her momentarily from fear. Leaving the ambulance, she stood for a moment, looking around her. Almost the entire length of one side of the street had been destroyed by the bombardment. Some people shuffled from the ruins, unnaturally cheerful, relieved to be alive. Others stumbled desperately through mountains of rubble, searching for relatives buried beneath the debris. Doctors and nurses tended the wounded, Heavy Rescue men levered aside fallen beams and floorboards, firemen aimed their hoses at the flames. The brick dust transformed everyone into an eerie terracotta army.

One of the doctors raised his arm and beckoned to

Faith. As she began to walk towards him, an ARP warden shouted at her, but she disregarded him, and continued to circle the perimeter of a large crater. She had recognized the doctor as Guy when the warden caught up with her.

'Are you mad? Didn't you hear me? There's a UXB in that hole!'

Faith looked back at the crater, and thought, how nice if the bomb had exploded as she had teetered round it. Certain, instant, unanticipated death.

She realized that Guy was staring at her. She made herself reply to the warden. 'Sorry. I didn't hear you.'

She turned to Guy. A small boy was trapped beneath a tangle of planks. Faith levered up a slab of wood. She heard Guy explain, 'Several of his ribs are staved in. And his lower leg is a mess.' He looked at her. 'Are you all right, Faith?'

'I'm fine,' she said, 'perfectly fine.'

She watched him as he worked. The precise, careful movement of his hands soothed her. After a while, one of the Heavy Rescue men called out: 'He's free now.'

Sally, the girl who now partnered her, helped Faith load the injured child onto a stretcher and slot it into the ambulance. On their way back from the hospital, their route was slowed by the fallen rubble of previous raids. Sally said, 'I'm dying for a pee. Stop a minute, and let me nip behind that hedge.' Faith pulled on the handbrake. Bunty's voice echoed inside her head. *Give me a tick and I'll check my mum's all right.* She could not bear to wait for Sally, but climbed out of the ambulance and wandered around the deserted shells of the houses.

Chairs and tables, coated with a brownish sludge, warped by the rain, stood in rooms that lacked a wall or a ceiling. A bed, fully made up with sheets and ragged blankets, had fallen from an upstairs room into a parlour, and was surrounded by a hotchpotch of broken-backed books, splintered shelves and shards of crockery. Hearing a footstep, Faith pushed aside a tangle of torn curtains, and glimpsed an old woman, crouched over a stove. A single candle on a rickety table illuminated the three-sided room. As Faith stood in the doorway, watching the woman, it seemed to her that she was watching a ghost, that her unsteady mind had conjured the figure up, a spirit returned to haunt the ruins of the house.

But the woman turned to her and said, 'I'm making supper for my boys.'

She was stirring a cooking pot. Faith realized that they were standing inside the battered remains of a kitchen. The sink hung at a drunken angle, and the shelves were scattered with dented tins and soggy packets. One side of the kitchen was completely open to the elements. The floor, a jigsaw of splintered tiles, was sheened with puddles.

The old woman wore a ragged coat over layers of filthy cardigans. She beckoned to Faith. 'Do you want to taste my soup?'

Faith stepped between the fallen plaster and tiles. There did not seem to be any coal in the stove. The wooden spoon, stirring the pot, moved slowly. Faith whispered, 'Why don't you let me take you to the rest centre?' but the woman disregarded her.

'Here's soup for you, dearie. Nice, hot soup.'

When she looked down, Faith saw that the pot was full of rubble, that the wooden spoon stirred a broth made only of bricks. She stared at the pot, then at the old woman, and then she stumbled out of the house.

*   *   *

The following afternoon, Faith was dozing at the kitchen table when she was woken by a persistent hammering on the front door. She ignored it at first, hoping it would stop and she would be able to sleep again, but when it did not let up she stumbled to the hallway.

Opening the door, she rubbed her eyes. 'Guy.'

'Can I come in?'

She showed him into the house. In the drawing-room, he looked around, eyes wide. 'Do you *live* here?'

She saw the house suddenly as he must see it: the unglazed windows, cracked plaster and fallen cornices, the dark patch on the carpet where the rain dripped through, the nest of blankets she had made for herself on the sofa.

'I sometimes sleep in here, and sometimes in one of the other rooms. Whichever is best at the time. It depends which way the wind is blowing – sometimes the rain comes through some places, and sometimes through others.' Glimpsing the expression on his face, she added defensively, 'It's not so bad, Guy. La Rouilly was a bit crumbly, if you remember. I'm used to it.'

'La Rouilly was *warm*. And you weren't on your own there.'

'Jake has leave every now and then. And so does Rufus.' In the kitchen, she rinsed out cups. 'Tea, Guy?'

'Please.' He sat down at the table.

She filled the kettle, placed it on the stove. Her back was to him when he said, 'Actually, I came here to apologize to you.'

She swung round. 'To apologize? What for?'

'For not being much of a friend,' he said simply.

Tears stung behind her eyes. She could bear neglect or even coldness, but kindness these days made her weep. She busied herself with spoons and crockery so that he should not see her face.

She heard him say, 'I've never forgotten how kind your family was to me that first time we met. I remember how Ralph found me at the roadside, and how Poppy asked me to stay to dinner. And how you made a bed for me in the barn. How old were you, Faith? Ten?'

'Eleven,' she whispered.

'I was in a frightful mess – no money, no friends – and you – all of you – you saved me. And then you put up with me visiting year after year . . . do you know, Faith, how much I used to look forward to the summer, and seeing you again? I used to count off the days. It was the best part of the year. And I've realized that since you came to England, I haven't—' He broke off suddenly. She was unable to disguise the shaking of her shoulders. 'Faith, what is it?'

She gasped, 'Oh, Guy, I miss it all so much! Everything! France – La Rouilly – and Genya – what has happened to Genya?'

He hugged her. For a moment she closed her eyes, enjoying the warmth and safety of his embrace. She heard Guy say, 'Genya's a survivor. She'll be all right.' Yet he did not sound confident.

'The kettle's boiling.' She slipped from his arms, and began, in a messy, inaccurate way, to make tea.

'There's something more, isn't there?'

She shook her head, unable to speak. Guy said bitterly, 'It's my fault. I've neglected you. I don't blame you for not wanting to confide in me.'

Faith's hand, clutching the teapot, trembled, and tea

scattered over the table. She whispered, 'It's not *you*, Guy. I can't possibly tell anyone.'

'Tell anyone what?'

She closed her eyes. 'It's too awful.'

He said sensibly, 'Nothing is so awful that it isn't helped by talking about it.'

'This is.'

He took her hand, enfolding it between his warm palms, and said gently, 'I know that these last few months I've been preoccupied and snappy and jealous – yes, I admit it, I felt jealous when I saw you with Rufus, that's why I was so foul – I suppose I'd got used to thinking of you as my particular friend, and couldn't stomach seeing you with anyone else.' She smiled weakly. 'Won't you let me make amends?' he said. 'Won't you let me help?'

She looked at him, and wondered whether to make the leap of trust. Before she could retract the impulse, she said, 'Guy, I think I am going mad.'

He did not laugh, or tell her not to be ridiculous. 'Tell me why you think that.'

There was a long silence. She pulled away from him, and, wrapping her arms around herself, looked out of the window. Birds were singing in the branches, blossom was forming on the trees. She gathered up her courage.

'I forget things.'

Guy paused before he said, 'Not . . . people's names, that sort of thing, I guess? You mean that you lose all memory of an hour, perhaps, or even a day—'

'Never a day,' she said quickly. 'I thought it was getting better, that it was going away, but then the other night I lost six whole hours.' She remembered the old woman making soup out of bricks, and she remembered arriving home at dawn and opening her front door. Between, there was nothing.

'I read some books in the library.' Her voice was unsteady. 'There's something wrong inside my head, isn't there, Guy?'

'Take my advice, Faith, and never read medical textbooks. When I was training, I thought I had every disease in the book. Yellow fever, malaria, tuberculosis . . .' He smiled. 'Faith, you are not going mad. You are just very, very tired, and under intolerable pressure. Losing your memory is something that happens when a person's under too much strain. It's not uncommon. The mind can't take any more, and it shuts off. It's a protection mechanism. Quite sensible, if you think about it.'

She wanted to believe him. 'But you, Guy, you're tired too. Do you lose your memory?'

'I smoke and drink too much. And I lose my temper. And I have nightmares, dreadful nightmares, about Oliver. I suppose we'd all like to think that extreme circumstances bring out the best in us. But it isn't necessarily so. Although Eleanor . . . Eleanor copes magnificently. She is at her best in a crisis.'

She looked up at him, her eyes serious. 'Do you mean it? That I'm not ill, or mad?'

'You're not ill, and you're not mad,' he said firmly. 'You're just exhausted, and if you were to have a week or two's rest, then I'm sure the blackouts would stop.'

She was aware of an overwhelming rush of relief. 'Oh, Guy, you can't imagine how hellishly worried I've been!'

He looked across at her. 'Have you leave due?'

'A couple of weeks. I want to go to Norfolk, to see

Ma – Pa says she's fine, but I'm not sure . . .' There had been an uncertain tenor to Poppy's letters recently: nothing Faith could put her finger on, but she was concerned nevertheless.

'Then put in for your leave, and go away as soon as you are able. And meanwhile' – he glanced around the crumbling kitchen – 'Faith, you can't possibly stay here.'

'I like it here, Guy,' she said quickly. Mahonia Road had, in the last eight months, become a home. 'I'm fond of it. I don't mind about the holes and things, and it's almost summer, so it'll be warm again.'

He looked dubious, but said, 'As you wish. But I insist that you come to lunch this Saturday. Eleanor likes to have guests for Saturday lunch, and she'll love to see you. You will come, won't you, Faith?'

In late May, Faith was at last granted a week's leave. Guy, meeting her at Mahonia Road, offered to carry her bag to the railway station.

'I haven't packed yet.'

Guy glanced at his watch. 'Then you'd better hurry. Anyway, you'll throw a few things into a bag, just as you always do. I've seen Mulgraves pack.'

'I've improved,' she said superciliously. 'I iron things.'

'Any more blackouts?'

'Not one.' She had not suffered from memory loss since she had confided her worries to Guy. It was almost as though the mere act of sharing the problem had rid her of it.

'Come here.' He took her hand and frowned. 'You are skin and bone.'

She wriggled away. Halfway up the stairs, she called

over her shoulder, 'You don't need to worry about me, Guy.'

In her room, throwing a few crumpled dresses in a bag, she heard him shout, 'And who else would worry about you? Nicole? Jake? Ralph?'

'I can look after myself!'

'Of course. You always were the sensible Mulgrave. You must have inherited it from Poppy.'

Running downstairs, bag in hand, she said sharply, 'Well, certainly not from Ralph.' Then she flung open the front door, and they stepped out into the drizzle.

He put up his umbrella, and they huddled beneath it. Catching sight of the bus turning the corner of the road, they decided to walk to the next stop. As they skirted the vast puddles that had formed in the bomb-damaged pavements, Guy said, 'Are you worried about Ralph?'

Faith sighed. 'You know that Pa comes to London a great deal. He adores the Blitz – he's always thought England dull, and with the bombs it isn't, of course. Well, I don't mind that, I don't mind him staying with me, there's just more washing-up, but I'm afraid – I'm afraid that he's made friends with some very *silly* people.'

He looked down at her. 'Some of the Lodgers were rather silly.'

'I know.' She tried to explain. 'But the Lodgers weren't silly in quite the same way that these people are. They egg him on, Guy, and . . . oh, I don't know . . .'

There were some things that she could not speak about even to Guy. She could not tell him, for instance, that she sensed a desperation in Ralph, an anguish that she found almost unbearable to witness. She knew

209

that Ralph's London friends did not love him as the Lodgers had loved him. She knew that Bruno Gage and his friends viewed Ralph as an Edwardian curiosity, a source of amusement in lean times.

Rain drummed against the skin of the umbrella. Guy asked, 'And Nicole? And Jake? How are they?'

'Jake's bored. Nicole is well.'

'She's expecting a baby, isn't she?'

'In September. She says it hardly shows at all.'

'Some women are like that. Good muscle tone.'

Faith tucked her hand round his arm. 'Dear Guy,' she said, 'I'm so pleased that we're friends again.'

Often Guy feared that the casualty services must collapse under the strain imposed by the Blitz, and that the wounded would remain stacked up in hospital corridors and reception rooms, groaning and weeping as, one by one, the doctors and nurses themselves broke down, gave up. He wondered how long one could survive without more than three or four hours' continuous sleep. He wondered how long it would be before the sight of another casualty, scarlet with blood and pierced with shards of broken glass, reduced him to actual nausea. His only consolation, Guy thought with grim amusement, was that the Luftwaffe was effecting a programme of slum clearance that he himself had long thought overdue.

The only way he could survive was to cut himself off from his emotions, to refuse to let himself empathize with those whose lives were his responsibility. He could not afford to feel for his patients, only to cut and stitch, and to decide with cold objectivity which bodies were worth expending effort on, and which were beyond repair. Sometimes he feared that his enforced detachment would spill over into the rest of his professional life, and that faced by women whose lives had been broken by the loss of their sons at sea, or by bewildered old men whose wives had died in the Blitz, he would feel nothing, and would write prescriptions and issue anodyne condolences, treating the body, disregarding the soul.

Until recently he had retained the capacity to feel intensely only for one person. For Oliver. Because of pressure of work, he had not seen Oliver between September, when Eleanor had taken him to Derbyshire, and late November, when he had been given leave. Then, Oliver had been almost a year old, lisping his first words, on the verge of taking his first few unsteady steps. Seeing his golden-haired, blue-eyed son for the first time in three months, Guy had felt such an overwhelming rush of love that he had had to struggle not to weep. Oliver's wholeness, his beauty, reminded him unbearably of all the dead and broken children he had taken from the ruins of London. There and then he had made a vow that Oliver should never suffer, that he would protect him from all the horrors life could inflict. That his son would always be loved and safe, that he would want for nothing.

Guy had remained in Derbyshire for three days, taking Oliver to see the ice that crystallized around the clear edges of the Dove, piggybacking him to the summit of Thorpe Cloud. He had returned to visit twice since then, both times with Eleanor. On each occasion, parting from Oliver when his leave ended, Guy had come reluctantly to the conclusion that Eleanor felt little of the aching pain at their son's absence that he himself suffered. She seemed, in fact, to have blossomed since she no longer had the responsibility of looking after a small child. Her WVS work absorbed most of her time; running the Holland Square house occupied the rest.

Their departure from Malt Street had been a campaign of attrition. Eleanor had worn away, and Guy had eventually given in. She had orchestrated their leaving of the home in which Guy had lived since babyhood with the brisk, self-confident efficiency that he had come to realize was characteristic of her. At Holland Square she revelled in the large, graceful rooms, the many familiar possessions. When he had once expressed a nostalgia for Malt Street's worn ugliness, Eleanor had looked at him blankly, and had said, 'Don't be silly, Guy, we're much more comfortable here. You have a dressing-room as well as a study, and it's such a relief for me not to have to struggle in that dreadful kitchen.' They shared the house with Eleanor's father. It was, on the whole, a satisfactory arrangement: Guy liked the older man, and their arguments, though frequent, were good-humoured.

Yet he sensed that, in returning to Eleanor's childhood home, they had lost something. Marriage was not quite what he had expected it to be. Eleanor had made it plain that she wanted no more children, and Guy sensed that in bowing to that and to her other wishes – evacuating Oliver to Derbyshire, moving from Malt Street to Holland Square – he himself had contributed to the dimming of his own ideal. Guy told himself that the romantic dream was an illusion, that the companionship and practical support that Eleanor gave him was the most anyone could hope for, and more than many got, and that the intensity that he had once sought had been nothing more than the fancy of a very young, and rather naive, man. Though his initial passion had faded, he told himself that was for the best. It was enough that Eleanor was his helpmate and the mother of his child. Her strength meant that he need not worry about her; for him to have felt concern for her would only have weakened him, a weakness he could not just now afford.

Leaving Liverpool Street station after seeing Faith onto the train, Guy was aware of an ache in his chest, a sense of loss. The ache was similar to the pang of grief that he experienced whenever he thought of Oliver. Yet now the image that lingered in his mind was of Faith: her bare, sandalled feet splashing through the puddles, her untidy fair hair blown in her eyes by the breeze. He recalled too the cool touch of her cheek when he had kissed her farewell at the station. Her thinness, her pallor, had worried him. He imagined taking her away from the battlefield that London had become – into the countryside, or to the sea, perhaps. He pictured himself walking beside her along a deserted beach, and then with a sudden jarring blow he remembered Eleanor, Holland Square, his marriage. He had, just for a moment, forgotten all that.

Guy pulled up the collar of his raincoat around his face, and began to walk fast through the busy streets.

CHAPTER SEVEN

Heronsmead in late May was silver and gold, a glitter of marsh and distant sea. Poppy had been working in the garden all day. She was stooping over the raspberry canes when she heard the gate open.

She looked up and saw her daughter. '*Faith*,' she said. She found that she wanted to cry, but she blinked the tears back so that Faith would not see them, and held out her arms instead. 'Oh, *Faith*. Such a lovely shock. Why didn't you tell me you were coming?'

'I wasn't sure they'd let me go until yesterday, so I didn't have time to write.'

'How long have you got?'

'A week.'

Poppy held Faith at arm's length, and looked at her. At twenty, she thought, Faith still retained some of the gangling awkwardness of adolescence, but there were marks of exhaustion like bruises beneath her eyes.

'But you're so *thin*, darling.'

'I'm fine, Ma. Just very tired.'

They went into the cottage. Filling the kettle with water, Poppy heard Faith ask, 'Where's Pa?' and she glanced at her daughter sharply.

'In London. I thought he was staying with you, Faith.'

'I haven't seen him for weeks. He must be with Bruno Gage.'

Poppy put cups and saucers on the table. Faith said curiously, 'Are you lonely when Pa's away?'

It seemed to Poppy that she had almost forgotten how to smile. More of a grimace than a grin, it twitched falsely at the corners of her mouth. But she said honestly, 'It's more peaceful here without him. Ralph thinks Heronsmead is dull, but I adore it. The soil is marvellous. When we were travelling, all my gardens were just stones and dust. Here, I plant seeds and they seem to spring up the next day.' She looked out of the window, to the fields and to the salt marshes, with their gently swaying reeds. 'The only thing that I mind,' she added, 'is not being able to reach the sea. Because of the barbed wire, Faith. I dream, sometimes, about running barefoot along the sand.'

She did not, of course, tell Faith everything. Some things one did not confide to one's daughter. She could not tell Faith, for instance, that she suspected that Ralph was having an affair.

Arriving at Heronsmead a year ago, Poppy had quickly become attached to the place. What Ralph loathed, she had loved. The bleakness, the isolation, was a balm to her. She had recognized that she no longer had any desire to travel, and that all need for adventure had left her. It was as though that last, dreadful journey from France had erased the lingering remains of her youthful restlessness. She loved Norfolk's broad skies, the shimmering salt marshes, the history and permanence of the landscape. She loved the tiny flint-faced cottage, and the garden whose high walls, built to protect the plants from the northern winds, reminded her of the walled garden at La Rouilly. Ralph saw their transition to England only as a loss, but to Poppy it was a homecoming.

The villagers, isolated and insular, had at first viewed the Mulgraves with suspicion. Poppy had been aware of words muttered behind cupped hands, lace curtains twitched aside as she and Ralph walked past. Ralph's clothing, considered suspiciously foreign by the inhabitants of the village; Ralph's habit of singing un-English songs loudly in the bath, with the window open (French or Italian songs mostly, but all foreign languages were equally damned in the opinion of the local population); and Ralph's unrestrained, multilingual cursing: all these had precluded their acceptance. In the September of 1940, at the height of the invasion scare, a policeman had called at Heronsmead. He had been prompted, Poppy had quickly realized, by malicious gossip; she had quelled his fears with tea and with the peculiarly English charm that she could still, if she could be bothered, unearth, and he had gone away and they had not been troubled again.

Though Ralph had never courted acceptance – had, indeed, gone out of his way to avoid it – Poppy had, during the past few months, begun to attempt to make friends. She made a point of stopping and talking to passers-by; she had even joined the Women's Institute. She went to church once, but Ralph's sarcasm was so intense, so all-encompassing, that she did not go again. She acknowledged her unhappiness of the past few years; she now saw that since the death of her baby she had needed to come home. She would, Poppy often thought, have been content had it not been for the war, and had it not been for Ralph.

The war sickened her. She never listened to the

wireless bulletins; she tried to avoid reading newspaper headlines. She could not bear to think what was happening in France, in Italy, in Greece. She had friends in all those countries. Fleeing France in 1940 she had learned what it was to fear. Her most vivid, most terrible memory of all was of her nauseated dread that they would be forced to leave Jake behind. Nowadays, the distant sound of aeroplanes jettisoning their bombs on the coastal towns of Norfolk always reinvented in her that terror. When German aeroplanes flew overhead, Ralph ran out into the garden and waved his fist at them, but Poppy hid in the broom cupboard. She thanked God that Jake had not yet been called upon to fight, and that Nicole was safely married. She worried for Faith, in London, but less, she thought, than she would in the same circumstances have worried for the other two. Faith had common sense.

When Ralph had first visited London, Poppy had been relieved. She had begun to dread the day that he would tell her to pack her bags and leave Heronsmead. Though she missed him, and though, without Ralph, the house seemed appallingly quiet, she had hoped that he might find a sort of equilibrium, that London might provide him with the company he craved, so that he could return to her and be content, for a while. But his sojourns in London had, if anything, made him more restless. Each visit had been for a longer period, and he had returned to Heronsmead for ever shorter intervals. During those homecomings he had been irritable, his temper uncertain. He seemed to find it hard to fill his days. Ralph, who hated to be alone, took to going for long, solitary evening walks. And for the first time since Poppy had met him, he had no grand design, no scheme certain of making the Mulgrave family fortune.

In March, Ralph had asked her to move to London with him. They could share Faith's house, he had said – there was plenty of room now that Jake no longer lived there. Poppy had refused. It would be madness to think of removing to London just now, and besides, she was happy at Heronsmead. To her surprise, Ralph had not argued. He had just shrugged his shoulders, and said, 'As you wish,' and had gone out for one of his interminable walks. She had not then realized the implications of her refusal to leave Heronsmead.

Until she found the note, she had assigned Ralph's moodiness to his uprooting to a country he disliked. Then, a month ago, there had been a sudden shower, and the washing had been on the line, and in her attempt to rescue it Poppy had grabbed the first coat she could find. Running out into the garden, she had jammed her hands into the pockets of Ralph's old black overcoat. She had discovered a scrap of paper, and she had unfolded it and glanced at it, expecting . . . a receipt, she supposed. A theatre ticket. Not a billet-doux.

She remembered standing in the garden, the rain blurring the ink on the paper. After a minute or two, she had no longer been able to read the words. But by then she had known them by heart.

Darling Ralph – don't you miss me already? L.

Her first thought had been, *How trite*. A love letter in a coat pocket. How *conventional*. Ralph, who prided himself on avoiding the commonplace. Then, when the hurt had begun, she had tried to persuade herself that she had been mistaken. That it had been the letter of a friend. That the note had said nothing compromising.

But she had been unable to convince herself. *Darling Ralph – don't you miss me already?* Such arrogance, she thought, in those seven words, such confident possession. She looked at Ralph anew, and saw that what she had previously perceived to be a dissatisfaction with his surroundings was in fact the moodiness of a lover. Secretly she followed him on one of his evening walks, hating herself, hating Ralph for goading her to this. He walked to the telephone box at the other end of the village. He talked for hours. He was talking, Poppy knew, to *L*.

Ralph had had flirtations in the past, always with Lodgers. The first one, Poppy guessed, had been after Nicole's birth, when she had been ill and tired, and they had been so short of money. And then there had been Louise in 1937, after they had escaped Spain. There had, she suspected, been one or two others. They had lasted a week, a fortnight at most, until Poppy had sent the girl packing, and Ralph had wept for her forgiveness. She had forgiven him because she had known that those women meant nothing to Ralph, that their function was to shore up his confidence, his egotism, at a difficult time.

But this affair was different. This time he *loved*. She could see it in his abstraction, his abjectness, when he was parted from the unknown *L*. She could see it in his constant lurches between euphoria and despair.

This time, Poppy was overwhelmed by misery. Glancing in the mirror, she saw that she looked every one of her forty-two years. She realized bitterly that somewhere over the past few years she had become middle-aged. Her golden hair was dulled with silver, and years of southern sun had not been kind to her delicate English complexion. There seemed, she thought, to be few consolations to being forty-two. She tired easily, and was prone to bad headaches. Her body had never completely recovered from the premature birth of her fourth child. The children had left home, and she missed them deeply, remembering the warm, sunny days of their early childhoods with nostalgia. She imagined *L* to be young, beautiful, her body still taut and unblemished by childbearing.

In her lowest moments, she wondered whether, if she were dead, anyone would really miss her. All her friends lived far away, her children had lives of their own, Ralph was in love with another woman, and she herself had been absent from England too long to be close to either of her sisters. Poppy thought of confronting Ralph with his unfaithfulness, but did not do so. She no longer felt confident of the outcome.

Johnny Deller, the Canadian airman, borrowed three rowing boats. Nicole had no idea where he had found them: Johnny was good at finding things, even unobtainable things like chocolate and nylons. In the morning, they rowed the boats along the clear, green waters of the Avon. Nicole organized races, and appointed herself cox of Thierry's boat, kneeling in the prow, Minette on her lap, counting out strokes as the lush banks and trailing willows blurred with the speed of their passing, hardly able to speak for laughter. When Johnny's boat won, she crowned him with a wreath of pondweed.

After they had picnicked, they swam in the river. Because she had not brought a bathing costume (the baby now showed when she wore close-fitting clothes, an odd round little pudding shape), Nicole just paddled at first, but when she slipped, ducking under the smooth surface of the river, she emerged spitting water coltsfoot, and struck out with her untidy crawl for the centre of the river. After they had swum, they lounged in the buttercup-strewn water-meadow, Nicole's damp head cushioned on Johnny's chest, her dress drying in the heat, the sun burning overhead. She felt Johnny's careful fingers disentangling the knots in her hair, but she knew that, from beneath the shadow of the horse chestnut tree, Thierry was watching her.

In the late afternoon, they went back to Compton Deverall. One of the Dutch boys cycled with Nicole perched on the crossbar. Laura Kemp was away, looking after her sister, who had had an operation, but there were still the evacuees and the weekend house guests. Nicole made an enormous goulash and sent the Dutch boy down into the cellar for some very old, very cobwebby bottles of wine. After dinner, they played charades and Felix's musical game, which was terribly complicated. Johnny abandoned the game in disgust, preferring the brandy bottle and his cigarettes, but Thierry won the first time he played. Thierry was very clever. Then one of Nicole's BBC friends suggested sardines. Compton Deverall, he said, with its priest's hole and its warrens of dark rooms, was perfect for sardines.

Upstairs, alone in a bedroom, Nicole stood at a window, enveloped in a heavy brocade curtain, and looked out at the stars. Hearing the door open, she glanced back and saw Thierry.

'You haven't hidden yourself very well, Nicole.'

'It's a silly game.'

'All games are silly,' he said companionably, and lit a cigarette. 'They're to help silly people pass the time.'

She said vaguely, looking at his cigarette, 'The blackout . . .' but he continued to smoke. The silence extended. She explained, 'And besides, I loathe hiding in cupboards and things.'

He was standing behind her, not touching her, but she thought that she could sense the heat of his body through the evening air. He said, 'When I escaped from France in 1940, I hid for two days and two nights inside a wooden seat in a train.'

She shivered. 'How awful.'

'You're cold, Nicole.' He wrapped his arms around her. She leaned back against him. After a while, she felt his lips press against the back of her neck. Then the palms of his hands traced the smooth curve of her belly beneath her cotton dress.

'Don't do that,' she said sharply.

'Did I hurt you?' His voice was concerned.

'No, it's not that. It's just that' – she searched for the right words – 'it reminds me of it.'

'Of the baby?'

'Yes. I prefer not to think about it.'

There was a silence. Then he said, 'Don't you want this baby, Nicole?'

It was the first time anyone had ever asked her that. Everyone else – David, Laura, Poppy, Ralph – took for granted that she wanted this child. Only sometimes, in Faith, had Nicole detected an unvoiced doubt.

She tried to explain. 'I don't like it being *inside* me. I feel as though it's taking me over. As though I belong to it.'

He said gently, 'It's the other way round, isn't it? The child will belong to you, Nicole.'

'It doesn't feel like that.' Briefly, she rested her hand upon the lump. 'I'm trying not to let it change me, but it will, won't it? I'll be glad when he's born, when it's all over.'

He said, 'When it's born, you'll love it. Apparently all mothers do, no matter how ugly or bad-tempered their baby.'

'Do you think so?' She smiled. 'If he has David's good nature and my good looks, then everyone will adore him.' Looking out of the window, she saw the dimmed headlamps of a car heading through the beech trees, towards the house. 'More visitors,' she said. 'I'll have to put them in the cellar.'

She left the bedroom, and went downstairs. The others had abandoned the game, and both the piano and the gramophone played very loudly. Johnny had fallen asleep in the fireplace, and people were folding paper aeroplanes and aiming them at the chandelier.

She heard a key turn in the front door. Someone grabbed her hand as she walked past, trying to coax her to dance with him. It was midnight. Nicole looked up as the new arrival walked into the Great Hall.

'David,' she said, and ran to him.

Just a few friends for the weekend, she explained. Then she saw how tired, how pale, he looked. How he sat down, unspeaking, in a chair, his head in his hands. She went to him and stroked his bowed shoulders. The others began to leave, treading quietly out of the front door, their boots crunching the gravel. Two men hauled Johnny to his feet; someone else switched off the gramophone.

'David,' she said. 'They're all gone now, darling.'

Slowly, he raised his head and looked at her. She whispered, 'You look *exhausted* . . .'

Deep runnels gouged his face from nose to lip. There

223

was no colour in his face. He looked nearer forty than thirty.

'Bad day,' he said, and tried to smile. 'Bad few weeks, actually.'

'Where have you *been*?'

'Can't say.' He rubbed his eyes and blinked.

'Out of the country?'

He did not reply, but she read the truth in his eyes. She whispered, 'Oh, *David*,' and, kneeling in front of him, rested her head in his lap.

'I've been driving for . . .' he glanced at his watch '. . . almost twelve hours. I shouldn't have turned up like this, I suppose, without warning you, but I longed to come home. I longed to see you, Nicole.' He added, looking around, 'Only when I came in, I hardly recognized the place. It was different. Those people—'

For the first time, she noticed the crumpled balls of paper, the empty bottles in the grate, the litter of dirty glasses and cigarette packets and sheet music.

She took his hands in hers. '*I'm* no different, David. I'm just the same. Apart from this, of course.'

She stood up, and let him rest the side of his head against her belly. He smiled at last. He was listening, he explained, for the baby's heartbeat. Nicole imagined it ticking away inside her, like the clock in the crocodile in *Peter Pan*. It was her present to him, she decided. The baby was her present to David, who was kind and good and uncomplicated, and whom she would always, whatever happened, love dearly.

In the October of 1940, after she had taken Oliver to Derbyshire, Eleanor had acquired an old van, fitted it out with kettles and crockery, and driven it to the areas of the East End suffering most in the Blitz. She had made soup and tea and toast for men and women who no longer possessed a teacup, let alone a kitchen, and she had served plates of pie and peas to exhausted, hungry firemen and rescue workers and doctors. A month later, she had acquired a second van, and fitted that out, and selected two reliable members of the WVS to man it. In the New Year, she had given over the task of driving her own van to a colleague, and had concentrated instead on searching for suitable vehicles and stocking and staffing them efficiently. She enjoyed organizing; serving cups of tea to people who looked as though they had worn the same clothes for a fortnight gave her little pleasure.

When the Luftwaffe turned its attention to England's great provincial cities – Coventry, Bristol, Southampton – Eleanor was asked for her advice. She travelled across England, sourcing equipment, wheedling for petrol, judging where the need was greatest. She had an eye for choosing the most reliable, most dependable staff. She was asked to help supervise the system of used clothing banks that the WVS had instigated. She delegated to others the task of sorting through stained underwear and holey jerseys, and concentrated on ensuring that the most serviceable clothes went to the people most in need of them. The mayor of Bristol himself thanked her for her hard work.

As well as her demanding voluntary work, Eleanor visited Oliver regularly. He was now eighteen months old, and possessed of a fair, fragile beauty. Arriving at the Derbyshire house, Oliver would run to her, greeting her with an enthusiasm that Eleanor had lately come to find unexpectedly gratifying. He seemed to regard her visits as a special treat, and would trail around the house and garden after her, holding on to her skirts.

His devotion was peculiarly touching. One day, Eleanor watched Oliver play at the stream. Splashing flat pebbles into the clear water he looked back every few minutes, as if to reassure himself that she was still there. Although Oliver was as fair as Guy was dark, the expression in his eyes – that blue intensity – reminded her suddenly of Guy, and of the early days of their courtship. Once, Guy had looked at her like that, with that same fervent, unmixed devotion. It occurred to Eleanor that it had been a long time since she had seen devotion in Guy's eyes.

The change in Guy's attitude to her had, Eleanor thought, coincided with the Mulgraves' arrival in England. He had become more critical, less eager to please. Long ago Eleanor had sensed that there were two sides to Guy's character. She herself answered the one side; the Mulgraves – Faith Mulgrave in particular – reflected the other. Though outwardly Guy conformed, there was a streak of rebelliousness in him. Eleanor knew that Guy had married her for her energy, her confidence, her certainty. He liked Faith Mulgrave for – Eleanor was never quite sure what. She was unable to comprehend what men admired in Faith. She saw only a scrawny, knobbly body, untidy hair of a colour that was not properly blonde, and a face made plain by too high a forehead and those doleful grey-green eyes. Confused, Eleanor had spoken to her father. Faith is an original, Selwyn Stephens said, she is her own person – which to Eleanor explained nothing. She concluded that men liked Faith because they sensed that she was available; because, in her slapdash ways and peculiar clothes, they saw an equally careless virtue.

Though she had always recognized her as a rival,

Faith's challenge had been diminished – virtually negated – by the mere fact of Eleanor's marriage to Guy. Running through Guy's character was a streak of almost Puritan idealism. Eleanor knew that Guy was not the sort of man who could easily indulge in casual affairs. The morals that both Guy's parents and his school, and his hard-working, unworldly upbringing, had bequeathed to him could not lightly be discarded. Faith, of course, was another matter entirely. Faith's early years would not have taught her to value constancy. It seemed to Eleanor that Faith Mulgrave, who happily stayed in other people's houses, who seemed to live in borrowed or second-hand clothes, and who casually charmed other people's friends, would not balk at stealing someone else's husband. Faith had regaled them all with stories about her brother Jake's many love affairs. Eleanor herself had heard gossip about the married younger sister. Why should slovenly, careless Faith prove any different from her siblings? And what man was capable of refusing what was offered to him on a plate?

It had seemed to Eleanor lately that the war itself, with its shaking up of London and its consequent shaking up of society, had added to the danger. Rules were being broken everywhere. The city in which Eleanor had lived all her life had changed unimaginably during the past year. The bombs, destroying slums and fine houses alike, had laid waste more than the landscape. Fur-clad ladies queued with down-at-heel housewives for meat at the butchers. Factory workers, emboldened by money earned through war work, danced at smart nightclubs. London had become a constantly changing kaleidoscope of all nationalities, all classes. You were no longer judged by your accent or by your name, but by the uniform you wore. These things disturbed Eleanor. Guy, she suspected, embraced them.

And the Mulgraves were, she thought, emblematic of the jumbled-up people of blitzed London. Homeless, stateless and penniless, they drifted recklessly through a city that sometimes seemed all but unrecognizable to Eleanor. Their many languages, their hand-me-down clothing, were nothing out of the ordinary in the London of 1941. They fitted into this changed world more easily than Eleanor herself did; they, and their like, had robbed her of her confident sense of her place in society, something that she had always taken for granted. She saw that what she had first admired in Guy – his iconoclasm, his fearlessness – allied him, in this battered, other London, more closely with the Mulgraves than with her.

She had seen Faith Mulgrave only occasionally until Guy had got it into his head that Faith was exhausted and unwell. We are all exhausted, Eleanor had wanted to say. Faith no more requires your concern than the rest of us do. Eleanor, too, commonly worked an eighteen-hour day; Eleanor, too, endured countless interrupted nights. Faith merely drove an ambulance; she did not have to think, to organize, and neither did she have to bear the weight of responsibility that Eleanor herself carried. So typical of a Mulgrave, Eleanor thought, to choose the more dramatic but less demanding task.

Guy wrote to Jake in Northumberland, who managed to get a weekend's leave. Jake made repairs to the Mahonia Road house; Guy invited him to supper. Jake was the most presentable Mulgrave. He had better manners and was less slovenly than Ralph, and lacked the deviousness that Eleanor suspected in Faith. Though he shared Faith's fair colouring, Jake's eyes were properly blue instead of that ugly grey-green, and he was tall and strong-looking. Jake complimented Eleanor on her cooking.

'The supper was absolutely splendid.' He seized Eleanor's hand, and kissed it. 'One of the best meals I've ever eaten.'

Eleanor, who never blushed, was surprised to find herself doing so.

Faith grimaced. 'Yuck, Jake – such a *sycophant*.'

Eleanor said, 'You're very hard on your brother, Faith.'

Faith rose from the table, and curled one arm round Jake's shoulder. 'That's because I know him of old. I see through him.'

Jake smiled, tugged Faith's hair, and said something extremely rude. Faith added, 'And because you've been so kind to me, Eleanor, I feel you should know the truth about my brother.'

Eleanor said stiffly, 'It's been a pleasure to see you, Jake.'

'Don't flatter him, Eleanor. He's very conceited. His head will get so big it will burst.' Faith turned to Guy. 'Do you remember, Guy, how Jake used to persuade Madame Perron to give him bon-bons?'

Guy frowned. 'She was the old dragon who kept the *épicerie* in the village, wasn't she?'

'Mmm. Nicole and I were terrified of her. We thought she was a witch. But she doted on Jake.'

Jake said, 'Genya loathed Madame Perron. Thought she fiddled the grocery bill.'

'They used to have awful arguments. Genya used to scream at her in Polish.'

'She used to curse *marvellously*—'

'Draw herself up to her full five foot one—'

'Do you remember, Guy—'

They had forgotten her. Selwyn Stephens smiled indulgently, and moved to his seat beside the fire, but Eleanor was aware of a deep, burning resentment. They had discounted her. She was not a part of the small, privileged circle of the Mulgraves. Guy was, but she was not. They tolerated her, but they did not welcome her. Their privilege lay in neither their wealth nor their status, but in the allowances that society made for them. If Eleanor had permitted herself their licence, then she would have encountered only derision. But different rules applied to the Mulgraves.

One hot summer's day, Eleanor had to make an unscheduled visit to the Malt Street house to see Guy after morning surgery. Walking up the path, she heard voices from the garden. Guy's voice, Faith's voice. They were arguing about something, but their argument was pitted with laughter.

Eleanor turned on her heel. She managed to catch a bus as far as Camden, and then she walked the rest of the way home. Her fast pace failed to exorcize her fury. Then, cutting through Queen Square, she caught sight of a familiar figure.

Ralph Mulgrave. She recognized the voluminous black overcoat, the battered wide-brimmed hat. She did not, however, recognize the woman he was with. She was tall and slim and platinum blonde, and she was dressed with the easy elegance that Eleanor knew she herself never quite achieved.

From the far side of the street, Eleanor watched as they embraced. A lover's embrace: such longing in the single-minded intensity of that kiss, such adoration in the way Ralph drew the woman to him, as if to make her part of him. Just for a moment she bitterly envied their passion, but then, walking away, she hugged her secret to herself, a weapon to be quenched, sharpened.

'Strawberries . . .' Looking at them, Faith felt dizzy with longing.

'They're from Compton Deverall,' said Nicole. 'We've pounds and pounds.'

That morning, a handsome young man in an RAF uniform had delivered a note to Mahonia Road, telling Faith that Nicole was in London, staying in the Devonshire Place house.

'You can eat them all, Faith. I'm sick of them, and anyway, I'm not hungry.'

At seven months pregnant, Nicole looked, thought Faith, like a beetle, with skinny limbs and a round body. Her face, legs and arms seemed to have grown thinner as her belly became fatter.

Guzzling strawberries, Faith said, 'Did David drive you here?'

'I haven't seen David for ages. Not since May. I hitch-hiked, actually.' Nicole giggled. 'Stood at the roadside in my hideous maternity smock and stuck out my thumb.'

Faith picked a plump green caterpillar from a strawberry. 'Another hitch-hiker.'

On the table stood a vase filled with huge cabbage roses. 'Put it in one of these,' said Nicole. 'Thierry gave me them.'

'Thierry?'

'He's French and given to romantic gestures.'

Faith placed the caterpillar carefully in the warm pink heart of a rose. 'It's awfully hot and dusty in

London. I would have thought Compton Deverall would have been nicer in the summer.'

'I was bored.' Nicole shrugged. 'We haven't had so many visitors since the bombing stopped. Last weekend there was just Laura and me and the girls' school.' She looked at Faith. 'Did you find me anything? I've been wearing David's old jerseys, but they won't do for a nightclub, will they?'

'These.' Faith tipped out the contents of her string bag. The two dresses, unpromising at first, were twisted into narrow sausages, but when she shook out the folds they flowed in glorious silky pleats.

Nicole held one up. '*Beautiful.*'

'Aren't they? Fortuny, of course. They should fit you – they haven't any waists.'

Nicole took off her smock, and pulled the frock over her head. The turquoise silk was the same colour as her eyes. 'You shall have champagne with your strawberries as a reward, dearest Faith,' said Nicole, and kissed her. 'I know an awfully clever Frenchman who has given me half a dozen bottles.' She ran her hands down the narrow pleats, but scowled when she reached her abdomen. 'I'll be so glad when the Lump's gone. Only another six weeks, thank goodness. It gets in the way of everything. Could you . . . ?' Nicole handed Faith the champagne bottle, and laughed again. 'I can't dance cheek to cheek any more. It's more belly to belly.'

Beneath Nicole's superficial cheerfulness Faith detected a darker mood. The cork shot out of the champagne bottle with a dull *thunk*. Faith filled the glasses, and handed one to her sister.

'Nicole, is something wrong?'

Nicole whispered, 'If I really loved David, then I wouldn't need other people, would I?'

Faith tried to sound reassuring. 'You said yourself that you've hardly seen him recently. You're just a bit lonely.'

'I suppose so.' Nicole pleated and unpleated the silken folds of the dress.

Faith wondered whether any marriage could have lived up to Nicole's expectations. 'Perhaps you can't expect one person to make everything all right.' She chose her words carefully. 'Perhaps that sort of thing only happens in books. I expect you're thinking these things because you're rather tired and unwell with the baby.' Faith heard the note of pleading in her voice. 'Guy says that pregnancy can make women feel a bit low.'

'Guy.' Nicole smiled. 'How is Guy? I haven't seen him for years. Is he still as handsome?'

Faith had drunk two glasses of champagne, and eaten an entire basket of strawberries. She felt extremely full, and rather sleepy. She too smiled. 'Guy works very hard, and scowls even more than he used to.'

'Guy always had a touch of the Heathcliffs,' said Nicole dreamily.

'We have lunch together quite often, at his house in Hackney.'

Later, at home, dozing on the sofa, Faith dreamed that the green caterpillar she had discovered in the strawberries had metamorphosed into the adder that had bitten her years ago in the woods at La Rouilly. In her dream, she could feel Guy's lips touching against her ankle, but he did not, as in that long-ago summer, suck the venom from her veins. Instead his mouth caressed the sole of her foot, her toes, her shin. A slow, ecstatic caterpillar-crawl to her knee, until her alarm clock woke her at seven o'clock, reminding her to go to the ambulance station.

Nicole did not particularly like the Devonshire Place house – the home of David's bachelor days, it was rather dark and plainly furnished – but she did not intend to spend much time there. Telephoning friends in London, she soon received invitations to bars and restaurants and nightclubs. She went out each evening, even though, as she had explained to Faith, the Lump got in the way. She received a letter of alarm and veiled reproach from Laura Kemp (she had left Compton Deverall on the spur of the moment), and she wrote back, reassuring Laura that she had gone to London to shop for baby things, as David had suggested she should. In the end, though, she did not buy rattles and nightgowns, but discovered a tiny Corot in an antique dealer's in Frith Street, and spent all the money David had given her on that. Outside, in the sunshine, she admired the painting's jewelled colours. A much better present for her son, she thought, than a boring teething ring.

The house in Devonshire Place took on an untypically bright ambience as Nicole's friends gravitated towards it. She went to the theatre, and to the Café Royal, and to Quaglino's. Yet certain questions plagued her, making her uneasy. If David was The One, then why did she need the others? If she truly loved David, then why wasn't she content to remain at Compton Deverall, waiting for him? Because the troubling thoughts only occurred when she was alone, she made sure that she was always in company.

Only Thierry seemed to notice her disquiet. In the early hours of the morning, he ejected the other guests from the Devonshire Place house and confiscated Nicole's wine glass and cigarettes. Then he made her a glass of hot milk.

'Good for the baby,' he said. 'Strong teeth and bones.'

He made her sit with her feet propped up on cushions on the sofa, while he perched beside her on the arm. As she drank the hot milk, he said, 'You should go home, Nicole. Back to your beautiful house in the country.'

'Soon,' she said, and smiled up at him. Thierry was darkly handsome, yet his high cheekbones and the downward curve to the corners of his eyes gave his face a sardonic cast. 'Freddy and Jerry are to visit tomorrow.'

Thierry shrugged. 'They are little boys,' he said dismissively.

'They're twins, darling, and they're terribly handsome, and terribly charming.'

He lit himself a small black cigar. 'You tire yourself out so that you don't have to think, Nicole. What is it that you don't want to think about?'

She scowled, but did not answer. He pressed her.

'Is it the baby? Are you frightened about having the baby?'

She said, 'I suppose it'll be awful because everyone says that it's awful, but I haven't really thought about it, to tell the truth. Actually having it, I mean.'

'Are you still unsure whether you want it?'

She rather regretted their earlier conversation. She had wondered, fleetingly, whether Thierry was The One, but, as she never felt completely at ease in his presence, had concluded with relief that he was not.

'Of course I want the baby.' She abandoned the hot

milk; there was a disgusting skin on it. 'David will be so pleased to have a son. There's been an unbroken line of Kemps since the sixteenth century, you know.'

'Really?' His smile was mocking. 'Of course David cares about that sort of thing. But you don't, Nicole, not in the least. You are a gypsy. Which is why, of course, poor David fell in love with you.'

'I care about David,' she said fiercely. 'I want to make him happy.'

'Only because you feel guilty about him.'

'That's not true! I love him!'

He looked down at her. 'Perhaps.' He smoked for a while in silence. Then he said, 'If you really want to make David happy, then you'll go back to your country house. You are tiring yourself out, Nicole.'

'Thierry the nursemaid!' she said derisively. 'You've missed your true vocation, darling. You should abandon your Spitfires and wheel prams in the park.'

She tried to get up, but that, these days, was not an easy venture, and to her annoyance he had to help her to her feet. He did not immediately let go of her but, standing in front of her, said softly: 'If it were not for this' – and he glanced down at the Lump – 'then I wouldn't make you hot milk and put cushions beneath your feet, Nicole. I would make love to you instead.'

She gave a strangled cry. 'How dare you!'

'Oh, I would dare. And you would let me.' The tips of his fingers stroked the back of her neck; her shiver was perceptible. 'I would, as I say, make love to you. But to do so when you are carrying David's child' – his hand left her neck, and he rested his palm very gently on her swollen belly – 'it would seem to me as though I were treading in another man's footsteps.'

She hissed furiously, 'I told you, I *love* David!'

He let her go. 'Of course you do. But perhaps not enough.' He gathered up his jacket and cap. 'Now go to bed, Nicole.'

The next day, with Thierry's discomforting words echoing in her memory, Nicole made sure that she was very busy. Lunch at the Savoy was followed by a picnic with Ralph and his friends on Hampstead Heath, then dinner at a British restaurant with some of her BBC acquaintances, and a revue at the Criterion. After the revue, they went to the Bag o' Nails in Beak Street. She wore one of the Fortuny gowns that Faith had given her: the colour of an oyster's shell, it emphasized her pallor. To her annoyance, Nicole saw that Thierry had attached himself to their crowd. To spite him, she danced a great deal, and laughed a great deal. Her legs ached and sometimes, standing up too quickly, she felt oddly muzzy, but she refused to give in to her exhaustion. To give in would mean that the baby was winning, that it had changed her, that she belonged to it.

A Canadian boy was teaching her a new dance step when the muzziness became particularly fierce, and the dingy interior of the nightclub was overlaid with bright stars and dark, greenish blobs. When she came round, she was lying on a bench. Someone said, 'Give her some air,' and flapped an RAF cap in her face. Someone else tried to make her drink brandy.

A woman's voice said, '. . . can't end up having her bloody baby in here!' and Nicole, who hardly ever cried, felt suddenly like doing so.

Thierry rescued her, scooping her up in his arms, placing her gently in the passenger seat of his car, and driving her back to Devonshire Place. She expected him to crow, but he did not do so. In the morning, she sat in bed, white and feeble, while he packed her things. Then he drove her to Compton Deverall.

Because it was high summer, she could not see the many windows, or the tall, barley-sugar chimneys, until they had left the heavily leaved avenue of beech trees behind. Then, the stone columns of the windows seemed like bars, and the great dark house towered over her, swallowing her.

Faith appeared at the Malt Street house one day during morning surgery. Guy came out of his consulting-room to call in the next patient, and there she was, sitting between a man with a septic finger and a youth with impetigo. He blenched – he actually felt the colour drain from his face – because the front of her frock was red with blood. Then she saw him and said quickly, 'It's not me, Guy, it's Raffles.' She was cradling a dog on her lap, a gangling, scruffy creature of indeterminate breed. 'I found him on the way here,' she explained. 'He's stepped in some broken glass. I've wrapped his leg in my petticoat, but it's still bleeding. I didn't know where to find a vet, so I thought that perhaps you . . .' She looked up at him hopefully.

Guy peered at the animal. There were few dogs in London these days: many had been evacuated with their owners, others had been reduced to mad howling by the noise of the bombardment and had had to be put down. The dog that Faith had found must have been made of sterner stuff.

He said, 'I'll have to see to my human patients first,' and dealt with the septic finger and the impetigo with great speed. Then, after he had covered the couch in his consulting-room with newspaper, he asked Faith to bring the dog in. The cuts were deep and lengthy. He cleaned them with disinfectant, and began to stitch them. After a while, he said: 'Why Raffles? He hasn't a name tag.'

'He was trying to steal meat from a butcher's shop. He's awfully thin, isn't he, Guy? I think he's a stray. I thought I might adopt him.'

Raffles was not only thin, Guy thought, he was also very smelly. The matted coat was alive with fleas. He would have to disinfect the surgery.

'He's a dog of advanced years. Look – his ears are going grey.'

'There's some old things of Eleanor's in the bedroom upstairs, Faith, if you want to change your frock. I can finish off here.'

She looked down at her bloodstained clothes. 'People were trying not to sit next to me on the bus.'

She went upstairs. Guy put in the last few stitches and went to the sink to wash his hands. When he returned to the couch, he saw that Raffles was lying ominously still. He put his stethoscope to where he supposed a dog's heart to be, but could hear nothing. He murmured, 'Shock, I suppose. Poor old boy,' and found an old sheet to wrap the animal in, and went upstairs to find Faith.

The door of the bedroom that he had once shared with Eleanor was partly open. He caught a glimpse of the soft, sloping curve of bare neck and shoulder before he turned away, coughed, tapped on the door.

'Faith? Can I come in?'

She turned to him, smiling, doing up the last button of a cream-coloured blouse. 'Eleanor has such lovely things, doesn't she, Guy? I haven't taken the best – and you must tell her that I'll wash and iron this with the greatest care, and—'

She broke off. She must have seen the expression on his face. He crossed the room and came to her, and told her about the dog. He was unprepared for what happened next: he was unprepared for the tears that slid from her eyes, and for the great, gulping sobs that accompanied them.

He almost said, *But he was just a diseased old stray*, but he managed to stop himself. He knew that she cried not for the dog that she had attempted to rescue, but for everything that she had seen over the past year. Stroking her hair, patting her back, he became aware of a new emotion. Desire, of such dark intensity that it shocked him. He wanted her here, now, on the bed that he had once shared with his wife. He wanted to tear off the blouse that she had borrowed from Eleanor, to see again the pearly flesh that he had glimpsed from the half-open door.

He did not even kiss her. He would have kissed her once – a friend's kiss – but he knew better than to do so now. *Friendship* – such a feeble, apologetic word for what he had felt for Faith for weeks, months – years, perhaps. With dazzling clarity he saw the extent of his self-delusion, and he let go of her, almost pushing her away from him, stumbling through the door and downstairs to the garden. There, he took a spade from the shed, and found a shady patch of earth. He welcomed the hard, physical work of digging the baked ground. As he dug, he forced himself to think back through the years. First she had been a child, a sort of adopted younger sister, part of the family he had never really had. Then she had become a friend, a companion. She had made him laugh; she had made him see ordinary things in a different light. Then, in a single year, she had seemed to grow up. The last time he had visited La Rouilly he had seen that she was no longer a child, that she had become a young woman. He remembered lying with her on the beach at Royan. He remembered her blue dress, and the weight of her head on his chest. How the smoke from his cigarette had drifted in wisps into the dark sky, and how he had twisted a lock of her straw-coloured hair round his finger. Had he loved her then, yet been too blind to see it?

He remembered, too, the violence of his anger when he had seen her in the street with Rufus. His anger had been born of jealousy. Sexual jealousy. His lack of perception disgusted him, but worse was his sudden, sickening understanding of the implications of his discovery. Had he, for the last few years, followed the wrong path? Knowing how much he loved Faith, what on earth was he to do?

After a while she joined him, and made a marker for the grave, tying two pieces of wood together with string, pencilling the name 'Raffles' very carefully on it. Her eyes were swollen and red, her face blotchy. Eleanor's clothes were far too generously cut. Others, he knew, might have thought she looked ridiculous and plain, just as others might have thought it ludicrous to bury with such ceremony a flea-ridden old dog. But to him she was beautiful. She always had been.

After he had laid the animal in the grave, she looked up at him and said, 'He's chasing rabbits in heaven, isn't he, Guy?' and he nodded, and stepped back, unable to speak.

He watched her for a while, envying the lock of hair that caressed her cheek, the ladybird that crawled up her arm. He said, 'You should go back to the house. There's a bottle of Scotch in the bottom drawer of the filing cabinet.' He did not want her to read the truth in his eyes. He needed to be alone; he needed to think.

He shovelled the remaining heap of earth onto the grave. It was hot: he rolled up his shirtsleeves and unknotted his tie. It seemed to Guy that the road he had recently uneasily travelled had divided at last into two irreconcilable routes. He did not see how he could love Faith, yet remain married to Eleanor. He had always prided himself on his honesty. He was unpractised at deception. He saw the choice he might be forced to make, and it appalled him. He saw also the only way he might spare himself that choice.

CHAPTER EIGHT

When Eleanor arrived home, Guy was sitting at the kitchen table, going through his notes. The room was warm and stuffy; flies beat at the windows. Eleanor took off her hat and gloves.

'The train was rather late. And I had to stand all the way from Crewe.' She pecked his cheek. She thought that he looked pale and tired. 'Busy day?' she asked him.

'Quite.' Guy put the top back on his fountain pen. 'Eleanor, sit down, won't you? Can we talk?'

'Just chat to me while I work, won't you, Guy? I have to make the filling for the pie, and Betty Stewart has made a frightful hash of the accounts this month—'

'Eleanor, *please*.' He poured her a cup of tea and placed it on the table. She noticed that his own tea was untouched, a pale scum forming on its surface. He held out a chair; she sat down.

She said, 'Guy, what is it? You're making me nervous. Has something happened? Is Father . . . ?' Selwyn Stephens was holidaying in Derbyshire.

'Your father's very well. He telephoned this morning. But it's about that, in a way, that I wanted to talk to you. Eleanor, I want Selwyn to bring Oliver home with him.'

Eleanor gave a short laugh. 'Guy, we've been through this so many times.'

He closed his eyes. There was a film of sweat on his forehead. Eventually he said, 'I think that Oliver should come home now. The Blitz appears to be over. There hasn't been a major raid on London for almost three months.'

'We can't,' Eleanor reminded him, 'read Herr Hitler's mind. London may be safe now, but who knows whether it will be so next week or next month?'

'Oliver will be as safe here as he's likely to be anywhere. You know that recently the worst raids have been on the provinces. You know that country villages are at risk, just as the cities are.'

Eleanor stirred her tea. Guy was right. Only a fortnight ago she had arranged for emergency clothing to be sent to a Dorset village that had been all but destroyed by a plane that had failed to locate Exeter, and had ended up jettisoning its bombs in the country-side instead.

'May I telephone and tell Selwyn to bring Oliver home?'

Eleanor remembered the first nine months of Oliver's life. The tedium, the isolation, the persistent feeling that each day brought no reward. The prospect of being marooned at home once more with a young child appalled her. 'No,' she said. 'No.' She went to the larder and began to take out ingredients.

'Why not?' Guy's voice was taut.

'Because Oliver's happy in Derbyshire.'

'He'd be happier here, with his parents.'

'He's settled.' She took a tablespoon out of the drawer.

'*Settled!*' The word resounded with barely suppressed anger. Measuring flour, Eleanor was aware of an answering anger in herself.

'Children need stability, Guy. They need a routine.'

'Children need their parents. If the war goes on for another two years, Eleanor, or for five – or for ten – will you insist that our son remains with your grandmother? And if so, will he even remember who we are?'

Chopping onions, she said coldly, 'Don't be ridiculous, Guy.'

'Is it so ridiculous? Small children have short memory spans.'

'I visit Oliver every month. Every four weeks exactly. Of course he remembers me.'

'I suppose it's written into your diary. Attend WVS committee meeting . . . check monthly accounts . . . visit son.' He turned away, and lit himself a cigarette. When he spoke again, the sarcasm had gone from his voice. He sounded, Eleanor thought, drained, and rather desperate.

'Eleanor, I need to be with my son. I need Oliver to come home.'

'And what,' she hissed, turning to him, 'what of what *I* need?'

'I rather thought that in the case of Oliver our needs should coincide.' His eyes were dark and hard, like basalt. She recognized his determination because it was matched by hers. She had, she thought, arranged her life well. She had left that dreadful little house in Hackney, and had returned to Holland Square, to live with her father. She had Guy: if his touch no longer had the power to make her shiver, as it had once done, still she saw how other women looked at him, and envied her. She had work which allowed her to use her talents.

House, husband, work: she did not intend to lose any of them.

She threw the sliced onions into the pan. 'Oliver's only eighteen months old,' she pointed out. 'Grandmother tells me that he still wakes twice a night.'

'I would attend to him at night, Eleanor. I did so before.'

'And when you're on duty at the hospital? He's too young for nursery school. Who would look after him if he were to come home?'

'We could work something out. You could cut down your commitments . . . I've a couple of hours free in the afternoon . . .'

'A couple of hours in the afternoons!' she repeated scornfully. 'What use is that for a child who needs someone watching him every moment of the day? When I'm with him he follows me around like a puppy dog!'

'If you spent more time with him, then he might not be so clingy.'

She just caught the muttered words. She cried out, 'Would you give up your precious work, Guy – would you abandon those feckless, verminous people that you care for to look after your son?' She slammed the knife down on the draining board. 'Would you go into partnership with Father, as I've asked you to time and time again? We'd have more money if you did so . . . and perhaps if we had more money it might be easier to find a nursemaid. And perhaps, if you didn't have to travel to Malt Street, you'd be at home more often. Would you do that, Guy? Would you do what *I* want, this time?'

The silence lasted longer. Then he said quietly, 'No, Eleanor, I won't.' He took his jacket from the back of the chair, and walked out of the kitchen.

She shouted, 'Where are you going, Guy? It'll be supper soon!' but he did not reply. When she heard the front door slam, she stood still for a while, digging her nails into her palms. Then she tipped both cups of cold tea down the sink, and began, with untypical heavy-handedness, to roll out the pastry.

Trimming the pie, brushing it with milk, she was aware of apprehension, mixed with anger. She had an uneasy feeling that she had missed something in that conversation; as though, in asking whether Oliver could come home, Guy had also been asking some other, different question. Eleanor dumped the pie in the hot oven with a crash of ceramic on metal rack. Then she went to the drawing-room and poured herself a drink.

In the aching heat of the August afternoon, Faith and Rufus left the Mahonia Road house. Rufus carried a rug and a portable gramophone; Faith clutched a picnic basket. Crossing the road, she heard a voice call her name and, turning, she saw Guy. She waited for him to catch up with her.

He looked dishevelled and slightly out of breath. He said urgently, 'Faith, I need to speak to you.'

'We're going on a picnic. Come with us.'

They walked to the park. Guy glowered and smoked and said little. Faith mentally shrugged her shoulders and ignored him, and talked to Rufus instead. At Mrs Childerley's house she collected the dogs and put them on their leads. At last, unable to bear the lengthening silence, she said: 'Oh, for heaven's sake, Guy, what is it? What have I done this time?'

He looked genuinely surprised. 'Done? You've done nothing, Faith.'

They had reached the park, and were walking down an avenue of lime trees. Pale green keys floated stickily through the windless air. Faith let the dogs off the leash, and they sloped around the trees, nuzzling fungi and dead leaves.

'Then don't be so cross, Guy. You always were shockingly bad-tempered.'

'It's not that, it's just that—'

Rufus interrupted. 'There's Stella and Jane, under the trees.'

They picnicked beneath the limes. Clouds misted the sun, and the air was so hot and still that it seemed to Faith she could have scooped it up in her hands. The heat endowed the late afternoon with a peculiar stillness, so that conversation seemed slow and disjointed, almost as if each word they uttered lingered suspended in space, like the lime keys. Faith and Stella and Jane chattered in a desultory fashion, but Guy sat, his back propped against a tree trunk, tearing the petals from a daisy, while Rufus, lying on the grass, smoking, also said little. Faith knew that at the end of each Atlantic crossing, Rufus found it harder and harder to return to his ship.

Stella said, 'Have you heard from that gorgeous brother of yours, Faith?'

'Jake's on leave, visiting my parents in Norfolk. Then he's coming here, but I don't know when.' Faith threw crumbs to a flock of sparrows, and watched Guy stand up and wander away from the trees.

Words fluttered beneath the lime branches.

'Bruno's giving another party.'

'Are you coming, Rufus?'

'I don't know where he finds the *food*. He must have friends in very high places.'

'Or very low ones.'

'Even Linda has used up her tins of salmon.'

'I haven't seen her for ages.'

'Someone told me she's having a very steamy affair.'

'One can't imagine Linda *steamy* about anything.'

'Who is he? Do tell.'

'She's very secretive . . .'

Guy was standing by himself, a little way from the others, his hands dug into his jacket pockets, looking out over the heat-scarred grass. As Faith walked towards him, both the conversation and the gramophone music became inaudible.

She said bluntly, 'What's wrong? Is it your work? Has it been awful?'

'Not particularly. Rather routine, in fact.' He was smoking; he offered her his packet of cigarettes, but she shook her head. 'I never thought I'd miss the bombs, but I almost did, the other night.' He grinned fleetingly. 'At least they kept me awake.'

'The ambulance station is very dull, too. I seem to play an awful lot of poker.' Faith looked at him. 'Have you quarrelled with Eleanor?'

He said, 'We . . . had a disagreement,' and dropped his cigarette butt on the lawn. The hessian-dry blades of grass smouldered scarlet. He watched them burn.

She wanted to reach out to him, but she did not do so. There was a distance about him, and an ominous brittleness. If she were to touch him, she thought, then his anger might shatter into a thousand sharp pieces, one of which might pierce her.

It had begun, at last, to rain: dark, heavy drops that quenched the smouldering grass. She said, 'What was it that you wanted to talk to me about, Guy?' but he glanced at his watch and shook his head.

'Another time, perhaps. I'm late at the hospital.'

He walked away from her. As Faith called the dogs, she was aware of a sense of unease, almost of dread. She was reminded of the moments between the sounding of the air-raid siren and the falling of the first bombs. The weather, she thought, as she watched the rain battering the dusty ground. The drumroll smothered the sound of Rufus's footsteps; when he spoke, she jumped.

'I don't think he appreciated the jolly crowd.'

She followed Rufus's gaze to where Guy, walking fast, was heading through the park gates.

'How are things between you?'

'Everything's fine.' Clipping the leads to the dogs' collars, she smiled up at him.

'You were in love with him.'

It seemed like an accusation. She said firmly, 'That's all over. We're good friends now.'

At first he was silent, but then he said, 'Do you really believe that?'

'Yes. Why not?'

'Because that sort of love can't change into friendship.'

'That's nonsense!' The others had run for cover; Faith gathered up the basket and the rug.

'Is it?'

'Of course it is. Anyway, what do you mean by "that sort of love"?'

'I mean passionate love. By your own admission, Faith, you've loved Guy Neville for nine years.'

She began to walk to the park gate, regardless of the rain that streamed down her face and soaked her thin cotton dress. She called back, 'I was a *child*. I wasn't *passionate* about Guy. I never have been.' Yet she remembered her dream about the snake bite, and was glad of the cold rain, stinging her burning face.

At the gate Rufus caught up with her. He said bitterly, 'And of course, he is madly in love with you, too,' and walked away into the rain, leaving her standing alone at the side of the street.

Two very large gins and tonic cooled Eleanor down a little. She saw, looking out of the bedroom window, that a heavy greyish cloud now covered the bronze face of the sun, and that raindrops had begun to trail down the window panes. She took off her creased clothes, and washed her face and brushed her hair. From her wardrobe she selected a red crêpe de Chine dress. There were still scrapings of lipstick and powder in the pots on her dressing-table; she applied them carefully. Then she glanced at her watch. Seven o'clock. Supper time. She was unsure whether Guy was on duty tonight, but even if he was, he usually came home for supper.

In the kitchen, she checked that the pie was golden and well risen, and that the vegetables were cooked just right. She laid the table and lit candles. Rain drummed against the paving stones in the courtyard, and trickled down the basement steps. Eleanor knew that Guy's rages were short-lived, the product of too much work, too little sleep. She knew also that, after some reflection, Guy would realize that she was right, and Oliver would remain in Derbyshire. Guy invariably agreed with her in the end. His hot-headedness could always be countered. Though he was stubborn, he disliked conflict. It was just a question of being sufficiently persuasive, sufficiently firm.

At a quarter past seven, Eleanor put the pie back in the oven to keep it warm. At half past, she blew out the candles. At eight o'clock, she poured herself another drink, and sat in the drawing-room, thin-lipped. At twenty past eight, when the doorbell rang, she assumed that Guy had forgotten his key, and she decided, in the distance between drawing-room and door, that she would, if he was sufficiently contrite, forgive him.

She opened the front door. Jake Mulgrave stood on the step. Slightly blurred by alcohol, Eleanor could only stare at him.

Jake said, 'Is Guy in?' and Eleanor shook her head.

'Or Faith? I thought she might be having supper with you. I've been to Mahonia Road, you see, but there was no-one in.'

Eleanor was seized just then by a horrible suspicion. Where would Guy have gone, having quarrelled with her, if not to seek solace from that woman? In spite of the closeness of the evening, she shivered.

'Guy will be back at any moment.' She had to concentrate to enunciate her words clearly. The gin, and an intense, boiling sort of emotion – anger, she thought – threatened her accustomed poise.

She forced herself to smile. 'And I haven't seen your sister recently. Won't you come in, Jake?'

He followed her indoors. She imagined Guy and Faith, together. Guy pouring out his troubles; Faith offering him comfort, capitalizing on his vulnerability.

'A drink, Jake?' In the drawing-room, Eleanor poured a whisky for her visitor, another gin for herself. She thought she had got hold of herself; she was pleased how normal, how unruffled, she sounded, yet as she replaced the stopper on the bottle her hand shook.

Jake explained, 'I've just spent a few days in Norfolk with my parents. I wanted to ask Guy about Ma. I'm worried about her – that's why I came to London early. She doesn't seem well. She won't see a doctor. I thought she might talk to Guy, though.'

'Your mother's probably just tired and anxious like all the rest of us,' said Eleanor. She wasn't really listening; the image of Guy and Faith together persisted. 'I'm sure it's nothing to worry about.' She glanced out of the window, and said, 'It's still pouring with rain,' and looked at Jake. His fair hair, cut short for the army, was slightly curled by the rain, and his eyes were very blue against his suntanned skin. And she had always admired a man in uniform. It was a pity, she often thought, that Guy was not in uniform.

'You'll have supper, won't you, Jake?'

'Well, I—'

'You don't mind eating in the kitchen, do you? So much more cosy.'

He began to demur, but she disregarded him, and went down to the basement. The kitchen was hot and close. Rain drummed relentlessly against the windows. Eleanor took pleasure in serving Guy's dinner to Jake Mulgrave. She drank, but did not eat. She could not have eaten; the food would have choked her. Instead, she watched Jake. He had the sort of face, she thought, surprising herself with an untypical leap of imagination, that with just a few rubbings-out or additional brush strokes one might have seen in a painting of quattrocento angels.

'Army life must suit you, Jake,' she said. 'You look well.'

He glanced up, and smiled. 'The army's bloody boring and unbearable, to tell the truth, Eleanor, but I'm very well.'

She did not comment on his use of bad language, as

she would have done to Guy. Indeed, it produced in her a frisson of pleasure, a sense that he was including her in his world. As though, sealed off from the rest of London by the thunderstorm, she and Jake were together breaking some sort of rule. She could not stop looking at him. There were tiny beads of sweat on his forehead, and he had rolled up his shirtsleeves. She thought that, much as she disliked the Mulgraves, she did not, perhaps, dislike Jake as intensely as the others.

'You'll have some more, won't you?' she said, and scooped the remainder of the pie onto his plate. She glanced at her watch. 'Guy must have been kept late at the hospital. So there's just the two of us. Well, I don't mind in the least, do you?'

Jake shook his head, smiled, looked down at his plate. 'You're spoiling me, Eleanor. I'll become hideously fat, and poor Guy will go hungry.'

She touched his hand. 'I'm afraid that Guy sometimes takes me for granted. That tends to happen with old married couples, you see.' Her laugh sounded, even to her, rather odd. Her hand still lay on his. His skin was cool; she sensed the muscle and sinews beneath. She longed suddenly for Jake's thumb to trace the hollow of her palm, for Jake's mouth to press against that same hollow. She did not often desire physical contact, so the unexpected depth of her need made her breath catch in her throat.

'What do you say, Jake?' Still that peculiar hoarseness to her voice. 'Shall we make an evening of it? Go out on the town? Just the two of us?'

He said, 'Sorry, Eleanor, I have to dash,' and, looking up at him, she understood the gravity of her mistake. He did not quite manage to disguise his shock, or his lack of interest, quickly enough. Jake Mulgrave, who, by all accounts, was not discriminating in his tastes, was utterly uninterested in her. Her sense of acceptance, of inclusion, had been an illusion. His hand slid away from beneath hers, and she was left cold, alone, unwanted. She felt as she had felt all those years ago, when she had met Hilary Taylor in Fortnum and Mason. Large, lumpy, housewifely. Old.

She took his empty plate from him, and went to the sink. She ran the tap. The plate clattered noisily as she dropped it into the water.

She heard him say, 'That was delicious, Eleanor. You really are the most marvellous cook. One can always rely on an absolutely splendid meal whenever one comes here,' and she knew that he had realized that he had hurt her feelings, and was trying to placate her. He did not want her as a woman, yet he presumed to mollify her with this half-hearted appreciation of her domestic skills. Her back to him, she wanted to scream, to spit, but she did neither. She had a sharper weapon.

She said, 'I saw your father a few days ago, Jake. He was with a friend. A very close friend, I should say. They were coming out of a house in Queen Square. A charming girl, I thought. Tall, elegant, platinum blonde – the real thing, I think, not out of a bottle.' Wiping her hands on a tea cloth, Eleanor turned and smiled at Jake. 'Do you know her?'

He did not reply. He had, she noticed, gone very pale beneath the tan. With vicious pleasure, she drove in the knife.

'Whoever she was, Ralph seemed very taken with her. So nice for your father, don't you think, Jake, to have such close friends in London.'

*　　*　　*

After he left Holland Square, Jake stumbled into the first pub he came across. He was halfway through his second double Scotch when his mind, frozen by shock and anger and fear, began to work again.

So nice for your father, Jake, to have such close friends.

Eleanor had implied that his father was having an affair with Linda Forrester. Jake forced himself to consider whether there could be any truth in her accusations. He remembered his mother as he had left her in Norfolk: pale, tired, apathetic. He had believed her unwell, which was why he had decided to call on Guy. Was it possible that he had confused illness with heartbreak?

Jake's thoughts slid to Linda Forrester. Beautiful, icy, amoral Linda. He himself had, when on leave in London during the past six months, visited her Queen Square flat. He had long ago read the invitation in those pale blue eyes, yet had never followed it up. Something in her smooth, blonde demeanour had unnerved him. As for Ralph . . . Jake, immured in an army camp in Northumberland, had seen his father only occasionally since the Mulgraves had arrived in England. Might Ralph, resenting his enforced return to a country he loathed, have chosen to distract himself by taking Linda Forrester to his bed?

Jake's fist clenched, and he struck the bar. Glasses rattled, and the publican glanced at him warningly. Only one way to find out, thought Jake and, knocking back the last of his Scotch, he set off through the rain for Queen Square.

He could hear, through the heavy door, the raucous, insistent chime. A rattle of chain, a clunk of lock, and she peered through the six-inch gap between door and jamb.

'Can I come in?'

'*Jake.*' Linda was wearing a pale blue satin negligée. 'It's late.'

'I'm only in London for the one night. I was hoping to catch you in.' He pushed open the door and entered the hallway. He heard her squeak of protest, and held his finger to her lips. 'Ssh. The neighbours.'

He climbed the stairs. She swept past him, a rustle of satin skirts. The door to her flat was open; he went inside.

She said, 'Drink, Jake?' and went to the cabinet and poured him a Scotch. As she placed the glass in his hands she looked up at him and frowned, and said, 'What is it?'

His confidence, born of anger, seemed to ebb away; he could not now find the words. *Are you having an affair with my father?* Voicing it would have made it seem more real. He stumbled, 'Someone told me—'

'What, Jake?'

He went to the window. The blackout covered the glass, enclosing them, trapping indoors the lingering heat of the day. He heard a crackle of thunder.

His back to her, he said, 'Someone told me they'd seen you with my father,' and he turned, needing to see her expression, yet finding her smooth features unreadable.

'Seen me with your father?' she repeated.

'Yes.' There was a silence. The dim light of the room shadowed her face, darkening its sculptured angles. Jake's head had begun to ache, and he felt slightly sick: the weather, or that gargantuan supper that Eleanor had shovelled down him, he supposed.

'Ralph is a friend of mine,' she began, and then she broke off, and glanced up quickly. 'You don't mean—' Her eyes were enormous, silvery pale in the lamplight. 'You don't mean that someone's told you that Ralph and I . . . that Ralph and I are *lovers*?'

He said nothing, just looked at her. She gave a peculiar laugh, and crossed the room to him. 'Jake, you can't possibly believe that I'm having an affair with your father.' She stared at him. 'You *do* think it, don't you? Good God.' Her expression altered. 'I think you'd better leave, Jake.' She went to the door, opened it. 'Now.'

He remained where he was, leaning against the window sill. 'Not yet. I'm not going yet. I need to know the truth.'

'You seem to have made up your mind already.' Linda's voice was cold. But when he did not move, she let the door swing shut, and sat down on the sofa.

'Who told you this nonsense?'

'No-one you know.'

'A friend, Jake?'

He remembered the loathing in Eleanor's eyes as she had turned from the sink and looked at him. He shuddered. 'Not exactly. No. Not a friend.'

Linda shrugged. 'Well, then.'

Jake closed his eyes, and rubbed his aching forehead. 'Why should she lie?'

'How should I know? Perhaps she was angry – or jealous.'

'Jealous?'

She sat back on the sofa and studied him. 'You're a very attractive man, Jake. Though I must say that just now you do look rather frightful.' Her voice had softened a little.

'Headache,' he muttered.

'Poor old you.' She patted the seat beside her. 'Come here. Come *on*, Jake. And do stop glowering so – no wonder you have a headache.'

Unwillingly, he sat down. 'Close your eyes, darling,' she said. With the tips of her fingers she began to massage his temples. As the pain in his head ebbed, he struggled to remember the exact sequence of the evening's events at Holland Square. Eleanor had insisted he eat Guy's supper, then she had taken his hand (a shock in itself: touch, previously, had been confined to a parting handshake), and then she had made a pass at him. In retrospect, it seemed unbelievable, but it was true: Eleanor Neville had made a pass at him.

'Better, darling?'

'Yes. Thank you.' Her touch had induced in him an unexpectedly delicious lethargy. He thought, *Eleanor made up those filthy lies because she was angry with me and wanted to hurt me*. He was almost overwhelmed with relief. He began to stand up. 'I should go.'

'Don't be silly. It's pouring with rain, Jake. You can't possibly go out in that.' With the palm of her hand she pushed him back into the seat.

'Then it's not true—'

'*Jake*.' She silenced him by pressing her lips over his own. He felt her small, tapered fingers undo the buttons of his shirt, and he felt her straddle him, so that she sat on his lap, facing him. He let physical desire take him over, drowning out the remnants of all those other tormenting thoughts. He slid his hands beneath the icy satin of her negligée, and ran them the length of her naked body.

*   *   *

At five o'clock in the morning, Faith let herself into the house, dumped her bag in the hall, and went into the kitchen. She was filling the kettle when she heard a movement behind her. She jumped, swung round, whispered, 'Rufus?' and then focused on the man sitting at the table.

'*Jake.*' She could make out only the pale gleam of his hair, and the gathering of light on the rim of the glass that he held. 'Is the electricity off again?'

'Don't know. Didn't try.'

She found the switch; light flooded the room. Jake was sitting at the table, his chin propped on his bunched fists. There was a bottle and a glass in front of him. He said, 'Drink, Faith?' but she shook her head.

'No thanks. I wasn't expecting you so soon, Jake.' She dumped her gas mask and mackintosh on the table. 'What are you doing?'

'Thinking.' He glanced up at her. 'Makes a change, doesn't it?'

The feeling of unease, which had begun the previous afternoon in the oppressive heat of the park, intensified as she looked at him. 'You're pickled, Jake. Go to bed and sleep it off.'

He ignored her. 'I'm trying to work things out.' She noticed that his hand shook as he raised his glass to his lips. 'I'm trying to make a considered assessment of the facts.' He smiled, looking up at her, but the smile did not touch his chill blue eyes. 'Bit of an effort for me – I'm more one for acting first and thinking afterwards, aren't I?'

She said, 'What facts? What are you trying to work out?' but he stood up clumsily, and went to the back door and opened it. Rain pounded the step and seeped into the kitchen.

'I came here yesterday, you see, Faith. I was looking for you. And for Guy. So I went to Holland Square. But Guy was out.'

'He was with me. Rufus and Guy and me . . . we went for a picnic in the park. Shut the door, Jake. The light—'

In the doorway, he raised his face to the rain. Drops of water trailed down his mouth, his nose, his chin. He said, 'But Eleanor was in. So I spoke to her instead. Or rather, she spoke to me.'

'*Jake.*' She dug her nails into her palms.

He swung round, facing her. The shoulders and the front of his shirt were darkened by rain. 'Eleanor gave me a drink. Fed me.'

'*Jake.*' Suddenly, she was frightened. 'What's *happened*?'

'Nothing.' When he looked down at her, the expression in his eyes lacked all sympathy – lacked, even, she thought, recognition. 'Nothing happened,' he repeated. 'Eleanor gave me a delicious meal, and we had a little chat. And then—'

She interrupted him. 'What has Eleanor said to you? Is Guy—'

'Guy's fine. I think. Didn't see him. She made me eat his supper.' Jake shivered. 'It was funny, though – all the time I was eating, I kept thinking of Hansel and Gretel and the witch. It was as though she was fattening me up for the oven. But she hardly mentioned Guy. No – she wanted to tell me about Pa.'

'*Pa?*' Faith was bewildered.

'Eleanor told me that Pa was having an affair with Linda Forrester.'

Her mind seemed cold, blank, slow. She stared at Jake, and he looked back at her, wide-eyed.

261

'Eleanor's a bitch, Faith. I didn't realize. God knows why Guy ever married her. Anyway, I went to see Linda. And she denied it, and I thought, well, that's all right then, of *course* Pa wouldn't. I mean – he just wouldn't, would he?' He frowned. 'Only, since I left her, I've begun to think – well, what else would she say?' His voice became a savagely mocking falsetto. '"Yes, Jake, I've been fucking your father for the last six months."'

Faith whispered, 'It's gossip, Jake. Hateful gossip.' Yet she remembered, with a sudden sickening squeeze to her stomach, the conversation in the park.

He seemed to see her change of expression. 'What?' He crossed the room to her. 'What is it?'

She shook her head. 'Nothing.'

He grabbed her upper arms and shook her. 'Tell me.'

She felt tears spring to her eyes. 'Someone told me Linda was having an affair, that's all. They didn't know who with.' His fingers bit into her flesh. 'Jake, you're hurting me!'

His hands dropped to his sides. His face was ashen. He began to button his shirtsleeves. She wailed, 'It's nonsense, Jake. Horrible nonsense. Pa wouldn't do that to Ma. He *loves* her!' Tears were streaming down her face.

Jake scooped up his keys and change from the tabletop, dropped them into his pocket, and grabbed his jacket. As he left the room, Faith cried out, 'Where are you going, Jake?' but her only reply was the front door slamming behind him.

He waited in a doorway opposite Linda Forrester's flat. He would wait for ever, Jake thought, if necessary.

He remembered Linda's apparent bewilderment, her

pique at his accusations, her sudden access of sympathy. He remembered her fingertips stroking his forehead, distracting him; her lithe, soft body pressing against his, erasing from his mind all other thoughts. Too easy, he thought savagely. Too easy.

The last ragged remains of the thunder growled uneasily, and every now and then the dawn streets were illuminated by lightning. Rain beat the pavement and slid down the gutter. The storm seemed to Jake an appropriately clichéd background music to the events of the last twenty-four hours. In the shelter of the doorway, he smoked cigarette after cigarette, and waited as the air-raid warden bustled home, as the milkman's dray clanked along the street, and as the paper boy's tyres skidded on the wet tarmac.

Then he saw a swirl of black overcoat and hat, and heard in the distance a familiar footstep. Jake dropped his cigarette stub and ground it into the pavement with his heel as he shrank back into the shadows. Against the haunted purplish light of the storm he watched his father ring the doorbell of Linda Forrester's flat, and wait. After a while, Jake glimpsed a fall of moon-fair hair in the dark slit of the open door. Last night, he had run that silky hair through his fingers; last night he had pressed handfuls of it against his mouth. The recollection made him shudder.

He saw her glance up and down the street. To check that he was not there, he supposed: he had made her nervous. A ragged bunch of flowers was unearthed from the folds of Ralph's overcoat. They kissed. Jake tasted bile. Then his father walked away from the flat. *Not today, darling* – she was keeping him on a leash.

He heard the click of the front door as it closed behind her, and he waited until Ralph had walked the length of the street and turned the corner. Then he crossed the road and leaned on the doorbell of her flat.

She did not, this time, unhook the chain from the door before opening it. He saw the shock on her face as she recognized him, and he jammed a foot and a shoulder into the aperture before she could slam the door shut.

'Jake—'

He said, 'I want to know why you took my father for your lover. Was it to spite me?'

He saw her struggle to recover herself. She gave a little laugh. 'Jake . . . I don't know what you mean.'

'It's a simple enough question. Did you decide to have an affair with my father to punish me for turning you down? I find it hard to believe that you couldn't resist his ageing body, you see. Or have you a penchant for older men? After all, poor old Harold must be fifty or so. Though one always assumed you married him for his money.'

Behind her, the door to the ground floor flat opened, and a head peered out. Linda trilled, 'Sorry to disturb you, Mr Lockwood – won't be a moment,' and then she hissed, 'Go *away*, Jake.'

He did not move. 'Not until you tell me the truth.'

A flick of her eyelids. She smiled. 'Ralph and I – I think you've misunderstood, Jake. If you saw us together just now, then you mustn't think—'

'*Don't*. Damn you, Linda – I may be stupid, but I'm not quite that bloody stupid.'

Her expression altered. 'It's really none of your business, is it, Jake? Ralph and I are both adults. What we choose to do is nothing to do with you.'

'And I suppose it's nothing to do with my mother either?'

She shrugged. 'Ralph's a man of the world. I'm sure I wasn't his first.'

It was hard to speak; his anger almost choked him. 'You didn't like me turning you down, did you? So when my father appeared, feeling sorry for himself, you saw an easy way of getting even. I don't suppose it was very significant to you. Just another trophy.'

An answering anger flickered across her smooth features. 'And I suppose last night was *significant* for you, was it, Jake?' Her eyes, pale glittering chips of crystal, focused on him. 'You want to know the truth, do you, Jake? Then I'll tell you. The truth is that I took Ralph as my lover because I was bored. Bored with this boring war – the boring food, the boring clothes, the way one is trapped in this beastly dull country. Ralph is refreshing, you see, and amusing.' She looked up at him. 'Do you know, Jake, that it's been rather thrilling to have the two of you. It's quite taken my mind off things. Father and son – I don't think I've ever managed *that* before.' She laughed, seeing his expression. 'Oh, come on, darling – you're not going to go all petit bourgeois at the thought of following in your father's footsteps, are you?'

He recalled, a sudden vivid vision, her naked body astride his. He whispered, 'If you have anything more to do with my father, then I'll kill you. Remember that,' and then, unable to bear the nearness of her any longer, he walked away from the building.

In the thin early morning light, Jake moved at random through streets washed clean by the storm. He did not hate her, he realized. He hated two people. His father, and himself.

* * *

Sometimes Faith knew that she had been right, that it was not possible that her father could be Linda Forrester's lover. Ralph would not betray Poppy. Ralph quarrelled, he sulked, he needed to see himself reflected in the company of admiring friends, but he did not betray. Yet a fragment of doubt lingered. Throughout the night, memories had drearily rewound themselves in her head, like an over-used newsreel. Ralph at Linda's dinner table, surrounded by Bruno's fawning friends. Ralph at Heronsmead, bored and isolated and resentful. The expression in Poppy's eyes as she had said, *I thought he was staying with you, Faith*.

At eight o'clock she ran a comb through her hair, splashed cold water over her face, and headed for Queen Square. The streets were sheened with puddles from the previous night's rain. Overhead, a barrage balloon, freed by the lightning, drifted in a ragged assemblage of silver tatters. At Linda Forrester's flat, she pressed the doorbell and waited, but there was no answer. After a while, walking on through Bloomsbury, she saw a public telephone box.

Inside, she stared at the handset. If she were, ringing round Bruno Gage and his friends, to track down Ralph, then what would she say to him? *Pa, it's Faith. Is it true that you're sleeping with Linda Forrester?* She left the phone booth.

The sun pierced the film of cloud, comforting her. Jake must have misunderstood Eleanor, she told herself, or Eleanor must have misinterpreted what she had seen. Eleanor – sensible, conventional Eleanor – must have witnessed a friendly kiss, and mistaken it for something more. Faith decided to go to Holland Square.

*   *   *

Eleanor made her a cup of tea, and plumped up the cushions before she sat down. Faith was searching for the right words when Eleanor, her back to her as she tidied sheet music from the piano, said: 'I'm so glad you dropped in, Faith. I'd been meaning to speak to you.'

Faith gave her tea a final, savage stir, sloshing liquid into the saucer. 'About last night?'

Eleanor replaced the music in the piano stool. 'Pardon, dear?'

'You wanted to speak to me about what you said to Jake?'

Eleanor looked blank. 'I wanted to speak to you about *Guy*.' Her voice became low and confidential. 'If you could just take up less of his time, Faith. He's so busy, you see, and he gets so tired. He won't say anything to you, so I must do it for him. You don't mind, do you, Faith?'

Her heart was beating very fast. She repeated stupidly, 'Take up less of Guy's time . . . ?'

'Yes. Guy knows how much you depend on him. He feels obliged to be kind to you.'

He feels obliged to be kind to you. She sat motionless and silent. Her face burned. She remembered Guy comforting her when she had thought that she was going mad, Guy carrying her bags to the railway station, Guy tending the wounded dog.

'He feels that he must repay the debt he owes to your family,' added Eleanor. 'He knows how hard you've all found it to adapt to England. I sometimes think' – a little laugh – 'that his sense of duty . . . his conscience . . . is a tremendous burden to him.'

Strange how a few words could put the past in such a different light. For the first time Faith saw herself as a burden, a misfit, someone deserving of pity. She whispered, 'Guy is under no obligation to me. No obligation whatsoever.'

'More tea, Faith? No? I think I'll have another cup.' Eleanor poured milk from a jug. 'You see, Guy is given to enthusiasms, impulses. He can, I'm afraid, be quite easily led.'

Faith forced herself to look into those opaque dark eyes. 'What do you mean, Eleanor?'

'Well . . .' The small laugh again. 'It isn't easy for me to talk about this. It's hard for a wife to admit that her husband may in some respects be . . . weak.'

The air in the wide, spacious drawing-room seemed to have become drained, lacking in oxygen. She wanted to leave.

'I understand,' added Eleanor, 'that your standards – the standards of your family – are different from mine, Faith. You think of me as an old fuddy-duddy, I expect.' That little laugh again.

'No. No, I don't.' Faith swallowed. 'In fact, I've always admired you, Eleanor. But I don't understand what you mean by "the standards of my family".'

'Don't you? Really?'

She saw that she had fallen into a trap. 'You mean . . . my father.'

Eleanor drank her tea and said nothing.

She said angrily, 'You must have made a mistake, Eleanor. What you told Jake last night – it can't possibly be true.'

'It is true.' Eleanor's voice was sharp. 'Oh, it is true. I may not be as . . . as *experienced* as you, Miss Mulgrave, but I assure you that I was not mistaken in what I saw. I thought it best to warn Jake. Divorce is such a shameful thing, isn't it? But perhaps, in a way, I

268

was mistaken. Perhaps the Mulgraves see things differently. The French, I believe, don't disapprove of extra-marital affairs. And you're such a well-travelled family, aren't you?'

Though her legs shook, Faith stood up. But Eleanor laid a hand on her arm, staying her, so that she sank back into the chair.

'I believe in constancy, Miss Mulgrave. And I believe in fortitude.' There was a warning in Eleanor's expression. The hard, quiet voice continued, 'And so, of course, does Guy. Where we differ is that he is capable of being beguiled. To live as your family lives would be impossible for him. He would be torn. He needs the security and the order that I have created for him. Guy may not think that he needs that, but he does. He loves his work, and he loves his son. He thinks that he might prefer a different way of life, but to abandon all I've given him would, I believe, destroy him. You see' – and as Eleanor turned to her, Faith glimpsed for the first time the cold dislike in Eleanor's eyes – 'you see, I *know* him.'

Faith's voice was small, quiet. 'But do you love him?'

A lift of the eyebrows. 'I've tried to make clear to you, Miss Mulgrave, that that's not your concern.'

She had to gather up all her courage. 'It may not be *my* concern, Eleanor, but it should be yours.'

Eleanor's composure slipped. 'How dare you! How dare someone like you presume to tell me my business!' Eleanor stood up. 'I think you should leave now, Miss Mulgrave. And I think you should remember that neither you nor your family are welcome in this house any more.'

* * *

After Thierry had driven her back to Compton Deverall, Nicole had tried to be a good wife. She had sat on the sofa all afternoon, as ordered by the doctor, playing with the kitten that Thierry had given her, and reading novels. She had even tried to knit baby clothes – she knew that was what expectant mothers were supposed to do – but the stitches kept falling off the needles, and the wool unravelled, and by the end of the week, when she had produced an inch of holey, greyish knitting, Laura Kemp tactfully reclaimed her sewing bag and knitted the matinée jacket herself.

Though she tried to keep herself amused, Nicole was nevertheless terribly bored. The girls' school billeted on Compton Deverall was taking a summer holiday, so there was only herself and the housekeeper and Laura in the great, echoing house. The housekeeper was deaf, and Laura was obliged to spend much of her time tending the garden, because if she had not done so they would not have eaten. Thierry drove down from Boscombe Down airfield every now and then and played cards with Nicole and took her out for little excursions in his car. She had neither seen nor heard from David since May.

Her enormous belly was squeezed uncomfortably against her ribcage, and her back ached all the time. She put up with the discomfort, gritting her teeth, uncomplaining, writing long letters to Faith. 'I look like a *whale* . . . I can't have baths any more – you would need a crane to haul me in and out of the tub.' Nicole passed the time playing the piano, and shuffling around the house and garden. But David's ancestors stared disapprovingly at her from dark, craquelured oil paintings, and the history of the house, which she had at first thought romantic, had begun to oppress her. Nowhere could she escape noticing how ineradicably the Kemps belonged to this place. Their insignia – three stars and a rather cross-looking griffin – was engraved on the silverware, was carved on the mantelpiece, and could just be distinguished, in faded, gaudy paint, on the ceiling of the Great Hall. Within these ancient walls she felt herself stilled, diminished, trapped.

She went back to her old habit of trying to count the windows in the house. Once a day she plodded slowly round the building. Nicole told herself that if there was an even number of windows, then it would be a boy, and she would be the sort of wife David wanted, and everything would be all right. But, try as she might, the answer was always different.

The nursing-home that Laura had booked her into had given her a pamphlet called *Your Baby*. Opening it, Nicole caught sight of an awful diagram, and immediately shut it again. Peasant women in Mediterranean villages had babies without reading books about it; Nicole resolved to do the same. When Laura tried to talk to her about childbirth, she pretended to listen, but in fact thought of nice things, like horses and music. She was supposed to pack her case for the nursing-home, but did not do so. It would have made it all seem real, and besides, there was still three weeks to go.

Laura had to go to Salisbury to shop; Nicole had intended to go with her, but it was too hot, and the thought of the sweaty, crowded bus was unbearable. Laura looked closely at her and asked her if she was all right – the shopping could wait until tomorrow – but Nicole smiled and reassured her. She did not tell Laura that she felt rather odd – not actually ill, just odd – and that her back ached worse than usual today. A deep, intermittent sort of ache. She waved as Laura walked down the drive, and then went back into the house, where she wandered around for a while, ending up in the nursery, with its cot and baby bath and nursing chair. She thought that the room looked rather dreary, and she remembered the painting that she had bought in London, and went and dug it out of her drawer, and hammered a nail into the plaster and hung it. The gorgeous colours, pinks and oranges and golds, made the room look brighter. In an old chest on the landing she discovered lengths of fabric – silks and satins and wonderful old brocades – and draped them around the cot and over the curtain rail. Then she went into the garden and picked armfuls of roses, arranging them in vases around the room.

By the time she had finished, the ache in her back had become worse. Walking downstairs, she had to pause, holding on to the banister as the pain gathered and coiled, ready to spring. She noticed that with each twinge, her swollen stomach hardened. She began to wonder whether something was wrong. Glancing at her watch, she saw that it was midday; Laura had told her that she would be home by three. Feeling suddenly very alone, she decided to look for the housekeeper but, plodding from room to room and up and down stairs, could not find her. In the dining-room she discovered the table laid for one: a covered plate of cold veal and ham pie and salad, and a note saying, 'Flan in larder.' She had forgotten that it was the housekeeper's day off.

She couldn't eat the food; she felt rather sick. She was horribly afraid that the pain was to do with the baby. She wished that Ma were here, or Faith. Her loneliness, the knowledge that if she cried out no-one would hear her, seemed worse than the pain. She had to escape the empty, echoing house, so she decided to take her mind off things by counting the windows again. Outside, in the midday sun, she wandered around the gables, Minette gambolling at her heels. Nicole counted very carefully, determined to get it right. When, completing the circuit, she discovered that there were one hundred and fifty-seven windows, an odd number, she told herself that she must have got it wrong. She must have forgotten one of the oriel windows, or that funny little round porthole in the attic. She began again, screwing up her eyes, sheltering them from the sun with the flat of her hand. The pain, at its worst, was truly awful. Worse than the time she had fallen off her horse and broken her arm, worse than the tooth abscess she had had in Naples. She wanted to weep, but made herself keep counting. If the baby was to be born soon, then she needed to know about the windows.

One hundred and fifty-five, one hundred and fifty-six, one hundred and fifty-seven. Nicole stood looking upwards, clutching her stomach. Then she heard the car on the drive, its wheels skirring as it came to a halt on the gravel. She watched the driver climb out, and she cried, 'David!'

He ran to her across the courtyard. 'Nicole, what on earth are you doing out here in this heat?'

She said, 'I was counting the windows.' She felt faint. 'You must go indoors.'

'I can't.' She was clutching the mass of old ivy that crawled up the wall for support. 'David, something awful is happening. I have such a pain.'

He said very gently, 'Nicole, you're going to have the baby, that's all.' Then he put his arm round her, holding her to him. After a few minutes he said, 'Where's your case?'

'I haven't packed it yet.'

'It doesn't matter. I think I'd better take you to the nursing-home straight away. Can you walk?'

She said, 'I don't think so,' and he scooped her up carefully in his arms, and put her in the passenger seat. Then he drove very fast to Salisbury.

At the nursing-home, they put her in a wheelchair and pushed her through long corridors covered with white ceramic tiles. She wanted David to stay with her but they would not let him. The nurse tutted when she explained that she had not brought her own night things. They bathed her and then they dressed her in a horrible hospital nightgown, and then they did unspeakable things to her. When she swore at them, they told her off. A doctor came and prodded and peered and did yet more humiliating things. When he had finished he said cheerfully, 'Well, you've a few hours to go, Mrs Kemp. But baby should be here by morning.'

She looked at the clock. Half past five in the afternoon. She found it impossible to believe that this could go on much longer. Her body felt as though it was being torn in two. Lying alone on the cold, high bed, she watched the hands of the clock move slowly round. For a long time there was no-one with her, but when eventually she began to shout and swear again a nurse bustled in and said sharply, 'Your husband's in the corridor, Mrs Kemp. You don't want him to hear you carrying on like this, do you?'

After that, she kept quiet. Mulgrave Rules, she thought: never let them see that you mind. The pain was more dreadful than she could possibly have imagined, but she did not make another sound. She stopped asking for David; she stopped watching the clock; eventually she no longer even noticed the pain. Doctors and nurses fussed around her, but she paid no attention to them, and when they clamped an oxygen mask over her face, she sank into a dark, quiet place inside herself where her consciousness ebbed and flowed. Sometimes she was in this nightmarish place, and sometimes she was at La Rouilly, rowing on the circular green lake with Faith and Jake and Guy.

The night skies had begun to lighten by the time her baby was born. They dragged the infant from her with metal forceps. Nicole heard a slap and a howl, and then she closed her eyes and escaped.

Guy was waiting for her outside the ambulance station. Faith did not see him until he stepped out of the shadows. He said, 'Faith. For God's sake. I've been looking for you all afternoon. Where have you been?'

She hunched her shoulders. 'Here and there.' She could not really remember. She remembered, though, every word of the morning's conversation with Eleanor.

She tried to walk away from him, into the building, but he grabbed her arm.

'I need to talk to you.'

'Let me go, Guy.' She paused, her back to him.

'I said, I need to talk to you.' One of the girls on Faith's shift, entering the building, stared at them.

'I have to go to work. It's six o'clock.'

Guy looked, for a moment, utterly defeated. His hand fell to his side, and he rested his shoulders against the stuccoed wall of the porch, and said, 'Faith. Please. Why won't you talk to me?'

Eleanor's voice echoed. *Guy knows how much you*

275

depend on him. He feels obliged to be kind to you. She shrugged.

'What do you want to talk about, Guy?'

'Not here.' People stumbled past them, going in and out of the ambulance station.

'You don't need to worry about me, you know.' She made herself smile, though she had not slept for more than twenty-four hours and felt dazed with tiredness. 'You don't need to feel that you have to look after me. You've nothing to repay us for, Guy.' Her voice had an unnatural brightness. 'We're all managing very well.'

He looked at her blankly. Then he said, 'I don't know what the *hell* you're talking about, but if you won't give me five minutes of your time, in private, then I shall set fire to this building.'

He took his cigarette lighter out of his pocket, flicked the flame. She muttered, 'Dear God,' and thought quickly. There was a small courtyard behind the ambulance station, full of dustbins and sandbags and fire buckets. She led him there, and sat down on a heap of sandbags. It had begun to rain again.

He said, 'I wanted to ask you something.' He had put up the collar of his jacket; rain dripped down his nose. 'I tried to speak to you yesterday, but I couldn't, because of the others.'

For the first time that evening, she looked at him properly. He was unshaven, and there were dark shadows round his eyes.

'What did you want to ask me, Guy?'

'I need to know how you feel about me.' His voice was abrupt.

Faith put her head in her hands. She thought of Jake, Ralph, Poppy, her dreadful interview with Eleanor, the whole intractable bloody mess of it, and felt exhausted.

'I can't make it any more plain,' he said, and she knew, looking at his dark, angry face, that Eleanor had told the truth, and that she had become for Guy an uncomfortable and wearying responsibility.

He said, 'I want to know whether we're still just friends – a sort of honorary brother and sister—'

She raised her shoulders, almost unable to speak. Tears ached behind her eyeballs, and rain dribbled down the back of her collar. 'I never meant to ask anything of you, Guy.' Her voice shook. 'I know that when the dog . . . and when I was ill . . . and in La Rouilly, when the snake bit me . . . but if you've begun to believe that you're obliged to be nice to me, then I really think that—'

He flung out his arms and shouted, 'What on earth are you maundering about, woman? I'm trying to tell you that I love you!'

Faith stared at him. After a while, she whispered, 'Pardon?'

Someone rapped on the window and shouted, '*Mulgrave!* For heaven's sake! It's ten past!' There was a flicker of white at the window.

She said, 'Say it again, Guy.' Eyes wide, she looked at him, her voice low and urgent, and repeated, 'Say it again. I need to hear you say it again.'

'I love you, Faith.' The anger seemed to slip away from him, and he sounded pleading, defenceless. 'It's taken a hell of a long time for me to realize it – I've been quite unbelievably dense – but I love you.'

She was aware first of an immense relief. Eleanor had been wrong. The disarrayed shapes of Eleanor's making fell into place. She stared at the pattern, wondering whether it would jiggle, shift, alter once more. Guy had come to her not out of a sense of duty,

277

but because he loved her. Her heart lifted and flew.

He rubbed his outspread fingers against his face, and said, 'But I've no idea what you think of me.' His voice was anguished. 'I believe that you care for me – but I don't know *how* you care for me.'

She thought, *I believe that I have loved you since I was eleven years old, Guy. I've loved you since I walked into the kitchen at La Rouilly and saw you for the first time, with dust all over your boots, and your eyes lighting up as you smiled at me. There hasn't been a time when I haven't loved you, one way or another.*

The window latch rattled; knuckles rapped on the glass. He said, 'You see, I've thought about it all day. I've done nothing but think about it.' He tried to smile. 'I almost plastered the wrong bloody arm this morning.' He looked spent, exhausted. His eyes were dark and red-rimmed. 'Do you love me, Faith? Could you love me a little?'

She went to him, and laid her head against his chest. 'Of course I love you, idiot,' she said softly. 'How could I possibly not love you?' A muffled groan, and then he wrapped his arms around her, and kissed the crown of her head. She thought that though one often does not recognize moments of perfect happiness until they are over, she nevertheless knew that this moment was complete. She wouldn't have changed anything: she wouldn't have changed the drip from the drainpipe that formed a puddle beneath their feet, or the rough sandpaperiness of his chin against her cheek as he kissed her. Only when she thought, *Eleanor*, did the moment darken a little, and tarnish at the edges. But then she closed her eyes, concentrating on the warmth of his arms around her and the utter delight of the present.

The latch rattled again. A head poked out. 'Equipment check, Mulgrave. At the double.' Inquisitive eyes stared first at Guy, then at Faith. '*Now*, Mulgrave. Or Deakin will tear you into little shreds, and sell your bones for glue.'

Miss Deakin was the supervisor. Faith muttered, 'I have to go, Guy,' but she heard him call out, as she ran to the front door: 'I can't go on like this, you see. I can't live a lie.' He caught up with her, and seized her shoulders, pulling her towards him.

Her breath hurt in her chest, as though she had run a very long way. She said, 'The park tomorrow morning – I'll meet you under the lime tree, Guy, at half past eight. Under the lime tree.'

Faith was glad that Miss Deakin, the supervisor, had chosen that night to check every item of equipment in the station. Counting pencils, checking bandages, she had little time to think. As she crawled around the ambulance, searching for a missing oil can, the bruises on her knees distracted her from the memory of Guy's embrace, and Miss Deakin's scolding erased temporarily her recollection of the hatred in Eleanor's voice.

At six o'clock her shift ended, and she walked home. Mahonia Street was cold and unlit. She called out, 'Rufus? Jake?' but there was no reply. As she moved around the house, throwing open doors to empty rooms, she lurched between elation and despair. Memories, half-finished sentences, incomplete fragments of thought, drifted through her head. She knew that she should rest, but could not, and continued to wander from room to room, unable to settle. She tried to remember how long it was since she had slept, but lost count, adding up the hours. Days, she thought. She glanced at her watch. It was half past seven.

In her bedroom, she opened a drawer, and stared at its contents. Her clothes, her dresses and scarves and hats, lay folded: neat, colourful reminders of the past. She touched the Douillet dress, running the back of her hand along its silky folds. Would she, wearing this dress perhaps, walk once more along a beach with Guy? Would she, dressed in her eau-de-Nil Schiaparelli, dine with him, to a background of candles and soft music? Carefully, she lifted the Holly Blue dress out of the drawer. Would he undo these dozen tiny pearl buttons? Would he slide this dress from her naked shoulders, and let it slip to the floor, a pool of lilac-blue crêpe de Chine?

She sat down on the edge of the bed, the dress cradled in her arms like a baby. She reminded herself coldly that if she took Guy as her lover, then she would be no better than Linda Forrester. She would have done to the Neville family what Linda had done to the Mulgraves. When she recalled the chilling hatred she had glimpsed the previous morning in Eleanor's eyes, she shivered. If she became Guy's lover, then she would deserve that hatred. She thought of Ralph with Linda Forrester, and she hunched her knees up to her chin, wrapping her arms around herself to quell her trembling. Could she humiliate Eleanor as Linda Forrester had humiliated Poppy? Closing her eyes, breathing in the lavender-scented folds of the Holly Blue dress, Faith acknowledged that she could. Just for a moment, then, she hated herself. She looked at her watch again. Ten past eight. If she was to be at the park by half past, she should leave.

She almost stood up, almost left the room. But then

she remembered standing beside Guy in the nursery of the Malt Street house, looking down at the sleeping child in the cot. The baby's small, perfect features; the love in Guy's eyes. What of Oliver? Though she might no longer care for Eleanor's good opinion of her, could she take Guy away from his baby son? Could she hurt an innocent child?

The euphoria of the previous evening faded, and she saw only the utter wrongness that becoming Guy's lover would entail. She forced herself to remember everything Eleanor had said to her. *He needs security and order . . . to abandon all I've given him would, I believe, destroy him.* She remembered Guy at La Rouilly: the neatly folded clothes in his rucksack, the care and precision with which he had dissected the chicken. She had recognized that very first day that he was different, that he was not a Mulgrave, that he kept to other rules. That had been part of his fascination. She gnawed her fingernails, and thought, *Eleanor is right, Eleanor told the truth.* Though Eleanor might not love Guy, she nevertheless understood him, and had something to offer him: the sort of measured, ordered existence that would allow him to continue with the work he loved.

Not one of us is measured, or ordered, she thought bitterly. We blunder through life, careless of our effect on others. The Holly Blue dress slid unnoticed to the floor, and Faith rested her aching forehead against her knees. She remembered Nicole, her belly swollen with her forthcoming child, telling her that she was no longer certain that she loved David. And with a twist of panic, she thought of Jake. His continued absence frightened her. Recollecting the suppressed violence in his eyes as he had said, *I'm trying to work things out.*

I'm trying to make a considered assessment of the facts, she felt sick with dread.

She thought, we are falling apart. We've never had much in the way of roots, and what few we have had have been cut away. The disintegration that had begun the previous year in France had speeded up, and was whirling out of control. Certainties that Faith had once taken for granted now seemed threatened. Her parents' marriage. Nicole's relationship with David. Jake's love for his father. The after-effects of their expulsion from France reverberated: destroying, dividing, splintering. She had once been afraid of the bombs, but the breakdown of the accustomed boundaries of her life frightened her even more.

For her there was only one place of safety. She remembered the lime tree, and the keys drifting from it in the heat. 'What of *me*?' she said out loud. She could do nothing for her family, but she could salvage some happiness for herself. She was seized by a sense of urgency. When she glanced down, the hands of her watch seemed to have turned with unnatural rapidity. Twenty-five to nine. She must hurry.

She ran downstairs, pulling a jacket from the peg, pushing her feet into the first pair of shoes she found. She could not find her door key. I might not need it, she thought. I may not come back. She flung open the door.

And saw a familiar figure, turning the corner into the road. Not Guy. Nor Jake. But Poppy.

She knew, seeing Poppy, that she had waited too long, that she had left it too late. At first she thought, she knows. Ma knows about Pa. The early morning sunshine blinded her. Her unnatural restlessness evaporated, and she felt drained with tiredness, and leaned against the door jamb, waiting. Poppy looked up.

'Oh, *Faith*,' she cried. She had been walking fast, and was gasping for breath. 'Faith, such awful news.'

She whispered, 'Pa . . . ?' but Poppy just looked back at her, dazed, her eyes dark pools in a bone-white face, and shook her head.

'David sent me a telegram.' Poppy's voice shook. 'Nicole has had a baby daughter.'

Faith could not speak. Fear gathered, a small, hard ball in the pit of her stomach.

'The child's very small and weak,' said Poppy. 'And Nicole is terribly ill. Oh, Faith, they're afraid that she may die.'

He waited until midday. The lime tree's leaves shivered in the heat; keys whirled, tiny parachutes, tumbling to the ground. When he was quite sure that she would not come, he walked to her house in Islington. Rufus Foxwell answered the door. She has gone away, Rufus told him, she didn't say where.

Guy went back to Holland Square. Waiting at the park, joy had transmuted to bewilderment; but now he was seized by despair. His way home was impeded by the drifts of rubble strewn across the pavements, and the fenced-off areas that lay in the shadows of the bomb-damaged buildings. Standing beneath the towering crags of bricks and mortar, looking up, he thought none of it was as unstable as love.

CHAPTER NINE

Poppy spent a fortnight at Compton Deverall, and then returned to Heronsmead. By then, Nicole was out of danger, and by then Poppy was able to acknowledge to herself that althought both Laura and David Kemp had been welcoming – they had, indeed, gone out of their way to ensure that she was comfortable – she had not felt at ease staying in their house. It had seemed to Poppy that both the Kemps and their beautiful home represented a way of life that she might once have chosen for herself. Her impulse on a beach at Deauville twenty-one years ago, and the passing of time, had excluded her from that way of life. Long ago, she, a Vanburgh, had been the equal of the Kemps; now she was an outcast, a vagabond. Her hair, her clothes, were, even in these straitened times, wrong. Sometimes she struggled to remember to choose the right cutlery; sometimes she thought that even the way she spoke betrayed her. Ralph would not have noticed, but she, who had belonged to people like this, did.

As soon as Nicole was well enough to leave the nursing-home, Poppy decided to go home. Faith and Laura would look after Nicole and the baby; there was no need for her to stay. Though Elizabeth was a delightful, dark little thing, Poppy held back from giving her heart to her granddaughter. Fear of loss, she acknowledged, warned her against loving. Five years ago her fourth child had died; in the summer of 1940 she had only narrowly avoided leaving France without her surviving son. When the telegram had arrived telling her of Elizabeth's difficult birth and Nicole's illness, she had stared out of the train window as she had travelled to London to collect Faith, filled with dread that she would lose both her daughter and her granddaughter.

Pausing at the verge, Poppy put down her case and took a deep breath. The level marshland extended to either side of the narrow road. In the distance the sea shimmered, a thin band of silk. Though September had only just begun, it seemed to Poppy that autumn had already touched the landscape, that it could be seen in the quivering seed-heads of the reeds and felt in the cold edge to the wind. In this featureless, shimmering world, she might have been the only scrap of life.

She tried to remember when she had last seen Ralph. Not for more than a month, she realized. He had left for London several weeks before Elizabeth's birth, and throughout the fortnight that Nicole had been in danger no-one had been able to trace him. Of all that Ralph had done wrong, that, Poppy thought, she could least forgive. Though Nicole had always been his favourite child, though he had spoiled and cosseted and indulged her as an infant, when Nicole had most needed him, Ralph had not been there.

She began to walk again. She could see in the distance the village, the church spire, and her own little cottage, straddling the border between hamlet and marsh. Suddenly, she longed to be home and enclosed within those familiar flint walls, lighting a fire in the living-room grate, and shutting the door, keeping out the world. She had become unsociable, she thought. She, who had for years been surrounded by people, now longed to be left alone with her misery and her anger, to nurse them in solitude.

Her shoulders ached with the weight of her case as she turned onto the rutted track that led from the road to the cottage. She smiled wearily as she opened the gate. The flecked walls of the cottage, the shifting reed-beds beyond, the mournful cry of the curlew, all seemed welcoming. Inside the cottage, she put down the suitcase with a sigh of relief and flung her hat and gloves onto a chair.

She was filling the kettle when she heard the footstep behind her. When she swung round, she saw Ralph, standing in the doorway. He looked more than usually dishevelled: the pocket of his coat had come away from the rest of the material, and the sole of one of his shoes flapped loosely, a fish's open mouth.

He said quickly, 'How is she? Tell me that she's all right.'

She looked at him coldly. 'I assume that you're speaking about Nicole.'

'For God's sake, Poppy . . . I've been out of my mind with worry.' There was a wild look in his eyes.

She took down the tea caddy. 'But not worried enough,' she said, 'to visit.'

'I didn't hear till this morning. I came back here last night. You were gone . . . you hadn't left a note . . . this morning that bloody nosy parker of a woman from the vicarage called and told me what had happened . . . took the greatest pleasure in telling me my daughter was dying. I tried to phone, but the blasted telephone wires are down again.' He seized her arm. 'For pity's sake, Poppy . . . tell me she's not . . . she's not—'

286

She saw that there were tears in his eyes. She said, 'Nicole's making a good recovery. They've allowed her to go home, though she's still very weak.'

As she pulled away from him, she heard him whisper, 'Thank God. Thank God.'

She poured boiling water into the teapot. 'Where were you, Ralph? Why didn't you come? There are trains, after all.'

He muttered, 'I'd run out of cash.'

He looks like a beggar, she thought. She said coldly, 'How much money do you have, Ralph?'

'One shilling and threepence,' he admitted. 'I had to cadge a lift. Been hitching lifts all week.' There was a lost, hopeless look in his eyes.

She hissed, 'Where have you *been*?'

'Oh, here and there,' he mumbled.

She thought, *You have been with* her. Her hatred dizzied her.

'I thought I'd come home.' He touched her shoulder tentatively. 'Got into a bit of a mess, Pops.'

Got into a bit of a mess, Pops. She was, she thought, supposed to forgive him, to kiss him, to make love to him. Just as she always had done.

'I have a headache,' said Poppy. She pulled away, unable to bear to be near him. 'I'm taking my tea to bed. I'm sure that if you look hard enough, Ralph, you'll find something to eat.'

Afterwards, Faith often thought that if Nicole had not been so ill during those first few weeks, then she might have got to know her daughter, might have learned to love her. As it was, she lay grey-faced and still in the nursing-home, and later, at Compton Deverall, sat propped on half a dozen pillows in bed, staring out of the window, Minette tucked under one arm. Faith or Laura fed the baby, bathed her, soothed her.

Elizabeth had fine dark hair, navy-blue eyes, and a pale, translucent skin. She was, Faith thought, quite perfect. She rarely cried, woke promptly for her feed at four-hourly intervals, and was tolerant of her aunt's initial clumsiness. She had a sunny disposition, smiling at six weeks old, laughing at eight. Faith loved her utterly. Elizabeth filled some of the gaps that her leaving of Guy had torn in her heart.

David returned to Compton Deverall when his daughter was two months old. Faith took Elizabeth for a walk in her pram while David spent time with Nicole. She was heading back through the woods when she caught sight of him on the path, and waved.

He ran to catch up with her. 'Here, let me.' He took the handles of the huge Silver Cross pram from her, and pushed. 'You're very brave, Faith, to steer this thing through the rabbit holes.'

'It's almost as bad,' she agreed, 'as driving the ambulance.'

He glanced at her. 'Will you go back to it?'

She shook her head. 'I've resigned. I told them a few weeks ago.'

There was a gust of wind; a few papery gold leaves drifted from the beech trees. David said, 'I think that this is quite my favourite time of year.'

'The trees do look rather splendid.'

'Autumn suits the house, don't you agree? Summer's too brash for such an ageing beauty.'

She laughed. He pushed for a while, and then he said, 'She looks better, don't you think?'

'Nicole?' His anxiety was written in his eyes. Faith said firmly, 'Nicole's almost well again. She told me yesterday that she was bored.'

'That night – the night that Elizabeth was born – I couldn't live through too many nights like that.'

She glanced at him and said mockingly, 'David, you're almost completely grey.'

'I know.' He ran a rueful hand over his head.

They emerged from the cover of the trees. 'I think,' said Faith, 'that I'll leave at the end of the week.'

'So soon? Faith, you can stay as long as you like – you mustn't feel that because I've come home—'

She shook her head. 'It's not that. It's just that Nicole's better now, and she'll want Lizzie to herself.'

She deceived him, though. She would go because, if she went, then Nicole must surely become acquainted with her daughter. As long as she stayed, Nicole could pretend that the child was not hers; that Elizabeth did not exist.

'We'll be sorry to lose you,' said David, 'but you've a life of your own, of course.'

'I suppose.' She remembered sitting in her bedroom in Mahonia Road, the Holly Blue dress cradled in her lap, trying to decide whether to go to Guy. Poppy's arrival and Nicole's illness had, in the end, made the decision for her. Day and night, she tried to convince herself her decision had been the right one. Since then, she had neither written to nor telephoned Guy.

'Will you go back to London?'

Faith shook her head. 'To tell the truth, I haven't the least idea what I'll do. I've been racking my brains for weeks. Perhaps I'll join one of the services. Can you see me in khaki, David, mending tanks?'

He laughed. 'Perhaps not. Though I'm sure that you could do whatever you chose to do.'

'It's the choosing that's so difficult, isn't it?' She

sighed. 'I only know what I *don't* want to do. You seem to have everything sorted out, David. How did you decide?'

'It was easy for me. I went to Marlborough because my father went there, and I went on to Oxford because that was what one did, and so on.' He looked at her. 'What sort of things do you like doing?'

She had become very fond of David: he was so comfortingly sensible and intelligent and unchanging. She thought for a while.

'I like to be busy. I hate to have nothing to do. I like – oh, making up my own mind about things.'

They had reached the garden. Faith sat on a stone bench; David rocked the pram as Elizabeth slept. 'You see,' she explained, 'I never went to school. I'm afraid that when they ask me what exams I've passed, and I tell them that I haven't passed any, then no-one will want me. That's what's happened to Jake, more or less.'

'Jake?'

She nodded. 'He's very bored, and always in trouble. Something . . . something awful happened in London just before Elizabeth was born, and I'm afraid—' She broke off.

'Tell me.' His voice was gentle.

She shook her head. 'I hadn't meant to say anything. What happened doesn't reflect well on my family.' She smiled at him. 'You have a way of making people confide in you, David. You'd make a wonderful torturer.'

He laughed. 'I'll take that as a compliment. Anyway – Jake . . .'

'He's in the army, as you know, but it's terribly dull. So he's acting the fool and getting into trouble, and I'm sure that he'll end up being court-martialled and getting shot at dawn.'

'It's more likely square-bashing or potato peeling these days, I'm afraid.'

'He's all right really, you see, David. Jake just needs to be needed.'

He glanced down at her. 'Your brother's fluent in French, isn't he?'

'And Italian, and Spanish. We all are.'

David looked angry. 'Appalling how such useful people can still slip through the net. Look, Faith, don't worry. I'll see what I can do about Jake.'

Elizabeth had begun to grizzle. 'It's getting cold,' David said. The sun was a dull, copper coin in a leaden sky. He began to push the pram across the lawn. 'I'd better take her indoors.' He glanced back. 'And you should think about the Land Army. It might suit you, Faith.'

Faith told Nicole that she was leaving Compton Deverall at the end of the week. Nicole looked dismayed.

'But what will I *do*?'

They were in the morning-room, which looked out to the lawns and the woods. Faith said firmly, 'You'll do all the things you normally do. Riding . . . and reading . . . and—'

'I've read every readable book in the library. There's only dreadful things like Cooper's *History of Wiltshire* left. Anyway, I meant, what shall I do about the *baby*.'

'Elizabeth,' said Faith. 'She has a name. Elizabeth.'

'I know.' Nicole sighed. 'I didn't choose it. So dreary.'

'I think it's a lovely name. Elizabeth Anne Kemp. It's nicely old-fashioned. And solid.'

Nicole left the sofa and went to the window. 'I was going to call it Edward after David's father. With Fitzwilliam after Mr Darcy for a second name. That would have been lovely, wouldn't it?' She traced patterns on the glass. 'She should have been a boy, you see.'

Faith said tentatively, 'Perhaps in the future—'

'No. Never. I shall never have another baby. It was all so unbelievably ghastly. So, you see, it should have been a boy. David needs a son.'

'David adores Elizabeth.'

'Girls don't keep the family name, do they? So I've let him down. There have been Kemps at Compton Deverall since the sixteenth century. Now, because of me, there won't be any more.'

'You've got to get to know Elizabeth. If you spent some time with her you would love her, and nothing else would matter.'

Nicole perched on the window seat. 'But she's so dull, Faith.' She sighed. 'I do try, I really do. I feed her, and she falls asleep. I sing to her and she falls asleep. I showed her the painting I bought for her the other day, and she wasn't in the least bit interested.'

'She's far too young to care about that sort of thing.'

'Then someone else can look after her until she's older,' said Nicole firmly. 'I'll like her in the future, when she's more amusing, I know that I shall. It's just that now she's so impossibly dull. Dogs are more interesting, aren't they? At least you can play with a dog.'

Faith felt defeated. She made one last effort. 'If you learned to look after her—'

'Faith, you know that I should be hopeless at looking after her.' Nicole smiled. 'I should forget I had her, and leave her on the bus or something. You know that I would.'

'But—'

'Laura will look after her. Laura likes her. As for me, I'll send her lots of presents, and when she's old enough I'll take her to the theatre and the opera. And you'll find her lovely dresses, and Jake will teach her to row and shoot.'

Faith thought, looking at Nicole, that the last two months had changed her a great deal. She was thinner, taller even, and the fine bones and planes of her face were almost visible through her pale skin.

'What are you going to do, Nicole?'

'I'm going away for a while. You know I can't bear to be in the same place for too long. I thought I'd like to live somewhere like this – somewhere old, somewhere with a history, but I can't seem to get used to it. It weighs me down.' Her tone was calm, matter-of-fact. The alterations in Nicole were not only superficial, Faith thought: the experience of giving birth and rubbing shoulders with death had made her grow up at last.

'Where will you go?'

'To London first, I thought. There's masses of people in London.'

There's masses of people in London. She sounded, Faith thought, like Ralph. 'And David . . . ?'

'I'll always love David. I only want what's best for him.' Nicole slid off the window sill. 'I'll come back, Faith, you'll see. You really mustn't worry.'

* * *

293

Nicole left Compton Deverall the following month. By then, Faith had joined the Land Army, and David had returned to his mysterious work. Nicole told Laura that she was going to London to buy baby linen and new clothes for herself. She was thinner than she had been before her pregnancy, and nothing fitted. Laura gave her all her clothing coupons and recommended a woman in the Edgware Road who made marvellous dresses out of unpromising scraps of fabric. Nicole hugged her, and kissed Elizabeth, and caught the train.

Travelling, she felt, as she always did, free. A weight seemed to slip from her shoulders; she was almost overcome by relief. She had been told that one did not remember the pain of childbirth, but she had found that to be untrue. She was haunted by remembered pain and loneliness, and worse, by the realization that even one's own body could seem not to belong to one. She tried to let her worst memories disappear into the train's fast slipstream, so that they were lost in the distance.

In London, she opened up the Devonshire Place house. The following day she telephoned a friend at the BBC, who promised to help her find work. In the evening Thierry knocked on the door of the house. He took her to a restaurant in Soho. Though the food was uninteresting, the small room, with its blacked-out windows and fallen plaster, was crammed with off-duty servicemen and women. A pianist, tucked into a corner of the room, played popular songs, and everyone roared the choruses. Between courses, they danced. The remainder of the weight of depression that Nicole had carried with her since Elizabeth's birth slipped away, and she felt light-hearted. She was, she reminded herself as Thierry steered her round the tiny dance floor, still only eighteen years old.

In the early hours of the morning, Thierry walked her back to Devonshire Place. In the shadow of the doorway, he kissed her. After a while he said, 'Aren't you going to ask me indoors, Nicole?'

She shook her head. 'No.'

'Why not?'

'Because you would assume things.'

He looked cross. 'What do you mean?'

'You know what I mean, Thierry. You'd assume that I wanted you to make love to me.'

'But you do want me to, don't you?' He sounded sulky.

It was true that her body, bruised and dulled by childbirth, had seemed to come alive again as he kissed her. She tried to explain. 'I believe that one should only make love to someone one truly loves, you see, Thierry.'

She saw the hurt in his eyes. He rarely looked vulnerable, but he did so now. He said pointedly, 'Then why are you here and not in your country house, waiting for your husband?'

'There are different kinds of love, aren't there? I thought David would be everything to me, but he wasn't.' For the first time she calmly faced the realization that she had shrunk from over the past few months.

'So you're going to leave the poor bastard.' Thierry took out his cigarette case.

'It's kinder to make things clear now, don't you think? Then he can look for someone else. I can't stay with David – even if I could keep on pretending that he was The One, I've still failed him.'

Striking a match, Thierry looked at her, eyes narrowed. 'How have you failed him?'

'I had a girl, not a boy. David needs a son. So it's better that I go now and then he can look for someone else who'll give him a son.'

Thierry smoked in silence for a while, and then he said, 'That's just an excuse, Nicole.'

She shrugged. 'You may believe that if you wish. But it's part of it, an important part of it. I know that I can't be the sort of wife David needs. And I can't be the sort of mother Elizabeth needs. I wouldn't be any good for either of them. I tried it, and it didn't work. So it's better that I go now. The longer I leave it, the more it'll hurt them.'

He said, 'But you won't sleep with me?'

She smiled. 'Not tonight, darling. Another time, perhaps, but now I need to be alone for a while.' The realization surprised her.

When, two days later, dancing in the Bag O' Nails, they told her that Thierry was dead, she did not at first believe them. *Shot down over Holland*, they said, *gone for a burton*. She was convinced that a mistake had been made, and that at any moment he would walk into the room, and look at her with those dark eyes of his, that seemed to see her too clearly. Others had died, of course – Johnny, who had rowed her along the silky green waters of the Avon, and the Canadian who had taught her to jive, and the Dutch boy who had let her ride on the crossbar of his bicycle. And so many more. But it had never occurred to her that Thierry should die. How could such a price have been asked of someone who had paid so much already?

*　　*　　*

At the beginning of November, Faith started work at Rudges' Farm. It was a dairy farm, set among the rolling hills of Somerset, not far from Taunton.

When she mentioned to one of the other Land Army girls that she was lodging with Mrs Fitzgerald, the girl stared at her, open-mouthed, and said, 'I say. You do know she's a witch, don't you?' Faith laughed disbelievingly, and the girl added, 'Betty Lismore was lodged with her. Couldn't stand it. Said she was a stuck-up, mad old cow. Betty left after a week, got a room with the postmistress.'

Mrs Fitzgerald's cottage was surrounded by woodland, at the end of a winding, muddy track. In the evenings barn owls shrieked, and beneath a sickle moon the asymmetrical roof of the cottage gleamed like pewter. To the original single-storey brick building had been tagged on a hotch-potch of little rooms made of packing cases and metal boxes, hammered out until they were flat. The metal walls still bore the remains of the advertisements for the products they had once enclosed. At night, in bed, Faith read the walls of her room. 'Knight's Castile prevents tired skin.' 'Ovaltine, the nation's nerve-restoring beverage.'

Mrs Fitzgerald herself, Faith often thought, matched the cottage. She was tall, in her late forties, her long, greying red hair heaped anyhow on top of her head. Her clothes were unconventionally styled, originally hued. She did not seem to possess a coat, but wore, on her rambles through the woodland, a long black cloak – the source of the witch rumour, Faith assumed. The walls of the cottage were hung with vast woven squares, the floors covered with striped rugs.

Faith's day began at four o'clock in the morning, when she ate a doorstep of bread and jam, washed down with tea, and cycled down the track from the cottage to the road that led to Rudges' Farm. In a freezing milking-shed, she cleaned the cows and washed their udders, and milked them. The milk was then bottled, a torment of tubes and metal gadgets and ice-cold liquid. By the time she finished, her hands were chapped and blue. She breakfasted at the farm, and then the cowshed and all the equipment had to be washed and sterilized. After dinner at midday, Faith would invariably fall asleep for an hour. Sometimes she curled up in the shed with the cows to keep warm. The whole process had to be gone through a second time during the afternoon. At half past six she cycled back to Mrs Fitzgerald's cottage, ate whatever supper had been left out for her, and fell asleep again.

By the end of her first fortnight in Somerset, Faith reckoned that she and Mrs Fitzgerald had exchanged half a dozen sentences – partly because Mrs Fitzgerald did not encourage conversation, partly because they were rarely in the cottage at the same time. She and Mrs Fitzgerald would have gone on like that for months, Faith often thought, hardly speaking to each other, if she had not worn the Holly Blue dress. She retrieved it one evening from the bottom of her ruck-sack, a remnant of better times. Shaking out the creases, she wanted to weep. But she forced back the tears, and, after bathing in the tin tub in front of the fire, she put it on instead of her sensible skirt and jersey.

Mrs Fitzgerald, coming into the kitchen while Faith was eating her supper, stopped and stared and said, 'Good heavens. Paquin.'

'Rather moth-eaten Paquin, I'm afraid.' There were several tiny holes around the hem.

'Better than those frightful breeches.'

Faith laughed. 'Though not as warm.'

Mrs Fitzgerald placed several jars on the draining board. 'When I was younger, I had a Paquin coat. I adored it. Wore it until it fell apart.'

'This belonged to a friend of mine, who lived in France.'

Mrs Fitzgerald eyed her. 'A very generous friend, to give you a Paquin dress.'

'Genya gave it to me for my collection. I call it my Holly Blue dress. After the butterfly, you know.'

'Your collection?'

'I like old clothes,' explained Faith. 'I used to have dozens. I rescued a few when I left France. I've a couple of Fortuny dresses that I found in a street market in Marseilles, and a lovely Douillet gown, and some other things.'

Mrs Fitzgerald said, 'What a surprising girl you are. I had assumed you were a dunderhead, like the rest of them. The last girl used to scuttle out of the room whenever she saw me. It was like living with a mouse.'

'They think you're a witch, you know.'

Mrs Fitzgerald roared with laughter. When she had recovered, she said, 'They've seen me collecting my samples by moonlight, I suspect.' She took one of the jars from the sink, opened it, and showed it to Faith.

Faith peered into the jar. 'Lichen.'

'Yes.'

'Does it have to be collected by moonlight?'

'Certainly not. I weave by day because the light's good, so I sometimes find myself scouting around the forest for plants at midnight.' She added impatiently, 'For dyes, girl. Brazil wood for red, woad for blue,

299

weld for yellow . . . and the lichens make marvellous ochres and browns.'

Faith glanced at the rugs, and the woven fabric slung over the old sofa. 'You made all these?'

'Yes. Do you like them?'

'They're glorious.'

'Not as glorious as a Paquin dress, though. Such a remarkable colour. How I should love to reproduce it . . .' Her eyes narrowed as she touched the filmy silk. 'But you should put a jersey on, before you die of cold.' She glanced at Faith. 'Drink?'

She was not, Faith saw, offering tea. 'Wine. How splendid.'

'You may not think so when you taste it. Parsnip. Made it myself. Last year's vintage.' Mrs Fitzgerald poured two glasses, and gave one to Faith. Then she sat down on the sofa, and half closed her eyes. 'I could almost imagine myself back in my palmier days . . . you, in that gown . . . a wineglass in my hand . . .'

'Did you own a Paquin dress?'

'Several. I sold the lot of 'em eventually. For a fraction of what they were worth, I suspect.' She looked fiercely at Faith. 'Let that be a lesson to you. Palmy days never last.'

'I never expect them to,' said Faith politely.

'Very wise.' Mrs Fitzgerald raised her glass. 'Then we shall drink to fortitude.'

'To fortitude,' echoed Faith.

'I dare say it requires a fair amount of fortitude to plough fields or hoe turnips or whatever it is you do for that rascal at Rudges' Farm.'

'I milk cows,' said Faith. 'And actually, I quite like it.'

'Why? Because you feel in tune with nature, or some such nonsense?' Mrs Fitzgerald's voice was scornful.

Faith considered. 'Because I don't have to think. Because I'm so exhausted at the end of the day that I just fall into bed and don't even dream.'

'Don't you like thinking?'

She said, 'Not at the moment,' and swallowed the remainder of her glass of wine. It was sharp and potent and it made her head feel pleasantly fuzzy.

Mrs Fitzgerald said brusquely, 'I won't pry. I can't bear people who pry. Can you face a second glass?'

Faith nodded, and looked around the room. 'Have you always lived here?'

Mrs Fitzgerald snorted. 'Not when I owned my three Paquin gowns. I lived somewhere rather more splendid then. But I ran off with a scoundrel, I'm afraid – Johnnie Fitzgerald was divorced, so you can imagine the scandal – and I lost everything.'

'Did you love him?'

'Madly.'

'What happened?'

'Johnnie fancied himself a racing driver. He put every penny I owned – he hadn't a farthing himself – into some ridiculous car – and smashed it and himself to pieces at Le Mans.'

'How awful.' The words seemed hopelessly inadequate.

Mrs Fitzgerald shrugged. 'My fault. Everyone warned me against him. But I wouldn't listen.'

'Do you' – Faith had begun to feel cold – 'do you regret it?'

Mrs Fitzgerald frowned. 'No. No, I can't say that I do. It's left me on my uppers rather, which is why I bought this place and take in lodgers . . . but no, I don't regret it.'

Faith had to gulp down her second glass of wine and

gather up all her courage before saying: 'Then you believe that one should follow the heart?'

Mrs Fitzgerald looked at her. She was silent for a while, and then she said, 'I sense a great deal of misery behind that question. My dear, I really have no idea. I did what I did, and no-one but myself suffered for it. My parents were dead, you see, and I'd only a guardian who really wasn't very interested. So I don't think I can answer you.'

Faith sat for a moment, looking out at the stars. Then she stood up. 'I must go to bed now. Good night, Mrs Fitzgerald, and thank you for the wine.'

'Constance,' said Mrs Fitzgerald. 'My name is Constance. But my friends call me Con.'

Guy had taken to going for a drink in the evening after surgery, before going home. It was the only way he could face Holland Square and Eleanor.

The months that had passed since his futile wait under the lime tree for Faith had reinforced in him his awareness of his own failure. He had seen that he was not perceptive, that he had misunderstood others and, most of all, he had misunderstood himself. Though he might be sensitive to his patients' needs, fears and pains, he had not been aware of his own. He had married Eleanor believing that her confidence, her strength of purpose, was necessary to him, only to discover that confidence could turn easily to obdurateness, and that strength of purpose might entail a blindness to others' needs. He knew, had known for a long time now, that he did not love Eleanor. He would have remained with her for Oliver's sake, but without Oliver there was nothing at all to disguise the emptiness of his marriage.

So he had immersed himself in his work, as he always did when he was unhappy. He had taken on extra sessions at the hospital, and as well as his own patients he now cared for the patients of an adjacent surgery, whose doctor had had a nervous breakdown after the Blitz. He spent as little time as possible at Holland Square. Eleanor put down his short temper and exhaustion to overwork. But Guy sensed that behind her forbearance there was triumph. He sensed that she believed that she had won.

None of the Mulgraves had visited Holland Square since those hot early August days. Neither Ralph, nor Jake, nor, of course, Faith. Seized by a mixture of fury and despair, Guy had once more visited the house in Mahonia Road. It had been autumn, and he had been rather drunk, and he had hammered at the front door until a dressing-gowned neighbour had emerged from the adjacent house and crossly told him that No. 17 had been uninhabited for months.

He had no idea where she had gone. He had only understood the implications of her leaving. Though she had told him that she loved him, she had not loved him enough. It had crossed his mind that he might never see her again, and he had been unsure whether to be relieved or whether to weep. Since then, his anger had faded a little, and his overwhelming emotion had been one of regret. If, years ago, he had understood – on that last brief visit to La Rouilly, perhaps – that he loved her, then he might have scooped her up and brought her back to England with him and been granted years of happiness. As it was, he had missed his chance.

Thus the two shots of whisky each evening. Guy drank in central London, invariably choosing an anonymous pub where he knew no-one, and where the barmen did not attempt conversation. He avoided the East End. His patients must not witness their doctor's attempts to steel himself before going home.

Tonight, Guy sat by a window in a saloon bar in a narrow alleyway off Piccadilly. The weather was foul: sleety rain oozed from a leaden sky and gathered in the pockmarks left in the roads by the previous winter's bombs. Now, at the end of the November of 1941, London was wearied by war. The great and proud city was tattered and tarnished, almost exhausted by the demands that had been made on it. From a corner of the bar room, the wireless announced in tones of refined cheerfulness another series of disasters: Germany's advance on Moscow, Rommel's counter-attack in North Africa, the Allied shipping losses in the Atlantic. Guy broke his rule, and ordered a third Scotch. Cradling the glass between his palms, he looked out of the window at the grey, dreary scene, and felt a sudden intense longing for a pre-war France, for summer, for the past, for a time when joy and optimism had been easy. In spite of the cold and damp, he could, if he closed his eyes, almost *smell* the long August days at La Rouilly, and the thick, bitter, garlicky scent of the woods where he had walked with Faith . . .

When he opened his eyes, and looked through the window, he saw her. It was as though his imagination had conjured her out of the ether. Fair hair bunched at the nape of her neck, her slight, graceful figure weaving through the crowds on the pavement. She wore a navy-blue raincoat and carried an umbrella. Guy slammed down his glass on the table, and dashed out of the pub.

Outside, he stared wildly around, searching for her.

Too many damn people. He cursed, and then caught sight of her again, turning the corner into Piccadilly. The pavements were overflowing. He wondered what the hell all these people were doing here – nothing in the blasted shops anyway and the weather was foul. He ducked across the road, weaving between the taxis and buses. He had lost her again; when he swore violently, a woman glared her disapproval of him. Splashing through icy puddles, he caught another grimpse of the navy-blue raincoat, heading down Berkeley Street. When he cannoned into a large man in a merchant navy uniform he saw the sailor's fists clench, and offered hasty apologies. Berkeley Street was slightly less crowded than Piccadilly, but she was walking at a fair crack, and his heart sank when he saw her raise her arm to hail a taxi. The taxi sped past her, sending up a tidal wave of grey water. Guy's ribs ached as he ran. Another taxi headed down the street. He muttered, 'Don't stop, damn you!' and then, as the cab drew to a halt beside the kerb, he yelled at the top of his voice, 'Faith!'

She did not immediately respond to his call. But when he shouted a second time, she paused in the act of opening the cab door, and looked back at him.

As soon as she turned, he realized his mistake.

'Nicole,' he said.

From the pavement, she smiled at him. 'Guy. Guy Neville, how marvellous.'

He struggled for breath. He felt dazed, and rather stupid. She was so similar to Faith, and yet so utterly different. Her hair was fairer, her eyes bluer, her body – he found himself noticing the slight curves beneath the navy raincoat.

He heard the taxi driver shout, 'Has she hired me or not, guv?' and he shook his head and called back, 'No. Sorry.' He watched her as she crossed the road to him. Nicole Mulgrave, he thought. He tried to recall how old she had been when he had last seen her. Thirteen . . . fourteen . . . A child. She was not a child now.

'Guy.' She took his hands in hers, and kissed him. The differences from Faith multiplied; he could not now think how he had confused them. Nicole's clothes were well cut, her haircut was chic, her bearing confident.

'Guy, how absolutely delightful. You haven't changed a bit.' She still held his hands. Her grip was surprisingly strong. 'Are you in a hurry? You're rather out of breath.'

'I was trying to catch up with you.' He explained, 'I thought you were Faith.'

She smiled. 'You were mistaken, I'm afraid. Will I do instead?'

He found himself blurting out, 'Yes. Yes, of course.' He was acting, he realized, more like seventeen than twenty-seven. He struggled to get hold of himself.

'Have you time for a drink, Nicole, or dinner?'

'Dinner would be delightful. I've been rehearsing all day, and I'm starving.' She looked at him. 'But won't your wife be expecting you, Guy?'

He had completely forgotten Eleanor. He said, 'I could phone Eleanor – tell her that I've been kept late at the hospital . . .'

'Can you? There's a phone box at the corner.'

They walked to it, he went in, dialled Holland Square, gave his message. It was only when he emerged from the booth that he wondered why he had felt it necessary to lie.

He said, 'We should look for a restaurant, I suppose.'

Nicole suggested a place in Soho. As they walked, the sleet thickened to snow, blotting out the shabbiness of the London streets. In the restaurant he watched her as she ate. His own appetite seemed to have deserted him, yet he felt oddly alive, focused and alert, as though all the muddle and confusion and disappointment of the last few months had begun at last to ebb away. At first, they discussed the usual things one talks about with an acquaintance one has not seen for some time – the weather and the war and the latest films and their work. She was quick and amusing and witty; several times she made him laugh. He realized that he was having fun. He had almost forgotten what it was like, to have fun.

Nicole touched his hand. 'You're staring at me, Guy.'

'Sorry.' He said suddenly, 'Is your husband in London?'

'I don't think so. His work's terribly top secret, so I never know where he is.'

'You were expecting a baby . . .'

'I have a daughter, Elizabeth.'

'Congratulations.'

'Thank you, Guy. Elizabeth is in Wiltshire with her grandmother. Faith told me that you have a son.'

'Oliver lives with Eleanor's grandmother.'

They had finished their pudding. 'Coffee?' asked Guy.

'I suspect it'll be made of dandelion leaves or something equally dreadful. I think that it would be a much better idea to go back to my house in Devonshire Place, don't you?'

He heard himself say, 'If you like,' and they left the restaurant. Outside, she tucked her arm through his and they walked for a while in silence. The snow had begun to settle, crystals glittering in the dim glow from the headlamps of the cars. The bruised, battered city, Guy thought, was being washed clean, given a second chance.

The Devonshire Place house was cold, empty, echoing. Nicole said, 'The blackout's not up to much because no-one really lives here. I did try pinning tablecloths up, but they kept falling down, so I tend to use candles at night.' She took his coat; Guy flicked his cigarette lighter and put it to the two candlesticks on the mantelpiece. The dim, golden flame showed him the sofa and chairs, the rows of books, the dark oblongs of the paintings on the walls.

She unbuttoned her raincoat. 'Drink, Guy?'

He knew that he should say, *Just a small one*, and knock it back quickly, and go home to Eleanor. It was ten o'clock. These days, Eleanor wanted excuses, explanations. The longer he remained with Nicole, the more he would have to lie. Yet he found that he did not particularly care. All that – Eleanor, Holland Square, the sham that his marriage had become – seemed strangly unreal.

He watched Nicole as she crossed the room to the cabinet. Her movements were graceful and fluid. He tried to recall whether she had always been so, and found that he could hardly remember her. She had been the youngest of three, tagging along behind her elder brother and sister.

'I'm trying to remember you,' he said, 'at La Rouilly.'

'You were Faith's friend, of course. I was only allowed to be with you two on sufferance.'

He began to protest, but she halted him, saying, 'Yes, it's true. You know that's how it was, Guy.'

He drank his whisky. A recollection flickered into his mind at last: Nicole howling to catch up with them as they walked through the woods. Tangled flaxen curls and plump little limbs and her face red and creased with fury.

'Did you mind?'

'Not really.' She laughed. 'I had my ponies, Faith had you.' She put down her drink and studied him. 'I should mind now, though.'

His heart slammed against his ribs. 'Mind what?'

'If you were just putting up with me.'

He thought, staring at her, that it was as though some god, dissatisfied with his earlier attempts, had taken the Mulgrave features and distilled them into something sublime, something magnetic. Something he could not stop looking at.

'I should mind,' she said, making it perfectly clear, 'if I were still second-best.'

He had lied to Eleanor; he did not seem able to lie to Nicole. He shook his head. A small gesture, but it seemed to Guy that he had crossed a chasm.

'Though of course, I wouldn't take you from Faith. Sisters are more important than lovers, aren't they?'

He spoke at last. 'Nicole, I have a *wife*—'

'But you don't love her, do you, Guy? If you loved her you would have invited me home, introduced me to her, asked me to stay for supper. And you wouldn't have come here.' She smiled. 'Don't look so worried, Guy. I'm only saying what's obvious. I've always hated prevarication. It's best to say what you think, don't you agree?' She shivered, and pulled her fur coat round her. 'Would you light the fire, Guy? It's so cold in here.'

As he stooped in front of the grate, he heard her add, 'And I've always thought that love makes everything all right. That without love, marriage vows are just words.'

The wood was damp, and he could only find one piece of newspaper. Crumpling it, he said angrily, 'Aren't you just rationalizing – romanticizing – a dishonourable impulse?'

'My life has seemed wrong for a very long time. As yours has, I would guess. The dishonour would seem to me to continue to live a lie.'

She only voiced what he had forced to the back of his mind for months. 'If you love someone,' continued Nicole, 'then pieces of paper and gold rings are unimportant. If you love someone, then you'll break the rules for them.'

He said bitterly, 'Love has to be returned, though, doesn't it?'

'Are you talking about your wife, Guy, or about Faith?'

He looked away from her. Nicole said, 'You've quarrelled with Faith, haven't you? She didn't talk about you once in almost three months, Guy. That's how I know that you've quarrelled.'

Stooping, he put his lighter to the paper, and blew to fan the embers. He said, his back to Nicole, 'Not *quarrelled*. I made the mistake of telling Faith that I loved her.'

'And . . . ?'

He shrugged. 'And nothing. Nothing at all. She just – walked away from me. It was a mistake, as I said.'

There was a silence. Guy seized a copy of Lord Chesterfield's *Letters* from a bookshelf, and flapped at the feeble flames.

'Faith wouldn't break the rules, then?'

He remembered waiting under the lime tree. The sun filtering through the leaves; the slow, grinding turning of hope and joy to bewilderment and then despair. 'No,' he said slowly. 'No, she wouldn't.'

There was a silence. Nicole knelt down beside him, took the book out of his hands, and tore pages from it, scattering them on the fire. The flames roared. 'There,' she said, and smiled at him. Gently, she brushed back the lock of hair that had fallen over his face.

'And you, Guy? Do you love Faith?'

'I think . . . I think that I hate her.'

She placed a silencing finger on his lips. 'Don't say that. Not *hate*. No-one should hate Faith.'

Her skin, the scent of her flesh, intoxicated him. He stood up, went to the mantelpiece. His back to her, resting the palms of his hands on the sill, he said thickly, 'I should go.'

There was a silence. Then she said, 'It's just a question of walking out of the door, Guy.'

He gathered his coat, his hat. Outside, in the street, his shoes crunched the thin snow underfoot, leaving a yellowish mark on the expanse of white. The tube journey, the walk from Russell Square station to his home, seemed onerous, taking him in a direction he did not want to travel.

He did not sleep at all that night. In the early hours of the morning, he slid quietly out of bed. As he opened the door, he glanced back at Eleanor, heaped beneath the eiderdown, her dark hair, in curlers, trapped under a net, her brushed cotton nightdress neatly buttoned at the wrists. For the first time in months, he regarded her with pity rather than dislike. In the kitchen, he drank weak tea and smoked until it was dawn, and then he dressed and took a bus to Malt Street.

Finishing afternoon surgery at six o'clock that evening, he travelled to the centre of town. As he emerged from the dark mouth of the tube station, he was struck by the beauty of the scene. The full moon caught the planes of white that iced every building and every tree with a bluish light. On pavements that were slippery underfoot, Guy walked to Devonshire Place. When he raised his hand to press the doorbell, he knew that he was about to step out onto the ice, and that he courted danger, and the deep, drowning embrace of the water below.

Nicole opened the door. After she had drawn him into the house, he kissed her fingertips, then her palm, then the delicate webs between the fingers. As he undid the small mother-of-pearl buttons of her blouse, he heard her whisper: 'How marvellous, Guy, that you should be The One.'

Faith received the letter at the end of the first week in December. It was from Poppy, and it told her, in a few spare, angry sentences, that Nicole had left her husband and child and was now living with Guy Neville. Though the letter was short, she had to read it three times before its meaning sunk in. She just had time to reach the cottage's cramped, icy bathroom before being violently sick.

Afterwards, she continued to work at the farm, to cycle to and from the cottage, to eat and drink. She kept going because that, she supposed, was what one had to do. Ralph or Jake, she thought, would have stormed and shouted, or run away, or caused some sort of violent scene, but she did not do so. She was incapable of the dramatic, she thought dully. The personality trait that had caused Poppy to elope with Ralph, or Jake to volunteer to fight in the Spanish Civil War, seemed to have passed her by utterly. *You were always the dullest of my children*, Ralph had said, and she found that she agreed with him.

She was glad that it was winter. Winter reflected the blackness of her mood, and focused her mind on the business of survival. The naked black branches of the trees surrounding the cottage were pasted against a heavy grey sky. She welcomed the dreariness of the scene: she could not, she thought, have borne summer just now. Inside Con's cottage she invariably wore three jerseys, as well as long stockings beneath the despised Land Army breeches. At night she heaped every item of clothing she owned on top of the bed to keep herself warm. Breaking the ice on the pitcher of water before washing each morning gave her physical discomfort rather than mental pain. Cycling to the farm along mud ruts frozen to a glazed and treacherous solidity concentrated her thoughts on something other than imagining Guy and Nicole, laughing and kissing.

Her friendship with Con Fitzgerald was a solace to her. She suspected that Con had guessed that something was horribly wrong, but Con asked nothing, and left her alone when she preferred to be alone, and offered her company when she seemed to welcome it. Con showed her the huge weaving loom, housed in an icy shed, and the wool she bought from a local farmer. 'It's difficult to lay one's hands on decent yarn,' Con explained. 'This wretched war.' In the evenings Faith helped Con unravel old jerseys and frayed blankets, so that she could re-use the wool. The repetitive task soothed her. One evening, after supper, Con sat her at the loom, and talked about warp and weft, shuttles and treadles. Faith's weaving proceeded with agonizing and uneven slowness, but glorious shades mingled in the length of woven fabric: taupes and ochres and sage greens and chocolate browns. Con said one night, 'You have an eye for colour,' and she felt immensely flattered.

One stormy winter's night, after the evening news bulletin had described the bombing of Pearl Harbor by the Japanese, Con said: 'America will enter the war now. It'll help us, of course, in the end. But one imagines it like a great, dark blight, spreading over the globe. When it's over, everything will have changed.' She handed a mug of cocoa to Faith.

'I suppose that I expect things to change.'

'Do you? Why? Most people don't, you know.'

'Because my family are nomads. Gypsies. We never really had a home. We borrowed a home each summer from Genya, who gave me the Holly Blue dress, but it wasn't *our* home. So I suppose I've lost less than a lot of people have.'

Though the Mulgraves had mislaid something, she thought. A sense of direction, perhaps. She did not want to think about Ralph and Linda Forrester, or about Nicole and Guy.

'But something's happened, hasn't it, Faith?'

As she stared into the flames, she heard Con add quickly, 'I'm sorry. Nosiness is such an unforgivable trait.'

'I don't mind talking about it now. I've got used to it.'

'Really?' Con's voice was disbelieving. 'You look to me as though you were caught up in the eye of a whirlwind. As though you're waiting for something even worse to happen. That letter . . . it was bad news?'

'Yes . . .' she admitted, 'but not death in battle, nothing *glorious*. Just . . . a betrayal.'

'*Men*,' said Con, with disgust.

'No. It was me. My fault.' Milking the cows, rinsing bottles, mucking out the shed, she had had plenty of time to think about that. She had been offered a choice, and, waiting too long that hot August morning, it had been she who had first betrayed. Though he, in changing allegiance so easily, had since proved to her that he had never truly loved.

There was a silence. Faith watched the flames as they roared up the chimney. 'You see,' she said slowly, 'I thought I was doing the right thing, but now I wonder whether I just wasn't brave enough.'

Often she wondered whether she had prevaricated not because of Eleanor and Oliver, but out of cowardice. She had not had the courage to face the consequences of loving Guy Neville. She had justified, she thought bitterly, Ralph's estimation of her. She had been the dull Mulgrave, the cautious Mulgrave, the timid Mulgrave, and because of that she had lost Guy to Nicole.

She tried to explain. 'You see, my family . . . what we once said about following the heart . . . My family believe that one should always follow the heart. But what if, in the process, other hearts are broken?' Her voice wobbled. She pressed the palms of her hands against her eyes to stem the tears. Amid grief and regret and confusion, she was aware also of shame. She thought of Elizabeth, who no longer had a mother, and David, who no longer had a wife. She knew that neither Nicole nor Ralph ever fully understood the havoc that they caused. The Mulgraves smiled their charming smiles as they cut a swathe through the valleys of other people's hearts.

From a cupboard, Con unearthed an ancient, dusty bottle, and poured a slug of brandy into each mug of cocoa. 'I keep it for medicinal purposes,' she explained. 'Perhaps it can mend broken hearts. And besides, I've always thought cocoa irredeemably vile.'

The brandy warmed Faith's throat and dulled some of the pain. She heard Con say, 'I've always thought that women waste far too much time and effort on love. I did so myself, of course. "Men must work and women must weep" – such nonsense. Women must dry their tears and get on with their jobs – as they've done, of course, both in this war and the first one. There are plenty of other things in life besides love.' She glanced at Faith. 'Or will nothing other than marriage and children do for you?'

Faith remembered how she had felt when she had held Elizabeth for the first time. That warm, tiny body, cradled against hers. Nothing else had seemed to matter.

'I adore babies. I looked after my niece after she was born.'

'But if you can't have this wretched chap—'

'Guy. His name is Guy.'

'I once knew an utter scoundrel called Guy. Terribly handsome, too.' Con's face softened for a moment. 'But if you can't have Guy, will anyone else do?'

She said honestly, 'I don't know. I really don't know.'

'In that case, you must think of something to fill the gap. You can't waste your life mooning over some chap who probably isn't worth a single night's lost sleep.'

'I don't intend to moon,' Faith said stiffly. 'I don't believe I've ever mooned.'

'Now, don't get huffy,' said Con equably. 'I simply meant – have you thought what you'll do when the war is over?'

'I suppose I haven't,' she admitted. She had lost the habit of thinking a month, a week, a day ahead. Immediate troubles pressed on her, surrounding her like brambles in a thicket.

Con poured out more brandy. Then she said firmly, 'You'll have to support yourself. You haven't a convenient inheritance waiting for you, I assume?'

Faith smiled. 'I'm afraid not.'

'You see, the men will come back, and then they'll milk the cows, and you'll be out of a job, my dear.'

She knew that Con was right. Rudges' Farm, in spite of the cold, in spite of the long, back-breaking hours, was merely a breathing space.

She began, 'The trouble is, I'm not much good at anything—' but Con interrupted her.

'If you're going to spout such ridiculous nonsense, then I'll regret having wasted the last of my brandy on you.'

'Sorry.'

'Apology accepted.' Con scowled.

Faith assessed her talents. The brandy was making her pleasantly muzzy. 'I can do first aid—'

'Not much use unless you want to train as a nurse. Appalling job, I've always thought. Only for saints.'

'I can milk cows, but I really wouldn't want to do that for the rest of my life.'

'I told you that you have an eye for colour. Most people haven't, you know.'

Faith thought of France, and the flea-market in Marseilles. 'I'm good at hunting out bargains.'

Con laughed. 'Squirrelling away Paquin gowns in the bottom of a rucksack . . .'

Outside, the wind howled, and the long, bare branches of the trees tapped at the chimneys. Faith had begun to feel warm and sleepy. 'What about you, Con?'

'Oh, I'll stay here, I suppose. Though I've always thought—'

'What?'

'I've always thought that it would be nice to have a little shop. A dress shop.' Con's lip curled. 'Not one of those frightfully genteel establishments you see in the side streets of every provincial town – "Madame Fleur's" or "Valerie's" or some such nonsense. I mean, somewhere special. Something *different*.'

'Beautiful fabrics . . . and wonderful colours . . .'

'I've always wanted,' confessed Con dreamily, 'to weave silk. Terribly difficult and ridiculously expensive, of course. But one could make such lovely things.'

'Like my Holly Blue dress.'

'Exactly. We could call the shop—'

'*We*?'

'Of course. Why not?'

Faith stared at Con. She did not know whether it was because of the brandy, or whether she had simply realized that she did have a future after all, but she found that she laughed. She said curiously, 'Do you think that after all this, women will still want beautiful dresses?'

'It won't be the same again, of course. Who'll be able to afford Vionnet or Fortuny, or whoever will come after them? But women will *particularly* want lovely things, to cheer themselves up after this awful time.'

Con divided the last of the brandy into the cocoa sludge at the bottom of the cups. 'Shall we drink to it? To our shop. To "Holly Blue".'

From the front window of the cottage, Poppy watched Ralph walk up the narrow track that led to Heronsmead. The slope of his shoulders, the downward tilt of his head, told her that he had failed.

She met him at the gate. 'Did you find her?'

'Eventually,' he said. He looked, she thought, old and beaten. His face was tinged purple with cold, his hands dug deep into the pockets of his old greatcoat.

'And . . . ?'

'And she refuses to return to her husband.'

She followed him inside the cottage, and watched him take a half-bottle of Scotch from his tattered pocket, unscrew it, and drink deeply. She whispered, 'But the *child*!'

Tears gathered in the corners of Ralph's bloodshot eyes. 'She says that the child will be better off without her.'

Poppy sat down suddenly, her legs unable to bear her any longer. Ralph had left Heronsmead the day that they had received the letter from Eleanor Neville telling them that Guy and Nicole had run away together. The letter had scarcely been coherent: Eleanor's fury had been obvious in every misspelt word, every blotted full stop.

She heard Ralph say, 'They're living in a couple of rooms in Bermondsey. Frightful little place. Money's obviously tight – after all, Guy has a wife and child to support as well.'

She said, 'Did you speak to Mrs Neville?'

He sat down and ran the back of his hand over his eyes. 'She was hysterical. Insulting.'

There was a silence. Then Poppy cried out, 'How could she, Ralph? How could Nicole leave her child?'

He did not answer. She watched him screw the top back on the empty whisky bottle, and she noticed that his hand shook. His abjectness, his humiliation, only deepened her anger.

He said, after a while, 'I ran into a friend of mine when I was in London. Jerry MacNeil – you remember him, Poppy, we met him at the Lovatts' place.'

The friends and acquaintances of the first twenty years of her marriage had blurred into an indeterminate mass. Poppy half-listened, her mind haunted by the image of Nicole's dark-haired baby. Of all the awful things, she thought, that she had had to face during the last couple of years, the worst was the realization that she had not known her own daughter at all. The pain that tore at her heart was, she thought, no less intense than that which she had endured when her infant son had died.

Odd phrases of Ralph's penetrated her misery.

'Anyway, we got talking . . . decent chap, Jerry . . . has an estate in Scotland, as you know . . . a cottage – bothy, I think the correct word is . . . we could have it for next to nothing . . . get us out of this hole . . . start packing this evening.'

She said, 'No.'

He looked up at her. 'Pardon?'

She could hardly speak for anger. 'As far as I understand you, Ralph, you're suggesting that we leave Heronsmead and decamp to some frozen hovel in Scotland. The answer is, *No*.'

'It's not a hovel – Jerry says that it needs a bit of work, but—'

She said, 'Nicole takes after you, of course, Ralph.

Cutting and running whenever things get difficult.'

She saw him blench. He whispered, 'What do you mean?'

'You know perfectly well what I mean, Ralph. Your . . . your *slut* has given you the cold shoulder, so you intend to turn tail and run to the other end of the country. And you expect me to follow suit. Well, I won't, you know.'

Seeing that he remained perfectly still, frozen into silence and immobility, she laughed. 'Did you think I didn't know about her? Do you know, Ralph, how transparent you are? Running to the gate to wait for the postman . . . spending half the day at the wretched phone box . . . did you really think I didn't know?'

He mumbled, 'It was nothing. Just a little flirtation.'

She screamed, 'Don't lie to me, Ralph! You love her, don't you?'

He covered his face with his hands. After a while, when she was able to speak again, she said, 'What I mind most of all is what you've done to the children. It's *your* example that has led Nicole to do this terrible thing. *You* taught her to know only inconstancy . . . it's because of you that she has left a loyal husband and a baby daughter. And Jake, too – what's happened to Jake? Why does he no longer write – or visit? And Faith—'

Ralph mumbled, 'Faith's all right. Had a letter last week—'

'Faith *loved* Guy Neville!' Poppy's fist slammed the table. 'She always loved him! Or were you too stupid to see that?'

She went to the window, unable to bear the sight of him any longer. She said slowly, 'You have humiliated yourself, and you have humiliated me. Was she worth it? Tell me about her.' When he did not reply, she said, 'I deserve a reply, Ralph.'

After a while she heard him say softly, 'She's beautiful. Young. Self-possessed. Yes – I think that was what I fell in love with. Her self-possession. I've never been self-possessed.'

Her back to him, she closed her eyes. Beautiful. *Young*. Now she wanted to scream at him again, to silence him. Yet she let him continue, though his words scoured her heart.

'I met her at a dinner party. I couldn't at first believe that she was interested in me. I was feeling . . . old, I suppose. I'm fifty-six, Poppy. Not a young man any more.'

She could see her reflection in the glass. There were lines on her face, and her hair was colourless and brittle. She pressed her arms against her chest, as though cradling a child. Her breasts were flat and empty.

He said, 'It stopped quite suddenly in August. Much the same time as Elizabeth was born. She wouldn't see me any more. Wouldn't answer my letters. Put down the phone when I said my name. I went to her flat, but she wouldn't open the door to me. She left town soon after that. I spent weeks chasing round the country looking for her, but I couldn't find her. A month ago, a friend told me that she'd found someone else.'

She felt, listening to him, utterly drained and exhausted. She stood quite still, staring out of the window. It was a fine, bright winter's day. The sky was the colour of Faith's Holly Blue dress. The distant sea shimmered like shot silk, and the marshland seemed to reflect the waves, a feathery, shifting ocean of reeds.

'I'm so sorry,' he said. 'I love you, Poppy. I always

have done. There's only ever been you. I've been such an idiot. But we can start again, can't we?'

She swung round to face him. She hissed, 'You may go to Scotland, Ralph. But you'll go by yourself!' and then she walked swiftly out of the room, pausing only to grab her coat from the peg in the hall as she passed.

She followed the path that led through the marsh to the sea. The breeze ruffled her uncovered hair, and a flight of geese formed a V-shape in the sky, heading inland. Muddy creeks meandered through the reed-beds. Each seed-head was seared into a miniature pennant by the frost. Her feet trod on dried sea lavender, releasing a summer scent that mingled with the salty air. As she walked, Poppy's anger ebbed.

She saw that, though Ralph had been at fault, she herself had not been blameless. Over the past few years, since her baby's death, she had retreated inside herself, nursing her wounds. Dreading that her aches and pains were symptoms of serious disease, she had not had the courage to visit a doctor. She had used Heronsmead as a sanctuary, a bolt-hole. In the summer, she could have stayed longer at Compton Deverall, she could have taught Nicole how to love her child, but a sudden perception of how she had slipped in the rungs of society had made her run home. She herself had given birth to her first baby at the age of twenty-one: she recalled how confused and exhausted she had felt, suddenly overwhelmed by the responsibilities of motherhood. No woman could anticipate the voracious needs of a newborn infant; but mostly, love compensated. Nicole had not given love time to grow. Nicole, not much more than a child herself, had not known how to love someone so helpless, so greedy.

She could see the beach. A length of marshland and

a barricade of barbed wire divided her from the sand. Beyond, the sea was a smooth, waveless expanse of silvery-grey. She wondered what she had expected, all those years ago, watching a man make a sandcastle on the beach at Deauville. She remembered how aimless she had been, and how she had longed for adventure, and for meaning. Ralph had promised her the company and excitement that she had craved. He had promised to take her to the loveliest places on earth; he had promised her that she would never be bored, never be lonely. And most of the time he had kept his promise. He had hurt her dreadfully, it was true – but, had she not loved him, would he have had the power to wound her? And if she still loved him, then could she find it in her heart to forgive?

Alone on the marshland, Poppy covered her face with her hands and wept. When she had exhausted her tears, she realized that she was cold and tired and wanted to go home. Ralph was part of home, she thought. Without him, any house seemed empty. She was unsure whether she could accustom herself to such emptiness.

The whine of an aeroplane snapped her out of her reverie. Turning round, she made out its silhouette, a sinister black bird against the pale blue sky. The marshland behind her and to the side of her was flat, featureless. No trees, no houses, no hedgerows. The aeroplane drew closer, its dark shadow tracking the pale land. Terror stayed her feet, forcing her to stand still. 'It cannot see me,' she muttered out loud. 'It cannot see me.' Surely from that high cockpit, she was no more than a rabbit, or a mouse. Her mouth was dry and her stomach cramped. The noise of the engine grew louder, filling her consciousness. She wanted to go to the lavatory. She wanted Ralph. As the plane swooped down from the sky, and as she saw the first flare of tracer fire snaking brightly towards her from the aeroplane's nose, she began to run, heading for the sea. There was another flash, like a second sun, a searing agony as the bullets struck her, and then she collapsed face down in the sandy earth.

For a moment the aeroplane's dark shadow covered her, and then it continued on its journey back to Germany. Gorse and marram grass bit into Poppy's face. The sleeves of her coat were wet with blood. Raising her head a fraction, she saw the beach, beyond the barbed wire. The sand was smooth and flat and unmarked by footprints. She could smell the salty tang of the sea. She tried to stand up, to walk forward, but she could not. Though the day was still sunny, the cold had become intense. It seemed to spread out from her heart, chilling her veins. Poppy closed her eyes.

Opening them, she discovered that she had reached the beach. Her feet, treading the white sand, left no mark. At the sea's edge, a man was building a sand-castle, a beautiful and extraordinary edifice, decorated with shells and seaweed. She waved, and he turned and smiled, and held out his arms to her.

Written On The Sand

1951–1953

CHAPTER TEN

The Skylon seemed to float in the air, a great, vertical, silver needle. Oliver Neville imagined what it would be like to be in the point of that needle, far above the Festival of Britain crowds. You would be able to see all of London – all of England, perhaps. It would be like sitting in the cockpit of Flash Gordon's rocket.

At the thought of Flash Gordon, Oliver smiled to himself, thrust his hands into the pockets of his school shorts, and made his way into another pavilion. Inside, it was yawningly dull ('twenty-five thousand photographs illustrating the wide range of British manufacturers') – as bad as a geography lesson. Ignoring the dotted red line that everyone else was following, he darted through the crowds, heading quickly for the exit. The blue skies and fresh air were a relief after the shaded rankness of the pavilion. He sat down on the grass and searched in his pockets for a sherbet dab, the last of six he had bought earlier that day at Paddington station. He liked to suck up the sherbet very quickly through the liquorice tube so that it hit the back of his throat in an explosion of sugar and lemon.

When the sherbet was finished, Oliver hunched his knees up to his chin and nibbled the liquorice, wondering what it would be like to have the Festival all to himself. No awful, scruffy oiks from the council schools, with their holey pullovers and scuffed shoes, no shuffling old people making the progress from pavilion to pavilion so boringly slow. He imagined Martian spaceships, green fire blazing from their magnetron guns, swooping down on the South Bank site. Everyone else would scream and run away and Oliver would be the only person left. He would be able to wander through the twenty-seven pavilions, looking just at the interesting bits; he would climb the spindly ladder-legs of the Dome of Discovery, and run round its silver, flying-saucer roof. He would go to the Pleasure Gardens at Battersea, and ride, all by himself of course, on the miniature railway, and sail a boat around the ornamental lake. He would take as many turns as he wanted on every roundabout and helter-skelter.

But no Martians appeared from the bland, blue sky, and he was starting to feel rather tired and rather lonely. He wished his great-grandmother were here. And he felt slightly sick, too: Oliver had never eaten six sherbet dabs before, and was beginning to pay the price.

'Such lovely tweeds,' lied Faith, her heart sinking at the dull green, grey and maroon heaped on the bed. 'But I'm afraid that we don't take tweed. Do you have anything lighter?'

'Marigold Lyle told me you took good-quality clothing,' said the Honourable Frances Brent-Broughton rather huffily.

'Holly Blue specializes in second-hand and original day and evening wear,' explained Faith, 'and it doesn't matter if it's rather falling apart, to be honest. As long as the fabric's good.'

'How extraordinary,' sniffed the Honourable Frances, but disappeared into the back of a wardrobe.

Faith glanced surreptitiously at her watch. Almost three o'clock. The party was due to begin at six.

She had almost, taking the phone call this morning, turned down Miss Brent-Broughton's invitation. Though she loved searching for treasures on market stalls or in antique shops, plundering the decaying grandeur of the once rich made her feel like a vulture. But Rufus had offered his van, and she had told herself that she must be businesslike, not sentimental. And besides, there was always the possibility that she might find something exquisite

But the tweed skirts, the patched hacking jackets, were not exquisite. Faith gazed out of the window at the sweep of parkland that lay beyond the Brent-Broughtons' house, soon to be sold to meet the 75 per cent taxes imposed by the government. To own such a place, and then to lose it: it was hard, Faith thought, to imagine such extremes of fortune.

'There are these . . .' said Miss Brent-Broughton doubtfully, emerging wide-bottomed from the wardrobe. 'They were Mother's.'

Faith took from her the wisps of water-coloured chiffon.

'Frightful old things really,' added the Honourable Frances. 'Women must have been a very peculiar shape then – no waists or busts.'

Faith went to the cheval mirror, and held a dress up against herself. From the Twenties, it was drop-waisted and beaded, with a handkerchief hemline.

Miss Brent-Broughton said, 'Well, do you want 'em or not? The moth has got them, I'm afraid, so I don't expect much.'

Faith smiled. 'I'll take them.'

Driving fast back to Soho, she sang to herself. When she reached the shop, she parked the van and ran inside. Con, wearing overalls, a bandanna tied around her head, was perched up a ladder. Faith called, 'Three glorious evening dresses from Patou, Con! A good omen, don't you think? One's almost eaten to bits, but I can use the fabric in my patchworks.'

'Clever girl.'

'Where's Lizzie?'

'Upstairs, making sandwiches.'

Faith hung up the dresses on a rail in her bedroom. Just for a moment she buried her face in the folds of silk and velvet and lace, and breathed in the slight, stale, mothbally scent that all old clothes seem to have. Then she went to find her niece.

The party was to celebrate the purchase of the lease of the shop. And to knock down the dividing wall between the two tiny downstairs rooms. Faith and Con had begged a pickaxe and hammers, and had made mountains of sandwiches and sausage rolls and bought gallons of beer and lemonade. They took turns swinging the pickaxe until the first brick was dislodged and light issued from one room to the other. Everyone cheered, and drank a toast to Holly Blue.

Gramophone music accompanied the hammering of the pickaxe. You could not, Faith thought, have squeezed in more guests if you had used a shoehorn. She said to Con: 'If they all buy clothes from us we'll be fabulously rich.'

'They won't all buy clothes. A few of them will buy a scarf, perhaps one or two a dress.' Con, frowning, looked around the crowded room. 'Who are all these people, anyway? I don't know the half of them.'

Faith said vaguely, 'Oh . . . they're friends . . . and the plasterer, and the carpenter and the next-door neighbours.'

'And Uncle Tom Cobbleigh and all . . . *really*, Faith—'

'And the van driver—'

Con snorted. 'Who won't buy so much as a needle and thread.'

Faith grinned. 'I can't imagine our more influential clients wielding a pickaxe.'

'We don't *have* influential clients, Faith. We've a handful of eccentrics who buy a dress or two when they can afford it.'

'*Loyal* eccentrics,' Faith reminded Con. 'Clio Bettancourt is here.'

'Is she? Dear Clio . . . I'll go and find her. If I can fight my way through the brick dust.'

Con disappeared into the room. There was another cheer as half a dozen bricks tumbled simultaneously from the wall. A hand tugged Faith's sleeve.

'Auntie Faith, can I knock down the wall?'

Faith often thought, looking down at Elizabeth, that Nicole's brief essay at motherhood had left little mark upon her daughter. Elizabeth was a small, feminine version of David Kemp: dark-haired, serious-eyed, at ten years old utterly reliable and sensible. Only sometimes, in her niece's sudden bright smile and in her talent for happiness, was Faith reminded abruptly and painfully of Nicole.

She smiled. 'Of course you can, Lizzie.'

*　　　*　　　*

Much later, sitting in the tiny backyard among the heap of bricks that had once been the dividing wall, Rufus came to join her.

'I've brought you a drink.' Faith smiled gratefully up at him. He waved a hand at the bricks. 'How do you feel?'

'Dusty.' She smiled. 'And delighted. And relieved.'

'Relieved?'

'It's taken so much longer than I thought it would. I was beginning to think it would never happen, that it would be like one of those monsters . . . I can't remember the name . . . that are always just out of reach—'

'A chimera,' supplied Rufus helpfully.

'Thank you.'

'You're welcome. The benefits of a classical education.'

'Ten years, Rufus. It's taken us almost ten years.'

He whistled. 'That long?'

'Con and I first thought of Holly Blue in the December of 1941. The day before Poppy died.'

She looked up at the black velvet sky, and thought that the two events had become inextricably linked. It was as though someone had drawn a line through her life, dividing an existence that had ended with Poppy's sudden death from that which had begun when Con had said, *I've always thought that it would be nice to have a little dress shop.* Amid the noise and the laughter of the party, she was aware of a terrible loneliness.

'The jobs I've taken to save up for this place, Rufus,' she said softly. 'The awful shops and restaurants I've worked in . . . the dimwitted little girls that I've tried to teach French . . .'

'You should marry me, Faith. I could take you away from all that.'

She laughed. 'Oh, Rufus, what should we live on? And where should we live – in the shoebox above the shop?'

'We'd live on honeydew and drink the milk of paradise,' he said equably. 'I'll keep asking, Faith. I'll wear you down, like water dripping on a stone.' Then he bent and kissed her, and went back indoors.

Faith sat for a while, thinking. She wondered what it would be like, to be married to Rufus. She wondered whether, if she married Rufus, and if she, perhaps had his children, the awful empty gap that seemed to reappear from time to time between her ribs would disappear. She had the shop, she had somewhere to live, she had countless friends, but there was still that gap, somewhere between the four points of her heart.

The telephone rang as they were getting ready for the party. Guy, vaguely hoping for a medical emergency that would allow him to escape from a tedious evening, took the call. As he listened to the voice on the other end of the line, he became increasingly anxious. He interspersed the verbiage with short, sharp questions. When the conversation was over, he made another brief telephone call, and then he put the receiver down and went to find Eleanor.

She was in her bedroom, seated at her dressing table. 'That was Whitelands,' Guy said. 'Apparently Oliver has run away from school.'

Eleanor's face was reflected in the dressing-table mirror. He saw her eyes widen.

'He hasn't been seen since this morning,' explained Guy. 'Friday's a half-day, so Oliver's absence wasn't

335

noticed until teatime. They wasted a couple of hours searching for him, and then they phoned me to find out whether he's come home.'

'Guy – he could have been *kidnapped*.'

'I really don't think so. We're hardly rich enough for that.'

'How can you make jokes – at such a time—'

'His school cap and blazer were missing. And his outdoor shoes. And there was no pocket money in his tuck box, and he'd persuaded another boy to lie for him to the games teacher. The chap who was organizing the cross-country run thought that Oliver was playing cricket, and vice versa. And as soon as that idiotic housemaster was off the phone, I called the nearest railway station. And yes – a fair-haired boy in Whitelands uniform bought a second-class ticket to London at midday.' Guy lit a cigarette. 'Oliver was in some sort of trouble, apparently. He was due in the headmaster's study tomorrow morning, so presumably he's done a bunk rather than face the music.' He laid his hand on Eleanor's shoulder. Her flesh felt slightly clammy. He said, with an effort at reassurance, 'He'll turn up. You mustn't worry. Oliver's very good at looking after himself.'

'But . . . London!' she whispered. 'All by himself! He's *eleven*!'

'If he isn't here by . . . let me see . . . eight o'clock, then I'll call the police. The school want me to put it off until tomorrow morning – they want to avoid scandal, naturally – but I'll not wait so long.'

There was a crease of worry between her eyes. 'Do you think that it'll come to that, Guy?'

'No, I don't.' He forced himself to sound confident. 'He'll come home as soon as he's tired and hungry, I'm sure of it. Meanwhile – would you prefer to call all this off?'

'All this' referred to the cocktail party that they were to host that evening. Eleanor had spent the last six weeks preparing for it.

She picked up her lipstick, and began to outline her mouth. 'As you say, Guy – Oliver will turn up.'

At seven o'clock, Guy escaped to his study. He did not think that he would be missed. All the most important guests had arrived (he had seen the list in Eleanor's diary, ranked in order of significance), and he had balanced sherry glass and vol-au-vent, had admired the tiny aspic moulds, vegetables glistening glassily within, and had moved, as he was supposed to, from guest to guest, exchanging a few meaningless sentences with each.

Now he closed the door on the muted, well-bred sounds of the party, and took the magazine from his desk drawer. It was a film magazine, not the sort of thing that he usually read. It had been abandoned in the kitchen by one of the girls that Eleanor had engaged to help with the party food. He had been about to chuck it into the bin when he had noticed the small review at the foot of the page.

'*Sailor Sally*,' the caption said, 'a musical. Sally Fairlie (Stella Delmar), recuperating from a broken engagement on a Mediterranean cruise, finds true love on board ship.'

Unknown stars and a tired storyline: Guy would not have normally given the article a second glance. Except that, at the foot of the paragraph, in italics, were the words, *Also starring Gray Banks, Diana Taylor and Nicole Mulgrave*.

Nicole Mulgrave. Not a name, of course, that could be mentioned in Holland Square.

Briefly, he touched with a fingertip the two italicized words. It had jolted him to know that she – that one of them – still existed. He had neither heard of nor seen any Mulgrave in almost ten years.

Guy lit himself a cigarette, and went to the window. The sky was a flawless blue, and sunlight gleamed on the roofs of the houses. He associated Nicole with winter. They had fallen in love as the first snow fell, and they had parted three months later, when the pale green shoots of spring had begun to show. They had had, he thought, a few weeks of euphoric happiness. Then Nicole had been told of Poppy Mulgrave's death, and from there he could date the disintegration of the affair.

She had left him one morning in March, scooping up her clothes into an old shopping bag, knotting her glorious fair curls on top of her head as she spoke. *I've met someone. I really think that he's The One. This was a mistake, wasn't it? You'll forgive me, won't you, Guy?* He had forgiven her, because he had known by then that without the physical passion that had consumed them during those first weeks, they were two separate people, with only their childhood memories and their adult betrayal of those closest to them in common.

He had lived on in the Bermondsey rooms for a month. Then Eleanor had called. She had found him at mid-afternoon unshaven, dressed in grubby corduroys and a shirt that he had worn most of the week. She had stated her terms. If Guy wished to see his son again, then he was, after the war was over, to return to Holland Square, to give up his Malt Street practice and

338

to work with her father instead. Meanwhile he was to re-enlist in the Army Medical Corps. By the time he came home, the scandal would be forgotten. Oh, and one final proviso. He was never to see any of the Mulgraves again.

He had accepted Eleanor's conditions, of course, even though he had known that she took him back to salvage her pride, and because she could not bear to lose him to a Mulgrave. It was generous of her to take him back at all. Her resentment of him only equalled his own self-loathing. He had deserted his son – what greater crime could a father commit? He'd broken his vow to do all that he could to protect his child – and for what? For a woman he had not even truly loved.

Discharged from the army in 1946, Guy had returned to Holland Square. Oliver had by then been living with Eleanor and Selwyn for a year. Guy soon recognized that what affection Eleanor was capable of, she had transferred to Oliver. He was no longer a demanding baby, but an exceptionally beautiful child, golden-haired and quick-witted, possessed of a self-contained reticence that sometimes seemed to Guy inappropriate to his age. Guy's own intense love for his son was sharpened by a nagging sense of guilt. When Eleanor insisted on the best schools for Oliver, and whatever toys and clothing could be bought in an exhausted, straitened London, Guy did not quibble, though to pay Oliver's school fees demanded of him long hours of work. He, too, wanted only the best for Oliver. When the National Health Service came into being in 1948, Selwyn, with Eleanor's encouragement, decided to remain in private practice. Guy was therefore forced to stand aside, watching the creation of his dream without being a part of it. He told himself that he did not mind, because everything he did was for Oliver.

Since his father-in-law had begun to show symptoms of heart trouble, Guy had taken over most of the work of the practice. He was successful; sometimes he even told himself that he was happy.

Now, though, he struggled to master his anxiety. He imagined Oliver, lost and alone in London. He glanced at his watch. Twenty past seven. He'd not wait till eight, Guy decided. Another ten minutes and he would phone the police.

The study door opened. 'Guy,' said Eleanor. 'What on earth are you doing in here? Our guests—'

Without another glance, he threw the film magazine into the wastepaper bin. He saw that Eleanor did not look angry. He said, 'Oliver?' and she smiled.

'He's safe. He's come home.'

Oliver was in the drawing-room with the party guests, talking to a consultant from St Anne's. Seeing his son, Guy felt a rush of love and relief. But he forced his features into a sterner mould.

'Oliver? What's all this about, then?'

'Daddy.' Oliver's great blue eyes met Guy's.

'We need to talk, old son.'

'*Guy*,' hissed Eleanor, 'he's tired and hungry. It can wait till tomorrow, surely.'

'I don't think so, Eleanor. I'll have to phone the school tonight, offer some sort of explanation.'

'Our guests . . . I must stay with them . . .'

Guy took Oliver's hand and led him into an adjacent room. He shut the door behind them. 'Tell me why you ran away from school, Oliver.'

Tears welled around the sapphire blue. Oliver

gasped, 'One of the other boys . . . Hayward . . . swapped me his Flash Gordon annual for some of my marbles . . . but Hayward told Mr Ganderton that I stole it, and Mr Ganderton told Dr Vokes.'

Dr Vokes was Whitelands's headmaster, Mr Ganderton Oliver's housemaster – a fluttering fool, Guy thought. He frowned. Oliver had clamoured for a Flash Gordon annual for his birthday. It was one of the few things that Eleanor had refused him. Comic books were, in Eleanor's opinion, common.

'Are you sure that this other boy – Hayward – understood that it was a swap, Oliver? Perhaps you were mistaken . . . perhaps he thought only to lend you the book.'

Oliver sniffed. 'It was a swap, Daddy. He took my marbles. He put them in his desk. I saw him.'

'It sounds to me as though there has been a muddle.'

'Are you cross with me, Daddy?'

'Not about this wretched book, no. But why did you run away, Oliver? Why didn't you stay and explain everything to Dr Vokes?'

Oliver bit his lip. 'I didn't want to sneak on Hayward.'

'Oh, *Oliver*,' Guy said and, remembering his own prep school days, held out his arms and hugged his son.

There was a stiffness about Oliver that Guy was always aware of in any physical contact between them. It was as though he always held a part of himself back. Guy had recognized long ago that Oliver was a private, secretive child, a loner with few close friends. Guy blamed in part the child's long separation from his parents during the war, but most of all he blamed himself. He was unable to rid himself of the conviction that his desertion of Oliver had left a scar.

The door opened and Eleanor came into the room. Guy released Oliver from his embrace.

'I think we've sorted things out,' said Guy. 'I'll telephone Dr Vokes. Oliver had better go back to school tomorrow.'

'*Daddy*,' whispered Oliver.

Eleanor looked at her son closely. 'You look pale, darling. Don't you think he looks pale, Guy?'

Oliver did, now Guy came to think about it, look rather green about the gills. 'What is it?' he asked gently. 'Sore tummy?'

Oliver nodded. 'I haven't been able to eat anything *all day*!'

'Perhaps it's appendicitis,' said Eleanor.

'I don't feel well enough for school, Daddy.'

'Poor darling. How unkind of Daddy to insist that you go back to school when you're unwell.'

'*Daddy*,' said Oliver, pleadingly.

Guy ruffled Oliver's hair. 'I suppose there's only another week of the summer term left.'

'I'll put him to bed straight away,' said Eleanor. 'And you must phone the school, Guy, and tell them that we won't be bringing Oliver back until September.'

The last of the guests left at midnight. Rufus set off for Islington; Con returned to her cottage in Somerset. Elizabeth had long since gone to bed in the room above the shop. Faith gathered up empty glasses and crumby plates and at one o'clock abandoned the mess and went upstairs to her flat and fell asleep on the sofa.

She dreamt, as she had not done for years, of La Rouilly. The château was as it had been before the war, the roofs and attics miraculously intact again. She was opening chests and wardrobes and taking out beautiful dresses. Silvers and golds and blues and emeralds gleamed in the rosy bands of sunlight that streamed through the attic windows. The bodice of one dress was made of iridescent birds' feathers; the skirt of another was pieced together from the kaleidoscopic scales of a butterfly's wing. Her arms were weighed down by dresses. As she carried them through the attic, she heard the first shots. They ricocheted against the window panes. Looking out, she saw that the building was surrounded by soldiers, who seethed around the gardens like dun-coloured ants. The bright colours of the dresses dulled to lovat green, to grey, to khaki . . .

Faith opened her eyes. At first, her heart pounded in rhythm with the guns, and then rationality asserted itself, and she was able to separate the hammering on the front door from the echoes of her dream. Pulling on her dressing gown, she ran downstairs and opened the door.

'*Jake.*'

His fair hair was picked out by the moonlight. He half fell into the shop. 'I've been looking all over bloody London for you, Faith. Had to wake up Rufus. Why didn't you tell me you'd moved house?'

Because I didn't know where you were, she thought. *Because you've neither written nor phoned in six months*.

'Almost went to bloody *Somerset*,' added Jake.

'Shh,' said Faith. 'Elizabeth's asleep upstairs.'

Jake held a finger to his lips, and said, in an exaggerated whisper, 'As quiet as a mouse.'

A rather large, scruffy mouse, she thought, looking at him. There was a quarter-inch of stubble on his chin, and his untidy fair hair touched the worn collar of his shirt. 'Come in, Jake.'

'A hug, first, for your favourite brother.' He flung his arms round her in a crushing embrace. His clothes smelt of cigarettes and alcohol.

She said, the words muffled by his chest, 'You missed our party.'

'Did I?' Releasing her, he looked down at her. 'A thousand apologies.'

She smiled at him. 'I'll forgive you if you help me clear up the mess tomorrow.'

Jake slept on the sofa that night; Faith squeezed in with Lizzie. Rising early, Faith made tea and brought him a cup. In the bright morning light she could see clearly his pallor.

'You've got awfully thin, Jake,' she said crossly. 'Where on earth have you been?'

'Oh . . . here and there.'

'Have you a job?'

'Not just now.'

'But your friend . . . You were going to buy a bar—'

'I tried it for a while, but it was very dull. Too much counting change and scrubbing floors.'

She had lost count of the jobs Jake had had since the war. A dozen, surely. More, perhaps.

He yawned, and stood up, and prowled around the room, glancing briefly and uninterestedly at her books, her pictures, her photographs.

'How's things, Faith? How's everyone . . . David . . . Rufe . . . ?'

'Rufus was here last night. He helped us knock down the wall. And David's away on business just now, which is why I'm looking after Elizabeth.' She nodded to the adjacent room. 'She's still fast asleep – I let her stay up for the party.'

'How is she?'

She thought, *She is the light of my life*, and smiled. 'She loves her new school. David could hardly bear to part with her, of course. Laura Kemp died in the spring, you see, so David had to bite the bullet and send Lizzie to boarding school.'

'I've brought her a present.' Jake crouched on the floor, fished in his rucksack, and drew out a paper snake on a string. 'I found it in Marseilles.' When he tugged the string, the snake wriggled sinuously across the lino. He let out a crack of laughter. 'Clever, eh?'

'She'll adore it.' Faith looked Jake in the eye. 'Pa isn't too good. He had bronchitis badly last winter. You should go and see him, Jake.'

He let go of the string and stood up, his hands in his pockets, and went to the window. She heard him say, 'No.'

'Jake—'

'Never.' His back was to her. 'He killed her.'

'Pa's old and frail, Jake. You could leave it too late.'

'Leave what too late?' He swung round. 'Are you still hoping for the touching reunion with the prodigal son? Still hoping that I'll shake his hand, weep a little perhaps, and say, "It's all right, Pa, I know you didn't mean it"?' His voice was savagely sarcastic.

She said bluntly, 'He loves you, Jake. He misses you.'

Jake's blue eyes were expressionless. 'And I . . . I *despise* him. Understand that, Faith.'

There was a long silence. She picked up the paper snake and put it on the table, and began to gather together dirty plates and cups, remnants of the previous evening's hurried supper. She felt exhausted, the interrupted night pressing on her shoulders like a weight.

Jake said, his tone of voice altered, 'I'm here to ask your advice, Faith.'

She looked at him. 'You've never in your life taken my advice, Jake. Or, I expect, anyone else's.'

'I'm a reformed character.' A sudden smile, and he dropped gracefully full-length on the sofa. 'The thing is,' he said, 'I can never quite work out where I'm going wrong. I mean – I'm twenty-nine, aren't I? Shouldn't I have . . . well . . . *things*?'

She perched on the sofa arm beside him. 'What sort of things, Jake?'

He sketched a vague gesture with his hand. 'Oh . . . somewhere to live . . . holidays . . . children . . . saucepans . . .' He shrugged, looking at her, bewilderment in his eyes. 'All that. Other people have things. Even you do, Faith.'

She laughed. 'I could squeeze most of my possessions into a suitcase, I expect. This flat – it's more Con's than mine, because she put more money into the shop. And I haven't managed children yet. I just borrow other people's.' Without intending it, her voice was bitter. She took a deep breath, and glanced at Jake, stretched out lazily beside her.

'But if that's what you really want, then you have to settle with one person, not go from one to another like you do, Jake. All that . . . all that lusting and chasing and bedding must take up so much *time*.'

He frowned. 'D'you think so?'

'Of course. And if you remembered to eat . . . and to sleep at night . . . and didn't get so angry with people . . . And you must get a job. People who own things usually have jobs. It doesn't matter what you do as long as you do something.'

'I do try,' he said. 'Only something always seems to

346

go wrong. Either I oversleep, or I forget what I'm supposed to be doing because it's so damnably dull and pointless, or the person I'm working for is wretchedly mean, or stupid—'

Sliding from the sofa arm, she said, exasperated, 'But you have to put up with it, Jake! That's the thing – you just have to put up with it!'

She began to hurl dirty dishes into the sink. She thought of the places where she had worked over the years – the dingy cafés, the tedious shops and offices. Suddenly, she could have wept into the washing-up water.

A hand squeezed her shoulder; he had come to stand behind her. 'Don't howl, old girl,' he said. 'Mulgrave Rules, remember?'

She sniffed. Jake held out a grubby shirtsleeve, and she wiped her face on his cuff.

'And don't worry about me. All I need is to borrow a couple of quid to get me through the week, and I'll be fine. I told you. I'm a reformed character.'

Faith went to Heronsmead for Ralph's birthday in August. Aunt Iris had allowed Ralph to remain at the cottage since Poppy's death The royalties from his novel had long since dried up, and Poppy's annuity had died with her. Though Ralph tended Poppy's vegetable garden with fanatical zeal, there were still bills to pay. Faith's long years of working in cafés, shops and offices had not only been for Holly Blue.

Walking with Ralph along the ribbon of sand between the shimmering planes of marsh and sea, she thought that he looked decidedly threadbare. No matter how often she repaired them, the collars and cuffs of his coats continued to fray. The cloth was shiny with age. Ralph was sixty-six now, and looked, Faith thought, every year of his age. Grief had aged him, just as sorrow and regret had tied him to this place. It was as though, in remaining tied to a land he had once professed to hate, he still hoped to call back the years, to make the past different.

They spoke of Holly Blue, of Ralph's garden, and of Elizabeth and David and Nicole. Poppy's ghost haunted this lonely, beautiful place between land and sea. They did not speak her name, but Ralph tucked his hand round Faith's arm, and their footprints converged on the impacted sand.

The following day, Faith took Ralph's ancient bicycle from the shed and went out for a ride. She rode north, with no particular destination in mind. She wanted to lose herself, to exhaust herself. She pedalled fast along paths barely wide enough to take a motor-car, hardly glancing at the grey-green landscape. At midday she bought a bag of broken biscuits and a bottle of Tizer from a village shop. Sitting on a bench, eating and drinking, she felt pleasantly weary. Some of her anxieties – about the shop, and for Ralph and Jake – had faded into the background. She remounted the bicycle and set off for home.

She became lost, truly lost among a maze of un-familiar fields and thickets. As she travelled inland the landscape swelled, the narrow lanes bordered by high hedgerows. It began to rain, conjuring a late summer scent of damp beech leaves and wet bracken. Drops of rain rolled from the dusty verges and gathered in puddles at the side of the road. She had brought neither raincoat nor hat. She glimpsed a turning from the road, tall beech trees growing to either side of it, their topmost branches touching overhead. She rode up the track, looking for shelter. The heavily leaved branches formed a dark tunnel, and rain hardly touched the dry earth beneath. The surface of the track was pocked with deep hollows; she dismounted from the bicycle. She continued along the track, curious to know where it led. She must have walked half a mile or so before she saw the house.

It lay, red-bricked and symmetrical, in a clearing at the end of the path. By the time she reached it, the shower was over and the sun had broken through. The house stirred a memory within her. She walked forward, trying to pinpoint the fleeting recollection. She noticed that the windows were, unusually for England, shuttered, and that each peeling, faded shutter was closed. The garden was tangled, and no careful owner, secateurs in hand, walked the winding paths looking for an overblown rose, a broken shoot. Thinking to ask for directions, she went to the front door, but knew at once from the empty echo of her clenched fist that the house was untenanted.

As she walked back through the garden, her shoulder brushed against the rain-dewed branches of the shrubs. A handful of blue butterflies – the last of the summer surely – drifted up into the warm air. From far away, Genya's voice echoed, *When all this horror is over, you will come back, and everything will be just the same*, and she had to clench her nails into the palms of her hands to stop herself weeping.

Oliver hardly recognized his great-grandmother. She seemed to have withered, to have become smaller and paler and somehow rather transparent, like a chrysalis. Her breath rattled in her throat.

He heard his father say softly, 'It's all right, Oliver.

Just take her hand, and tell her that you're here.'

He went to the bed, but he did not take his great-grandmother's hand. He knew that if he touched it, it would crumble to dust, like a dead leaf.

'Hello, Nana,' he said.

Slowly, she opened her eyes. 'Oliver. My best boy.'

He said, 'I have to go back to school today. I'm in 3A this term, and I expect I'll be Form Captain.' He didn't really – Lessing would be Form Captain, Lessing was always Form Captain, but his father had explained to him that his great-grandmother was dying, and he thought the lie might cheer her up.

'You're a clever boy, Oliver,' she whispered. And then the moment that he had dreaded. 'Give me a kiss.'

She put her head to one side. He bent, and smelt the familiar scents of powder and lavender water. But when he touched his pursed lips to her cheek, he detected another underlying, ranker perfume. He could smell death, he thought, and he jumped back. His great-grandmother had already drifted off to sleep again, so only his parents saw him bolt out of the bedroom door.

Their footsteps followed him. He heard Mummy say, 'I told you it would be too much for him—'

And his father: 'Better this than the unexpected telephone call at school.'

'Just because you—'

Oliver turned towards them. He hated them to quarrel. 'I was too hot.'

'It was rather stifling in there.' His mother ruffled his hair. 'Grandmother isn't very well, Oliver, so she keeps a fire on all day.'

'Nana's heart isn't working properly any more, you see,' said his father. Oliver, steeling himself for the inevitable scientific explanation, shifted his features into what he thought of as his listening face (it came in handy for really boring lessons at school). As his father spoke of valves and blood flow, Oliver imagined himself flying a spaceship high over the valley of the Dove, looking down at the hills and the twisting river.

When his father had finished, Oliver said politely, 'Can I go out and play now?'

'Of course you can. Your mother and I will go and sit with your great-grandmother.'

'Don't play by the river, darling. And don't get your school uniform muddy.'

When they were gone, he did not go outside, but wandered around the house, peering into cupboards and drawers. He had lived in the Derbyshire house until he was five; it was an odd mixture of strangeness and familiarity. The rooms, though otherwise just as he remembered them, seemed smaller. The garden, which he had once believed vast, had shrunk. Even Thorpe Cloud itself was no longer the mountain of his memory.

He found it hard to believe that the wheezing, wizened person he had just seen was really his great-grandmother. Fleetingly, he imagined that Nana had been taken away and hidden in another house (so someone could steal her money, perhaps) and that hollow, chrysalis-woman substituted for her. But the fantasy collapsed almost immediately; he was too old to believe that sort of thing any more.

Oliver went into the morning-room. It was a large, bright room, facing out onto the garden. When he was a little boy, he had liked to play at his great-grandmother's writing desk. All her familiar possessions were arranged there. Her fountain pen, her blotter, her ink bottle, her writing pad. And her paperweight, made of Blue John stone. Oliver touched the paperweight, wondering how it remained cold while the rest of the house was so hot. Then he opened the drawers of the writing desk.

The photograph albums were boring, mostly pictures of little girls with bows in their hair, and when he came across snapshots of himself, horribly fat and wearing rompers, he slammed the book shut. He looked at the letters. There were heaps and heaps of them, tied up with ribbons. Oliver recognized his mother's handwriting. She wrote to him twice a week at school – long letters, though Nana's were always funnier. He thought about not getting letters from Nana any more, and the familiar ache started behind his eyes. He pressed his fists against his sockets to stem the tears. Only cissies cried. Patterson, at school, was a cissy. To take his mind off things, he read the letters. Boring stuff about boring things like wallpaper and carpets and boring grown-up parties.

Oliver pulled out a second bundle of letters. The ink was so faded that the uppermost page was almost unreadable, but the contents of these letters were more interesting – wizard stuff about bombs and fire-watching. He was about to put them back into the drawer, when a sentence leapt out at him. 'I have decided to take Guy back.' It seemed to Oliver a very odd thing for his mother to write. As though Guy (his father, of course) was something faulty she had tried to exchange at a shop. He read on. 'The wretched affair only lasted a few weeks. A (a few words that looked horribly like French), and best forgotten, I'm sure you'll agree.' Oliver concluded that this was something to do with his father coming back after the end of the war. He had been six, and he had come home from his day school, and there had been a man sitting in the drawing-room, and Mummy had said, 'Daddy's come home, Oliver.' The man had hugged him and talked to him, and Oliver had longed to go and play with his train set.

Oliver heard footsteps. He shoved the letters back in the desk, picked up the Blue John stone paperweight, put it in his pocket and ran out of the room.

His parents were talking. 'A week – no longer, I think . . . a release for the poor soul . . .' and he gave a sigh of relief. They weren't quarrelling. Patterson's people had divorced, and one of the other boys had got hold of the newspaper article about it, and everyone had ragged Patterson, and Patterson had cried, the cissy.

After tea, they drove on to Oliver's school. There, he kissed his mother goodbye, but he resisted his father's embrace, and instead held out his hand. He remembered the smell of death, and he wanted to punish his father for making him endure that.

The following day, Guy was required to call on a Mrs Myers in Curzon Street. He was shown by a uniformed manservant (did such people exist these days? Eleanor struggled to find even a competent charwoman) to an upstairs room where he was introduced to Mrs Myers and to her daughter, Susan. Susan Myers neither glanced at nor spoke to him, but continued in a sullen fashion to inspect her fingernails; Mrs Myers looked at him as though she had discovered a cockroach scuttling across her carpet, and said: 'Where's Dr Stephens? We always see Dr Stephens.'

'Dr Stephens is unwell, I'm afraid, Mrs Myers.' Guy

had at last persuaded Selwyn to undergo investigations for his heart trouble. 'Will I do?' He made himself smile.

'I suppose you'll have to,' said Mrs Myers icily.

'Then what seems to be the trouble?'

'My daughter is unwell.' Susan shuffled and stared at her feet through a curtain of lank, dark hair.

Examining Miss Myers in an adjacent room, it did not take Guy long to ascertain the nature of Susan's ill health. Susan was seventeen, and about three months pregnant. She was also unmarried. When he gently explained to Susan her condition, she said grumpily, 'I know. A bore, isn't it?'

'Would you like me to talk to your mother?'

She stared at him. 'Mummy knows, of course. That's why she sent for you.'

'You'd like me to arrange antenatal care?'

The stare filled with scorn. 'Don't be silly. Mummy wants you to get rid of it.'

Guy struggled to disguise his shock. His back to her, as he put things into his bag, he said, 'Then I'll explain to your mother that I don't do things like that.'

'Not you personally.' Her contempt for him was audible. 'I mean – you can recommend a clinic, can't you? Lorna Cummings told us that Dr Stephens had fixed things for her.'

He said coldly, 'I told you, I don't do things like that.' He looked back at her. 'Can't you marry the father?'

There was an open box of chocolates on the bedside table. She began to cram sweets into her mouth. 'Don't be silly,' she said again. 'He's a groundsman at my school.'

Guy left the room. In the adjoining chamber, he said

to Susan's mother, 'Your daughter is three months pregnant, Mrs Myers. Plenty of rest and a good diet will ensure that she remains perfectly healthy. If you'd like me to recommend a good obstetrician, then I'll do so.' He left the room before she could reply.

He carried out his last few visits with a robotic absence of thought. The calls were, fortunately, routine – a sore throat, an ingrowing toenail, a twisted ankle. When he had finished, he did not immediately return to his surgery. The depression that had begun the previous afternoon, parting from Oliver at his prep school, had intensified. He went into a pub and ordered a drink. It took the first Scotch to persuade him not to go to the clinic in which Selwyn was incarcerated and demand an immediate explanation. The second to predict Selwyn's reply if he were to do so. *If I didn't tell her somewhere decent to go, then she might end up at the mercy of some incompetent struck off the list ten years ago.* He did not even know whether Selwyn would have been right or wrong. He had seen the consequences of a botched abortion too often in his Malt Street practice to feel any moral triumph at his refusal. He only knew that the Myerses' assumption of his compliance had left him feeling tainted.

The Scotch failed to lighten his despair. Walking back to the surgery in Cheviot Street, he remembered parting from Oliver the previous day. Oliver had refused his embrace, and had instead, for the first time, held out his hand. Guy remembered shaking Oliver's hand and saying, *Have a good term, old chap.* A caricature of the middle-class English father. The grief that he now endured, thinking of Oliver, seemed to Guy worse than all the other griefs he had suffered. He knew that the fault lay with him, and that his absence

– enforced at first, it was true, by Eleanor, but considerably lengthened by his own foolish affair with Nicole Mulgrave – was the root cause of Oliver's ambivalent attitude to him. Returning to Holland Square after overseas service in 1946, he had felt like an interloper.

In Cheviot Street, Guy climbed the stairs to the reception area, intending to collect some unfinished paperwork and then leave for home. But as he entered the room his receptionist, Sylvia, hissed at him: 'There's someone to see you, Dr Neville . . . The name's Mulgrave . . . it's not on our list. Looks a ruffian . . . I explained that you don't hold an evening surgery . . . Shall I call the police?'

The name's Mulgrave . . . Suddenly, Guy's heart was pounding. He realized that Sylvia was staring at him, waiting for a reply. She repeated, 'Shall I call the police, Dr Neville?' and he blinked, and shook his head, and said, his voice steady, 'No, Sylvia, it's all right, I'll deal with this.' He went into the waiting-room.

When he focused on the figure silhouetted against the window, his heartbeat quietened a little. 'Hello, Jake,' said Guy.

'Had a bit of an accident,' explained Jake. They were in the surgery; Jake was sitting in a chair, holding a dirty piece of cloth to one side of his head while Guy fetched bandages and disinfectant. The cloth was stained crimson with blood. 'Went to the hospital, but there were about a hundred other poor bastards in the casualty department – a bus had crashed, someone said. I couldn't face waiting, and I remembered a girl I knew who'd trained as a nurse, so I thought I'd look her up and maybe she'd sort me out. But she wasn't at home, and I was bleeding like a stuck pig, and then I thought,

Guy – what about old Guy?' Jake smiled, pleased with himself. 'I know it's been a long time—'

'Hell of a long time.'

'Quite. So I looked you up in the phone book.' He glanced around the room. 'I say, very splendid, Guy. A Chippendale desk and . . . let me see . . . Stubbs prints on the walls.'

'Reproductions,' said Guy briefly. He had never quite got used to the new premises' splendour. He and Selwyn, persuaded by Eleanor, had bought the Cheviot Street surgery three years earlier. It would be more appropriate, she had said. She was tired of patients trudging through Holland Square.

'Really?' Jake attempted to stand up.

Guy shoved him back into his seat. 'Really. Sit still, won't you, Jake?'

'You must've gone up in the world, Guy. Whereas I . . . I have been concentrating all my efforts on going down.'

Guy unpeeled the piece of cloth. There was a deep gash on Jake's forehead. 'And have you succeeded?'

'Pretty well.' Jake considered. 'Yes, pretty well.'

'I think this'll need a couple of stitches . . . I can give you something for the pain, if you want.' He looked at Jake. 'Though you've had a bit to drink, haven't you?'

'I should say so.'

'What happened, Jake?'

'Some bastard in a pub . . . twenty quid he owed me. Won it in a card game. He wouldn't pay up, you see. Said I'd cheated.' Aggrieved, Jake looked up at Guy. 'I don't cheat, do I? Not one of my sins.'

'Of course not,' said Guy soothingly.

'Anyway, we got into a bit of a fight, but I must've had more than I thought, because he got the better of

357

me.' He looked up at Guy. 'I am in mourning, you see.'

Guy paused in the act of selecting sutures. 'In mourning? For what?'

'For my lost freedom.' Jake flinched as Guy put in the first suture. 'I've decided to get a job.'

Guy concentrated on the task in hand. He noticed that Jake had gone very pale. 'If you think you're going to pass out, just tell me, and I'll stop.'

'Not – going – to – pass out.' Jake screwed up his eyes, took a deep breath. 'Faith told me to.'

Guy's hand was perfectly steady as he put in the final stitch. 'Faith told you to what?'

'To get a job. A proper job. I asked her what to do. She said, get a job. And other stuff, but I can't remember. I was living in France, you see, but it didn't work out.'

'Faith lives in France?' Guy's voice was sharp.

'Of course she doesn't. She lives in London.'

Guy paused, bandage in hand. Jake glared at him impatiently. 'In Soho, Guy.'

Soho. He tried mentally to calculate the distance between Cheviot Street and Soho. A mile or two, surely. He found his voice. 'Has she lived there long?'

'A few months. Since June.'

He thought, somehow, that he should have known. When he had considered Faith – and he had been, he had believed, quite successful in putting her out of his mind – he had always imagined her a long way away. Somewhere warm and sunny with white beaches and dark pine woods. The landscape of the past.

'She has a shop,' said Jake, 'called Holly Blue.'

The name rang a bell, but Guy could not place it. 'What sort of shop?'

'Dresses. She makes rather odd things out of scraps.

Works with an alarming woman called Constance Fitzgerald.' A little colour had returned to Jake's face. 'Of course, Guy, it was such a bloody surprise when you ran off with Nicole, and not Faith.'

'It was a long time ago,' said Guy curtly. 'And a bad mistake.'

'I'll say.' Jake laughed. 'Nicole's been married twice since. Once to a poet – he called himself a poet, anyway – who got himself killed in a plane crash – and once to a Yank. They were divorced. I don't think she's married just now.'

'Ralph,' said Guy. Over the last decade he had sometimes, often when he least expected it, found himself missing Ralph. 'How's Ralph?'

Jake shrugged. 'Haven't a clue.'

Guy felt confused. 'He's travelling again . . . ?'

'I told you, I haven't a clue.' And couldn't care less, Guy thought. Jake's rigid posture and cold voice suggested both anger and resentment. Guy, forcing himself to swallow his curiosity, voiced instead the question he most wanted answered.

'And Faith? Is she married?'

'Faith?' Jake laughed again. 'Of course not.'

There was a long silence. Guy looked at Jake's battered face. 'You're going to have a splendid black eye, I'm afraid.'

'Isn't one supposed to apply steak?' Jake grimaced. 'Though in my case, I could only afford luncheon meat.'

Guy said kindly, 'Have you somewhere to go, Jake? I can't invite you home, I'm afraid.' An absolute embargo on all Mulgraves, concussed or otherwise.

Jake's one good eye, brimming with a sardonic intelligence, met Guy's gaze. 'All this' – and the sweep of his hand indicated the desk, the thick carpets, the fine furniture – 'I never imagined you'd go in for all this. Blood money, was it, Guy?'

He muttered, 'Something like that,' and started to clear up.

Jake said, 'Faith'll let me sleep on her floor. Good old Faith.' He dropped his head into his hands. 'God, I'm thirsty!'

Guy filled a glass with water, and handed it to Jake.

'Bastard,' said Jake equably. 'I bet you've a bottle of Scotch stashed away in there.'

'I have, but you look as though another drink would finish you off.' Guy leaned against the edge of his desk. 'What sort of job are you thinking of?'

Jake looked despairing. 'God knows. I've tried everything.' He stood up, and went to the window. 'Butcher, baker, candlestick maker – I've done the bloody lot.'

'Teacher?' suggested Guy.

Jake snorted. 'Oh, come on . . . I'm hardly a role model – how *not* to grow up, perhaps.'

The last ten years had changed Jake, Guy thought. There was a bitterness, a cynicism behind the easy charm, that had not been there before.

'I just thought,' he said, 'that as you speak French . . . You could hardly be any worse than the French masters I had at my school.'

'Generous of you, Guy.'

'A half-decent suit . . . a haircut . . . it wouldn't take much more.'

'I'll think about it.' Jake went to the door. 'Bloody awful idea, but I'll think about it.' He paused, halfway across the threshold, looking at Guy. 'Will you go and see Faith?'

Guy shook his head. 'I don't think so.'

360

But he did go, of course. He was walking home after visiting a patient in Knightsbridge. He was making a detour, stretching his legs. He told himself that he was just going to explain, to put the record straight.

He found the shop in a narrow street still scarred by memories of the Blitz. A seedy-looking club to one side, and to the other a patch of open ground, laced with fireweed and the stumps of the walls of the houses that had once stood there. It was raining, stair-rods of water that drilled steel-grey holes into the derelict land. Yet the name on the shop front caught him, a splash of colour. Holly Blue, in light cobalt and gold: once more the words stirred memories. A twist to the compass of the heart. Crossing the road, he studied the dresses in the window of the shop. The designs were simple and lacking in frills, the fabrics light and airy, clean shades of pink and lemon and mint. Ice-cream colours, very different from the navies and cherry reds that Eleanor favoured.

Retreating to the pub opposite, Guy ordered himself a beer, and sat down and watched. Several people went into the shop. One or two came out carrying large cardboard dress boxes. He did not see Faith.

Guy took a coin from his pocket. Heads he'd go home and never walk this way again; tails he'd go into the shop. He tossed the coin. Heads. He went into the shop anyway.

Holly Blue's interior was like the inside of a sea-washed shell. The walls were washed with ivory and azure and mother-of-pearl, and there was the same absence of fussy ornamentation that Guy had noticed in the dresses in the window. The room was simple, streamlined, a breath of fresh air. He thought that if he closed his eyes and filled his lungs, he would scent, in the distance, the sea.

The shop was busy. Women inspected with single-minded intent the dresses on the rails; from a nearby fitting-room a disembodied voice said loudly: 'The one with those gorgeous trumpet sleeves, darling. I wore it on my first night.'

But still he could not see Faith. He had half expected to feel relief if she were not there; instead, he was aware only of a crushing disappointment. The opening of a door made his heart hammer. But only a temporary quickening: an older woman, her long grey hair escaping from a pleat at the back of her head, her large frame encased in one of the cream-coloured dresses, approached him.

'Can I help you, sir?'

He grabbed the first thing that came to hand: a scarf, an intricate jigsaw of shimmering scraps of material.

'I'll take this.' He watched her fold the scarf, and wrap it and a card bearing the name of the shop in tissue paper.

'That's two pounds, seven shillings and sixpence, sir.'

He paid the money, and walked quickly out of the shop. Outside, the rain had thickened. It streamed in a yellow torrent along the gutter. 'Fool,' he muttered out loud to himself. A passer-by turned and stared. 'You fool.' And he dropped the scarf into the nearest litter bin.

A voice halted him as he reached the corner of the road. 'Guy!' she called. 'Guy!' And he turned and saw her.

*　　*　　*

She had been in the changing-room with a customer, Faith explained, when she had heard him speak. She did not, though, tell Guy how her knees had buckled, how the blood had pounded through her veins. She said, 'I recognized your voice. Voices don't change, do they?'

He stared at her. 'I hardly said a word.'

She had once known the echo of his footsteps. She stood beside him in the rain, uncertain that he would not disappear, dissolve, retreat once more to memory and dream.

'I say, you're getting soaked.' He unfurled his umbrella.

'I must go back to the shop.' Suddenly she longed to escape to the safety she had created for herself. 'I've left one of our best customers standing in her slip with my tape-measure in her hand.'

'When do you close?'

She glanced at her watch, then knotted her hands together. 'In twenty minutes.'

'I'll wait in the pub.'

She went back to the shop. She felt slightly sick. Con, at the till, whispered, 'Go-to-bed eyes and a Savile Row suit – be careful, Faith,' and she darted into the changing-room. Looking at herself sternly in the mirror, she thought, *You are being ridiculous. You are thirty years old. You should have let him walk away.*

After the shop closed, she found Guy sitting at a table in the corner of the pub. There were two drinks in front of him, both untouched.

She said, 'Was it an accident? Chance?'

'I ran into Jake a couple of weeks ago. He told me you were working here.'

She slid into the seat opposite him, and raised her

glass. 'To our glittering careers. Yours is obviously glittering, Guy – such a splendid suit.'

Their glasses touched. 'I'm in private practice now,' he said, 'so the suit's obligatory.' He looked at her. 'I'm old and rich and changed. But you . . . you look wonderful, Faith. So elegant.' He looked dazed.

'Do you think so?' It was going to be all right, she told herself. He had become, after ten years' parting, a remnant from another life, an old friend whom she could regard with distant, incurious affection. 'I'm attempting to be *soignée*. Don't you think a person who owns a dress shop should be *soignée*?'

'Tell me about your shop. Tell me about Holly Blue. Jake said that you've only been in business for a few months.'

'We're still running at a loss, which is rather worrying. We've been doing private dressmaking for years – Con worked at Lucille's when she was younger, and I've been to evening classes. I do all the bookkeeping, and quite a lot of the buying. We've a few loyal clients already. They're mostly artists and writers and dancers, those sorts of people. Plenty of women think that our clothes are peculiar, but a few love them. I hope *enough* of them love them.' She saw that a few small lines crinkled the corners of his eyes, and grey peppered the hair around his temples. He has told the truth, he is not the same, she thought, and was relieved.

'After the war,' she explained, 'we used to make over old dresses. You couldn't get new material, and I've always liked to rummage through jumble sales, you know that, Guy, so I started making patchworks out of the things that were beyond repair, and making them up into scarves and blouses.' She looked at him. 'Like the scarf that you threw in the bin.'

'You made that?' She nodded.

'Then I shall rescue it immediately.'

She heard the double doors of the pub swing shut as he walked out into the rain. Alone, she clutched her arms round herself, and watched him through the window. Rain, streaming down the pane, blurred his image, distorting his dark figure.

He elbowed open the door, a battered package clutched triumphantly in his hand. 'There.'

'*Guy.*' Rain had glued his hair to the side of his head and blackened the shoulders of his grey overcoat. 'You're soaked . . . your lovely coat . . .'

She heard him ask, 'Have Jake and Ralph fallen out? There was something Jake said—'

'Jake hasn't spoken to Pa in ten years, Guy. He has always blamed Pa for Poppy's death.' She added bleakly, 'Pa was having an affair. Ma found out. They quarrelled, and she went for a walk to calm down, and the German plane shot her. So Jake blames Pa. And Pa blames himself, of course.'

'Good God. I didn't know.'

'No.' She looked at him. 'You wouldn't, would you? You were otherwise occupied.'

He flushed. She pushed her empty glass aside. 'I'm sorry. I should go.'

'Please don't go. I want to explain.'

'You fell in love with Nicole, Guy.' The hurt remained. That in itself angered her. She forced herself to speak calmly. 'It happened. It was a long time ago. It doesn't matter now.' She turned to pick up her bag, but his hand gripped hers.

'I was infatuated by Nicole. I never *loved* Nicole. I thought I did, but I didn't.'

'Love . . . infatuation . . . what's the difference?'

'One lasts, I thought.'

While he touched her, she could not move, but was stayed by an emotion akin to dread. She heard him say, 'I was obsessed by Nicole—' and she said, too loudly, '*No*. No, Guy – I don't want to know—'

'Please. I ask too much, but . . . Please, Faith.'

She pulled away from him, but did not have the will to leave the pub, and sat looking out of the window at the rain as he spoke.

'After you left London, I felt at first bitterly angry. It all seemed . . .' He sighed. 'One day you told me you loved me, and the next day you'd gone. And not a word of explanation. I assumed . . . I assumed that you'd changed your mind. Or that you'd been trying to placate me, perhaps. That my declaration had been unwanted . . . embarrassing, even.' He drank the last of his whisky, and added, 'After you'd gone, I felt so empty. Everything seemed so futile. And then I met Nicole in London. I hadn't seen her for years. I can't explain what happened because I've never fully understood it myself.' Guy's brow creased; he took a deep breath. 'When I was training, I once took a whiff of ether by mistake. It made everything seem different. The world seemed to shift on its axis. Meeting Nicole was like that.' His voice hardened. 'I'm not trying to make excuses, though. And I'm not trying to diminish what I did, or how I felt. But passion isn't enough. It was what I'd misssed all the years I'd been married to Eleanor, but by itself it isn't enough. We – Nicole and I – we did not know how to live the rest of our lives. When we were not in bed we were strangers, two people who'd accidentally found themselves living in the same room. We didn't know what to eat, how to live, how to get through the hours. We wouldn't have been able to survive the smallest difficulty. I knew that after the first few weeks. So when something terrible happened—'

'Poppy,' she whispered.

'Yes, Poppy.' He paused. 'If we'd truly loved each other, a tragedy like that might have brought us together. It didn't. It tore us apart. We would have parted anyway, of course, it only hastened the end, but . . . I'd known heaven, and then I knew hell. I could offer Nicole no comfort, no consolation.' He gave a peculiar sort of laugh. 'Strange, wasn't it, that she should leave her husband and her child without a backward glance, yet the death of her mother almost destroyed her. I feared for her sanity sometimes. Such grief.'

Faith herself hardly recalled the months following her mother's death. They possessed a uniform bleakness, an absence of the event and emotion that makes the past memorable.

'And then, suddenly,' Guy went on, 'Nicole changed once more. She started going out to clubs and theatres and to the few friends' houses where we were still welcome. Without me, though. And then she told me that it was over. I was expecting it. I was glad. I'd begun to resent her ability to pick up the pieces, to survive. I knew by then that my own life was in ruins. I'd lost my family, my home, my career. And I'd lost you. Yet she – she'd suffered terribly, but in the end it seemed to fall off her, leaving her untouched. If she'd stayed, I would have hated her.'

Faith made herself look at him. 'So you went back to Eleanor?'

'I went back to *Oliver*.'

She thought of Elizabeth, of the intense, painful love she had always felt for her small niece.

'How is Oliver?'

Guy smiled. 'He's very well. He's doing so well at school, they've decided to put him ahead a year.'

'That's wonderful, Guy.' She looked down at her hands. 'And Eleanor? She has everything she wants, so I suppose she's happy.'

'No.' He lit a cigarette, and shook his head. 'No, I don't think that Eleanor's happy. She was happy during the war, working for the WVS. She's never managed to find a substitute for that. She applied for a few jobs after the war, but either she was too old, or they didn't want to employ a woman, or the work turned out to be too routine.'

Faith always pictured Eleanor Neville as she had last seen her, a gleam of triumph in her dark eyes. It was hard to believe that Eleanor, too, had suffered.

'Eleanor now devotes her considerable energies to her family,' said Guy drily. 'To me because she can achieve status through my position, and to Oliver because she loves him.' He inhaled his cigarette. 'I made a bargain, you see, Faith. Eleanor took me back and let me see my son again on condition that I became a partner in her father's practice. I'd lost most of my own patients. If a doctor abandons his family for a scarlet woman – and that was how they thought of Nicole – his patients tend to scatter. It doesn't do, you know. I was not the model of rectitude they believed me to be. Without Selwyn's help, I'd probably never have practised again. So it's all worked out for the best, I suppose.' He smiled crookedly. 'Only sometimes, recently, I've thought that I've paid too great a price. When I saw Jake – and he was half-cut, Faith, and beaten almost to a pulp by some ruffian in a pub – when I saw him, I felt somehow *less* than him.'

'Don't lie to me, Guy. Don't counterfeit emotions you don't feel.'

'But it's true. I mean it.'

'Jake has nothing, Guy.' Her voice was raw. 'Nothing that lasts. Neither a home nor work. I've lost count of the jobs, the women . . . I've lent him money that he's never paid back, I've bailed him out of police cells when he's drunk too much. I tidy up the chaos that he leaves behind him. He has chosen to destroy himself, and most of the time I feel that there's nothing I can do to stop him. So why should *you* envy *Jake*?'

'Because he, at least, is honest. Whereas I . . . I've learned to live a lie. I've become rather good at justifying to myself what I do. I tell myself that the rich need good medicine just as much as the poor, and that money brings its own problems. All those specious, self-deceiving equivocations. You see,' he said bitterly, 'sometimes I think that I've sold my soul. And that in doing so I've poisoned all of us – me, Eleanor, even Oliver.'

When she looked out of the window Faith noticed that the rain had eased, and that only a few widening circles disrupted the surface of the puddles that glazed the roads. She said, 'We lived through extraordinary times, Guy. The rules kept changing. We muddled through.'

He quoted, ' "Stick together whatever the cost. Never let them see that you mind," ' and she smiled.

'Mulgrave Rules . . . How extraordinary that you should remember.'

'I remember everything.' His voice was fierce. 'I remember La Rouilly . . . I remember rowing on the lake behind the house . . . I remember the woods and the adder . . .'

369

Yet she could not now recall how it had felt, those twin stab wounds in her skin. She heard him say, 'Have you been back?' and she shook her head.

'Jake has. He went back during the war. In 1943. He worked for the Resistance in France, you see. David Kemp arranged it, because Jake knew France so well.' She broke off; she did not want to talk about, or to think about, La Rouilly.

He frowned. 'Was La Rouilly destroyed? It was so near Royan . . . Was it bombed in the 1944 landings?'

'No, Guy.' Seeing that she must tell him, she took a deep breath, and said expressionlessly, 'In the August of 1940, the Germans decided to requisition the château. Genya tried to stop them. She always said that she would. She set fire to the building with herself and Sarah inside it. Only it isn't as easy to burn a house down as you might think it is. Only the roof and attics were destroyed. And Genya and Sarah survived the fire.'

There was a silence. Faith forced herself to go on. 'They were sent to a concentration camp. Genya was Polish, of course, and Sarah was a Jew. Jake made enquiries after the war. They both died in Auschwitz.'

'Dear God,' he whispered.

After a while she said, 'A few months ago I was cycling in Norfolk, not far from where Ralph lives, and I came across a house that reminded me of La Rouilly. It was much, much smaller, of course, and in England, not France, but there was just something about it. Shuttered windows and woodland and a wild garden. It was empty . . . for sale . . . it's been so for a few months.'

She had told no-one else of the house in the woods.

Not even Con. She wondered why she told Guy. A peace-offering, perhaps. A gesture of forgiveness.

'Are you thinking of buying this house?'

She laughed. 'Guy, it has no running water or electricity or proper drains, but it still costs far more than I can afford. But I've started a fund, I have to admit. I have a jam jar, which I put my sixpences into. It's my dream, I suppose.'

He smiled, and delved in his pocket and drew out a sixpence. 'Let me make a contribution, then. You should pursue your dreams. I abandoned mine a long time ago.'

The bitterness in his voice was audible. Guy glanced at his watch. 'I have to go. Supper time.' He stood up. 'You could telephone me, if you want. My surgery's in Cheviot Street. The number's in the phone book.'

As he turned to go, he said, 'I loved Nicole for her similarities to you, Faith. The differences always grated.'

CHAPTER ELEVEN

Faith locked up the shop, and walked to Leicester Square to meet Rufus. Wisps of fog bound themselves around the street lamps and shop signs. In the restaurant, after they had dined, Rufus handed her a package.

'Happy birthday, Faith.'

She unwrapped the paper. Inside was a small watercolour of a pair of Holly Blue butterflies. '*Rufus*.' She hugged him.

'Do you like it?'

'I'm supposed to say, "You shouldn't have", aren't I? But I won't, because I'm so glad you painted it for me, and it's so lovely.' She propped the painting against her glass.

Rufus offered to walk her home. The fog had become thick and yellow; beads of moisture clung to his tousled coppery hair. She heard him say, 'There's something I wanted to talk to you about, Faith. The thing is, my father's been on at me for decades to work in the family business. I've always said no, but I think that I might change my mind.' Rufus's father ran a timber-importing business.

'But your painting, Rufus – you told me—'

'I know. I always said that I'd never sully my artistic soul with anything as sordid as commerce, and that I'd starve for my art, all that.' The tip of his cigarette was a red pinpoint in the gloom. 'Only I can't paint any more, and that's the hell of it.'

'You painted my lovely watercolour.'

They had reached Shaftesbury Avenue. Traffic crawled slowly through the fog, headlights looming like pale, shifting moons. Rufus said, 'That was on a good day. And I was doing it for you. That helped. Oh, I can still manage the odd little thing now and then. But nothing serious. I was going to be a great painter, Faith, do you remember? Someone who'd make a difference. Well, the war put paid to all that. The sort of visions I have, no-one would want to hang on their walls.'

She took his arm to cross the road, weaving through the dark shapes that appeared suddenly out of the mist. 'But Rufus, office work—'

The fog crushed Rufus's voice, robbing it of timbre. 'I used to think it quite impossible, but recently I've thought . . . well, it wouldn't be so bad, would it? You come in at the same time each day, you answer letters and make phone calls, and you go to meetings. I used to despise the predictability, the sameness, of it, but I don't any more. In fact, it rather appeals. I'd know what I was supposed to do. An artist has to construct his own day – his own life. I can't seem to do that any more. And even if the job never meant much to me, then it might let me have the things that did mean something. It would let me buy a house . . . it would get me out of that dump in Islington. It would mean that I had something to offer.'

Though filaments of icy mist were strung through the air, her face felt suddenly hot. Rufus said, as she had known he would: 'I'm asking you to marry me, Faith. I know that I've asked you before, and I know you've always said no, but I want you to think this time.'

They were walking through the narrow maze of streets that made up Soho. From one doorway drifted the raucous clamour of a saxophone, and in another a man and a woman argued, their curses, and the flat of her hand against his face, muted by the mist.

'I could give you something better than this.' Rufus's voice was urgent. 'I could give you a decent home, a nice house with a garden. I know I used to sneer at that sort of thing, but I don't any more. And if you were there – well, I couldn't ask for more.'

She could hear the love in his voice. She said feebly, 'But the shop, Rufus—'

'I wouldn't ask you to give that up. I know how much it means to you. We could live in the suburbs somewhere, and you could take the train in.' It was half past ten; blurred figures spilled out of a pub, jostling them. When she looked up at him, she saw him smile. 'A semi in Metroland, how about it, Faith? I could buy a Ford Prefect, and you could bake cakes and go to bridge parties. If that's what you wanted. We could have children – as many as you like. I know you adore children. I've seen you with Lizzie.'

They had reached the shop. A crumpled newspaper, a few uneaten chips still adhering to it, uncurled in the doorway. He said, 'You can't want *this*,' and she saw that in the darkness, the gilt lettering of the shop sign looked faded and tawdry.

'I love you, Faith.' He took her hands in his. 'I've loved you for years and years. I know that you don't feel the same way about me, but you do at least *like* me. And that could grow, couldn't it, if you let it? I can give you security and comfort and love. That's not so little, is it?'

She whispered, 'It's a great deal, Rufus.' But she pulled away from him.

In the silence that followed, she pressed the tips of her fingers against the window of the shop, and watched the cold water seep down the glass.

She heard him say slowly, 'But it's not enough for you.'

When she did not reply, he said, 'I see. Just tell me, are you still holding out for that doctor chap?'

She hated herself. 'Guy's been married for fifteen years, Rufus.'

'That didn't stop him running off with your sister, did it?'

She said desperately, 'If I had any sense, I'd say yes. You'll make someone very happy.'

'You shouldn't assume that you're the only person capable of constancy.'

She winced. 'I'm sorry. I'm so sorry, Rufus.'

The sound of his footsteps lessened as he walked quickly away. She pulled up the collar of her coat round her face, and fitted her key into the lock. *Are you still holding out for that doctor chap?* Rufus's words clamoured in her head, a provoking, insistent chorus to the dispute that had taken place in her heart since Guy had called at Holly Blue. Nine weeks, she thought. It was nine weeks since she had seen Guy.

She let herself into the flat, and tipped the contents of her purse onto the table, to take out the sixpences. It was too cold to take off her coat. She slit open the letters that had arrived that afternoon. Notes from Ralph and Elizabeth, cards from friends. Nothing from Jake or Nicole. She could not think why she minded. Neither Jake nor Nicole ever remembered birthdays, their own or anyone else's. 'Happy birthday, Faith,' she muttered to herself. She looked around the room, focusing on the card that Lizzie had made for her, the fountain pen that David had sent. Her gaze drifted to the jam jar, now almost full of sixpences. She pressed her fists against her eye sockets. She was thirty-one years old, and she was spending her birthday alone, surrounded by gifts from someone else's husband, someone else's child. Tonight she had rejected what she longed for, what so many women took for granted – a home, a family. Her dream – the house in the wood – was unattainable, as impractical as any of Ralph's more extravagant fantasies.

She looked out of the window. 'You are feeling sorry for yourself,' she said out loud, sternly. 'You chose to be alone this evening; you have chosen not to marry Rufus.' Scolding didn't help. The flat still seemed small and claustrophobic, and fog pressed against the panes. Faith walked downstairs to the shop. There, she stroked with the back of her hand the thick pile of the velvets, and the cool, shimmering silks; there, she tidied a drawer, and swept a speck of dust from the counter. The telephone occupied only a corner of the counter, but it seemed to fill the room, until it was the only thing she could see. She said to herself, *You have this. You have work that you love and a place to live, and that's more than many people have. You have lots of friends and you have your family. You've travelled, you've seen as much of the world as you care to. That should be enough.*

The tips of her fingers touched the telephone receiver and traced the circular indentations in the dial. She thought that Rufus had been right, it was not enough. There was something missing. She lacked adult love. She had had love affairs – four or five since the war –

but they had never lasted more than a few months. She had devoted all her energies to Holly Blue, not to her lovers. Now, she could hardly remember what they looked like. Her heart seemed to have grown smaller and colder. *You were always the dullest of my children*, Ralph had said, long ago, and everything she did seemed to prove him right. She wondered whether this was what growing older, into one's thirties, meant: a shrinking of opportunity, a closing of doors. Yet she remembered standing in the changing-room, tape-measure in hand, hearing Guy's voice and feeling the blood rush through her veins. She said out loud to herself, 'He is a married man. What can he offer but fragments of his life?' She left the counter, and walked around the room once more. She had draped three of her scarves across the back of a chair. Scraps of material, but they glittered, they were beautiful. She went back to the counter and picked up the telephone receiver. She did not need to look up the number; she had learned it off by heart. He would not be at his surgery. It was late; he would have gone home.

But there was a click and a whirr and a voice said, 'This is Dr Neville. Can I help you?'

She swallowed. 'Guy, it's Faith.'

'*Faith*. Where are you?'

'At home. In my flat above the shop.'

'Shall I come?'

She did not pause. 'Yes, Guy. Yes.'

She opened the door. Tiny pearls of moisture, spun by the fog, gleamed on the shoulders of his coat. He said, 'Damned weather . . . couldn't see my way . . .' but she drew him to her, so that he folded his arms around her in a crushing embrace. When he pulled back it was to kiss her: her eyes, her forehead, her mouth. And then her throat, lingering in the hollow at the base of her neck, his lips tracing the swell of bone beneath skin. His hands unthreaded the buttons of her blouse; she buried her fingers in his dark hair. Again, she drew him to her. She had not realized until he touched her the depth of her need. As they fell to the floor his hands clawed at her skirt. She heard the ripping of a seam as the last of her clothing was flung aside, and then she was aware of nothing but his flesh, gripped by hers, and the glorious swelling of pleasure inside her. She felt him shudder, and she heard herself cry out as her climax gathered and stung.

After a while, he said, 'Faith, dearest Faith – speak to me.' He touched her face. 'You're frozen, my love. I shall buy you a carpet to cover this wretched lino.'

He held her until she had stopped shaking. She thought that she had waited for ever to sit like this, skin touching skin, bone clinging to bone. Eventually, he took her hands in his, and said, 'You're still cold. I'll make you a cup of tea. Not very romantic, I know – it should be a champagne cocktail or whatever – but this place is like a damned icebox.'

He pulled on his trousers, and went into the kitchen. She wrapped his discarded shirt around herself. He was searching through the larder for a packet of tea when she called out to him, 'I used to think that because you saved my life – the adder, Guy, do you remember? – that I'd be yours for ever.'

'You are.' He emerged momentarily from the kitchen door, tea-strainer in hand. 'Of course you bloody are. That's the thing. And vice versa, naturally.'

She sat listening to the rattle of teacups and trays, her arms wrapped around her knees. When he brought through the crockery, he said, 'You do still believe that, don't you? Good God, Faith – I've never been here before, but I feel that I've come home.'

She watched him pour the tea; she let him fold her chilled hands round the cup. Then Guy knelt on the floor and began to fiddle with the gas fire, trying to extract more heat from its miserly bars. His back to her, he said: 'But you haven't always felt the same, have you? In the war, when you went away . . . I've been trying to work things out. You said that Jake found out that Ralph was having an affair. Jake told you about it, I suppose. Was that why you didn't turn up at the park? Was that why you went away? Because, at that time, extramarital affairs seemed particularly sordid?'

'Partly.' Though it was ten years ago she still recalled clearly that hot, oppressive August day. 'I waited too long, you see, Guy. I couldn't make up my mind. I knew what I *wanted* to do – but I knew what I *should* do as well. Eleanor had made that perfectly clear to me.'

He said sharply, 'Eleanor?'

'I spoke to her the previous morning. Didn't she tell you? No, of course not. Anyway, she let me know that she thought that I – and the rest of my family – were promiscuous, untrustworthy and unreliable.' She laughed. 'And of course, a great deal of what happened afterwards proved her right.'

'So Eleanor' – Guy thumped the side of the fire with the flat of his hand; blue flames flared – 'Eleanor warned you off?'

Faith nodded. 'So I dithered, and then Ma turned up and told me that Nicole was very ill – she almost died after she had Elizabeth, you see, Guy – and by then it was too late. I went to Compton Deverall to be with

Nicole, and yes – it seemed to me better to leave you alone, to get out of your life.'

'And then I ran off with Nicole . . .' He shook his head and muttered, 'Good God, you should hate me for that.'

Faith put aside her tea, and knelt beside him in front of the fire. 'Do you think, Guy, that we could put by a bit of our lives for each other?' Smiling, she reached up and brushed back the lock of dark hair that had fallen over his forehead. 'Like I save my sixpences in a jam jar?'

He began to kiss her. His nearness seemed just then to be overwhelming; she had imagined these moments for so long that the reality was almost too much happiness to bear. Suddenly she needed time, silence, solitude to absorb such a change of fortune.

She glanced at her watch. It was almost eleven o'clock. 'You should go, Guy,' she said softly. 'Eleanor will be expecting you.'

'I don't want to go.' He drew her to him, burying his face in the crook of her shoulder.

'You must.' She kissed him, letting her mouth linger on his silky dark hair. At last he dressed and left the flat.

After he had gone, words, images, remembered sensations fluttered through her mind like a water-falling pack of cards. She curled up on the sofa, wrapped in a blanket, watching the fire, breathing in the scent of him that still lingered on her skin.

They made rules. Different rules from Mulgrave Rules. Stolen meetings in a museum or a park – ten minutes that transformed a routine day into a joyful one. Occasionally an hour or two, making love in a hotel room. When they could not meet, there were the telephone calls, the painful, wonderful telephone calls, when neither of them wanted to be the first to put down the phone. No letters, lingering to betray. If no-one knew, they told themselves, then no-one would be hurt.

He wanted to buy her presents, to bring her gifts, but she refused – his money was Eleanor's, she said. Once, when both Eleanor and her father were away, they spent a whole night together. They did not sleep until the chill dawn painted the roofs of London silvery-grey.

A winter of sixpences in the jar. She had never been happier.

Jake started teaching at Heatherwood Court Preparatory School for Boys halfway through the spring term of 1952. He had resisted the idea, planted the previous year by Guy Neville, for as long as possible, but then, seeing that without work he would become like Ralph – a drifter, a sponger, a good-for-nothing – he had answered an advertisement in the newspaper. To his surprise, the headmaster, Captain Munday, had written back to him, engaging him immediately.

Heatherwood Court perched on the wild grey coast of North Cornwall. The school occupied a large Edwardian house, furnished with dun-coloured linoleum, and cream and pea-green walls. On his first day, watching small boys bid anguished goodbyes to their parents after the half-term holiday, Jake, appalled, said aloud, 'But they look like refugees!' The history master, an older man called Strickland, turned to him and said, 'They're privileged to be here, Mulgrave. Never forget that.' There had been a trace of mockery in Strickland's voice.

Jake found the school rules hopelessly confusing. There were different stairs for the boys and for the masters, and in many apparently random parts of the school the pupils were not allowed to talk. Every Wednesday afternoon everyone pounded onto wind-swept fields to play games that, even after a month at Heatherwood, Jake still found incomprehensible. He was relieved when a cough absolved him from super-vising rugby practice. The matron, an angry Pole who had a son in Jake's form, gave him a jar of liniment and told him to get some fresh air. Jake threw the liniment away, but went for a walk along the cliffs.

Far below, graphite-coloured waves hurled them-selves at needle-sharp rocks. Jake, treading carefully along the narrow path, decided that he'd give the school another couple of weeks, and if it didn't become any more bearable he'd chuck it at the end of term. He'd go abroad – to Italy, perhaps. He hadn't been to Italy for years. He'd go to Italy, and drink himself to death, and then at least he'd die happy and not be a bother to Faith any more.

A voice said, 'Mulgrave. What on earth are you doing here?' and Jake jumped.

'Contemplating my own end, Strickland.'

'Rather chilly way to do it, old chap. And you'd disrupt the gannets.' Strickland was holding a pair of binoculars.

'I didn't know you were a birdwatcher.'

'It's my cover. To tell the truth, I'd go insane if I didn't get away from the place once a week. My leg – or rather, the absence of it – saves me from having to cavort on playing fields.' Strickland had been injured thirty-five years before at the Battle of the Somme. He glanced at Jake. 'And you?'

'A cough.'

'Did you seek succour from the Horrible Hungarian?'

'Mrs Zielinski is Polish. And she's not horrible – she's quite beautiful.' Jake, visiting the infirmary, had noticed that the school matron had black hair and a blue-white skin, and eyes like chips of glittering Cornish granite.

Strickland was scathing. 'Everyone's tried. Denman . . . Lawless . . . not me, of course, I'm past that sort of thing. Did you get anywhere?'

'Mrs Zielinski prescribed liniment, and told me not to smoke.' Jake offered his Players to Strickland, and lit a cigarette for himself.

Strickland took a hip flask from his pocket. 'Swig?'

The whisky warmed him. Strickland said, watching him, 'I wondered if that was your poison, actually.' They began to walk along the path. 'We're all crocks,' Strickland explained. 'That's how Captain Munday appoints his staff. I've my leg, and Lawless likes a bet, and Denman was sent down from Cambridge, and Linfield . . . Linfield is a sadist, of course.'

Jake laughed. 'I wondered how I got the job. I haven't a qualification to my name.'

'The good captain can pay us less, you see. Keeps the fees up and the salary bill down so that he can retire sooner rather than later to his bungalow on Canvey Island or whatever.' Strickland glanced at Jake. 'Still, he was lucky to get you, though I don't suppose he realizes it.'

They had reached the headland. The tussocky ground was springy with sea pinks. Jake looked at Strickland. 'Why do you say that?'

'Because you're good at your job.'

Jake roared with laughter again. 'I have to teach Latin – I wasn't supposed to, I was engaged for French and German – but the fellow engaged to teach Latin didn't show up. I'm one lesson ahead of the boys, Strickland. I read up the primer the night before.'

'You like the little buggers,' said Strickland equably.

'The boys?'

'Yes. I loathe them, you see. Whereas you like them.'

A curl of wind hit Jake in the face. He blinked. 'Yes, I suppose I do.'

'The rest of it doesn't matter. You like the boys, and you do your best for them – the ninnies and numbskulls and milksops included – and that makes you a good teacher.'

Jake chucked his cigarette stub into the churning waves below. In the distance a bell rang. 'Back to prison,' said Strickland glumly.

Jake realized after a while that he welcomed the pocketing of each day into little sections: lessons, games, prep, lunch and dinner, recreation. He welcomed not having to make decisions, not having to forge meaning from an existence that he had long since found capricious. His loathing of the bleak, grey Cornish countryside ebbed a little, and he began to dislike less the rugged coastline, and the empty, haunted moorland. His own small study-bedroom, with its inadequate heating and brown lino floor, became familiar. Entertainments were few – a drink with Strickland and Denman, the English master, in Strickland's study once a week or so; a chilly dalliance with a local barmaid on the moors that surrounded the school. There were few women at Heatherwood – the terrifying Mrs Munday, wife of the headmaster; a huge and ancient cook; and a couple of downtrodden chambermaids, whom Jake pursued in a half-hearted fashion. And the school matron, Mrs Zielinski, whose tongue was as sharp as the needle she used to lance boils.

Heatherwood Court itself remained bewildering. Most disturbing to Jake was the school's reliance on corporal punishment. Even the army, Jake thought, did not beat its recruits with a leather strap. The strap hung in a case in the school hall; recalcitrant boys were sent to fetch it, thus enforcing their compliance in their own pain and humiliation. Jake never resorted to the strap – the look of the thing nauseated him – but most of the other masters used it occasionally. Mr Linfield, the maths teacher, frequently beat boys with the strap. Mr Linfield, Jake sensed, enjoyed it.

One night, returning to his room after supervising prep, he came across Mr Linfield speaking to one of the pupils. The corridor was gloomy (Captain Munday economized on electricity), and Jake had to squint to make out the identity of the boy. Kirkpatrick was in Jake's form. Consummately untidy, shortsighted and adenoidal, hopeless at games, he was an unpopular and unprepossessing lad. His parents lived in Africa; during the shorter school holidays Kirkpatrick was consigned to the care of a bachelor uncle. Jake found it hard to imagine a much more miserable existence than Kirkpatrick's.

Linfield was telling Kirkpatrick off. The poor kid must have muddled his equations, thought Jake, or stumbled over his times tables. Any moment, Linfield would send the boy for the belt. But instead, as he approached, Jake saw Linfield remove Kirkpatrick's glasses, and hit the boy hard across the face with the flat of his hand. The sound of the blow echoed in the corridor.

He could never afterwards remember the bit between Kirkpatrick's anguished gulp, and the crack as Linfield's head struck the wall. There was a sort of black, empty void. Jake's hands were round Linfield's neck; his thumbs were pressing Linfield's bony windpipe. Kirkpatrick had gone – a scuttle of boots, a small face wet with tears. Linfield struggled and spluttered and gasped, 'Damn you, Mulgrave, let me go,' and began to cough. His face changed from red to white to blue. The colours of the Union Jack, thought Jake. He kept pressing. Then, suddenly, he felt someone trying to pull him away, and he heard Strickland say, 'For God's sake, Mulgrave, you'll kill him,' and his hands slipped from Linfield's throat. Linfield slid, coughing, to the floor.

Jake walked out of the corridor, out of the school, across the games field towards the cliffs. The path was a narrow trench of slippery mud. Waves crashed against the ragged coast. Gobbets of foam, thrown up by the wind, dampened his eyelashes. Standing on the cliff edge, he thought how easy it would be to fall, to tumble into the abyss, to look up and see the water close over your head. He despised himself for not being able to step forward, for knowing that it was that first step that was difficult, and not the rest of it.

After a while, he heard a voice call out his name, and he turned and saw Mrs Zielinski, the school matron, running towards him.

'Mr Strickland and I have been looking for you everywhere, Mr Mulgrave.' She was out of breath; patches of pink lit her pale face.

Jake chucked his cigarette stub into the waves.

'You smoke too much,' she scolded him. 'Your cough will come back.'

He said, 'I'll give them up, then,' and threw the Players packet, too, into the sea, and sat down on the grass. 'There. That'll make everything all right.' He wrapped his arms round his knees, hugging them to his face.

She looked down at him. 'I came to tell you that Mr Linfield will be fine,' she said. 'I had a look at him – there's only a little superficial bruising.'

'I rather hoped,' Jake said, 'that he was dead.'

'Then you are very foolish, because then they would hang you, and you would be dead too.'

He rubbed his nose with the back of his hand, and looked out to sea and said nothing. She said, 'When I saw you standing there, I was afraid. I thought that you might do something stupid.'

He looked up at her, surprised, and laughed. 'I haven't the nerve.'

'Nerve? Why do you say that?' Her voice was fierce. 'To go on takes courage. That's the easy way out.'

'Good God. You sound as though you've been reading too many women's magazines. I'd thought better of you, Mrs Zielinski. I'd thought you a malcontent like me.'

'Linfield is a horrible man, of course. I don't blame you for doing what you did. It was stupid, but I don't blame you.' She glanced at him again. 'Are you coming back to school, Mr Mulgrave?'

She thinks I mean to drown myself, Jake thought, and smiled. He shook his head. He felt empty inside.

'It's cold.' She shivered, pulling the two halves of her cardigan together. 'You'll catch pneumonia . . . it's foolish just to sit there, on the wet grass.'

'Then I'll walk,' he said, and stood up.

She followed after him, her small footsteps pitter-pattering on the impacted earth. After a while, he swung round and said angrily, 'Go home. For God's sake go home.'

'It's almost dark. You might slip and fall.'

'So? No great loss if I do.'

'More foolish words, Mr Mulgrave.'

He resented her tenacity, her interference. 'Go home, Mrs Zielinski. I'm not worth saving. I'm no better than Linfield, you see.'

'Now you are talking nonsense. You're not like him at all.'

He said, more calmly, 'Linfield enjoys hurting boys. I enjoyed hurting Linfield.'

He saw, and took pleasure in, the bewilderment in her eyes. 'I mean it,' he said. 'I enjoyed it.' As he flung the words over his shoulder, the wind almost stole them, and he forced himself to remember the first time he had experienced that cold, exhilarating rage. In Spain, during the civil war, perhaps. Or on that night-mare journey through France, when he had woken to find the man filching the bicycle that he himself had stolen.

'I wanted to kill him,' he called back to her. 'If Strickland hadn't come, I dare say I would have done.'

'It's not the same at all!' She pushed forward, drawing level with him by mounting the narrow grassy ridge at the edge of the cliff. 'Kirkpatrick's a little boy.'

'And Linfield is an asthmatic crock who takes his own feebleness out on those weaker than himself.' Yet, strangely, he could not bear to see her there, poised between two worlds, the land and the sea. He said, 'Get down from there. You might slip.'

'What do you care? You don't care about anything.'

He seized her hand, pulling her to safety. '*You* should care. Your son—'

'George is not your business. No-one's your business.'

He saw her take a step back towards the brink. He thought for a moment that he would hurt her, as he had hurt Linfield, but instead he tugged her roughly towards him. His voice muffled by her body, he said, '*Don't.*'

She was shaking – with cold, with fear, he did not know. A quick, steady tremor beneath the flattened palms of his hands. He took off his jacket, and wrapped it round her.

She whispered, 'Thank you, Mr Mulgrave.'

'Jake. For pity's sake, my name's Jake.'

They had almost reached the place where the cliff shelved down to a small, rocky beach. He knew that he stood on a different brink from the one on which they had teetered only a few moments ago. He looked down at her, and smiled crookedly.

'It's usual, Mrs Zielinski, when someone introduces themselves, to respond likewise.'

The pale face became slightly pink. 'My name's Mary.'

'I'd expected something exotic. Something Polish.'

'I am English, now, Mr Mulgrave. I mean, Jake. I am English, and George, my son, is English.' Her voice was proud. 'Now will you come back to the school?'

They had walked into the comparative shelter of the cove. The wind ruffled her hair; there was still a bluish tinge around her mouth. She made a small gesture, of impatience, of confusion.

'I'm finished, aren't I?' he said. 'They're hardly going

to welcome me back with open arms, having tried to strangle another member of staff.'

For the first time, she smiled. 'You haven't worked here as long as I, Jake. Captain Munday will do nothing. Believe me. He'll want to avoid scandal, and besides, he's lazy, and won't wish to look for another language teacher.'

The icy wind blistered Jake's skin. He knew, though, that it would happen again. At least, he thought wryly, he understood himself. His saving grace, self-knowledge, the awareness that sooner or later he himself would destroy the temporary sanctuary that Heatherwood had become.

He said, 'Has Strickland told you his theory? That we've all got something to hide? I told you, Mary, that there's a part of me that enjoys violence. It's been quite useful in the past, but I've a feeling that it's going to be a bit of a liability here.'

She said, 'You're speaking of the war, I guess. You were in the services?'

'I was in the army, twiddling my thumbs at first, and then I was in France for a while.' He tried to make her understand. 'It separates you, you see, Mary. I saw things – I did things – that have set me apart from other people. I'm unfit for the world, and yet I despise it too. People care about such little things . . . what they'll eat for dinner . . . what so and so said to them . . . and it all seems so ludicrously unimportant.'

She did not offer the facile comfort: *Talk to me, tell me, sharing it will make it better.* Instead, he heard her say, 'I felt like that once. When I found out that I was pregnant, I felt just like that.'

He was surprised. 'But George . . . you adore him—'

'Of course I do.' There was a long silence, and he

sensed that she was coming to a decision. Eventually she said, 'I was unmarried, you see, Jake.' She dug her hands deep into the pockets of his jacket. 'I've never been married. Zielinski was my maiden name. I tell you this – and no-one else knows – to show you why you must go back. I, too, wanted to give up. But I didn't, and I'm glad of it. I took this job because it gives George and me a roof over our heads. And because it gives George an education.'

He snorted. 'Of sorts.'

'An *English* education.' Her voice softened. 'You, too, Jake – you must put the past behind you. You must think of other things.' She added severely, 'You must be like me, Jake. I'll help you.'

Her eyes were a dark, inky grey. For a moment her gaze held his, and then he looked away. The waves crashed at the shore, battering the great boulders to grains of sand. She had pulled up the collar of his jacket round her neck. She looked small, defenceless, against the vast expanse of the sea and the great weight of the boulders. He felt, just then, the beginnings not only of desire, but of liking, and was aware of an appalled anticipation of all the pain and responsibility that liking entailed.

Better to nip it in the bud. 'It's no good, Mary. I don't fit in here. I thought I might do, but I don't.'

'But we're all misfits, aren't we? George buys those sweets at the tuck shop . . . I can't remember their name . . . they are yellow and pink and black and white—'

'Allsorts,' he said.

'That's it. Allsorts. All jumbled up together.'

He smiled, and fumbled in his pocket. 'My cigarettes—'

'You threw them into the sea.'

'Damn.' He looked at her. 'Damn you, Mary. You're an interfering woman. You remind me of my sister.' He took her strong, white fingers in his, and said, 'You're still cold,' and tucked her hand under his arm. And then, because he could think of nowhere else to go, he walked with her back to the school.

Jake did not get the sack. Captain Munday, protested to by Linfield, merely admonished him. 'Worried about the publicity,' explained Strickland as he tapped ash from the bowl of his pipe. 'Looks bad, you see, one member of staff trying to murder another.'

On their afternoons off, Mary Zielinski devised days out for them. Trips in a fishing-boat around Padstow harbour; a visit to the artists' colony at St Ives. Jake borrowed Strickland's battered A35, and they drove to Tintagel. Orchids and sea pinks bloomed among the ruins. They travelled inland, to the dark wasteland of Bodmin Moor, where a circle of menhirs cast long shadows. From beneath the shelter of the stones, he watched her. Her black hair hung free to her shoulders, and the thin drizzle stung her pale face. He saw how laughter lit up her grey eyes as she began to chase George, running in and out of the circle, weaving patterns among the stones.

Faith was thinking of getting ready for bed when the doorbell rang. She thought *Guy* and dashed downstairs and pulled open the door. Nicole stood on the door-step.

'How gorgeous to see you, Faith.' A crushing hug. 'Now, where's your bathroom? I'm dying for a pee.'

She said, 'Upstairs, on the right,' and watched,

dazed, as Nicole climbed the stairs. It was, she estimated, two years since she had last seen Nicole.

The hall was littered with suitcases and parcels. Faith gathered them up. Nicole, emerging from the bathroom, explained, 'There was only an awful chemical toilet in the plane, and queues miles long at London Airport.' She flung off her coat, a pale blond wool much the same colour as her short curls. She twirled round. 'Do you like it? Very Liz Taylor, I thought.' Her close-fitting sweater and flared skirt emphasized her small, curving figure. 'And Faith, you look marvellous. Such a lovely dress. And your hair. You must be in love.' She took Faith's hands in hers. 'Do you mind? Is this all right? I was going to go straight to Compton Deverall, only what with not being able to find a bathroom—'

There had been a time when she had minded seeing Nicole; a time when she had only been able to think that Nicole had had everything that she herself had wanted, and yet had thrown it all away. But Nicole was untroubled by conscience, and it had proved impossible, faced with such blithe indifference, to nurse much bitterness. It had always been easier to love Nicole. Only a faint wariness lingered, a small distance that had not existed in their childhoods.

'It's perfectly all right. A drink?'

'Oh, yes, darling, *please*. You're so wonderfully clever, as always.'

'I thought you were to be in a film . . . When you wrote, in January—'

'It didn't work out. Such awful songs – you can't believe how awful they were, Faith – I kept imagining what Felix would have thought.' Nicole screwed up her face. ' "My love is like the moon in June, I'd like to float away like a red balloon." ' She giggled. 'Well, *really*!'

Faith handed Nicole a gin and tonic. 'Weren't you under contract?'

'*Sailor Sally* didn't do as well as they'd hoped. So they made a bit of a fuss, but they didn't mind too much. I'll find something else. Something better.' Nicole's glass chinked against Faith's. 'I've met the most marvellous man, Faith. He's a Texan, called Michael, and I'm absolutely sure that he's The One. He's away on business just now, and my heart was breaking, so I thought I'd take my mind off things and fly over and see everyone.' She looked at Faith. 'And you?' Nicole's blue eyes narrowed. 'When I came here . . . you were expecting someone else, weren't you?'

She said, 'Not *expecting*,' and stopped, angry that she had given so much away.

Nicole knelt beside the cases on the floor, and began, flinging clothes and shoes carelessly aside, to unpack. 'I've brought some lovely things for you. This, and this.' She heaped boxes and packages onto Faith's lap. 'I won't ask any more. Only you look happier than you have for years, and if that's the reason, then I'm so pleased for you. And I know that you've only ever loved Guy Neville, and if it is Guy, then I'm especially pleased. Eleanor and I – we only ever borrowed Guy. He was always yours, Faith.'

Nicole thought, arriving at Compton Deverall, how nice it was that she could enjoy again that first magical glimpse of the house, just as she had when she had driven here as David's fiancée. The roofs and windows glittered in the sunshine.

She found them on the terrace, behind the house.

David was pulling weeds from between the paving stones; Elizabeth was sitting at an old wooden table, scribbling. For a few moments, Nicole just stood in the shadow of the house, watching them.

David looked up. 'Nicole!'

She smiled and crossed the terrace to him. 'Don't ask me why I didn't phone to say I was coming. You know that I never do.' She looked up at him. 'I like to tell by people's faces whether they're happy to see me.'

When he held her to him, she closed her eyes, enjoying, as always, the touch of him, the comfort of him. After a long time, he let her go and she held out her arms to her daughter.

'Darling Elizabeth, how *grown* you are.' She felt slightly bewildered. Elizabeth's appearance was fixed in her memory from her last visit, two years before, in 1950: a little girl in a pink party dress. Now, aged eleven, Elizabeth was wearing a rather dreadful pleated skirt and knitted jersey, and she was, Nicole estimated, only a few inches shorter than she herself was. Elizabeth was strong and well built. *Strapping*, thought Nicole, rather taken aback. She had never imagined herself having a strapping daughter.

She said, 'I've brought lots of presents for you both, but I'm not sure whether the clothes I've bought will fit you, Lizzie.'

David fetched Nicole's case from where she had left it at the front of the house. Nicole knelt and opened it. 'Now, David, I bought you a book – a first edition of *Moby Dick*. I found it in a bookshop in Boston – I tried to read it, but I couldn't, it was too horrible – the poor whale. And some wonderful shirts – such lovely cotton, aren't they – and these dear striped socks.'

He said, 'I'll be the talk of the City.'

'And I couldn't resist this.' She watched him un-wrap the miniature Studebaker. 'See, there's a cigarette lighter in the headlights, and the boot opens up – only they call it the trunk in America – and you can keep your pipe tobacco in it. Oh, and there's this.' She took out a flat package and grimaced. 'I made a gramophone record – it's the most awful song, I'm afraid, from my film. You can use it as a table-mat, if you like.'

She knelt again, and took more gifts from the case. 'Lizzie, see this lovely doll – she has the sweetest little buttoned shoes, and look, her eyes close. And here are some dresses and a skirt, though I think I'll have to let down the hems for you. And I found these in Florida.'

Opening a small leather box, Nicole showed Elizabeth the single row of river pearls. 'Do you like them, darling?'

'They're lovely, Mummy,' said Elizabeth dutifully.

'I think,' said David, 'that we should put them away safely until you are a little bit older, Lizzie.'

'Yes, Daddy.'

'David, how dreary of you!' Nicole stood up. 'I wore my mother's pearls when I was six! I remember when we were in Naples, and I wore one of Ma's old silk camisoles as a dress and her pearls, and Faith passed around a hat, and I sang and danced, and we made *pots* of money—'

'Nevertheless,' said David, 'I think we'll put the pearls away.'

Elizabeth handed her father the case. Nicole said, 'I suppose you're right. They unthread so easily, don't they, and they're such a bore to restring. But I'll buy you something else to make up for it, darling. You must come to London with me next week, Lizzie. We'll go to the ballet and to the theatre and to all the wonderful shops—'

'Lizzie has to go back to school next week,' said David gently.

'Surely it wouldn't matter if she missed a week or two?'

'I've a tennis match, Mummy.' Elizabeth threaded her fingers through Nicole's. 'It would be lovely to go to London with you, but I can't miss the match. And I've almost finished knitting my blanket.'

'Blanket?'

'It's for the poor children in India. We have to knit lots of squares and sew them together. It's taken me ages.'

'I suppose it would, darling,' said Nicole faintly. Looking down at her daughter, she stroked her dark, silky hair, and she thought how strange the child was. It had crossed her mind occasionally in the past to wonder whether that awful nursing-home had made a mistake, and had somehow swapped her baby for someone else's.

Yet she dismissed the idea immediately. Elizabeth was unmistakably David's. Her dark eyes, her composure and tranquillity were all his. As she touched the back of her hand against her daughter's face, she heard David say: 'Isn't it time to feed Pansy, Lizzie? Run along now. Your mother looks as though she could do with a drink.'

The child scampered away. Nicole sighed hugely, and sank into a deckchair. 'An absolutely enormous gin and tonic please, David. And is there ice? Does Compton Deverall have such a thing as a refrigerator yet?'

He smiled. 'I'm afraid not. But I keep the tonic in the cellar, so it shouldn't be too warm.'

When he returned five minutes later with two drinks, she said, 'You're very protective of Elizabeth, aren't you, David?'

'I want her to be happy. To spare her from hurt.' He sat down beside her.

'I meant, you protect her from *me*.'

'I'm sorry if it seems like that.'

'It doesn't matter. I quite understand. You don't want her to grow up like me.'

He looked at her. 'I'd like her to possess your beauty . . . your spirit . . . your courage.'

She said, 'I wonder why on earth I left you, David. I shall always adore you.'

'You left me,' he said lightly, 'because there were still continents to travel and a thousand new friends to make.'

They sat in a companionable silence, watching the trees' inky shadows lengthen across the lawn. She heard him say: 'Tell me how things are with you, Nicole. Are you to be a famous film star? Are we to see your name in lights in Piccadilly?'

She laughed. 'I'm afraid not. Too dull, darling, all that standing around. You wait for hours and hours and then they shoot you for a few minutes.'

'What will you do, then?'

'Oh,' she said carelessly, 'I'll sing . . . I prefer that. I prefer to see my audience.'

'It sounds . . . uncertain.'

'I've never been one for certainty, have I, David?'

His gaze met hers. He shook his head. 'Are you all right for cash?'

'Fine. Absolutely fine.' She looked at him. There were leather patches on the sleeves of his jacket. 'And you, David? Do you still work in London?'

'I've stayed with the Foreign Office. I'd like to give it up and concentrate on the farm, then Lizzie wouldn't have to go to boarding school. But it just isn't practical.'

She touched his hand. 'You look tired, darling.'

'I'm forty-four.' He smiled at her. 'I am old and grey.'

'Like me.'

'Never,' he said. 'Never.'

'I'll go and find Lizzie. I have to leave tomorrow morning.'

'So soon?'

'Yes. So I must have a good natter with my daughter.'

She found Lizzie in the stable, grooming her pony. Nicole stood for a while, unnoticed, watching her daughter combing out the horse's tail, listening to her gentle murmur. She saw that Elizabeth loved the pony, just as she herself had loved her donkeys and dogs and kittens and all the other creatures she had cared for when she was a girl. Nicole felt for a moment unbearably sad, as though without realizing it she had lost something irreplaceably precious.

Yet the following morning, leaving Compton Deverall, she looked back at the glinting, many-paned windows that she had once tried to count, and she knew that she could not have done otherwise, for she enjoyed only the journey.

CHAPTER TWELVE

In the summer of 1952, almost a year after Holly Blue
had opened, they made for the first time a profit of a
hundred and fifty pounds in a single week. Faith and
Con celebrated in style with beer from the pub opposite, and oysters bought from Harrods' Food Hall.

'Should be champagne, of course,' said Con, 'but I've
always thought beer was nicer. Less *spiky*.'

It was half past seven. The shop had closed, and they
had cashed up and swept the floor, and retreated to the
kitchen of Faith's flat.

'Do you think,' said Faith, 'that we'll be rich?'

'Fabulously.' Con's tone was dry.

'It would be nice to have a shop assistant.'

'Or a cleaner.'

Faith slid an oyster down her throat. 'Or a day off.'

Con looked at her. 'To spend with your chap?'

Con was the only person who knew about Guy. Con
always referred to him as 'your chap'. There was a
proprietorial air to the phrase that Faith liked. As
though Guy were truly hers, and not just hers for the
odd bits of the day when neither his work nor his
family required him.

She said glumly, 'Even if *I* had a whole day free, then
he almost certainly wouldn't.'

'The wages of sin, my dear.' Con flipped the top

from a beer bottle, and refilled Faith's glass. 'But you can have a few days off, if you like. Go and see your father, perhaps.'

Faith thought of Heronsmead, and how nice it would be to walk along the beach in the late summer haze.

'Oh, Con, that would be wonderful. But how would you manage?'

'I'll ask the girl who does our beading whether she wants some extra work. She's very reliable.' Con tipped down another oyster.

After Con had gone home, Faith cleared up and took the shop's books up to her flat. As she worked, she became aware of a low, familiar ache in her belly; the same ache that she had experienced every month since turning fourteen. She felt a pang of disappointment: she had been five days late, and she had hoped—

For what? she thought, suddenly angry with herself. Had she hoped for a baby? For Guy's baby? Had she hoped that Guy, who was always so careful, might have made a mistake?

She made tea, found aspirins, and curled up in her eiderdown, a hot-water bottle on her stomach. Each month the same fantasies, she thought, hating herself. The same stupid, impractical fantasy about having Guy's baby. And the even more stupid and utterly shameful fantasy about Guy abandoning his wife and child and living with her in the house in Norfolk. The house with the overgrown garden and the shuttered windows.

Looking around the flat, she made herself imagine it cluttered with a cot and pram and a high chair and wet nappies. I dream, Faith thought bitterly, about living with a man I can't marry in a house I can't afford. After a while she got up and fetched the order books from the kitchen, and made herself go through them, checking invoices and bills with rigid and single-minded concentration.

The summer lingered, herringbone clouds flecking a vast azure sky. At Heronsmead, Faith found Ralph in the garden, picking blackberries.

'Damn things are mildewed. Wretched plant – spent the entire summer ripping myself to pieces on the thorns, and now the blasted thing's got mildew.' He emerged from the brambles and gave Faith an enormous hug.

'I made you a cake,' she said, showing him the tin.

'Pink icing. My favourite.' Ralph looked around vaguely. 'We could have tea in the garden. Kitchen's a bit untidy, I'm afraid.'

Faith went indoors. The kitchen was a disaster. Potato peelings, black with age, lingered in the sink, and the contents of a milk jug grew lumpy on the window sill. As always, her heart ached with the absence of Poppy. You didn't come to terms with it; you only grew accustomed to it.

She made tea and took it out into the garden. Ralph was hauling decaying deckchairs out of the garden shed. After she had poured out the tea, he said, 'I had a letter from Nicole,' and handed her a piece of paper from his pocket. From the worn folds and tattered edges she could guess how often he had read it.

'And Jake?' asked Ralph, after she had read Nicole's letter. 'Have you seen Jake?'

'At the end of July. He's doing fine, Pa. He's been working at the school for five months now. He's very busy.'

She cut the cake to fill in the silence, and tried not to

imagine how she might feel if she had not seen Lizzie in ten years.

'A teacher,' said Ralph proudly. 'Jake, a teacher. I'd never have believed it.'

The following afternoon, she walked to the telephone box. She thought, Pa did this, walked out here secretly and phoned Linda Forrester, and she felt for a moment bitterly ashamed of herself. Then she shut the thought away, as she always did, in a cupboard in her mind. Sometimes the cupboard door threatened to burst open. She muttered to herself, 'If no-one knows, then no-one is hurt,' and tried to believe it.

Guy asked after Ralph.

'Ralph's fine, Guy. A bit old and creaky, but fine.'

'I should so like to see him. If only I could—' He broke off. 'Tell me about Heronsmead, Faith. Describe it to me. I need to hear your voice.'

She told him about the cottage, the garden, the beach.

'If I were to come to Heronsmead, where could I meet you?'

Her heart seemed to pause. She thought quickly. 'There's a triangle of grass where the lane to the village turns off from the coast road—'

'I'll meet you there at – let me see – ten o'clock tomorrow morning. Eleanor and Selwyn are spending the weekend with Selwyn's old tutor in Oxford. We'll have a day, Faith, a whole day in a place where no-one knows us, where we can go where we want, and do what we want.' She heard the joy in his voice. 'Do you mind being away from your father for a day? Will Ralph mind?'

'I was planning to go for a bike ride. Oh, Guy,' she said. 'A *whole day*.'

He was waiting in his car at the grass triangle when she freewheeled down the incline the following morning. Jumping off the bicycle, she flung herself into his arms and kissed him.

'I've brought a picnic,' he said. 'Dressed crab and Cox's apples.'

They drove north to Blakeney. The sea glittered. They parked the car and walked along the shingle isthmus of Blakeney Point, marooned between the salt marsh and the sea. Jellyfish, flung up by the tide, lay glazed and solidified on the pebbles. The last yellow blooms of horned poppies shivered in the breeze. Faith gathered flints and fragments of coloured glass, smoothed to dull jewels by the waves, and he wrote their names on a patch of sand. Picnicking, she fed him fragments of crab. In the thin, late summer light they lay together, his arm curled round her shoulders.

She took him to see her house. Driving up the tree-lined track, he said, 'Are you still saving your sixpences?'

'I've opened a bank account at the post office. Aren't you impressed, Guy?'

'Very.'

'I had to count out all the sixpences. I had over thirty pounds. But the house costs six hundred and fifty.'

'I wish you'd let me help.'

'You know that I won't.' The car rattled and shook on the uneven track. 'It's a quest, isn't it, Guy? Something I have to do alone for the good of my soul.' She looked up. 'There it is. Isn't it perfect?'

He slowed the car, peered through the windscreen. 'It's quite extraordinary. A witch's house.'

She opened the gate. Ivy had bound the shutters to the walls. The roof was patched with lichen, so that the tiles were dotted sage green and gold. In the garden, Old Man's Beard festooned what had once been a shrubbery, and brambles invaded the lacy, yellowing remains of a vegetable patch. A few roses lingered on a rambler, pink and scented and overblown. Behind the house, dandelions studded the grass. Dropping a stone into the well, she listened, but heard only a thrush, beating a snail shell against a stone, and the breeze shaking the leaves of a willow.

With a rattle of shutter and latch, Faith opened a window. She tried to haul herself onto the sill. 'I want to see what it's like inside,' she said, and smiled. 'If I'm to live here . . . Give me a leg up, Guy.'

He cupped his hands, and she swung up onto the sill, and slid into the room. She was in a scullery: stone jars stood beneath a huge butler's sink, cobwebs binding them together. Copper saucepans, green with age, hung from nails on the walls. A scattering of straw and a few feathers told her that a bird had once nested in the rusty Oxo tin on the draining board.

She went into the adjacent room. When she pulled back the rotting curtains, letting up a cloud of dust, she heard Guy, behind her, cough.

'The kitchen.' She rattled the door of the ancient range, and opened the gloomy larder.

'All mod cons . . .' Guy traced his fingertip along a shelf.

'What are you writing?'

'What else?'

She read what he had scrawled in the dust. 'Guy

loves Faith.' He pulled her to him and began to kiss her.

'Not here,' she whispered, and said, between kisses, 'There are probably ghosts.'

'Rats, more likely.' But he steered her through a doorway, his arm round her waist.

They climbed the stairs. In a room looking out over the front garden (slats of light through peeling shutters, a fly-spotted mirror on the chimney breast), he made love to her, stripping off her clothes so that she stood naked in front of him. In the mirror, she saw him shut his eyes for a moment, as if unable to bear the nearness of her. When he knelt in front of her, and kissed her toes, and the soles of her feet, and her ankles and calves, she shivered, fleetingly uncertain whether she was experiencing pleasure or pain.

When, finally, they turned from each other, and lay satiated, watching the spiders' slow journey across the cracked ceiling, the afternoon sun had begun to dim. The shapes of their bodies were imprinted on the dusty floor. She saw him rise and walk naked out of the room, returning a few minutes later with a bucket of water.

'All I could squeeze out of that well. You're piebald, my darling.'

'Do you still love me piebald?'

'I'd love you black, white, red or green.' He dipped his handkerchief in the bucket. 'Or striped. Or spotted.' He washed her feet, her legs, her arms, her breasts.

Dressing, returning downstairs, she noticed the flurry of dried leaves, blown through the open window. Outside, in the garden, the petals of the rambler had begun to fall, pink blots on the emerald grass. Driving back along the track and through twisting country lanes, they said little. When they reached the coast road, she saw that the tide had come in, and she knew that it would have washed the evidence of their morning's visit away: the picnic crumbs, the hollows where their heads had rested, and their names, written on the sand.

In the summer holidays, Heatherwood Court was pleasantly transformed. With the departure of Captain Munday and his wife for their annual holiday ('Motoring in Buckinghamshire, dear boy. Marvellous roadhouses'), tension seemed to evaporate from the empty corridors and classrooms.

A handful of boys remained, unfortunates whose parents lived overseas, too far away to reclaim their offspring in the summer. The masters, too, went their various ways: Strickland to birdwatch in Spain, Denman and Lawless to chase girls in Blackpool. Even Linfield scuttled one morning down the driveway, wearing a sports jacket instead of his dusty academic gown, a cardboard suitcase tucked under one arm.

Though, with Strickland, Jake had toasted the end of term, and though he had pretended, like the rest of them, to long to escape Heatherwood's grey, granite walls, he found himself strangely at a loss. He, who had travelled the world, could not think what to do, where to go. The unchanging nature of Heatherwood Court, its inability to adapt to the realities of post-war Britain, had sustained him for the past six months. He dreaded tipping that precarious balance, losing himself once more in the chaos of the outside world. Yet when Mary and George left for the bus stop, rucksacks on their backs, Jake, too, threw a few belongings into a bag, and headed for the railway station.

He spent a fortnight looking up old friends, and then, with something akin to relief, returned to Heatherwood. When Mary welcomed him with tea and scones and stories of her week camping at Lulworth Cove, he felt as though he had come home. That night, he took her to the cinema in Boscastle. The film was dull and unconvincing, and in the darkness he drew her to him. Her hair smelt of flowers, and her skin, against his lips, was cool and soft. He knew, suddenly, kissing her, that it was Mary who drew him back, Mary who made Heatherwood seem familiar.

But after a while she pushed him away, straightening her clothes, tucking her hair back behind her ears. 'Not here. Someone might see us, Jake.'

It was always the same. *Not here. Someone might see us.* Yet they spent whole days together, walking for miles, pausing only to eat vast cream teas, or to drink still, clouded cider in a village pub. Once, they hired a fishing-boat, and Jake showed George how to trail a line to catch mackerel from the rain-pitted, jade-green sea. Exploring the coast, they searched for fossils, and watched sea anemones wave puce-coloured tentacles. George's presence, and Mary's fear of discovery, acted as chaperon. In the evenings, she cooked supper in the tiny kitchen attached to her flat. Afterwards they played cards or listened to the radio. Yet Jake remained unsure whether she thought of him as much more than a friend. He was permitted to hold her hand; he was allowed a goodnight kiss. Once or twice the kiss became prolonged, yet still she drew away from him. He struggled to hide his anger, which was born of a suspicion that she kept him company merely to pass the time.

In September, the leaves on the beech trees surrounding the school became tinged with bronze, and the blue of the sea shifted to grey. The knowledge that the summer holidays were to end weighed heavily on Jake. Soon Heatherwood's antique, stifling routine would grind once more into gear. He feared the return of his habitual restlessness; if he let himself think long enough, he knew that Heatherwood was a respite, no more.

On the penultimate day of the holidays, they walked for miles along the headland. It had become colder; white foam flecked the blue-grey waves, and clouds scudded across the face of the sun. Conversation rose and died in brief, inconclusive entanglements that left both of them irritable and drained. He never managed to say what he wanted to say; he did not know what he wanted to say.

Back at the school, Mary gave George his supper and put him to bed. In his own room, Jake poured himself a large Scotch, lit a cigarette, and stood, his back against the desk, smoking and drinking. Through the open window the stars were dull pinpricks in a cloudy sky.

He heard Mary's footsteps in the corridor. When he opened the door to her, she said, 'George is fast asleep already. The walk must have worn him out.'

She leaned her head against Jake's shoulder, and threaded her arm round his waist. Turning to her, he began to kiss her. He felt her respond to him, her body pressing against his, her lips yielding, allowing his tongue to explore her mouth. When he undid the buttons of her blouse, and caressed her naked skin, she did not protest. Just a small gasp of pleasure or surprise. He took her nipple into his mouth; her soft flesh pressed against his face. But as he fumbled with the fastening of her shorts, she pulled away, and said sharply, 'Jake,' and began quickly to fasten hooks and eyes, and to tuck in loose flaps of clothing. She scrubbed her face with the back of her hand. As though he had hurt her, and she was rubbing away the pain.

Jake swore. Mary looked up at him. 'What is it?'

He began, 'Every bloody time—' but he did not finish his sentence. She was staring at him, her eyes narrowed.

'I don't come up to scratch. Is that it, Jake?'

He stubbed out his cigarette, which was charring a neat round black hole in his desk. 'What do you mean?'

'I'm not as easy as you thought I would be.'

'What in God's name are you talking about?'

'About you, Jake. And about me.' Her eyes were as hard as graphite. 'You assumed that because I had a child out of wedlock, I'd sleep with you.' She moved away from him. 'Why do you look so angry? I'm right, aren't I?'

He could hardly speak. 'The hell you are.'

'Did you mean to tick me off your list? Like that fat girl from the Rose and Crown that you used to fuck behind the gorse bushes – or that silly little chambermaid?'

His hands flexed. He wanted to hit her. Of all the things he had done, he thought, he had never hit a woman. Not even Linda Forrester. He went to the window and clenched his fists, pressing his knuckles against the sill until they hurt. When he was calmer, he said, 'If that's how you feel, then why do you waste your time with me?'

She raised her shoulders expressively, but said nothing.

'Because you like being seen with me in public? After

all, there's not a lot of choice, is there? Strickland's too old, and Denman's bald, and Linfield's hardly human . . . I suppose I'm at least presentable, aren't I?'

There was a silence. She sat down in his tattered armchair, her leg tucked under her, her arms wrapped round herself, protecting herself. After a while she said angrily, 'Why have you been so cross with me today? We had a nice time – I thought we had a nice time – and yet you've become crosser and crosser. It's because I won't let you make love to me, isn't it, Jake?'

'*No.* Damn it, Mary—'

'Don't you want to make love to me?'

He looked at her, at the swell of her breasts under her blouse, at the narrowness of her wrists and ankles, and his anger died, and he said, 'Of course I want to make love to you. But only if you want me to. And you've made it clear that you do not. Which is why I wonder whether you love me at all.'

She repeated slowly, 'Love. It's the first time you've used that word, Jake.'

It was not a word he was accustomed to; lack of use had made it rusty on his lips. He felt suddenly weary. He said bleakly, 'I don't know how you think of me. I don't know how you feel about me. And yes, I do want to make love to you. Because I desire you, because you're beautiful, but also because it would prove something to me.'

'That you are the handsome man – the ladykiller?' Her hands twisted and kneaded the folds of her sweater. After a while, she said, 'I'm sorry, Jake – you didn't deserve that.'

Another silence. At last she spoke. 'He made love to me just once, you see.' Her voice shook. 'He told me that he loved me. We'd been dating for months. And then, when I let him, it was in a park, and there were other people not far away, and I felt so ashamed.' She took a deep breath, and spread out her fingers in a gesture of finality. 'And that was it. Crossed off a list. A tick against my name.' She hunched her knees up to her chin, wrapping her arms round them.

Jake said, 'George's father?'

She nodded. 'Someone told me that he boasted about it in the pub.' Her voice trembled. 'You can imagine, can't you?'

In the dim light of the room, her eyes glittered. Jake poured another Scotch and put the glass into her hand. When she tried to drink, her teeth juddered against the rim of the glass.

'Did he know that you were pregnant?'

'He said, "How do I know that it's mine?" I hit him, Jake. I actually struck him.' She gulped the whisky. 'He was called up soon after that.'

'What did you do?'

She tossed back her hair, pursed her lips. 'I thought at first of getting rid of the baby. Someone gave me an address. But I couldn't, I don't know why. I had nowhere to go – my family were in Poland, and because of the war I couldn't go home. I slept rough for a few nights. I felt so degraded and bitter. I thought of killing myself. I thought of that many, many times, Jake. I almost did it.' A short crack of laughter. 'I was living in a dreadful little room, and it was so cold, and I put my head in the oven, and turned on the gas. But, Jake – here's the joke – I hadn't paid my bill, and they had cut off the gas!'

He held her until she had stopped weeping. After a while, she said, 'I realized then that I was meant to stay alive. I didn't know why – for the baby, I supposed. So

I found work in farms and orchards, and I saved as much money as I could. I wore loose dresses and tight girdles so that my employers wouldn't know I was expecting a child. I thought that when my baby was born, I'd have it adopted. But again, I couldn't. Instead, I lied – I invented a past, a husband who'd died flying for the RAF.' She looked up at Jake. Tears had glued her lashes together, like the points of stars. 'I wouldn't have got the job if they'd known the truth, you see, Jake. Schools don't employ unmarried mothers.'

The room had become cold. Within the course of the day, summer had changed to autumn. He knelt in front of the grate, and began to build the fire.

'You can't hide from love all your life because of one bastard.'

'I don't hide from love. I love George more than I have ever loved anyone else in the world.'

'I meant,' he said, striking a match, 'men.'

The crumpled newspaper flared. Mary slid off the chair to sit on the rug. 'And you, Jake?' she said. 'Where is your wife, your children, your cottage in the country?'

He smiled wryly. 'I haven't the knack of making things last. I fight for the wrong side . . . I fall for the wrong women. If I've fathered children, then their mothers haven't let me know.'

'Do you want . . . all that? A lot of men don't.'

'Family life?' He considered. 'I once thought that my family was the only thing I could count on. Then something happened, and I realized that I was wrong. You can't count on anything, can you?'

'You have a sister, don't you?'

He had told her about Faith, and about Holly Blue;

he had given her one of Faith's strange patchwork scarves for her birthday. He chucked lumps of coal on the fire. 'I've two sisters. The younger one lives abroad. And I have a niece.'

'No parents?'

He shook his head, but for the first time the lie troubled him. 'And you?'

'My parents died in the Warsaw rising. My brothers were killed when the German army invaded Poland.'

'Poor Mary.'

She smiled. 'Not at all. I have George, I have my flat and my job, and . . .' she looked at him '. . . and sometimes I think that I have you, Jake.'

He took her hand in his. 'Of course you have me. If you want me.'

With one finger, she pushed back the lock of hair that had fallen over his eye. 'Oh, I want you,' she said softly. 'Though I sense that you're transient, Jake. That you won't stay.' The tip of her finger outlined his brow, and the bridge of his nose, and the channels that had begun to form to the side of his mouth.

As her fingertip found the outline of his lips, he bent and kissed away the remainder of the tears from her lids. She whispered, 'Can you imagine that you'll still be here in ten years' time – or in five – or even in a year?' but he did not answer, and instead caressed with his mouth the pale interior of her wrist, then the hollow of her elbow, then the curve where neck and shoulder joined.

This time she did not protest as he undressed her. In the shifting light of the fire she lay naked on the rug, as with his mouth he traced the path from shoulder to breast, breast to navel, and from her navel to the black

414

curls between her legs. Her body arched as he entered her, and she shuddered as she climaxed.

Afterwards, she said, 'George . . . he sometimes wakes and calls for me . . .' and began to pull on her clothes.

He watched her leave the room. After a while, he too dressed, and walked along the corridor, down the stairs. From the moonlit garden he picked lavender and Michaelmas daisies, great armfuls of them, breathing in their scent, glancing up every now and then at the pale, perfect moon.

She hadn't enough jam jars for the flowers. Jake cooked breakfast for the three of them, and insisted they take a bus to the coast. 'But the boys come back tomorrow,' Mary protested, as he bundled her out of the school. From a tiny sea-front shop crammed with souvenirs, he bought her a jewel box covered in shells. They dined on eggs and chips and bread and butter in a beachside café postered with peeling exhortations to drink more milk. The sun glared, the sea glinted. George sucked a milk shake noisily through a straw.

As they left the café, Jake had to shade his eyes from the light. Faces danced in the shadows. He looked, and cursed.

'What is it?'

His arm was round Mary's waist. He drew his hand away, as though his touch might sting her, but he knew that it was too late.

'Linfield,' he said. 'Across the road.'

'Did he see us?'

He had seen the slight widening of Linfield's eyes. 'Yes. Hell.' He said suddenly, angrily, 'He'll use it, of course. To pay me back for the other thing.'

'That was a long time ago. He's probably forgotten.'

'I knew men like him in the army. They don't forget. They nurse grudges.'

Mary looked frightened. 'Do you think that he'll tell Captain Munday about us?'

'Probably.' Jake clenched his fists. 'Yes, probably.'

It seemed to Faith that, as the months passed, the cold weather shut around herself and Guy, trapping them in a small, tight box. At first they met in the British Museum or at the National Gallery, one waiting for the other beneath some vast scowling stone Pharaoh, or beside the opalescent mists of *The Fighting Téméraire*.' They abandoned both the museum and the art gallery when Guy narrowly avoided being seen by one of his colleagues. Ducking behind the Rosetta Stone, Faith had stifled her laughter; later, at home alone, she felt sick with fear.

Their illicit affair excluded them from the light and air that others enjoyed. Their love was separate, vacuum-sealed, unfit for daylight. Faith wondered whether such a thing could continue to exist, or whether, deprived of oxygen, it must shrink and die. She minded that she must see her favourite films without Guy, that she must browse in second-hand bookshops alone, that she must cook for one, and not two. She minded that the evenings spent in corner houses or jazz clubs could not be shared with the person she loved most. She minded that she refused invitations, waiting indoors alone for telephone calls that never came. The winter taught her that she and Guy existed on one side of a line, other people on another. Through the coldest months of the year they haunted smoky parks and scruffy backstreet cafés, retreating to places that no-one they knew would visit.

Ralph suffered from bronchitis throughout the winter. Faith shuttled between London and Heronsmead. At the weekends she shopped and cleaned for Ralph, during the week she served in the shop, sewing and writing up accounts. When, at the end of January, the sea broke through the defences of the east coast, Ralph had to be evacuated from his flooded cottage. For almost a fortnight he shared the tiny flat above the shop, adrift, noisily disconsolate, pining for home. When the waters permitted, Faith took him back to Heronsmead, and spent a week scrubbing muddy floors, and repairing or replacing sea-washed rugs and curtains. The cottage smelt of damp and mould.

Holly Blue was closed on Wednesday afternoons. On the Wednesday afternoons that Guy too was free, they met in a small hotel in Battersea. Sometimes Faith found herself thinking that without those few precious hours the affair would have just fizzled out – no dramatic quietus, just a quiet death from neglect.

In the hotel, there was green linoleum on the floor, a whiff of cabbage and Brown Windsor soup, and an uninquisitive landlady. Lying on the bed, watching the rainwater stream down the window pane, Guy said, 'We could go somewhere better than this, you know. Some of the smart hotels are very discreet.'

'I'm fond of this place. I adore it.' Faith lay curled in the crook of his arm.

He twisted a lock of her hair around his fingers. '*Faith*. It's vile.'

'I like the awful sheets that are almost transparent in the middle – and the eiderdown—'

Guy looked down at the eiderdown. 'What colour would you say it was?'

'Ochre. No – mustard. It's beautiful. And so is the funny little garden that seems only to grow horse-radish . . .'

'. . . and the cats yowling outside the kitchen. I suppose they're beautiful, too?'

'Of course they are, Guy.' She kissed his ribcage. 'It's all beautiful, because it's our room.'

He glanced at his watch. 'I'll have to go.'

'Already?'

'I told Sylvia that I was visiting a patient in Hampstead. There's a limit to how long one can spend visiting a patient in Hampstead.'

'If she was very, very ill—'

'She could have every disease in the medical diction-ary, but I'd still have to be back in time for evening surgery.' He sighed and pulled on his shirt. When he was dressed he said: 'It's still raining. Let me drop you off in Leicester Square.'

'Too risky, Guy, you know that. I'll get the bus, as usual.'

His lips lingered on her skin. 'Then I'll phone from the surgery.'

Driving back to central London, Guy thought that that was the worst of it. Not being able to take care of Faith, not being able to make her life easier. He knew that she worked long hours, and that many of her weekends were spent travelling on rackety trains to Norfolk to look after Ralph. He understood why she would not accept a penny from him, but he hated it. He knew that it was sensible of her to refuse his offer of a lift, but he despised himself for leaving her in a draughty bus shelter, shivering in her mackintosh.

He parked his car behind the surgery and went

upstairs. Sylvia, his receptionist, looked up as he came in. 'I tried to telephone you at Mrs Danbury's, Dr Neville,' she complained. Mrs Danbury was Guy's fictitiously ill Hampstead patient. 'But you weren't there. She said she hadn't asked you to call.'

Guy's heart began to hammer. He said smoothly, 'I'm here now. What did you want to speak to me about, Sylvia?'

'Mrs Neville telephoned. She wants you to ring her back urgently.' The phone rang again. 'I expect that'll be her now, Dr Neville.'

In his surgery, Guy lifted the receiver and said his name. As Eleanor began to speak, lies and excuses flickered rapidly through his mind *Some sort of a muddle . . . just thought I'd call on old Mrs Danbury . . . Sylvia must have made a mistake . . .*

'Guy? Guy, where were you? I've been trying to contact you all afternoon.' Guy cleared his throat. Yet Eleanor did not wait for his answer. 'Guy, something terrible has happened.' Eleanor's voice shook. 'Oliver has been expelled from school.'

Guy went home straight away. His son's disgrace absolved him from further deceit; Eleanor did not question his whereabouts that afternoon. Guy found her sitting in the drawing-room, a glass in her hand, looking white and strained.

'Where's Oliver?'

'They're putting him on the train tomorrow morning. He's to sleep in the school infirmary tonight . . .' Eleanor covered her face with her hands.

Guy put his arm round her shoulders. It felt strange to touch her. They had slept in separate rooms since his affair with Nicole Mulgrave; for twelve years they had avoided touch and its electricity, its ability to shatter the brittle façade of their marriage.

She trembled beneath his embrace. He handed her his handkerchief. After a few moments, she blew her nose and sat upright, shrugging his arm from her shoulder.

'Tell me what's happened, Eleanor.'

She pressed her fists together. 'Dr Vokes telephoned at midday.' Eleanor swallowed. 'He said that Oliver had stolen something from another boy.'

'*Stolen?*' Guy was incredulous.

'Some wretched toy.' Tears welled from Eleanor's eyes.

Guy felt bewildered. He heard her add, 'Apparently it wasn't the first time,' and he recalled Oliver's escapade of a couple of years ago. Running away from school, and some yarn about a Flash Gordon annual, for which Oliver had had a perfectly plausible explanation.

He, too, needed a drink. He went to the cabinet and poured himself a large Scotch. After a few mouthfuls, he said, 'I'll telephone Vokes. Get the whole story out of him.'

Guy rang the school from his study. As he listened to the headmaster's account, he felt sick, empty, ashamed, deeply aware of his own failure as a father. He went back to Eleanor. When she looked up at him, he saw the hope in her eyes. He crushed it quickly.

'There's no mistake. The only grain of comfort is that the school has agreed not to say anything to Missingdean.' Oliver was due to start at Selwyn's old public school in September.

Eleanor whispered, 'But we gave him everything—', and Guy thought, *Not quite everything*. Not consistency, not the sort of certain, undemanding love that a child needed. Oliver's childhood had been marked by war: by the conflagration that had first taken him away from London, and by the subtler, colder conflict that had persisted between his parents since his home-coming. Just now Guy hated himself for having been, when this crisis erupted, in bed with Faith Mulgrave; for having been, when Eleanor and Oliver most needed him, unreachable.

He heard her say, 'It'll be all right, won't it, Guy?' and he turned back to her. Distress had aged her, slackening the skin round her eyes.

'We'll work something out. We'll get to the bottom of this, I promise you, Eleanor. You mustn't worry.'

Oliver arrived home the following morning. After lunch, Guy spoke to him in his study.

'Dr Vokes told me what happened. You wanted to swap something with this boy – I can't remember his name—'

'Canterbury,' supplied Oliver. His face was chalk white.

'You wanted to swap something of yours for Canterbury's spaceship, and he refused. So you stole it.'

'I borrowed it, Daddy.'

'Without Canterbury's permission? Why? I don't understand, Oliver. You've plenty of toys, and you're not short of pocket money.'

Oliver shuffled from one foot to the other. He said again, obstinately, 'I borrowed it.'

'The book that you claimed to have been given last year . . . Did you also borrow that?'

A quick widening of the eyes; a flick of the lids. Guy glimpsed fear behind the stubbornness. He said sternly,

'Come, Oliver, you haven't answered my question. Why did you take it?'

Oliver gasped, 'Because I *liked* it.'

'We can't have everything we like, Oliver. And if you wanted it, then why didn't you ask Mummy to buy you one for Christmas?'

'But I wanted it *now*! I was going to give it to Farthing, for his birthday!'

Guy went to the window, and leaned, his hands gripping the sill, looking out. From his study on the top floor of the Holland Square house, he could see the new buildings rising, clean and shining, from the ashes of the Blitz. He felt exhausted, unequal to the situation. His fortieth birthday fell this year; he had never before felt so middle-aged, so possessed of the remnants of values that belonged to a different era.

'Farthing?' he asked, without turning round. 'Who's Farthing?'

'He's head of Drake House. And he's super at cricket. He scored fifty-four runs in the match against Holywell.' A hand tugged the sleeve of Guy's jacket. 'Daddy.'

Guy looked down at his son. He was struck anew by Oliver's beauty: the flaxen hair, the chiselled features, the sapphire-blue eyes. Because of that beauty, because Oliver would always be the only child, and because of his own guilt, they had always given the boy everything he wanted.

'Daddy? When will I go back to school? I haven't finished my Latin prep, and I'm going to be in the cricket team . . .'

He put his arm around Oliver, and said gently, 'Whitelands won't take you back, I'm afraid, Oliver. Dr Vokes made that quite clear.'

Oliver's eyes were enormous. 'But what shall I *do*, Daddy?'

'I don't know.' He could hear his own weariness. 'I don't know, Oliver,' and as Oliver began to weep Guy drew his son to him, and held him, stroking his soft golden hair.

Halfway through a strained, silent supper, Guy remembered that he had not, as he had promised, telephoned Faith the previous evening. With the excuse of needing to stretch his legs after the meal, he walked to a phone box. As he dialled Faith's number, a small voice echoed in his head. *Because I liked it . . . I wanted it*. Father and son, he thought grimly, taking what was bright and beautiful and forbidden.

When she picked up the phone and said her name, he could hear the anxiety in her voice.

'Faith. It's me.'

'*Guy*.' A huge exhalation of breath. 'Guy, has something happened? You didn't telephone – I was afraid—'

He interrupted, 'No, it's all right, we're still safe. Something's happened, but it's nothing to do with us.' Yet, explaining to her about Oliver, he could not avoid mentioning the near-disaster: Eleanor's telephone calls to his surgery, his receptionist's attempts to trace him.

She listened in silence; when he had finished, she said, 'Poor Guy. Poor all of you. How's Oliver?'

'Chastened. Quiet.' Though he found it hard, as always, to read Oliver: he was unsure whether Oliver's regrets were for what he had done, or for what he had lost.

'What will you do?'

'I'm not sure.' He traced a finger along the misty

423

interior of the phone booth, 'Guy loves Faith', and then erased the words with the flat of his hand. 'He's to start at his public school in September, you see, so it's hardly worth finding another prep school. And besides, they'd ask questions, and for Oliver's sake this has to be kept as quiet as possible. Eleanor wants to engage a tutor, but I don't know . . . I feel—'

'What, Guy?'

'I feel that in some ways a tutor would be the worst possible option. It would both isolate him and reinforce his sense of his own exclusivity.' He sighed. 'I wish I could take him away. Go camping with him on the Continent, perhaps, show him all the places I love. Make him rough it a bit. That's what he needs. But I can't, just now, because of my work. Selwyn's still not well, you see, though he won't admit it, and if I took time off, he'd insist on filling the gap, and I honestly don't think he's up to it.'

Guy became aware of the world outside: the buses and cars that hurried past the telephone booth, the queue of people waiting to make a call. He closed his eyes for a moment, shutting them out, envisaging her face, her dear familiar features. Then he forced himself to say, 'I don't know when we'll be able to meet again, Faith. This is going to take some sorting out.'

A silence. He could hear, along the telephone wire, the echo of her breath. At last she said, 'Are you trying to tell me that you don't want to see me any more, Guy?'

'*No.* Dear God, no.' Faces pressed against the glass, urging him to finish his call. 'I shall never say that, Faith,' he said fiercely. 'Don't you understand? You are what makes all this bearable. You are what makes it all right.'

'But it isn't all right, is it? It's wrong, what we are doing.'

'How can it be wrong when we love each other? How can love be anything but good?'

'Just because something feels good, it doesn't mean that it's *right*.' Her voice was raw. 'I have to go, Guy. Con's waiting for me. Ring me when you can.' The phone went dead.

Breakfasting alone with Eleanor, Guy told her his decision.

'Oliver can attend the local school during the summer term. King Edward VI's.'

Eleanor looked up from her boiled egg. 'Don't be silly, Guy. King Edward VI's is a council school.'

'It's a grammar school.'

'Oliver can't go to a *council* school.'

'Of course he can. It's only for a term, and he's already passed his Common Entrance, so it won't matter if he has to retread some of the work he's done in the past. It's ideal – only a bus ride away, so he can live at home during the summer. I'll ring the school this morning, and see whether they can take him.'

'Guy, it's out of the question.' Eleanor refilled her coffee cup. 'I will not let Oliver go to a place like that.'

He buttered a piece of toast. 'It's a decent school, by all accounts. Half a dozen sixth form boys got into Oxbridge last year.'

'That's not the point.'

He sliced the toast in half, but did not yet eat it. 'Then what is the point, Eleanor?'

'I don't want Oliver mingling with that type of boy.'

He looked up at her. 'What type of boy?'

'Rough boys. He might pick up bad habits.'

'I would have thought,' said Guy coldly, 'that the greater concern should be that other boys might pick up bad habits from him.' He put aside his plate. He could not eat: even the sight of food sickened him. 'Oliver is a thief, Eleanor. We have to face up to that. Oh, he only takes little things now, but who can say what might take his fancy a few years from now?'

Her lip curled. 'So you think that he'll become a bank robber . . . or a housebreaker.'

'Of course not.' He tried to make her understand; a last attempt to drag some meaning from the ashes of their marriage. 'Perhaps Oliver has had some things too easy. We've brought him up to believe that he can have whatever he wants as soon as he wants it. A few months spent among less privileged boys might teach him to value what he's got.'

'I won't consider it, Guy. Oliver, go to a council school? Never.'

He knew that she hadn't even listened to him. There grew within him a primitive need for revenge. He, after all, held the purse strings. He said, 'I won't pay for a tutor, Eleanor.' There was a small pleasure to be had in seeing the change of expression on her face. 'Whitelands won't refund next term's fees. And you know how expensive Missingdean is. We can't afford a private tutor.'

Her cup thumped angrily down onto her saucer. 'You could take on more patients—'

'But I won't.' He longed for a drink; at half past eight in the morning, he longed for a drink. Instead, he took out his cigarettes. 'I won't.'

Eleanor stood up. 'Then I'll ask Father. He has savings.' She paused in the doorway. 'I didn't think that even you could be quite so unreasonable.'

Yet Selwyn, to Eleanor's consternation, backed Guy up. Guy telephoned the grammar school, and arranged an interview for Oliver.

It was Oliver's reaction to the news that took Guy by surprise. He went greenish-white, and Guy thought for a moment that he was going to be sick. He put his arm round the boy, and gently explained that King Edward VI's was just a stopgap, something to tide them over until he went to Missingdean. Come September, they could put all this behind them. But Oliver just whispered, 'I hate you. Nana would never have made me go there. I hate you.' Then he left the room.

After the first few weeks of term had passed without incident, Jake wondered whether he had been mistaken in believing that Linfield had seen him and Mary together that morning by the seaside. Mistaken, too, in thinking that Linfield would bear a grudge. Relieved, he slipped back into the now familiar routine of lessons and prep and marking.

Then, one Sunday, when she met Jake at the foot of the cliff path, Mary's face was pinched and white, and her replies to his attempts at conversation were monosyllabic. Cormorants and shearwaters dived from the craggy headlands, and waves pounded against the cliffs. The path was too narrow for them to walk side by side; Mary strode ahead, her small, hunched figure seeming to welcome the violence of the wind.

Jake caught up with her. 'What's wrong?'

'Nothing.' She jammed her hands deeper into her pockets.

'Mary—'

'I told you, Jake, nothing's wrong.' Her voice was sharp. 'So let's walk, shall we, or I'll die of cold.'

They had reached the place where the cliff shelved away, permitting a path to the small, private crescent of beach. In the warm September weather they had made love there. But since then autumn had bitten, and the rocks were slippery with seaweed, creviced with a soup of crushed shells and salt water, lashed with spray.

Jake watched Mary doggedly skirting the rock pools. He called out, 'If you're sick of me, then for heaven's sake say so.'

She glanced back at him. 'Always so vain, Jake. I have concerns other than you.' She perched on a rock, hunching her shoulders, and looked out to sea.

A few feet away, the waves lapped at the sand, sucking it from beneath their feet. After a while, her defences seemed to falter a little, and she muttered, 'It's George.'

'Is he ill?'

'He was beaten. With the strap. Mr Linfield beat him. He said that George was talking in chapel. I asked George, and he told me that he'd whispered a word or two – there was a spider on the pew, or some such nonsense – but many of the other boys said more, and Mr Linfield didn't beat them. I hate him.' Her voice was low, violent. 'I hate to think of him hurting my child!'

She walked away, stumbling along the rocks that jutted out into the sea. Waves crashed to either side of the small headland, the spume colliding in midair. Every now and then she slipped on the barnacled stone. Her knees and her knuckles bled. She paused only on the furthermost rock, surrounded by sea, her raincoat soaked, her black hair twisted to seaweed. Because he sensed that in some obscure way she blamed him, he did not follow her. Yet neither did he leave the beach until she turned and walked slowly back to the cliff path.

Ten days later, Linfield thrashed George a second time. Again, three weeks after that. Jake recognized the method of the practised torturer. Leave it long enough each time for the victim to begin to hope. It's the crushing of hope that is hardest to endure. When Mary accused Linfield of fault-finding, she was met with supercilious denial. George's round, cheerful little face assumed a cowed expression. Though Linfield studiously avoided being alone with him, Jake noticed in the other man's eyes a gleam of triumph. He knew that he himself was the intended victim, and that Mary, and even poor George, were incidental. He, Jake, had humiliated Linfield, but now Linfield humiliated him. He could not protect his lover's child.

After a while, the solution became obvious. In the linen room, surrounded by heaps of pillowcases and towels, Jake asked Mary to marry him. The leap into permanence, that once would have daunted him, no longer did so.

As he made his proposal, she continued to mark sheets. After he had fallen silent, she said, 'It would make no difference, Jake,' and licked her pencil, and printed 'Heatherwood Court' neatly on a hem. 'It wouldn't stop that man hurting my son.'

'Munday might disapprove of an illicit affair, but he could hardly object if two of his members of staff were respectably married.'

Mary replaced the sheets on a shelf. 'If we were married,' she said calmly, 'Mr Linfield would probably beat George more. Perhaps he's jealous. Perhaps he too desires me.'

The thought of Linfield lusting after Mary nauseated him, and somehow tainted his own feelings for her. Looking at her, Jake knew that she was withdrawing herself from him, climbing back into the protective shell that she had worn when he had first arrived at Heatherwood.

The room was small and airless. He shoved his hands into his pockets and tried to think clearly. 'Then we must send George to another school.'

'That's the solution, of course. George and I shall leave Heatherwood.'

Jake felt cold inside. 'And me?'

She did not, as he half expected her to, scold him for thinking of himself. Instead, she said, 'It doesn't seem likely, does it, Jake, that we'll find a school in need of both a language master and a matron, which also has a place for a ten-year-old boy?'

He said angrily, 'You're playing into Linfield's hands – you're doing exactly what he wants you to do!'

She paused in the act of folding a pillowcase. 'Perhaps. But I have to protect George, you see, Jake.'

A few days later, he went to see Captain Munday. The headmaster was sitting at the desk in his study, account books in front of him. A pipe, balanced in an ashtray, cast a rank fug over the room.

Jake said, 'I've come to complain about Mr Linfield. He's picking on one of the boys. Singling him out for punishment.'

Munday's mustachioed mouth twitched in a grimace Jake eventually realized was intended as a smile. 'Perhaps the boy deserves punishment, Mr Mulgrave.'

'I don't think so. George Zielinski is a good-natured, conscientious little fellow.'

Munday began to clean his fingernails with a toothpick. 'Have you considered the possibility, Mulgrave, that Zielinski may be less assiduous at mathematics than at French?'

Pedantic, self-regarding little man, thought Jake, but swallowed his anger. Munday opened a desk drawer.

'Shall we consult the punishment book?' He thumbed through a ledger. Every master was obliged to enter the cause and quantity of each beating they administered into the punishment book.

'Talking in the cloakroom . . . ink on his fingers at lunchtime . . . incomplete preparation . . .' Captain Munday slid the book over the desk to Jake. 'It all seems to be in order, Mr Mulgrave.'

Jake glanced down at the list of petty misdemeanours. George's name appeared with horrible regularity. Looking up at Captain Munday, Jake said angrily, 'You condone *that*?'

'Without good discipline the school wouldn't function.'

'So you'll allow a sadistic oaf like Linfield to take out his vindictiveness on a little boy?'

'Be careful what you say, Mulgrave.' The bluff good humour slipped. 'Mr Linfield is a valued member of staff. He has taught at Heatherwood for eighteen years. You haven't yet been here one.' Captain Munday retrieved his pipe, and began to push black shreds of tobacco into the bowl. He looked consideringly at Jake. 'I recall that you come from a somewhat unconventional background. You've lived abroad a great deal, I believe?'

He managed, thought Jake, to make foreign travel sound like an infectious disease.

'I wonder whether you fully appreciate the English school system. It's the envy of the world, you know. And the boys *prefer* a thrashing.' Munday nodded complacently. 'They say that it gets the punishment over with quickly.'

* * *

In France, the night before D-Day, Jake had hunted a man. A railway official, a Nazi sympathizer, he had been trailed like an animal, Jake following his scent until he had trapped him alone and out of earshot of his friends. Then he had slit his throat.

He cornered Linfield on the way back from chapel, prayer book in hand. It was a fortnight before the end of the spring term, and they had just prayed for Heatherwood Court's success in the last rugby match of the season. Jake fell in beside Linfield, walking through the copse that lay between church and school.

'A word, please.'

Linfield's small feet scurried through celandine-studded grass. 'I don't have time for conversation, Mulgrave.'

'This won't take long. I want to talk to you about George Zielinski.'

'Zielinski's algebra is adequate, but his grasp of the geometric theorem still leaves room for improvement—'

'Lay off him, Linfield. Leave him alone. If you want to hurt someone, pick on someone your own size.'

'And if I don't?' Linfield had begun to wheeze. His words punctuated his furious struggle for breath. 'What will you do, Mulgrave?'

Jake shrugged. The copse smelt of beechmast and fear.

'Will you kill me? Is that what you'll do?'

'Perhaps,' he said, but he knew that he lied. He could not just then have touched Linfield. The small, smooth, almost hairless skull, the blue-veined transparent hands, repelled him.

'Leave George alone. Your quarrel's with me, not

with that child.' The canopy of trees had become oppressive; Jake began to walk away.

'I suppose you're going to seek consolation from your tart! Your tart and her bastard!'

Jake swung round. His heart pounded. As a denial rose to his lips – too late, already too late – Linfield's eyes gleamed.

'So it's true. The kid's a bastard. I always wondered.' Linfield shook out the crumpled folds of his gown. 'Well, well. Now wouldn't Captain Munday like to know *that*.' The wheezing became distant as Linfield walked out into the sunshine, leaving Jake beneath the trees, his hands impotently bunched at his sides.

He told her. He could not have done otherwise. Mary listened in silence, her face set like stone, and then she said, 'It's not your fault, Jake.' But he thought that it was. The whole bloody mess was his fault. If he had not the previous year punished Linfield for hurting that boy, if he had turned aside and walked away, just as everyone else did, then none of this would have happened.

Two days later, Mary told him that she had been offered a position at a school in Wales. For a moment, looking at him, her shell seemed to crack a little, and she touched his arm and said tentatively, 'You'll write to me, won't you, Jake? You'll keep in touch?'

He did not reply. He knew that the inevitable had begun. He would lose her, as he had lost everything of importance in his life. Nothing lasted: he had realized that a long time ago, cycling through the hot, tragic France of the summer of 1940. He saw that she waited for his answer, but he pulled away from her, and went to the window, and after a while he heard the door slam.

CHAPTER THIRTEEN

One Wednesday afternoon in April they went to their
Battersea hotel. The smell of boiled cabbage in the
entrance-way, the slippery mustard-coloured eiderdown on the bed. Everything seemed just the same, but
Faith sensed a slow, insidious alteration, a desperate
need to prove that they still found pleasure in this
place, and in each other. They made love, she thought,
to show that passion remained, because passion justified anything, everything.

Afterwards, she wrapped herself in the sheet and
went to the window. In the spring sunshine, the
cramped little garden that had amused her in winter
seemed ugly, signifying only lack of hope.

She heard Guy say, 'A penny for them.'

'I was wondering whether we should see each other
again.' The words were out before she could draw them
back.

'Faith—' He sat up.

'It's been five weeks – five weeks, Guy, I counted it –
since we had more than half an hour together.'

'I'm so sorry, darling.' He came to her, and laid his
hand upon her shoulder, but she did not turn towards
him, and after a while he said desperately, 'You know
that I have to be careful. That time when Oliver—'

'I know. Of course.' She remembered the sickened

434

feeling that had gripped her stomach when Guy had telephoned her the night after Oliver had been expelled from school: *Eleanor was looking for me all afternoon . . . luckily she was too upset to question me.*

'But I'm tired of being careful.' Yet she spoke too softly for him to hear.

Behind her, he began to pull on his clothes. 'Eleanor's taking Oliver on holiday for a fortnight in August – we'll have all the time we want then.' His voice coaxed her.

'It's not that, Guy.'

'What, then?' He paused, his tie half knotted. 'Or do you no longer feel the same?'

'Oh, I still love you, Guy,' she said. 'I'll always love you.' She thought, but there is no joy in it any more. Only loneliness and guilt and fear.

He put his arms round her waist. 'If it doesn't hurt anyone, it can't be wrong.' The old familiar mantra, yet even he no longer sounded convinced.

She cried out, 'But how can we be sure? We can't, Guy! We were lucky that time, that's all! We could so easily have been found out—'

'But we weren't. We weren't!' He pulled her towards him and began to kiss her. She sensed the desperation in his touch. 'Don't talk about parting, I beg you, Faith. I need you so much.'

He held her for a while, her face against his, his only movement the rise and fall of his lungs. 'We belong to each other,' he whispered. 'We always have done. You won't forget that, will you?'

At first, Oliver loathed his new school. An undistinguished red-brick building set in a busy London street, it attempted to emulate the public school system –

435

house colours, prefects and a school song – while lacking both the finances and sense of conviction of those it parodied. The work was not difficult – Oliver was ahead in classics, behind in science – and the boys were dull rather than dislikable. He was bored a lot of the time, but then he had been bored at Whitelands. If a term at King Edward VI's Grammar School for Boys had not been enforced upon him as a punishment by his father, then perhaps he would not have minded.

His mother perpetuated his sense of indignity. 'So unfair of Daddy sending you to that awful place! Well, we must grin and bear it, I'm afraid, Oliver. At least it means we may spend the summer together.' His mother seemed to have forgotten the cause of his homecoming; her anger was directed solely against Daddy. At night, lying in bed, his parents' quarrels echoing through the house, Oliver jammed his fingers in his ears to block out the disturbing sound. By day, an air of tension, of undeclared, unresolved war, lingered in the Holland Square house.

Once a week, he and his mother had tea at the Lyons' Corner House in Marble Arch. Oliver would eat a knickerbocker glory or a chocolate éclair while his mother poured tea from a silver teapot. Sometimes she talked about the war, which was boring, because she rarely mentioned bombs or aeroplanes or any of the exciting bits, and sometimes she talked about the hospital for which she had once worked, which was even more boring. And often, especially after the evening arguments had been particularly vocal, she talked about Daddy. She told Oliver that she sympathized with him for having to put up with Daddy's unkindness, because he was sometimes unkind to her as well. She told him that because Daddy had been quite poor as a boy, he had never lost the habit of being mean with money, and that without her help, he would still be as poor as a church mouse. She told him that Daddy's insistence on sending him to the grammar school showed that Daddy did not love him as much as she did.

Oliver wanted to comfort her, to say the right words, to cheer her up. Sometimes Oliver enjoyed his mother's confidences because they made him feel grown-up and important, but at other times the Corner House's tasteful decor, and the muted murmur of well-bred conversation, made him want to run from the place, kicking over tables and throwing teapots to the spotless floor as he escaped.

A few weeks after the beginning of term, he became acquainted with a boy called Wilcox. Wilcox was a year older than Oliver, and in the lowest stream, and thus not the sort of person he would usually have made friends with. They met in the corridor outside the headmaster's study, where, at lunchtime, a collection of miscreants gathered, waiting to receive punishments for their various wrongdoings. Wilcox stood next to Oliver. Lounging against the wall, Wilcox drawled, 'Aren't you in the wrong bloody queue, Neville? Shouldn't you be at Phillips's room, waiting for a pat on the head like all the other nancy boys?'

Oliver shrugged. Wilcox said, 'What did you do? Hand in your prep five minutes late? Forget to polish your shoes?' He glanced at Oliver. 'No. The *servant* polishes your shoes, doesn't she?'

Wilcox's shoes looked as though they had never seen a tin of blacking. The leather was coming away from the sole. His tie was a small, hard knot to the side of his neck, and braid unravelled from his blazer.

'Actually,' said Oliver, 'we don't have a servant.'

'Actually,' mimicked Wilcox in a piping falsetto, 'we don't have a servant.'

'And,' said Oliver, 'I'm here for smoking in the bogs.' He had learned to smoke at Whitelands; now, every so often, he filched a few cigarettes from his father's case: a sort of revenge, he always thought, for the humiliation of this place. He looked at Wilcox. 'What about you?'

'Cheeking Brownlie,' said Wilcox casually. Mr Brownlie was the games master, ex-army, with fists like hams.

'At my last school I put some nitrogen tri-iodide in the masters' lavatory, so that when the headmaster sat on the pan, it exploded.' He hadn't: another boy had suggested it, but no-one had had the guts to do it, but Wilcox wasn't to know that.

Wilcox roared with laughter. 'Right up his arse!'

That evening, Oliver went into his father's study and took four Players from the box in the desk drawer. He took them to school the next day. At break, he sought out Wilcox, and offered him a cigarette.

'Not here, thickhead – Brownlie will see.' Yet Wilcox slid the cigarette into his pocket.

After lessons were over, Wilcox waited for him outside the gates. In a dusty square off Great Portland Street, they shared out the cigarettes. Oliver lay on his back and watched the blue smoke drift into the sky. Wilcox coughed after his first cigarette, retched after his second. When he had recovered, he said: 'Bet you live in a house like that.' He pointed to the tall, thin houses that surrounded the square.

'I do, actually.'

'Your father rich or something?'

'He's a doctor. So's my grandfather. I'm supposed to become a doctor too.'

'Lucky sod.'

'Why?' He added honestly, 'I can't stand ill people.'

'You'll be paid to feel girls' tits.' Eyes narrowed, Wilcox looked at Oliver. 'Or don't you like girls?'

'They're all right. I suppose I don't know many. I haven't a sister or cousins, anything like that.'

Wilcox said, 'You're not a nancy, are you? I wouldn't want to be lying on the grass with a nancy.'

Oliver looked blank. Wilcox said, exasperated, 'Don't you know anything?' and launched into a detailed explanation.

After Wilcox had finished, Oliver felt slightly sick, but he shook his head and said, 'No, I don't like that sort of thing. I really don't.' His voice wobbled a bit, as it tended to these days.

Wilcox fished in his pocket and drew out some postcards. 'Have a look at these. Smashing, aren't they?'

They were all photographs of girls without any clothes on. As Oliver studied them, he heard Wilcox say, 'I could get some for you if you had the cash. Cost you a bob or two, though.'

Wilcox showed Oliver parts of London he had never seen. The docks, with their exciting confusion of cranes and crates and ships. Stevedores yelling to each other, and, painted on the bows of the ships, their ports of origin. Buenos Aires . . . Calcutta . . . Canberra. The words themselves gave Oliver a strange sort of excitement, a glimpse of hot sun and unknown languages and freedom.

Soho offered a different sort of excitement. Soho

might have been light years away from Holland Square for all Oliver knew of it. He knew Derbyshire, a hundred miles north, far better than he knew Soho, almost on his front door. The strange music issuing from peeling doorways, the litter and the colour and the girls in their flashy clothes at first repelled him, but then fascinated him. Wilcox explained about the jazz clubs that stayed open all night, and about the places where girls took off their clothes for money. They tried to get into one of those places, but the doorman shooed them away. Wilcox blamed Oliver, whose voice still lurched embarrassingly between soprano and bass. At night, Oliver studied the postcards he had bought from Wilcox. His favourite was a girl of gypsyish appearance, with black hair and huge dark eyes, and heavy breasts that hung pendulously to the sides of her chest. To look at her made him feel both happy and guilty at the same time.

Wilcox told Oliver about a shop in Soho that sold magazines full of pictures of naked girls. He'd buy one for him, he said confidently, if Oliver got the money. Oliver wondered where on earth he would hide such a magazine – his mother tidied his bedroom every day – but he nevertheless went to his father's study that night and took a pound from his wallet.

A faded, dog-eared piece of card fell to the floor as he drew out the pound note. Oliver glanced at it. 'Holly Blue,' it said, beside a drawing of a butterfly. 'Ladies' Day and Evening Wear, 3 Tate Street W.1.'

Mulgrave Rules, Jake: never let them see that you mind. He managed rather well, Jake thought, chatting to the other masters in the staffroom at break, taking the boys for cricket practice on Friday afternoons. He kept his temper, and when he drank, he drank alone.

Yet he did mind, of course. He minded desperately that Mary had gone. He minded that a thin, busy, middle-aged woman had taken her place in the infirmary; and that when he walked the cliff path he walked alone. Once he went to the cove and wandered among the rocks and the pools, and threw pebbles into the sea. And was always aware of the deep, boiling anger that he nursed inside him.

Mary had written him letters since her departure; he had not replied. He would not voice the anguish he felt, because to do so would mean that he would be exposed, defenceless. He knew that he would not stay at Heatherwood. He knew that she had been right, that he would move on. Yet he bided his time, he waited. Everything he had always loathed about the place – the hypocrisy, the snobbery, the undercurrent of violence – had, with Mary's leaving, become intolerable. Linfield, he realized, was only a symptom of a disease. Heatherwood and places like it existed to enforce conformity; people like Linfield flourished in such circumstances. The narrowness of Heatherwood's sights, and the greyness of both the school and the countryside that surrounded it, made him long for escape.

For the first time it occurred to Jake that had Ralph remained all his life in England, he himself would have been sent to such a school. Ralph had been the son of a conventional middle-class family; Ralph had been educated at a school like this, and had been inculcated with values similar to Heatherwood's. Had Ralph not chosen to be different, then he himself would have been obliged to follow unquestioningly in his father's footsteps. Jake understood that to pull away from all this must have taken courage. For the first time in more than a decade he began to think of Ralph with something other than contempt. He wondered what Ralph would have done in his situation, and knew that he would not have sat meekly back, accepting it all.

Jake told Captain Munday that he would like to present a prize at Founder's Day at the end of April. There were prizes for classics, prizes for history, prizes for geography, but nothing for French. Captain Munday, having first made sure that Jake would cover the full cost of the award, was agreeable.

On Founder's Day, Jake breakfasted on neat whisky. In the staffroom that morning, Strickland took him aside.

'Isn't done for the masters to appear blotto *before* such an occasion, old chap. We generally wait till the whole wretched business is over.'

'Just acquiring some Dutch courage.'

'For what?' Strickland looked at him suspiciously. 'You've only to endure an afternoon's boredom.'

'I have to make a speech. Haven't quite sorted out the text.'

Strickland placed a hand on his shoulder. 'You're not going to do anything stupid, are you, Mulgrave?'

He saw that there was genuine concern in Strickland's eyes. Jake shook his head vigorously. 'I loathe public speaking.' He would miss Strickland, he thought.

Flanked by parents and masters and boys, Jake ate dry roast beef and stringy beans for lunch, washed down with Scotch sneaked from his hip flask. In the afternoon, he dozed through a cricket match, and then sat at the back of the dais with the other masters, yawning through the speeches. Then the prize-giving. Colours for cricket and rugby. Awards for prefects and form monitors and every other damn petty official. Prizes for Hard Work and Improvement. Prizes for mathematics, poetry, and Latin translation.

Captain Munday beckoned to Jake. Jake, a little unsteadily, walked to the podium. He looked out over the assembled audience of parents and boys.

'There's been a slight change of plan. I told Captain Munday that I wanted to present a prize for modern languages. The Mulgrave prize for French, or some such nonsense. But I've had second thoughts. Come up with a better one. Something more appropriate to this place.' Jake smiled. 'The Mulgrave prize for hypocrisy, I thought.'

The bored coughs and shuffles, the whispers of the boys, tailed off.

'Of course, there are rather a lot of contenders. There's the good captain himself, of course.'

Captain Munday hissed, 'Mulgrave! Stop that immediately!' The atmosphere in the hall had suddenly become electric, erasing in an instant the mid-afternoon, postprandial torpor.

'Now, Captain Munday pays a pittance to the misfits and crocks who teach your sons, while charging you the top whack. Then he pockets the difference. Clever, don't you think?' Jake rubbed his forehead, and pretended to look down at his notes. 'Who else could we put forward for this prestigious award? Well, there's Mr Linfield—'

A buzz of conversation had replaced the silence. Someone said loudly, 'The fellow's drunk!' and Jake, looking up, wide-eyed, said, 'That's quite true. Only way I can stomach this dump. Anyway – Linfield. Now, Linfield likes little boys. Of course, when I say that he *likes* little boys, I don't mean that he respects them, or that he cares about them, I mean that he likes hurting them. Gives him a thrill. Probably can't manage it any other way. *Le vice anglais*, as they say on the Continent.'

A hand tugged at his sleeve. He struggled to focus on Strickland. 'Come away, old fellow, before you do yourself any more harm.' Strickland's voice was gentle.

Jake shook his head. 'I'm enjoying myself,' he said loudly. And yet some of his exhilaration had already begun to die. He pushed on.

'And besides, I haven't presented my prize. There are other contenders.'

Some of the parents were already leaving the hall. Jake raised his voice. 'Of course, you'd all make promising candidates. I mean you, ladies and gentlemen.'

A few people paused in the aisles. Jake called out, 'That's right, you, the parents of these poor, benighted children.' His voice was almost lost in the hubbub. 'After all, it's you who send your sons away to this place. You know that they weep for you at night. You know that they're beaten. You notice, don't you, how they've altered when they come home at the end of their first term. They've learned not to show their feelings – they've learned to dissemble. You've taught them your hypocrisy.'

'Jake,' said Strickland.

The PE teacher was standing on the other side of the podium from Strickland. Jake said, 'All right. Almost done.' He felt exhausted; the heady joy of rebellion had drained suddenly out of him, and he could have curled up and wept. He rested his elbows on the podium, and took a deep breath to steady himself.

'Don't go, ladies and gentlemen. I'm about to make

the award. Don't you want to know who I'm giving it to? I'm giving it to myself, of course.' He had to shout over the noise. 'I'm presenting the Mulgrave prize to Jake Mulgrave. Who else? For kidding myself that I could fit in. For letting myself go along with all this. For being no better than the rest of you. For—'

Hands grabbed him, dragging him from the podium. The hall was in uproar. Through the din, Jake heard Captain Munday's voice: 'Please keep your seats, ladies and gentlemen! I'm afraid that Mr Mulgrave appears to have had some sort of a breakdown!' But the sea of well-dressed men and women continued to the exits.

Jake was hauled to the side doors. There he shook himself free, and walked alone upstairs. Packing, he looked for a last time around the small, tidy room that had been his home for the past year. He and Strickland had played chess at the table by the window; he had made love to Mary on the rug in front of the fire. As he began to fling clothes into a rucksack, he heard the door open.

A voice said, 'I don't think I've ever seen a man slit his own throat with quite so much relish.'

Jake said easily, 'Oh, I've always been one for lost causes, Strickland. I joined the International Brigades – did I ever tell you that? And I was sure that the Germans would never take Paris. I just thought I'd have a go at reforming the English school system.'

'It's unreformable, didn't you know? It satisfies a purpose.'

There was a silence. Jake glanced at the books on the shelf. 'Can you use them, Strickland? Don't think I'll be needing them, and they'll be too heavy to lug around.'

Strickland came to stand beside him. 'What will you do?'

'I've no idea. I don't suppose any other school will employ me.'

'I shouldn't think so.' A pause. 'Unless they like stimulating speech days.'

Jake buckled the straps of his rucksack. Strickland said, 'Are you all right for cash?'

He wasn't, but he said, 'I've a bit put by.' He held out his hand. 'I'd better go, I think.'

They shook hands. As he walked out of the door, Jake heard Strickland say, 'I shall miss you, of course, but perhaps it was worth it. One of the finest moments of my life, I think, to see the expression on Munday's face.'

After school, Oliver wandered around Soho. But the rackety whine of the saxophone, drifting up from cellar doorways, and the tattered, gaudy shop signs and advertisements failed today to distract him. He hunched his shoulders and lit himself a cigarette, and turned down a narrow street, the sort of street, he thought, where gangsters lurk with flick knives in darkened doorways. He tried to look taller, tougher, more confident. He almost wished some hoodlum would jump out and attack him: he'd fight them off, and then they'd be proud of him, and everything would be all right again. But only a couple of girls, taffeta petticoats rustling, passed him, giggling as they wobbled on their stiletto heels. Today, Oliver could not even be bothered looking at their breasts, as Wilcox had taught him to. He dragged at his cigarette and scuffed the soles of his shoes on the pavement.

He reached a square of derelict land. The remains of the foundations of buildings could be seen like bones showing through the skin of briar and nettle. He'd always liked bomb-sites. He pictured the bombs falling from the sky, smashing through brick walls and tiled roofs. With savage delight, he imagined the Russians dropping an atom bomb on London: a whine and a whoosh and a great mushroom cloud, and all this – Soho's seedy clubs and Holland Square's smart houses alike – would be gone. What buildings would rise out of the devastation? Great, new, tall, shining columns, perhaps, like the illustrations of the Martian cities in his copy of *The War of the Worlds*.

Beside the derelict land there was a shop. Just a boring clothes shop: Oliver was going to walk on when he read the shop sign. *Holly Blue*, in light blue and gold. The name seemed familiar, though he could not at first think why. Then he remembered the card he had found in his father's wallet. Oliver stood at the window for a while, looking in, and then he went inside.

Bright colours, blues and pinks and lemons, decorated the walls. Rugs, their colours a muted, waving turquoise and green sea, were scattered on the floors. The chairs and lamps and side tables were simple and streamlined, so different from the fussy, tasselled crimson and beige of Holland Square. Oliver thought that this room could have come from another world, perhaps another planet.

Racks of dresses were stacked against the walls. Slung on the back of a nearby chair were several scarves, of a fine, sparkly material. Oliver glanced at a price tag. Three guineas. For a *scarf*.

A voice said, 'Can I help you, sir?' and he jumped. A tall, grey-haired woman stood beside him.

'I'm just looking,' he answered, in his mother's haughtiest tones. The woman went back to the cash register to attend to a customer.

Oliver looked carefully around. There were only two shop assistants: the tall woman, and a younger lady in a green dress. The shop was busy, women drifting in and out of the changing-rooms, others examining the dresses on the racks. The older shop assistant was wrapping up a purchase; when the telephone rang, the woman in the green dress answered it. Oliver slid the nearest scarf from the back of the chair into his blazer pocket. Then he left the shop.

He didn't run; he made himself walk steadily. It would have looked suspicious to run. His mouth was dry. He had almost reached the end of the road and was about to let out a huge sigh of relief, when he saw her standing in front of him. Light hair and eyes the colour of his mother's onyx brooch: the woman in the green dress, the woman from Holly Blue.

Faith said, 'The scarf, please,' and held out her hand.

He looked so frightened, so bewildered, she almost felt sorry for him. She explained, 'There's a back way. A short cut.'

'Oh,' he whispered, and slid the scarf out of his pocket and gave it to her.

'Will you tell the police?'

'I might do.' She, too, was puzzled. Shoplifters were not usually so young, so smartly dressed.

'Oh,' he said again, and blinked. 'Please don't.'

She looked at him and thought, exasperated, *And what on earth am I to do with you? Call the police, telephone your parents or give you a hug and tell you not to cry?*

She said, quite gently, 'What's your name?'

'Oliver.'

'That's a nice name. Well, Oliver, you don't want

448

me to call the police, but what do you think I should do?'

He shook his head. 'I don't know.' His eyes, a wonderful deep blue, were wide and terrified and fixed on her.

Standing on the busy pavement, she tried to make up her mind. He was thirteen or fourteen years old, she guessed, strikingly good-looking, and obviously well cared for.

'The thing is,' Faith said slowly, 'that I don't understand why you'd want to steal one of my scarves. Not many boys come into the shop, to be honest. A few at Christmas, I suppose, buying presents.' She narrowed her eyes. 'Was that it? Was it a present for someone?'

He nodded mutely.

'Your girlfriend?'

'Haven't got one.'

'Who then?'

His eyes glittered. There was a small café across the road. She steered him into it. 'We'll talk about this over iced buns and Tizer,' she said. 'You like iced buns and Tizer, don't you, Oliver? They're my favourite.'

She spoke to the waitress, allowing Oliver time to recover. She remembered being in Madrid, aged eight or so, and getting lost, and minding dreadfully about being lost, but minding much more about crying in front of strangers. When he had stopped biting his lip and was sucking his Tizer through a straw, she said: 'Tell me who you wanted to give the scarf to, Oliver.'

'To my mother. To cheer her up.'

'Is she unwell?'

He shook his head. His hair was properly gold, she thought, with a sheen like the best raw silk. He began, 'Mummy is – and Dad . . .' He blinked again, and looked down at the table. 'They quarrel a lot.' The muttered words were almost inaudible.

Faith said gently, 'Adults do quarrel sometimes, I'm afraid. It doesn't mean they don't love each other.'

He said fiercely, 'They're always quarrelling! I hate it! It makes me—' He broke off. 'I just hate it, that's all.'

He began to tear pieces from his iced bun. Looking at him, Faith remembered how she used to feel when Ralph and Poppy had argued. That sick, panicking feeling in the pit of the stomach; the dread that your whole world, of which your parents were of course the cornerstones, was about to collapse.

'They had a beezer row last night.' Oliver forced a more casual tone as he scooped up with his fingertip the icing that had fallen onto his plate. 'Me and Grandad, we turned the radio up really loud, but we could still hear them.'

'Poor Oliver.' Faith tried to fill in the gaps. 'So your mother looked unhappy this morning . . .'

'She'd been crying.'

'So your mother had been crying, and you wanted to get her something to cheer her up?'

'Yes.' Then, looking down at his plate again, he whispered, 'It's all my fault, you see.'

She forgot the scarf, and felt suddenly quite painfully sorry for him. 'It isn't your fault, Oliver,' she said. 'Not really. Children often feel that when their parents fall out it's because of them, but it isn't. It's just something that happens.'

'You don't understand.' He looked up, his eyes defiant. 'I did something awful, you see.'

She said firmly, 'Whatever you did, Oliver, I'm sure it wasn't that awful. You're just—'

'I was expelled from school,' he said.

His words seemed to strike her in the stomach. *I was expelled from school.* She put her glass down very carefully, and knotted her hands together to stop them shaking. *Oliver*, she thought. Thirteen years old. Expelled from school. And he took the scarf from the shop . . .

'See.' He glared at her. 'I told you it was awful.'

She said, 'You were expelled for stealing?' and his defiance changed to shame.

'That's why I'm home this summer. I usually board. Dad said I should go to the grammar school, but Mummy didn't want me to. It's all my fault.'

'Oliver,' she said carefully, 'what's your surname?'

Yet she knew his answer before he gave it.

'Neville,' he said.

Because she could not yet bear to go back to the shop, because she knew that Con would see her shock and guilt written on her face, Faith sat on the square of derelict land beside Holly Blue, watching the butterflies flutter in the ragwort. Tall spikes of rosebay willowherb, not yet in bloom, had forested the uneven ground. She hunched her knees up to her chin, and said to herself, *It's over*.

She realized that she had known for many months that it was coming to an end. She had just lacked the courage to deliver the final blow, to put a stop to the last breath. It had been a slow death, not for lack of love, but for lack of air. She had learned that love could not survive such a separate existence, that it needed other people, places, an exchange of energy to feed off. The deceits that had been necessary since the start of the affair had multiplied rather than diminished. Love could not live off deceit, because deceit poisoned whatever it touched.

She wondered too whether her love for Guy had always been fated. Whether the single-minded passion she had felt for him since her earliest days had not been in itself both seductive and dangerous. Had she unnaturally prolonged an adolescent obsession with Guy because he had been a part of a happier, safer past? Had she simply lacked the courage to start again, to commit herself to the new world that both the war and her family history had made?

She felt, after a while, calmer. The late afternoon sun kissed her shoulders and the top of her head. The months of uncertainty, of doubt, were over. She had just one awful thing to get through, and then she must start for herself a different sort of life. She didn't know how she would manage without him, but she knew that she must.

He telephoned the following evening. She said, picking up the receiver, 'Guy, we have to meet.' She knew that he would guess by the tone of her voice that something was wrong.

'Where?'

'Not here. Our café at lunchtime tomorrow.' She put the phone down.

He was waiting for her when she arrived. There were only three other customers: a cloth-capped old man eking out a cup of tea, and two boys with slicked-back hair and leather jackets, smoking.

Guy stood up when she came in. 'You've come to tell me that it's over.'

She had a hundred times rehearsed in her mind what

she would say to him, but now, looking at him, she could not find the words.

He said desperately, 'I know you hate the secrecy, and so do I, but—'

'Guy,' she said, 'Guy, Oliver came to the shop.'

His face blanched. The waitress arrived; Faith grabbed the menu, and ordered the first thing she saw. When they were alone again, he whispered: 'Oliver? *My* Oliver?'

She nodded. Now, looking at him, she could see the similarities between father and son. Different colouring, but the same fine-boned features. The same intensity, struggling for existence behind a conventional exterior.

'*How?* I don't understand . . .' Guy looked suddenly frightened. 'Does he *know?*'

'Oliver told me that he likes Soho – he often wanders around the area after school.' Faith shook her head. 'He doesn't know about *us*. But apparently he found one of Holly Blue's cards in your wallet.'

He stared at her. 'I kept it. That first time . . . when I bought the scarf, I kept it . . . I couldn't bear to throw it away . . .'

The waitress put two plates in front of them: Welsh rarebit topped with a glistening fried egg.

'My wallet . . . ?'

'He was, as he put it, borrowing a pound.' Faith's voice was grim. 'In the shop yesterday, he tried to steal a scarf. I saw him, and ran after him. We talked.'

Guy looked dazed. 'Stealing . . . Good God. I thought I'd put a stop to that.'

'He was upset, Guy. I took him to a café, and tried to talk to him.' She drove in the knife. 'And I told him

453

that a gentleman asks before he smokes in front of a lady.'

His eyes widened. 'Oliver *smokes*?'

'Yes, Guy.' Savagely, she stabbed the yolk of her egg with her fork. An orange rivulet trailed over the cheese. 'He had a packet of Woodbines. Didn't you know that your son smokes?'

Mutely he shook his head. 'What a bloody mess I seem to have made of it . . . being a father.' He took out his own cigarettes, offered the packet to Faith; she shook her head.

After a long time, he said, 'I suppose I'll have to speak to him again.'

'Not about the scarf, Guy. Or about the Holly Blue card. You can't, because it would implicate us.'

'Yes. Yes, of course.' He sounded small, diminished. 'I hadn't thought of that.'

'And besides, he told me about the card in confidence.'

Oliver had told her other things in confidence, things that she could never share with Guy.

'You seem to have made friends with him.'

'I liked him a lot.'

'Really? In the circumstances—'

She almost smiled. 'The circumstances were not propitious, but really, I liked him a lot.' She studied Guy. 'Though he seemed to me a rather unhappy little boy.'

'Unhappy?' He looked, she thought, haunted.

'In a funny sort of way, he reminded me of Jake. So bright and good-looking, and desperately searching for approval.'

Guy said bitterly, 'Oliver doesn't care a jot for *my* approval.'

'That's nonsense, Guy, and you know it.' She spoke coldly. 'Did you also know that Oliver believes that he is responsible for your arguments with Eleanor?'

He flinched. 'Poor kid,' he muttered. 'Poor little kid.' Ash showered from the tip of his cigarette and scattered the shining, untouched surface of his egg.

'Oliver believes that you and Eleanor quarrel because he was expelled from school. Whereas you and I . . . well, we know differently, don't we?'

Guy stubbed out his cigarette at the side of his plate. 'I don't argue with Eleanor because I love you, Faith, if that's what you mean. Eleanor and I argue because we dislike each other.'

'And before we started seeing each other?' Dear God, she thought, such a euphemism. *Seeing each other*. 'Did you quarrel as much then?' Her voice was hard, unforgiving.

He closed his eyes for a moment. 'No,' he admitted. 'No, I suppose we didn't.'

There was a silence. At length she said slowly, 'I suppose I'd never really thought of Oliver as a person. If the person you are betraying is just a name, a character in some drama that revolves only around you, then they don't matter so much, do they?'

He groaned, and buried his face in his hands. 'I told myself it would never affect him . . . never hurt him. Yet he believes himself responsible . . . I can't bear that, Faith. I can't bear it.'

The old man in the cloth cap shuffled out of the shop. Faith watched him walk away from the café, his overcoat buttoned in spite of the heat. She said, 'You still have the chance to mend things with Oliver. He loves you, Guy, I could see that he does. But as for us . . . We mustn't see each other again. Never, Guy. If we should pass each other in the street, we must be strangers.'

He cried out, anguished, 'But what shall I become, Faith? Without you, what shall I become?'

She said, 'A better father. A better husband,' and looked at him for the last time. Then she picked up her bag, and walked out of the shop.

After he left Heatherwood, Jake's first intention was to travel to the Continent. He needed a sun that burned high in the sky, and he needed dusty vineyards, and people who understood passion and spontaneity. He got as far as Southampton, with its bustle of docks and streets still scarred by bomb-damage, and there he ran into an old army friend in a pub in Bargate. The next morning, Jake woke up with a parched mouth, an agonizing headache, and a spine sore from having slept on a park bench. He could not recall the journey from pub to park. There was no sign of his old friend, or of his wallet.

The last of his anger, the last of the rapturous indignation that had carried him through his final few weeks at Heatherwood, began then to leave him. He looked at his actions of the past few months in a colder light. He saw that he had helped no-one – neither George, nor Mary, nor himself. There were things he could have done – quieter, less flamboyant things – which might have in the end achieved something. *Always the dramatic gesture, Jake old son*, he said to himself, as he wandered the streets of Southampton. Always the dramatic, futile gesture. Always the self-indulgent need to react with the heart, not the head. It occurred to him that the world had moved on, and that it regarded both heroism and passion with a colder, more cynical eye.

He telephoned a school in Northumberland which was advertising for a teacher of modern languages, but when they asked him for a reference he put the phone down. Each night, he dreamed. His dreams were colourful and complicated, and accompanied always by a fast, frantic commentary that echoed in the back of his skull. Sometimes he was sitting on a beach – in France, he supposed. It was Ralph's birthday, yet it was not summer, for the sky was a cold violet-blue, and the sea was pocked with dull, ragged waves. Guests came to the party. He saw the numbers tattooed on Genya's and Sarah's wrists. He waved to the Comtesse de Chevillard, but he could not tell whether she saw him or not, because her eyes were hidden behind dark glasses. Rufus offered him a drink; Nicole threw a ball to Minette. The railway official whom he had murdered in France smiled at him: Jake saw the thin scarlet line drawn across his throat.

He knew what Faith would say if he told her about his ghosts. *Get a job, Jake, so you're too tired to dream.* He found work in a pub. He remembered that Faith had also told him to sleep, to eat. Yet he could not eat, and the ghosts lingered. So he drank instead. When the odd tot of whisky became half a bottle filched from the pub's cellar, he was given the sack.

He decided to go to Wales, to see Mary. He thought that with her, he had managed, he had been all right. Because he had only a few pounds in his pocket, he hitched rides from Southampton to Swansea. From Swansea, he walked the twelve miles inland to the school. It was May, and the countryside was crisp and new. Jake began to hope again. He would talk to Mary, explain everything, tell her that he loved her. He would get on his feet again, find a decent job. He would write his own bloody reference if he had to.

The school where Mary worked was set in parkland. Jake climbed over the fence and walked through gently undulating lawns, beneath trees heavy with spring-green leaves. The school lay in a shallow valley, the building mock-Palladian, a cast-off, he assumed, of the once rich. He had reached a gravel drive that threaded between a huddle of cottages and garages, when a voice called out to him. A cloth-capped man – some sort of groundsman, Jake guessed – strode out from one of the cottages. The groundsman said something incomprehensible in Welsh, and then, seeing the blank look on Jake's face, spat on the ground, and, in English this time, told Jake to leave the premises. Jake explained that he was calling on a friend. The groundsman pointed out that it was half-term and that the school was almost empty. And anyway, Redstones didn't welcome Jake's sort.

His sort. Jake felt the anger rising inside him, but then he caught sight of his reflection in one of the cottage windows. He saw his dirty, tattered clothes, his unshaven chin. He realized that he could not remember when he had last had a bath, or when he had visited a launderette. He knew that he could not have borne Mary to see him like this, so he picked up his rucksack and started down the drive.

He went back to Southampton simply because he could think of nowhere better to go. In a pub by the docks he bought himself a double of the cheapest Scotch. He saw some navvies eyeing him – his overlong hair, his smart accent, the slight differences that he had never ironed out in all his years in England – and he knew that they, like himself, were spoiling for a fight. Jake smiled, and flexed his wrists.

Faith rearranged her life. Guy was part of the past, and she saw that she should have long since put the past behind her. She no longer saved her sixpences. She would forget the house in the country, the house that reminded her of La Rouilly, and would save up to buy a flat in Camden Town, or a west London terrace. She sorted through the apartment above the shop, and amassed a pyramid of photographs, postcards, mementoes, which she hauled down to the dustbin. She crumpled every one of Guy's love letters into a ball, arranging them in the stove. Then she put a match to the paper and watched the grey, lacy fragments vanish up the flue. Late one night she took the Holly Blue dress from her wardrobe. Age had caused one of the seams to fray; moths had nibbled the hem. She completed the work that time had begun, ripping seams, tearing sleeve from bodice, collar from neck, until the dress was a tangle of pale blue rags.

She telephoned friends she had neglected throughout the duration of her affair with Guy Neville. With them she watched films, went to the theatre, accepted invitations to parties. In an elegant, whitewashed house in Richmond she drank cocktails and danced with a stranger. His lips touched the crown of her head; his unfamiliar hands traced the bones of her spine. At midnight, they left the party. In a room cluttered with books, papers and typewriter, he made love to her. It was not as it had been long ago with Rufus; she knew now how to extract pleasure from such encounters. Guy had taught her well, she thought, and she looked up at the ceiling and smiled.

In the early hours of the morning, her lover rose from the bed and brought her coffee. 'Sorry, no milk or sugar. Do you mind? I forgot to shop.' He sat naked on the chair beside the desk, watching her. In the grey dawn light she could see that his flesh barely covered his ribs. Looking at the books heaped on the floor, she asked, 'Are you a writer?' and he answered, 'I'm writing my autobiography. I thought I'd call it *Destroyer of Worlds*. You remember . . . Oppenheimer's words when he watched the first atomic test: "I am become Death, the destroyer of worlds." ' He lit a cigarette. 'I was a prisoner of war, you see, when they dropped the A-bomb on Hiroshima. I saw the white flash. Often, when I close my eyes, I can see it again. It's like a second sun.'

She drank her coffee, and dressed. When he asked for her address, her telephone number, she prevaricated. She sensed a need in him, and she did not want to be needed. She wanted to remain disconnected from the days, the times, the people she encountered. At the weekend, visiting Heronsmead after an absence of a month, she had to bite her lip to stop herself exclaiming with anger at the chaos. A mountain of dirty clothes had gathered in the bedroom and beneath the sink a washer had come loose, so that washing soda, soap and scouring powder had coagulated into a thick, grey soup. Rinsing Ralph's shirts, phoning a plumber, she was filled with a deep resentment. Two days later, leaving Norfolk, she did not once look back from the carriage at Ralph, waving from the platform.

One Friday afternoon, she was in Holly Blue when the phone rang. She picked up the receiver, and said her number. Jake's voice said, 'Faith? Is that you?'

*   *   *

Jake was in a police cell in Southampton. He had been prosecuted by the police on a drunk and disorderly charge. He hadn't enough money to pay the fine. 'Faith?' said the small, disembodied voice on the other end of the line. 'Faith, I'm so sorry. I've got into a bit of a mess.'

She drove to Southampton. Red, white and blue flags flapped limply in honour of the forthcoming Coronation. Pictures of the new Queen, cut from magazines and newspapers, decorated the shop windows. She hated it all. She wished it had been winter, so that the landscape might reflect her closed, cold heart.

She paid the fine; they led Jake out of the police cell. There were large, purple bruises along his jaw, and one eye was ringed black and yellow. He had been given everything, Faith thought – looks, intelligence, charm – and he had squandered it all. She whispered, and her voice shook, 'What have you *done* to yourself!' and then she walked quickly back to the van.

Driving back to London, she swerved at speed around slower vans and cars. When she almost collided with a moped, she had to brake, pause at the side of the road, and force her pounding heart to slow. Jake slept; she kept her gaze on the road ahead, hardly able to bear to look at him. As she parked the van on the derelict land beside the shop, she heard Jake say, 'Faith – I'm sorry – don't worry, I'll pay you back,' but she turned on her heel, slamming the shop door behind her, leaving him to go up alone to the flat.

In the shop, all the most tiring, most tedious tasks waited for her. Dusting the shelves, chasing up late deliveries, pinning up hems. After she had cashed up, Ralph telephoned. He talked at length about the weather, the garden, the bird's nest in the eaves, but she hardly listened, and after a while she interrupted him, and put the phone down, and went upstairs. Jake was in the kitchen.

'There doesn't seem to be much food.'

'I haven't shopped.' It was an effort to speak to him. His face was pale, hollowed. He had wrapped a tea towel round one of his hands.

'So I made this.' He indicated a salad, bread, a square slab of luncheon meat, pink and glistening. 'Hope it's all right.'

'What have you done to your hand?'

He looked at it, his eyes blank. 'Cut it, opening this.' He gestured to the luncheon meat tin. 'Damn things.'

She unpeeled the tea towel. There was a gash the width of his palm. He grinned. 'Should've managed to do it a bit lower down – on the wrist perhaps – then I'd be out of your hair.'

'Don't be stupid, Jake.' Her voice was cold. She went to the bathroom to fetch plasters and cotton wool.

She heard him say, 'I'm sorry, Faith, for being such a bother,' and her fingers, holding the bottle of disinfectant, shook.

A bother . . . The demands of her family were, she thought, a cage, crashing down, enclosing her.

Jake came to the bathroom door. Just for an instant, she glimpsed in his eyes the despair that hid always, she sensed, behind the charm. Then she smelt the alcohol.

'You've been drinking.'

'Just a couple of beers in the pub.'

She hissed, 'Fifty pounds, Jake! I had to pay fifty pounds to that wretched court! And there'll be a solicitor's bill. I suppose you'll expect me to pay that as well!'

'I'll get a job.' Around the rainbow bruises, his skin was bleached.

'You *had* a job!'

His gaze dropped. He went back to the other room, fumbled in his pocket for his cigarettes, and perched on the window seat. His clothes were grubby, his chin unshaven.

'What happened, Jake?'

'I left the school a couple of months ago.'

She laughed. 'A record, wasn't it? You actually stuck it for a year, didn't you? What happened, Jake?' She remembered Ralph's justifications of the odysseys of her childhood. 'Did you get bored?' Her voice was mocking. 'Wasn't it quite the thing?'

He muttered, 'Something like that.'

'If you were fed up with that school, why didn't you just move to another one?'

'I hadn't a reference.'

'Why not?'

He evaded her gaze. 'I . . . left under a cloud.'

A pause. 'You drank?'

'It wasn't that. Not really.'

'Tell me the truth, Jake.'

He was fidgeting with a loose button on the cuff of his jacket. 'It was more of a disagreement of principle.'

'*Principle?*' She was almost incoherent with anger. 'So my savings – my future – have been sacrificed to your precious *principles*?'

'I told you.' The button snapped from his cuff and rolled onto the floor. 'I'll pay you back.'

'Do you know the number of times that Pa has said that to me? When the chimney caught fire . . . when he left the shopping on the bus . . . whenever the bills need paying . . .' She stared at Jake, folded gracefully on the window seat, and said bitterly, 'It's so ridiculous that you and Pa don't get on. You are so alike.'

Jake's eyes darkened. 'Faith – shut up, for God's sake.'

'Do you know how like him you are?' Now that she had begun to speak, she could not stop. She was aware of an exhilaration in voicing thoughts that she had pushed to the back of her mind for years. 'Never able to stick to anything . . . forever living in borrowed houses . . . living on other people's money. You have so much in common!'

Jake said, 'Of course we do. We shared the same woman, didn't we?' and she was suddenly silenced, the remainder of her words frozen on her lips.

'Didn't you know?' He smiled. 'Didn't you realize that I slept with Linda Forrester?'

She sat down heavily on the arm of the settee. She felt sick.

'I thought you wanted the truth.' Jake's eyes were a wide, deep blue. 'Don't look so horrified, Faith. Although, I have to admit, when I realized that I'd . . . followed in his footsteps, shall we say . . . I felt pretty revolted myself.' He smoked for a while in silence. Then he said, 'You're right, of course. I am like him. I realized that a long time ago.'

'Which is why you hate him.'

'Rather a trite analysis.' He considered. 'I don't hate him. I used to, but I don't now. In fact, I feel sorry for him.'

Tears pressed at the back of her eyes. 'But not sorry enough to visit him?'

Jake said nothing. Faith twisted her hands together. When he looked at her, his slick defensiveness seemed

464

to falter, and he said, 'Faith . . . what's happened? You're not usually like this.'

Her anger returned, cold and unforgiving. *You're not usually like this*. She was not, just now, good old Faith, the reliable Mulgrave, the sensible Mulgrave, the *dull* Mulgrave.

'All of you – you keep dragging me back. You won't allow me to be free—' She broke off, staring at him. 'Pa is an old man now, you see, Jake. He has grey hair, and sometimes he gets ill, and he's never managed terribly well without Ma anyway. Have either you – or Nicole – ever wondered who supports him? Have either of you ever wondered who makes sure that he has food in the house, or coal for the fire? Has it ever occurred to either of you to share the burden?' When she touched her ribcage with the tips of her fingers, Faith could feel her heart pounding. '*I* have looked after Pa all these years, Jake – me, on my own, since Ma died—'

He said slowly, 'We have leaned on you rather.'

'Leaned on me!' Her throat was raw. 'You've sucked me dry, all of you. "Stick together whatever the cost" – you have all cost me too much, Jake! I wanted a family of my own, children of my own – and look what I have instead! A sister who took the man I love . . . a brother who has shared my father's mistress . . . a father who contributed to my mother's death . . .' Her laugh was odd, cracked. 'Good God! It's like some wretched Greek tragedy!'

'Faith . . .' He stepped towards her, reaching out to touch her, but she clenched her fists, warding him off.

'I've had enough, Jake. You see, I've changed. In future, I mean to live like the rest of you. I'll follow my heart and be damned to everyone else. I'll live on everyone's money but my own. I'll chase my own dreams, keep to my own principles, and care less about the harm it may do to others.' She looked up at him. 'Will you let me do that, Jake? Or will you turn up in six months or so, asking me to bail you out again? You and Pa . . .' Her voice rose. 'How can I ever plan *anything*?'

He looked grey with exhaustion. 'What do you want me to say, Faith? What do you want me to say?'

She whispered, 'I want you to leave me alone. I want all of you to leave me alone. I want you to let me get on with my life.'

He remained for a moment quite still, looking at her, and then he bowed his head. 'Then I promise you that I'll never bother you again.' He picked up his rucksack.

She heard the sound of his footsteps on the stairs, and the door slamming behind him. She saw the supper, uneaten on the table, and, glancing out, glimpsed Jake crossing the road, and walking fast down the street. Suddenly she ran to the window and tried to open it. But the latch jammed, and though she called out, she knew that he had not heard her. And then his figure blurred, and, for the first time since she and Guy had parted, she began to cry. For Jake, for Guy, for Poppy, for all that she had lost.

He didn't blame her for chucking him out. He knew that he was guilty of everything she accused him of.

Jake walked west, heading for the Bath Road. In a pawnbroker's in Ealing, he sold his watch and his fountain pen, his only possessions of any value. He exchanged most of the cash for a postal order, and with the remainder bought a pad of writing paper and some cheap envelopes. Then he hitched a lift to Bristol.

It took him two days to travel from Bristol to

Cornwall. Cars and vans transported him from one road to another. The cities were replaced first by villages, then hamlets, and the bleak roads were hedged by wind-stunted trees. The last leg of his journey took him along the north Cornish coast. It was a fine day, and only a few wispy clouds drifted across the face of the sun. Jake remembered that other, long-ago journey, cycling south from Paris in the summer of 1940. He was glad that this English sun lacked the harsh, merciless quality that he associated with the burning heat of those nightmare days. That this time he felt none of the urgency, none of the dread he had then endured.

He reached his destination at midday. If he had walked inland from the coast, through the trees, he would have seen Heatherwood. He did not do so. He stood on the clifftop, remembering the day that he had gazed down to the sea, the day that he had realized that it was the first step that took courage, and not the rest. After a while he followed the path to where the cliffs bowed and crouched, forming the little cove with the rocks and pools. The breeze was quiet and the sea was the turquoise-blue of the Mediterranean.

Jake sat down on a rock. Waves sucked at the sand beneath him. The sun warmed his limbs, and it was delightful to shrug off his rucksack and jacket. He sat there for a while, watching the sea, remembering, and then he took the pad of paper and envelopes out of his rucksack.

First, he put the postal order into an envelope which he addressed to Faith. Then he addressed the second envelope, and for a long time stared at the blank writing pad in front of him. He could not, though, think what to write. What did one say to the father one had not spoken to for twelve years? His mind still felt clouded, burdened by the events of weeks, months, years. After a while, he folded the piece of paper, put it in the envelope, and replaced the envelope in his rucksack. The sun had burnt through the clouds, and a trickle of sweat ran from his throat down his chest. He undid his boots and peeled off his socks. His feet were raw and blistered. The sea had crept into the cove; shuffling down the rock, Jake dipped a toe into the water. It felt cool and delicious. He slid down until he was standing on the soft sand, the water lapping around his toes and ankles.

Jake closed his eyes, enjoying the sensations that assailed him. The waves, washing away his blisters and bruises, the hot sun beating on his back. He did not, at that moment, want anything more. When he opened his eyes, the sea spread out before him, a vast landscape, cool and blue and welcoming. That sea touched all other seas; beneath that sea whole continents lay unexplored. Jake unbuttoned his shirt, peeled off his trousers, and placed both on top of the rock beside his rucksack. Then he waded forward, heading out of the cove. The water lapped his calves, his knees, his thighs, and then, with strong, steady strokes, he began to swim. As the sea embraced him, it seemed to Jake that he was washing away the past, starting again.

On the evening before the Coronation, there was a knock at the front door of the shop. When, opening it, Faith saw the police officer, she knew that something dreadful had happened. In her tiny sitting-room, the policeman told her that Jake's belongings – his clothes, his rucksack – had been found abandoned on a beach in Cornwall. 'They're searching the coves and beaches along the coast,' the constable explained gently, and she knew he meant that they searched for a body, sea-bloated, spat up from the waves. When, the following day, she walked to the postbox, letters to David and Nicole clutched in her hand, the flags and bunting in the streets and the flickering glimpses of cheering crowds and regal processions on television sets mocked her. The rain pummelled the pavements, streaming in rivulets down the back of her neck.

She could not sleep, could not eat. The last words that she had said to Jake chimed in her head, a passing-bell. *I want you to leave me alone. I want you to let me get on with my life.* She went to Heronsmead. Ralph met her at the railway station. She threw herself against him, burying her face in the familiar, dusty folds of his overcoat, and wept. Patting her back, he offered her a ragged grey handkerchief, and said: 'I can't think why you are making that noise. I told you on the telephone – Jake will turn up.'

They began to walk through the town. 'So obstinate of you,' added Ralph as he strode along the pavement, 'to insist on believing that he's dead. You always were stubborn, Faith. Jake is alive. I've told you over and over again.'

Faith shook her head. 'No, Pa.' She had wept so much that her voice was scoured of emotion. 'Jake drowned. That's what the police think. They just don't know whether it was an accident or whether he killed himself.'

'Killed himself? Jake? What nonsense. Why on earth should Jake want to kill himself?'

She thought, because he had nothing left. Because for Jake, nothing of value ever lasted.

'Of course he didn't kill himself.' Ralph sounded truculent. 'I know that he didn't.'

She cried, 'But how can you know, Pa?'

They crossed a road, Ralph tugging her through the traffic, regardless of the squeals of brakes and tyres. Flung up on the far pavement, her shoes were soaked from the puddles, and her breath was taut in her throat. Ralph said smugly, 'Jake was writing me a letter.'

The police, looking for an explanation, had shown her Jake's letter. The envelope bearing Ralph's address, and the blank piece of paper inside. Of all the pathetic debris of Jake's life, which she, seeking the truth, had been forced to pick through, that mute letter had hurt her the most.

Faith dug her hands into her pockets and walked on. The clouds had pulled apart, a fragile lacework letting through narrow bands of sun. If Ralph, she thought, gained comfort by believing that Jake was alive, by believing, perhaps, that his son had forgiven him, then who was she to deny him that comfort?

Ralph continued to lecture her. 'And how could the boy possibly have drowned? He was a good swimmer – I taught him myself.'

'Yes, Pa.'

'Do hurry up, Faith. We'll miss the bus if you don't get a move on.'

'Yes, Pa,' she said again. She scuttled beside him, struggling to keep up with him, wishing that she had not worn high heels.

Ralph made her search through the jumble that filled the attic for a piece of sheet music that Felix had given him twenty years before; Ralph insisted she scour Norfolk with him by bus, in search of a nursery that grew vines, so that he would be able to make his own wine; Ralph made her stand beside him on the upstairs landing while he leaned out of the window, reloading his pre-war shotgun as he took pot-shots at the rats that stole the hens' food. At the end of a week, reeling with the jangling exhaustion that always accompanied her sojourns with her father, Faith cycled, longing for silence and uninterrupted thoughts, along the coast.

She abandoned her bicycle at Cley Eye, and climbed to the peak of the long shingle spit that jutted out into the sea, dividing land from water. Though it was midsummer, the wind buffeted her. She would walk to Blakeney Point, she decided. She had never walked the entire length of the shingle isthmus: she and Ralph had once sailed to the headland from Blakeney village, but, walking, she had always turned back partway. It was too far; the wind, blowing off the North Sea, had discouraged her, and the pebbles, shifting beneath her feet, had slowed her down.

She pulled the brim of her hat down low, jammed her hands into her pockets, and began her journey. Seals raised their grey-green heads from the waves, and seemed to glance fleetingly at her, like disinterested mermaids. Gulls wheeled in the leaden sky. She made herself pause at the place where she and Guy had picnicked, and found herself looking for an apple core, or a bottle top, some evidence that he and she had once existed. But there was nothing, of course, only a few blackened strings from a fishing net, and a clump of sea lavender.

After an hour or so, her ankles ached from the constant shifting of the stones beneath her feet. The Point, hazed by a greyish mist, seemed no nearer. Though she continued to place one foot in front of another, her destination seemed to remain unreachable.

It had begun to rain, fine needlepoints of spray that were cold against her face. Pausing for a few minutes in the shelter of the sand dunes, she looked out to sea. She wondered if she could do what Jake had done – strip herself naked, and walk into the grey waves – and knew that she could not. Something in her made her keep going, she thought, in spite of her fractured heart. *Stubborn*, Ralph had said.

A fisherman, walking back along the isthmus to the mainland, greeted her with a nod; an artist, his head bent over his windblown sketchbook, did not even glance up as she passed by. And then there was only herself and the gulls and the seals, and the swell of land ahead of her, rising up from the North Sea like a clenched fist, that had become at last better defined, separate from the water that surrounded it.

At mid-afternoon she reached the Point, and stood surrounded on three sides by sea and mudflats. The rain had cleared at last, and the thin sunlight made the reed-beds shimmer. Faith sat down on the shingle and pulled off her shoes. Her feet were patched with blisters; every stitch of her clothing was soaked by the rain. Hunger gnawed at her stomach. The insanity of it, she thought: to walk along this beach, in these shoes, in this weather. And as she lay back on the stones, her entire body aching with exhaustion, she thought suddenly of the Catholic churches in Brittany, with their colours and gilt and plaster saints. *This is penance*, she thought. *I am doing penance, just as those black-shawled women, kneeling at the altar, counting their rosaries, were doing penance. Just as Ralph, marooned on the cold, inhospitable coast of a country that he once loathed, is also doing penance.*

She thought, *I loved Guy. I loved Guy, and I wanted*

to live with him, and I wanted his children. She put her latticed fingers over her lids, protecting her eyes from the sunlight. She knew that in telling herself that her feelings for Guy had been only calf love, some sort of horribly delayed adolescence, she had been deceiving herself. She knew also that because she had lost Guy, and because she had not been able to bear that loss, she had also lost Jake. Because she had been angry and grieving, she had found it too hard to forgive Jake. Now she must do something far harder. She must try to forgive herself.

The sea was rushing back into the channels gouged between the mudflats and reed-beds. Faith squeezed her sore feet back into her shoes, and stood up. Then she began to walk home.

Favourable Winds

1959–1960

CHAPTER FOURTEEN

It was late afternoon, and Holly Blue was empty except for a dark-haired girl sitting at the till, reading a magazine. Oliver threaded through the racks and clothes stands.

'Hi.' He looked down at the girl. She was tall, sturdy, her well-scrubbed face innocent of make-up. He could imagine her pounding enthusiastically round a hockey pitch. He gave her his best smile, more out of habit than anything else.

'Could I speak to Miss Mulgrave?'

'She's not here.' Her downcast eyes hidden by a long fringe, she continued to thumb through her magazine. Oliver, craning his neck, saw that the magazine was not, as he had expected, *Woman's Own*, or even *School Friend*, but a very dull-looking political journal.

'I'm a friend of Faith's. Is she in her flat?'

At last the girl looked up, and focused on him. 'Sorry. I thought you were some awful salesman. Auntie Faith went out this morning, actually. I'm not sure when she'll be back.'

Oliver was disappointed. His visit was unannounced: he had only thought of visiting Faith Mulgrave as the train had pulled out of Princes Street station.

'Can I help?' She flushed slightly.

'It was just a spur of the moment thing. It doesn't

matter.' Yet the remainder of the day stretched emptily before him. Outside it had begun to rain, silver-grey rods pounding the littered pavements.

'Do you want to leave a message for Auntie Faith?'

Oliver, looking at her, said, 'You must be Elizabeth.'

'How do you know?'

'Faith told me all about you.' A lie: Faith had once briefly mentioned her niece, and had then changed the subject. But he was bored, and it was raining, and he did not yet want to go home, and he might as well enjoy the game of flirting with this plain, dumpy schoolgirl.

'Really?' Her blush had deepened.

'I've forgotten your surname, though.'

'Kemp. My name's Elizabeth Kemp.' She held out her hand. 'And you're—'

'Oliver Neville.' They shook hands. She wore dark corduroy slacks and a shapeless black sweater, and seemed incongruous among the bright, feminine colours that surrounded her. Her thick, dark hair – probably, Oliver thought judiciously, her best feature – was hacked off anyhow at the shoulders.

She said suddenly, 'Would you like a cup of tea?'

'If it's not too much trouble . . . I wouldn't want to keep you from your work.'

She snorted dismissively, and said, 'I wouldn't call this *work*,' and disappeared into a back room. Oliver flicked through the magazine she had been reading. It was called *The Universities and Left Review*, and was full of dull articles about the Bomb.

He called to her, 'Don't you like it here?'

Carrying two mugs of tea, she came back into the shop. 'I just help out sometimes, in the school holidays.

478

Sugar, Oliver?' She offered him the bowl. 'Tell me how you know Auntie Faith.'

Well, she almost had me arrested for shoplifting . . .
He said easily, 'I bought something here, oh, donkey's years ago, and we got talking.' He shrugged. 'I just call in once in a while.'

Oliver always found it hard to explain to himself why he had continued over the years occasionally to visit Faith Mulgrave. Because, he had eventually concluded, he liked to divide his life up into small, separate corners. That way, if one part fouled up, there was always something to fall back on. There was a corner (put aside, finished off) for Nana and Derbyshire, another for that stupid part of his life when he had stolen things to impress others (he had since learned that his looks and brains were sufficient guarantees of attention), another corner for medical school, and yet another was reserved for the girls that he slept with. Faith Mulgrave occupied the patch in his heart that enjoyed the unconventional, the Bohemian, the free-spirited. Oliver often thought it strange that he possessed such impulses: they did not seem to go with the rest of him.

'I can't think why anyone buys anything here,' said Elizabeth, looking around the shop. 'It's all so ghastly. I can't think why people bother about clothes when we could all be dead tomorrow.'

Oliver blinked. 'That's rather pessimistic, isn't it?'

'Don't you care about the Bomb?'

He recognized the flare of passion in her brown eyes and said hastily, 'Of course I do. I think it's dreadful.' Though he had always been fascinated by the enormity of atomic power: its capacity for instant annihilation.

'Are you going on the march, then?'

'What march?'

'The Aldermaston march, of course.'

Oliver dimly remembered television pictures of serious people in duffel coats, walking in the rain. He muttered something noncommittal.

From the back of the shop, there was the sound of a key in a lock. Elizabeth said suddenly, 'If you want to find out more about the march, there's a meeting on Friday night in the Black Cat café – it's near Chelsea Bridge, do you know it? A few friends of mine . . .' Her face had become petunia pink.

A voice called out, 'Lizzie? I'm back!' and Elizabeth snatched up her magazine. Faith Mulgrave, drops of rain peeling from her mackintosh, opened the door of the shop.

Seeing him, she put down her umbrella, and said, 'Oliver . . .' Her voice shook a little.

He thought she looked tired. He said, 'I just dropped in on the way home from university. I'll go if it's a nuisance.'

But she smiled and said, 'Not at all. It's lovely to see you, Oliver. We'll have a drink upstairs.' Faith turned to Elizabeth. 'Lizzie, there are some errands, I'm afraid. The weather is vile, but if you wrap up well . . .'

'A bit of rain won't bother me.' Elizabeth pulled on a coat, wrapped a scarf round her neck. 'Just tell me what you want me to do, Auntie Faith.'

In the flat above the shop, Faith, using the pretence of needing to dry her hair, had to escape to the bathroom; in reality she needed to quiet her pounding heart. The sight of Oliver and Elizabeth together had shaken her. Oliver, Guy's son; Elizabeth, Guy's lover's daughter. Rubbing her hair with a towel, she forced herself to

480

breathe steadily, and not recreate that moment of panic.

She should, she told herself angrily, have years ago put an end to such an unwise relationship. She had been weak and self-indulgent in allowing Oliver Neville to visit her. Yet she remembered the long-ago morning that Oliver had returned to Holly Blue. It had been five and a half years ago, the early autumn of 1953, and she had been exhausted, crushed by the end of her affair with Guy, and by Jake's death. Oliver's visit had, she thought, marked her return to humanity. She, who had been burnt out, able to feel nothing but regret, had been touched by his reappearance. To come back to Holly Blue must have demanded such courage of him. He had been red-faced, clutching a bunch of flowers, muttering well-rehearsed apologies. She could not have been cold to him; she could not have refused the flowers, or sent him away. A few months earlier, she had sent Jake away, and Jake had drowned himself, and it had seemed to her at that time that forgiveness was part of the responsibility of simply being human.

Since that first visit, Oliver had continued to call once or twice a year at Holly Blue. Each time she tried gently to put him off, explaining that she was busy, or that she had an appointment; each time he left Faith half expected, half hoped, never to see him again. She was a middle-aged spinster, she told herself; he would become bored with such an unconventional friendship. Yet Oliver Neville had continued to call at Holly Blue. She never spoke about the past to him, rarely talked about her family. Their conversations were wild, colourful leaps from subject to subject that left her dog-tired yet exhilarated. Though she saw clearly his faults – his pretences, his capacity for manipulation –

she recognized that they were, in spite of his apparent sophistication, a means of dealing with a world he often found bewildering. She did not think that she enjoyed Oliver's company because he was a last, second-hand link with Guy.

Back in the living-room, she poured gins and tonic for both of them. Oliver lounged on the sofa, his long limbs in stylish disarray. A single lock of dark gold hair fell every now and then over his forehead, and he swept it back carelessly. They must fall at his feet in Edinburgh, Faith thought wryly, and was doubly glad that she had sent Lizzie out. Oliver's type of dangerous, amoral charm might easily sway someone as innocent and over-protected as Lizzie.

She was slicing a lemon, when she heard him say, 'She isn't at all like you.'

'Lizzie?' She was calm now. 'She takes after her father.'

'How old is she?'

'Seventeen.'

'I thought she was younger . . . those clothes, I suppose.'

'Her mother hopes Holly Blue's style will rub off on her.' Faith dropped a slice of lemon into each glass.

He said disapprovingly, 'I can't understand why some girls dress like men. Especially girls who—'

He broke off. Faith handed him a glass. 'You sound as though you are fifty years old, Oliver. Perhaps girls choose to dress like men because they want to be treated on equal terms with men. And especially *which* sort of girls? Do explain.'

He had gone red. 'I just meant . . . I think . . . It doesn't matter.'

He had meant, she knew, especially rather plain girls.

She was not offended. She could only be relieved that Oliver was not yet old enough to appreciate Elizabeth's solemn, old-fashioned beauty.

She enjoyed watching him wriggle for a while, and then, sitting down beside him, changed the subject. 'How's Edinburgh?'

'Hideously cold and dreary.' Oliver grimaced. 'It's snowed for the past week. My landlady insists on serving me buckets of porridge each morning because she thinks I need building up.'

Faith laughed. One of the things she liked most about Oliver Neville was his ability to make her laugh. 'And medical school?'

'Oh, fine.' His tone was cool, disinterested. 'We had to dissect an eyeball last week. Two of the chaps passed out.'

Half an hour later, she saw him off into the rain. Then she unpacked the samples she had brought back that day from a supplier on the south coast, holding the fabrics close to the light to see their colours clearly.

From below, she heard a door slam. She called, 'Up here, Lizzie!' and heard her niece thunder up the stairs.

'I've done everything, Auntie Faith. Paddy wasn't in, so I just stuffed everything through his letter box.' Paddy Calder was Holly Blue's accountant.

'Help yourself to a drink as a reward. I don't know what I would do without you.'

Elizabeth looked down at the floor. 'Have a cleaner drawing-room, probably. Sorry – should have taken off my wellies.'

A puddle had formed round her feet. Elizabeth fetched a mop and dabbed at the floor. 'There. All done.' She squeezed out the mop. 'I'd make a good cleaner, wouldn't I? Do you think Dad would approve?'

'I'm not sure that's quite what David has in mind for you, Lizzie.'

'Much more useful than being a boring debutante.' Gloomily, Elizabeth replaced the mop and bucket in the kitchen.

Elizabeth was to leave boarding school in the summer. In September, David planned to send her to a finishing school in Paris, where she would stay for a year. After that, Queen Charlotte's ball, and what remained of the deb circuit. Elizabeth was unenthusiastic, but had come up with no practical alternative. David had confided his worries to Faith. 'I don't want her just to *drift*, you see, Faith.' Faith knew that he had meant, *I don't want Elizabeth to end up like Nicole*.

'Have you thought any more about secretarial college?'

'I suppose it might be all right.' Elizabeth perched on the window sill, chewing a lock of dark hair.

Faith refolded the lengths of material. 'You don't have to do anything, you know, Lizzie,' she said gently. 'You can stay at home, look after your horses, that sort of thing. You could give riding lessons, perhaps.'

Elizabeth scowled. 'It seems so useless, doesn't it? Just the sort of thing someone like me would do – give riding lessons to rich little girls.' She fisted her hands. 'I want to *do* something, Auntie Faith! I want to make things better!' Tentatively, she looked up at Faith. 'I saw a film about India – all those poor children sleeping out on the streets . . . so awful! I thought I could go and work there. I could nurse, perhaps.'

Faith said patiently, 'India's a very long way away, darling. Your father would miss you terribly. And really, you'd be far more useful if you had some training before you went. Why don't you talk to your father about becoming a nurse?'

Sometimes she felt sandwiched between Elizabeth's passion and idealism, and David's over-protectiveness. She wanted to say to Lizzie, *Wait, you've plenty of time*; and to tell David that he must let his beloved only daughter go, allow her to grow up. But she knew that neither would listen.

She heard Elizabeth sigh, 'Three years, though! You have to train for three whole years! I'd be twenty-one by the time I finished! *Old!*'

Whenever Oliver was in Edinburgh he loathed the grey, Puritan grimness of it all, and longed for London; yet in London, a blanket of apathy and irritation seemed invariably to settle over him. Last year, he had scraped together enough cash to spend Easter in France; this Easter, because of Marie, he was broke.

Unlocking Holland Square's front door, dumping his suitcase in the hall, Oliver walked from room to room. He thought at first that the house was unchanged, just as it always was, but then he began to notice the small alterations. The heap of old newspapers on the coffee table, the unwashed cups in the sink. Oliver, who disliked mess, felt unsettled and slightly disgusted.

He went upstairs. The door of his father's study was half open; Oliver peeped through the aperture. Guy was working at his desk. There was a sheaf of paperwork in front of him.

Oliver opened the door. 'Hi, Dad.'

Guy looked up. 'Oliver! How marvellous – why didn't you tell us you were coming? I'd have met you at the station. Come in.' A quick, clumsy hug. 'You're soaked.'

'Bloody awful weather.' Oliver pulled away, and took off his coat.

'It's rained for a week.'

'Snow in Scotland.'

'Really? Late in the year even for Edinburgh, isn't it?'

The *banality* of it, thought Oliver, gritting his teeth. The appallingly English *banality*. To travel hundreds of miles to see one's closest relations, and to talk about the *weather*.

Guy stoked up the fire. 'There, stand in front of that and dry yourself out, old chap.' He stood up. 'You look well, Oliver.'

'You too, Dad.' A lie. His father looked *old*. Old and tired and gone to seed, like the house. Bloodshot eyes and a hollowness to his face. 'Are you busy, Dad?'

'Very.' Guy gestured to the paperwork on his desk.

'Where's Mother?'

'Out,' said Guy vaguely. 'She's working for some charity or other . . . something musical . . .'

'The house is a mess,' said Oliver.

'Is it? I hadn't noticed. Mrs Thing left, I believe. Our vanquished Mrs Mops must be in double figures by now.'

It was a sort of feeble, laboured joke between them, his mother's inability to keep a daily help for longer than six months at a time. Oliver forced a smile.

'Drink, old chap? Cigarette?'

Oliver shook his head. The two gins he had drunk with Faith had been large ones; he, who disliked feeling out of control, felt slightly woozy. And he had given up smoking at sixteen.

'You don't mind if I do?'

486

''Course not, Dad.' Oliver watched Guy pour himself half an inch of whisky, and light another cigarette. The room, though not particularly warm, was stuffy.

'How's college?'

'Great,' said Oliver. The lies were piling up depressingly. He tried to remember what on earth he had been studying this term – odd, if a relief, how distant it seemed already. 'Got an A minus for my essay on the vascular system.'

'That's terrific, Oliver. Terrific.' Guy looked delighted.

Oliver swallowed, and took a deep breath. 'Dad . . . the thing is, Dad . . .'

'Spit it out.'

'The thing is, Dad – I'm a bit short.'

Guy went to his desk and drew a ten-pound note out of his wallet. 'Will this help? Look upon it as a belated "well done" for your essay.'

Oliver felt as though he was poised to dive into a very deep swimming pool. 'Dad, thanks for the tenner and all that, but the thing is, it's not enough.' Before he had even finished speaking, he knew that he had chosen the words most likely to antagonize his father.

'Not enough? What do you mean, Oliver?'

'It won't tide me over till next term,' floundered Oliver. 'I've had to pay for—' He wondered, momentarily, on what on earth he had spent his admittedly generous stipend. On Marie, he supposed. Marie, who had for the last six months made Edinburgh bearable, and who required a great many expensive presents. He had thought that he was in love with Marie, yet just now he found it hard even to remember her. Black hair; those pale, shrewd eyes and small, sharp teeth. His recollections of her remained separate, like pieces of a jigsaw he could not quite fit together.

'Oliver?'

'I had to buy some warm sweaters . . . And books . . .'

'Your grandfather's bequest to you was quite substantial. You can't have spent all of the term's allowance, surely, Oliver. Most students have to live on a lot less. When I was at medical school—'

Oliver shut himself off while his father droned on. He had heard it all before. The deprivations of studying medicine in the Dark Ages. Not being able to afford coal, having to sell his only overcoat in exchange for Gray's *Anatomy*. Oliver, edgy with resentment and frustration, wanted to leave the room, slamming the door behind him like a touchy adolescent. But he forced himself to remain.

Guy said gently, 'I know that it must be hard to see men of your age who are already in work, who are able to go out every night, who can afford to run their own cars – but it'll be worth it in the end, won't it, Oliver?'

Oliver shrugged. When he glanced up, he saw that his father was looking at him.

'You're still sure that medicine's the right thing for you, aren't you, old chap?'

Oliver evaded his father's gaze. ''Course I am, Dad. What else would I do?'

A small silence, then Guy said, 'I'm glad. Your mother and I are very proud of you, you know.'

He would offer to take his father out for a drink, Oliver thought. Soften him up with a pint or two and a bit of filial conversation. Get round him that way.

Before Oliver could speak, the telephone rang. Guy answered it.

'Sylvia . . . yes? Yes . . .' Guy sighed, and glanced at his watch. 'In half an hour or so, then. It doesn't sound urgent, but just to be on the safe side.' Guy put down the phone, and smiled ruefully. 'I'm going to have to go out, I'm afraid. We'll talk later. But Oliver – it's not such a bad thing to suffer a little for one's ideals, is it?'

Hypocrite, thought Oliver, focusing on the cut glass whisky tumbler, the box of expensive cigarettes on the desk. *You absolute, bloody hypocrite.* But he only said, in resigned tones calculated to induce guilt, 'It doesn't matter, Dad. If you can't help, you can't help. I'll get by somehow.' Then he left the room, shutting the door behind him with exaggerated quietness.

His mother, more sympathetic, gave him twenty pounds ('How stingy of your father not to help you'); a mixture of pride and weariness stopped him asking her for more. Oliver began to regret having come down from college early. All his London friends seemed to be otherwise engaged: they were either doing something enviable, such as skiing in Austria, or worthily working in a bar or factory through the Easter vacation. Heaving metal girders around a foundry seemed to Oliver even more appallingly awful than the suffocating tension of Holland Square.

On Friday night he accompanied his mother to the opera. He loathed opera, he could not see how anyone could find it enjoyable, but his mother seemed to, so he kept his thoughts to himself. Boredom soon reduced him to a state of almost catatonic torpor. Perched high in a box, he felt curiously separate from it all. The small, caterwauling figures on the stage; the glittering, well-dressed audience; even Eleanor, sitting beside him, seemed hardly to inhabit the same world as he.

At the interval his mother introduced him to endless flurries of her friends.

'Penny – Larry – you've met my son, Oliver, haven't you?' or, 'Simon – June – this is my son, Oliver. He's studying medicine.'

To which they would reply, 'Medicine! How clever!' and then stare at him as though he were some sort of strange exhibit gleaned from a museum. Or they would say, 'He must take after his father,' and Eleanor would respond crisply, 'His grandfather, I always think. My father died two years ago, but he would have been so delighted by Oliver's achievements.'

At the end of the evening, Eleanor drove them both home. 'Cocoa, darling?' she asked, fitting her key to the lock.

Oliver looked up at the house, at the empty eyes of its square, black windows. A sudden wave of panic, swelling in his lungs, squeezing the oxygen out of him, took him by surprise. He said quickly, 'I think I'll go for a walk, if you don't mind, Mother. Too much sitting still – I need to stretch my legs.'

Ignoring the hurt on her face, he headed down the road. He walked fast, in no particular direction, trying to shake off the black mood that had settled on him. The further he travelled from Holland Square, the easier he seemed to find it to breathe. He needed company, he thought, and perhaps a drink or two, something to take his mind off the weight of his parents' love and expectation. Who, though? He could not think of a single available acquaintance. He thought of going to Soho, to a club, but knew that he hadn't enough cash. Then he remembered Faith's niece's red-faced, blurted invitation.

'Not your *type*, Oliver old son,' he muttered to himself. Yet he began to walk towards the river.

The Black Cat café was a small, studenty place, its bare brick walls plastered with posters advertising obscure French films. One small room, leading off the street, was scattered with tables covered in gingham cloths. Oliver, searching through the crowds, could not see Elizabeth. He glimpsed a flight of steps leading down to a basement.

Pausing at the foot of the stairs, he looked around. The room was as dark as a cave. Candles flickered around the black perimeter; a single dim light illuminated a girl perched on a stool, playing the guitar. As she finished her song, there was a ripple of applause. A voice called out Oliver's name.

He caught sight of Elizabeth, and threaded through chairs and tables to reach her. In the candlelight, her eyes were shining. She patted the stool beside her, and Oliver sat down.

'How marvellous – I didn't think you were going to come.' Bubbling with happiness, she stumbled over the words. She seemed to be wearing the same baggy black sweater and corduroy slacks that she had worn in the shop. The other people at her table were similarly dressed. Oliver, in evening dress, felt slightly silly.

'Sorry about the penguin suit. Just been to the opera.'

She made a face. 'Poor you. My mother sometimes takes me, and it bores me to tears. Let me introduce you to everyone.'

She reeled off a list of names that he forgot instantly. Looking at the other people seated round the table, Oliver felt only contempt. The fraying sweaters, the

491

university scarves, the Ban the Bomb badges. So earnest. So dull.

Elizabeth said, 'Oliver's coming on the march.'

A bearded man glanced at him. 'Super. The more the merrier.'

Someone else said, 'Janetta's coming over from Brittany. Getting the overnight ferry, same as last year.'

'Do you remember the fellow who cycled from Cornwall? Collapsed from exhaustion on Falcon Field? First-aiders had to bring him round.'

'I came up in Jimmy Partridge's car. Damn battery packed up at Andover, so we didn't dare stop until we reached Aldermaston.'

'Supposed to be the biggest turn-out ever this Easter. The politicians'll have to take notice.'

Oliver stopped listening. He could not imagine feeling such enthusiasm about anything. Perhaps, for a while, for a girl. Or for a new car, even. But not for some vague, amorphous, futile ideal.

The girl with the guitar began to sing again. The room quietened. The man sitting beside Oliver tapped the table softly in rhythm with the music. A wave of boredom, as stupefying as anything he had experienced at the opera, swept over Oliver.

'Oliver?' Elizabeth touched his elbow. 'Oliver, are you all right? You look a bit fed up.'

He blinked. 'I could do with a drink, actually.'

'Coffee? Milk shake?'

'I meant,' he said, 'a real drink. Beer or something.'

'Oh.' She looked embarrassed. 'They haven't a licence, I'm afraid. You can bring your own wine if you have a meal, but—'

'It doesn't matter,' he said.

'We could go somewhere else, if you like.'

He looked at her. 'Your friends . . . haven't you things to do?'

'Everything's sorted out. I'll make the banners, and Brian and Geoff will work out train times and things. I was going to drive home now, actually, but I don't have to go straight away.'

'Won't Faith worry about you?' It was almost midnight.

'I mean home, not Auntie Faith's. She's gone away for the weekend, to visit Grandpa. I live in Wiltshire, you see. All the stuff to do the banners is at home.' She said suddenly, 'Would you like to help?'

'With what?'

'With the banners.'

He was confused. 'I thought you were going to Wiltshire.'

'I meant, you could drive back with me.' A short silence. Her head ducked, the fall of dark hair masking her eyes. 'No. Of course not. What a silly idea. You must have masses of important things to do.' Though he could not see her face, Oliver sensed that she was blushing.

He said, 'Do you mean, drive back with you to Wiltshire?'

'Sorry. You must think me an idiot. Your people will be expecting you.'

'I could telephone them.' He heard her squeak of surprise and pleasure, and he imagined escaping London, driving through the night beneath a canopy of stars, and was filled with longing.

'Won't your parents mind you bringing someone home?'

'They're both out of the country.' She began to rattle on about the whereabouts of her family; he did not

493

listen. He had always loved journeys. Especially unexpected ones. He would, no doubt, have to paint a few banners and pretend more devotion to the Movement, but for that glorious sense of freedom and escape, it would be worth it.

The party was in Clio Bettancourt's house, south of the river. There were ormolu mirrors on the walls, and a great many portraits of Clio, who was an actress. Faith glimpsed her own reflection multiplied in the glass: olive silk dress, fair hair heaped on top of her head, jet necklace and earrings that had once belonged to Poppy.

A hand touched her elbow, and a voice said in her ear, 'Darling Clio must be planning some vast and expensive project. All the great and the good are here tonight.'

She turned and smiled at Paddy Calder, Holly Blue's accountant. He was a large, thickset man, with shaggy fair hair and a reddish complexion. It was always easier, Faith thought, to imagine Paddy working on a building site or at the docks than behind a desk.

'Paddy. How lovely to see you.' She kissed his cheek.

'I've found you the perfect house, Faith.' Paddy was trying to persuade her to invest her savings. He added, 'Three storeys plus basement. Original doors and fireplaces still intact. And it's in an area that's about to become very fashionable.'

She said, 'That's sweet of you, Paddy, but I'm quite happy where I am.'

He knocked back his sherry. 'I told you, you can't keep your assets sitting in a bank, Faith. It's ridiculous.'

'Is it?' She teased him. 'Where should I keep my money, then? Sewn into my mattress? Beneath a loose floorboard?'

'Wretched woman,' he said equably, and helped himself to another glass of sherry. 'You're not poor, Faith – you've no need to live like a gypsy. And I meant, of course, that you must put your money into property, as I've been trying to persuade you to do for decades.'

She said meekly, 'I like my flat, Paddy. I'm used to it – I'm fond of it. I stumble downstairs to work in the mornings, and I—'

'You don't have to *live* in the house that you buy.'

'What would be the point of that?'

'To make money, my dear Faith,' said Paddy patiently. 'To make money.' He took a notebook and pencil out of his pocket, and scribbled a few lines. '*That* is the rate at which your savings will increase if you leave them in the bank, and *that* is the rate at which they'll increase if you put them into property.'

She had never understood graphs. Working for Holly Blue, she had laboured hard to fill in the vast gaps in her education, and could now add, subtract, multiply, and divide with ease. She could also interpret profit and loss sheets, and understand the difference between turnover and profit. And often her life seemed to be governed by cash flow. She had made herself learn these things, for Holly Blue. But graphs remained an arcane mystery.

'The thing is, Paddy, that I'll have to keep the flat going because it's convenient, and you know that I go to Norfolk most weekends because of Pa, and it would seem . . . well, rather . . . *prodigal* to shuttle between three houses.' She caught a glimpse of his expression, and added hastily, 'But I'll look at the house, if you want, Paddy. I promise.'

'After this wretched affair is over?'

She blinked. 'If you like.'

He grabbed a tray from a passing waitress, then looked down at it unenthusiastically. 'Oh dear. Vol-au-vents. The worst of both worlds, I've always thought. Pastry that splinters in your mouth like ash, filled with an unidentifiable slop.' He tipped three vol-au-vents into his mouth, and waved the tray in Faith's direction. She shook her head.

Through a mouthful of crumbs, he asked, 'And your prospective buyer . . . have you heard from him?'

She grimaced. Since the beginning of the year she had received a number of letters, all anonymous, all trying to persuade her to sell Holly Blue. The wording of the letters had been unpleasant, slightly threatening.

'I had another letter at the beginning of the week,' she admitted.

'Have you been to the police?'

She raised her shoulders. 'I did, but they told me that they can't do much at the moment. There's nothing to go on. No signature, just a London postmark. And he's not *hurting* me, is he?'

Paddy said, 'Not at present.'

'*Paddy*—'

'I'm not trying to alarm you Faith. But the site's worth a lot, I've explained that to you. It's in central London . . . and though on its own it's fairly useless, with the derelict land next door—'

She said firmly, 'I won't sell, Paddy. And I won't be driven out.'

'Of course not.' She could see the concern in his eyes. 'But there are some unscrupulous characters about these days. I don't like to think of you there on your own.'

'I'm used to being on my own, you know that,

496

Paddy. And when he doesn't get anywhere, he'll give up, I'm sure of it.' She looked at him. 'Subject closed. Please.'

Paddy sighed, and asked, 'How's Con?'

Faith smiled. 'Con's enjoying her retirement immensely. She's spending most of her time weaving. She makes the most beautiful fabrics, Paddy. She's getting very long-sighted, though, and will insist on working with fine yarns. It makes her terribly bad-tempered.'

'And your father?'

'Pa's very well. He and I are having a holiday soon. It's a sort of very late birthday treat.'

Paddy brushed crumbs from his dinner jacket. 'Where are you going?'

'France. It's years since Pa's been to France. I want to give him a really wonderful holiday, so I'm booking us into all the best hotels. Such planning, Paddy,' she added ruefully, thinking of the heap of brochures and timetables in her flat. 'It's taking me hours, but I want to make it all just right. I don't want him to have to worry about—'

A voice shrieked, 'Darling Faith! Such a wonderful dress! You must make me one just like it!'

'Clio.' She hugged her hostess.

'But lime green, not olive. Lime's my colour.'

Faith was sucked up into the crowd. She did not see Paddy Calder again until three hours later, when she emerged from the overheated house into the cold spring night. He helped her on with her coat and hailed a taxi. They travelled in silence for a while, and then, glancing at her, he said, 'You look frozen. Give me your hands.'

He hugged her chilly fingers between his huge, meaty paws: like the filling in a sandwich, she thought. After a while they stopped in an unfamiliar street. Paddy paid the driver, and took a key from his pocket.

'It's not even on the market yet. My brother tipped me the wink.'

Paddy's brother was an estate agent. Over the past year Paddy had taken her to see innumerable houses dotted around London.

He opened the door and flicked on a light. They walked from room to room. 'Fantastic cornicing . . . and look at the floors . . . solid beech . . . sash windows . . . south facing . . . five bedrooms.'

At the top of the house, they paused. The moon, framed in the attic window, smeared the bare boards with silver.

'It's a bit grubby, I know, but . . . what do you think, Faith?'

'It's a lovely house, Paddy.' She tried to inject some enthusiasm into her voice.

'A real investment.'

'But it's too big . . . five bedrooms . . . What would I want with five bedrooms?'

He shrugged, and went to the window. Just before he turned aside, she glimpsed the expression in his eyes. He ran his fingers along the sash cord.

'I thought you might want a family. Most women do.'

She said lightly, 'I've Ralph, and Elizabeth, and Nicole and David. And Con and you, Paddy. That's family enough, isn't it?'

'But . . . children. What about children?'

She looked at him. 'I'm thirty-eight, Paddy. I've left it rather late, don't you think?'

'My mother was forty-two when she had me. I'm trying to ask you, Faith . . .' He let out a quick, despairing breath, and shook his head. 'I'm not very good at this.'

She tucked her hand round his arm, and said, very gently, 'There's Ralph, and there's Holly Blue, and I don't seem to have time for much else, Paddy. I'm sorry.'

But later, back at the flat, she wondered whether she had spoken the truth. That house – and Paddy himself – had she rejected both because she could fit neither into a full, busy life, or because there remained within her a kernel of doubt, a lingering seed of suspicion that neither was quite what she wanted? She lay awake for a long time, drifting eventually into an uneasy sleep, where the elegant splendour of Paddy's house mingled with the cobwebbed simplicity of the Norfolk one in which she and Guy Neville had once, long ago, made love. In her dream, she tried to count the houses in which she had lived. From the years of her infancy, when Ralph and Poppy had roared around the world, babies and Lodgers in tow, to the flat over the shop in which she now lived. Numbers and images flickered through her mind. A church bell, ringing unnaturally loud and fast, tolled the passing years.

She woke. The telephone was ringing. Faith glanced at her watch, and saw that it was three o'clock in the morning. *Pa*, she thought, panicking, *something has happened to Pa*, and in a slither of blanket and night-gown she half fell out of bed and grabbed the receiver.

'Yes?'

'Miss Mulgrave?'

She did not recognize the voice. Male, slightly hoarse. Pa's doctor, or the police, or—

'Have you thought any more about selling the lease of the shop, Miss Mulgrave?'

Her fear changed to shock. He had given up writing

letters, then; he had taken to telephoning her instead. 'Who are you?' Her voice shook with fury. 'How dare you phone me at this time of night?'

'I've sent you a present, Miss Mulgrave. Go and look at the front door. And then think again.' The line went dead.

The phone slipped from her hand. She stared at the curtained window. *I've sent you a present.* She wondered whether he was out there, watching her, waiting for her to go downstairs. He would hide in the shadows of the shop, and then—

Yet she could not bear to remain here, waiting, not knowing. She pulled her coat on over her nightdress, and took the rolling pin from the kitchen drawer. Tiptoeing downstairs, she thought the black hollows in the stairwell rose up in menacing shapes. She opened the door to the shop. If she turned on the light, *he* would know that she was there. The amber glow from the street lamps filtered through the window blinds. Inky shadows flung themselves across walls and floors. Something lay on the mat beneath the letter box. She heard her own sob of fear. She squinted, trying to make it out. It was small and dark and elongated in shape. A bomb, she thought ridiculously: she would go to it, and in doing so set off some sort of fuse, and then the scratchy voice at the other end of the telephone line would not have to bother demolishing the shop after he had bought the lease . . .

Such nonsense, she told herself sternly. The shadow on the doormat seemed to grow larger as she approached it. Then, when she was near enough to make out what it was, her legs folded beneath her, and she knelt on the floor, her arms wrapped around her, rocking with laughter.

A rat. He had hoped to frighten her into selling Holly Blue by posting a dead rat through the letter box. If they had known, she thought, wheezing with disproportionate, relieved hilarity, of the rats in the barn at La Rouilly. Or of the rats in the Blitz: how the fires had forced them out of their hiding holes, sending them scurrying over her feet as she loaded stretchers into the ambulance. She wasn't afraid of rats. She glimpsed the rolling pin, still clutched in her hand, and her laughter doubled. Then she rubbed the tears from her face with her coat sleeve, and picked the creature up cautiously by its tail and dumped it in the dustbin in the yard.

The sky had cleared and, once they had left the city behind, Oliver could see, looking up, the constellations. The Plough, and the Great Bear, and Orion's Belt. Elizabeth drove her pea-green Morris Minor with a speed and expertise that took him by surprise. Towns and villages rushed past. The landscape rose and swelled. Trees, their outstretched branches outlined by moonlight, loomed out of the darkness. Oliver's gloom lifted with their retreat from the city, and was replaced by a mixture of excitement and relief.

Sometimes he dozed and, waking suddenly, did not know how much time had passed. He thought Elizabeth might be tired, and offered to take the wheel, but she shook her head and said, 'It's very kind of you, Oliver, but I love driving. Auntie Faith taught me. She was an ambulance driver in the war, did you know?'

He fell asleep again, and when he awoke he saw by the car's headlights that they were driving through a vast, empty plain.

'Where are we?'

'My second favourite place.' She touched the brake. 'Look.'

The circle of great stone columns rose out of the night, vast and ageless, painted by starlight.

'Stonehenge?'

'Isn't it wonderful?'

Oliver shivered, feeling horribly small and insignificant. As they left the stone circle behind, he glimpsed on the horizon a slight paling of the sky. 'Only a few more miles,' she said. Trees relieved the bareness of the landscape as they descended through the valley. Oliver yawned, and ran his fingers through his tousled hair. Elizabeth swung the car off the main road, up a driveway bordered by beech trees. Feeling rather crumpled, Oliver began to straighten out his clothing. Elizabeth said, 'This is it. This is Compton Deverall.'

When he looked up, his hands fell away, leaving his collar unstudded, his tie untied. He saw the house, with its windows and turrets and courtyards, and could not speak.

The size of it. The history of it. *We're home now, Oliver.* He thought, to live somewhere like this. To be a part of somewhere like this. Such freedom. Such power.

Elizabeth said, 'Are you starving? I am. I could cook you something. Or would you prefer a nap?'

'I'm not tired.' They were in the hall. The hall at Compton Deverall had, Oliver thought, little in common with the hall at home. The Holland Square hall was a longish, narrowish corridor, with a peach-coloured carpet that showed dirty shoeprints far too easily, and a half-moon table that held the day's letters, two photographs (himself and Grandfather), and a vase of flowers. The hall at Compton Deverall was *breathtaking*.

Faded heraldic emblems were painted on the ceiling. Huge, dark pieces of furniture cast inky shadows. No cocktail cabinets or television consoles, nothing *vulgar*. Only carved chests and buffets and sideboards and chiffoniers, and a vast, ornate fireplace that towered to the ceiling.

He realized that he was gawping, and assumed a more offhand expression, and said casually, 'Breakfast would be lovely, actually.'

He followed Elizabeth into the kitchen. As she cracked eggs and cut the rind from bacon, he looked at her, and saw her differently. There was still a hole in the elbow of her awful sweater, and her nails were still bitten to the quick, yet she no longer seemed just an ungainly schoolgirl: money and property had given her mystery.

He asked, 'Are you an only child?'

She nodded. 'And you?' She placed a coffee pot in front of him. 'It would have been nice to have had brothers and sisters, don't you think?'

Oliver poured two cups of coffee. 'It might have made things easier, I suppose. One wouldn't have to be so damn perfect.'

'I haven't even cousins.'

'Nor me. Not an aunt or an uncle. I used to feel rather cheated at Christmas.'

'I've Auntie Faith, of course.' She flipped over the bacon rashers. 'And I used to have an uncle, but he drowned.'

Oliver muttered vague condolences, and then, unable to stop himself, said, 'So one day you'll inherit all this?'

She was buttering toast. 'Yes. Ghastly, isn't it? I

should like to give it to someone who really needs it, but there's all sorts of trusts and things, so that would be difficult. And besides, I do love it. Some of my friends are shocked at the lavs and how cold it is, but I love it.'

She placed a plate of bacon and eggs in front of him. 'I'll show you round the house, if you like,' she said. 'I'll show you my favourite bits.' When she spoke, she looked at him in such a way that a shiver – of possibility, of escape – ran the length of his spine.

Oliver ate, his heart pounding. When they had finished breakfast, she took him on a tour of the house. Sunlight streamed through mullioned windows, and made diamond shapes on old oak floorboards. Mould flowered on the plaster walls of some of the most distant rooms, and when he ran a hand down the timber laths, the wood felt damp to touch. Grotesques – demons and green men – were carved in the beams, leering at him as he ducked beneath low doorways. When he stuck out his tongue and rolled his eyes in imitation, Elizabeth leaned against the wall, helpless with laughter.

In a gallery that spanned the length of the house, she showed him the portraits of her ancestors. Generations of dark-eyed, solemn-faced Kemps focused coldly on him. He felt out of place, rootless, shallow. Elizabeth had scraped back her messy fringe in an Alice band, displaying her high forehead, her long, straight nose, her hooded eyes with their sketchy arched brows. Oliver saw that he had been wrong in believing her plain, and that her features simply belonged to another age, to the era of those pale Tudor chatelaines with their box headdresses and stiff, low-fronted gowns. He found himself wanting to stroke that clear, unblemished skin, to feel the weight of her silky dark hair, and he felt faintly embarrassed, and walked on, out of the gallery, down the stairs. He preferred sophisticated women to naive schoolgirls; a night without proper sleep was making him irrational. Yet he felt very awake, very alert.

She said, as they reached the foot of the stairs, 'It's such a lovely day, we could do the banners on the courtyard. There'd be enough room to lay them out flat, and it wouldn't matter if we got paint on things.' She looked at him. 'Would you like to borrow one of my father's jerseys?'

Oliver was still wearing his dinner jacket. 'Please. If you don't think he'd mind.'

As she dashed back upstairs, Oliver waited, leaning against the newel-post. Fleetingly, he tried to imagine belonging to a place like this. He pictured himself flinging his umbrella into the stand, chucking his coat casually onto a peg. He closed his eyes, then opened them again, hearing the thump of Elizabeth's shoes on the stairs.

She gave him a sweater. 'It's a bit holey, I'm afraid. Daddy never buys himself new clothes, so he only gets them when Mummy visits, and she hasn't been for ages.'

Oliver pulled the ancient cashmere over his head. 'Your mother doesn't live here?'

'Oh no. She sometimes lives in America, and sometimes in Europe. They're divorced, you see.'

'Sorry. It must be—'

'I don't mind.' Her eyes, a clear dark brown, focused on him. 'Really I don't. People at school used to think I should mind, but I don't. She left when I was a very

505

small baby, you see, so it's not as though I can remember anything different. I can't remember *losing* her.'

They hauled armfuls of old sheets and half-full paintpots and brushes out onto the courtyard. Lichens blossomed on the surface of the paving stones, mosses grew in the crevices between them. Elizabeth spread the sheets out on the terrace. 'I'd better sew them together. I'd like the banners to be the width of the road, so they're really eye-catching.'

Oliver fetched her sewing machine, and found staves in an outhouse to support the ends of the banner. Elizabeth's practical nature surprised him: he had expected vagueness, incompetence, to go with the woolly ideals. He knew that her efforts were a pointless waste of time, but it was surprisingly pleasant to run errands for her, to paint slogans and symbols on lengths of sheeting, to be released from the burden of thought. The sun shone, and around midday Oliver put down his paintbrush and wandered back into the house. From the kitchen he took a slab of cheese, a loaf of bread, a bag of apples and a bottle of wine. Looking around, he saw that wadding extruded from holes in the sofas, and that sunlight had faded the brocade curtains so that their original colour could no longer be distinguished. He was at first shocked: in Holland Square the furniture was replaced as soon as it began to wear, and his mother insisted every five years on new curtains and carpets throughout. Oliver himself had always preferred the new, the clean, the streamlined to Holland Square's over-upholstered fussiness. Yet now, roaming through Compton Deverall, it occurred to him that his own tastes were second-rate.

He assembled his finds in a wicker basket, took a

couple of wineglasses from a dining-room cupboard, and returned to the courtyard.

'*Oliver*. How *clever*. I love picnics.' Elizabeth put down her paintbrush.

They carried the basket to the meadow beyond the lawn, and cooled the wine in the stream. The Compton Deverall estate, Elizabeth explained, was bordered by the stream. Her father sometimes considered selling off a few acres to raise enough cash to make repairs to the house, but never seemed to get round to it. Oliver thought of London, where office blocks were being squeezed onto the smallest plots of land, and where rows of old terraced houses were knocked down daily to make way for high-rise flats. The *money* you could make out of this place. When Elizabeth pointed to a field beside the woodland – not even sheep grazing there, not put to any use whatsoever as far as he could see – Oliver found himself picturing the rows of houses that might fill in the empty spaces.

His back against a tree, he was almost dozing off when Elizabeth said suddenly: 'Oh, look – how marvellous – there's Geoff and Phil and the others.'

Opening his eyes, Oliver saw the small black figures on the courtyard balcony.

'They said they might come and help.' Elizabeth threw her apple core into the stream and shouted and waved. After she had gathered up the picnic things, she galumphed across the lawn towards her friends.

Oliver himself dawdled back to the house, hands in pockets. The unusual clarity of the day persisted, but it had begun to antagonize him, to grate upon his nerves, so that the heartiness of the visitors' voices, their scruffy appearance and overloud laughter, irritated him. He watched, standing back, as Elizabeth proudly showed the new arrivals the banners, the placards.

'I say, you've done awfully well.'

'Super colours.'

'They're expecting a hundred thousand people in Trafalgar Square, after the march, so all these'll make a jolly good show.'

'There's still a few more sheets,' said Elizabeth. 'Could you give me a hand, Oliver?'

He followed her into the house. In her bedroom, the floor and furniture were almost hidden beneath lengths of cloth and sheaves of literature about the Bomb. She pointed to a heap of sheets on top of a chest of drawers.

'Could you carry those down?'

As he gathered up the sheets, something fell out onto the floor. He picked it up.

'What's this?' He looked at it. It was a tiny oil painting, six inches square. The broad bands of colour – red and gold and amber – seemed meaningless when he looked at them close to, but, holding the painting at arm's length, they formed into fields, trees, rivers.

'Oh.' She was unravelling a length of string. 'The hook came off the wall. It must have got caught up in the sheets.'

'It's a Corot.' Oliver saw the hole in the plaster, marking the place where the picture had hung. 'You can't just leave a *Corot* lying about among all this rubbish, you know.' He felt suddenly very tired, and his tone was more short-tempered than he had intended.

'It's only a painting.' Elizabeth sounded hurt. 'It doesn't matter.' She put the picture back on top of the chest of drawers.

'Of course it matters. Paintings *last*.'

She left the room. As they went downstairs, she said,

'None of this would survive a nuclear explosion. You know that, Oliver. All of this – Compton Deverall, my painting, you, me – everything would be gone. That's why what we are doing is so important. It's much more important than the painting.'

They had reached the courtyard. He said loudly, 'But none of this will make any difference, you know,' and Elizabeth's friends looked at him, he thought, as though he were something unpleasant and translucent that had crawled out from under a paving stone.

'Of course it'll make a difference.'

'It won't.' He looked at them all contemptuously. 'It can't. Oh, there'll be pictures on the telly, that sort of thing, but it won't change anything.'

'Oliver.' The man with the beard spoke with a patience that set Oliver's teeth on edge. 'We can all make a difference, you know. I know it doesn't seem like that sometimes, but you mustn't lose hope.'

Phil said, 'We're pressing the Labour Party conference to adopt a unilateralist resolution.'

Oliver, leaning against the wall, said, 'The Labour Party's unlikely to win the next election, so what does it matter what bloody resolutions they adopt?'

'I suppose you're a Tory.'

He shrugged. His eyelids were heavy with exhaustion. 'Possibly. By default. For want of anything better.'

'But it's nothing to do with politics.' Elizabeth was staring at him. 'Nuclear weapons are wrong. They're evil. That's all that matters. Think of Hiroshima – of Nagasaki—'

He said savagely, 'Think of the Japanese prisoner-of-war camps. Think of Hitler's concentration camps. They were wrong, weren't they? Perhaps the nuclear threat will stop that sort of thing happening again. And anyway, that's not the point. The point I was making is that whatever you do won't make any difference. Oh, you *might* sway the trade unions, and they *might* sway the Labour Party, and you never know, the Labour Party might even get into power. But it still won't make any difference because Britain's irrelevant now. We just' – and he smiled – 'don't count.'

'Britain has influence in America.'

'Rubbish. Absolute rubbish.'

'The American people might take their example from the British—'

'Even one less Bomb—'

'We can't do *nothing*!'

He swung round to her. He could no longer be detached, nonchalant, he felt only the familiar tedium, overlaid just now with fury. 'You *are* doing nothing. All this' – and he waved a hand in the direction of the banners – 'is just to make you feel better. It is – *nothing*.'

Elizabeth's face seemed to crumple, her eyes very dark against her white skin. Yet she did not weep, but said with quiet dignity, 'At least we try,' and she knelt on the paving stones again, and took up her paintpot and brush.

Oliver walked back through the house, out of the front door. It was late afternoon, and the blue of the sky had paled to white. He walked fast, wanting this house, and the girl, whom he had found himself beginning to like, to be far behind him. When, eventually, he heard the sound of a car's engine, he did not look back, but continued to stride on, only turning aside as she caught up with him, halfway down the avenue of beeches.

She was driving her pea-green Morris Minor. She

slowed, inching parallel with him, and said: 'Your jacket, Oliver.'

He realized that he was still wearing her father's jersey. He peeled it off, handed it back to her through the car window, and slouched on his jacket.

'Where are you going?'

'To the railway station. My parents will be wondering where the hell I've got to.'

'I'll give you a lift.'

'I'd like the walk.'

'It's six miles, Oliver!'

'Still. I'd like the walk.' He kept on, crunching the gravel underfoot.

He heard her call out, 'You're not coming on the march, then?' and, turning, pausing just for a moment, he shook his head.

'No. I don't think so. Thanks for the breakfast and all that, but I don't think so.' He walked on down the drive.

Guy said, 'You can get dressed now, Sir Anthony,' and replaced his stethoscope round his neck.

'What's the verdict, then, Neville?' Guy detected anxiety behind his patient's customary cheerfulness.

'Your blood pressure's up a bit.'

'Is that bad?' Sir Anthony Chant's voice was muffled behind the screen.

'It puts stress on the heart.' Guy washed his hands and blew his nose. He had the beginnings of a head cold: pressure drummed behind his brows.

'More pills and potions then?'

'You might consider losing some weight.'

Sir Anthony Chant emerged from behind the screens.

'Lose weight?' He patted his broad stomach. 'What on earth for? How?'

'You eat less,' said Guy drily, and then recollected himself. 'Just a suggestion, Sir Anthony. It would be better for your heart.'

'Can't see how.'

Guy began to explain the link between heart trouble and overeating, but his patient interrupted him.

'Just give me some of those thingummies you gave me the last time. They'll do the trick.'

Guy opened his mouth to speak again, but then, focusing on Sir Anthony's bland, complacent face, closed it. Writing out the prescription, he found that he had to swallow down his anger.

After his patient had gone, he rose and went to the window. His consulting-room, with its wall to wall carpeting, its tasteful prints and reproduction furniture, oppressed him. Yet the view from the window offered him no relief, for not a patch of green could be seen among the tightly packed buildings. London was composed of drab greys and browns. Guy tried to shut out his aching head and sore throat by remembering his youthful wanderings around pre-war Europe. He found himself longing for a splash of scarlet hibiscus, or a flutter of bright butterfly wing. After a while, he turned aside and heaved a stack of paperwork into his brief-case. Then he locked the surgery and walked the short distance to Holland Square.

He glanced through the heap of letters on the hall table, gathering together the bills and bank statements before he climbed the stairs. Eleanor called to him from the drawing-room, reminding him that they were to go out that night. He had forgotten: in his dressing-room

Guy changed into his dinner suit and fortified himself with aspirins.

The cocktail party – one of those awful affairs where you juggle glass and plate while carrying out polite conversation – was at the house of a colleague, Wilfred Clarke, who lived in Richmond. The guests were a mixture of doctors and aimless, horsy girls, invited, Guy guessed, largely as decoration. Guy ate little, which solved the problem of carrying the plate, but was unable, on moving from one guest to the next, to recall what each previous conversation had been about.

'Dr Neville?'

Guy had taken sanctuary in a corner beside a large pot plant. He looked round. A red-haired young man, wearing an ill-fitting suit, stood in front of him.

'My name's James Ritchie. I'm a junior doctor at Bart's.'

They shook hands. 'Dr Clarke told me that you trained at Edinburgh, like myself,' said Ritchie. Guy detected a Scots accent. 'I wondered what your speciality was.'

'I'm in general practice.' Guy held out his cigarette case. Ritchie shook his head.

'I'm thinking of going in for paediatrics. I plan to work in Africa, you see. In the Belgian Congo. I've a cousin who's a doctor there.'

Guy stifled a cough. 'Sounds interesting.' He offered Ritchie a drink from the bottle he had liberated and hidden beneath a hart's tongue fern.

'I don't, thank you.'

'Not at all?'

'I was brought up a teetotaller.' A slightly apologetic gesture. 'Don't let me stop you, Dr Neville.'

Guy shook his head. 'I've a splitting headache already. I seem to have caught a chill. I've no wish to give myself a hangover on top of it.' He smiled. 'Distract me, Dr Ritchie. Take my mind off this tedious minor ailment. Tell me about Africa. What do you hope to achieve there? Africa always sounds distinctly hot and uncomfortable.'

'But the *need*, Dr Neville! The need is so great.' Ritchie's eyes shone. 'So many children are dying of easily curable diseases – measles, stomach upsets, and so on—'

Listening to James Ritchie, the longing that Guy had experienced earlier that day, looking out of his consulting-room window and thinking of France, returned. The longing was unfocused, and it was mingled with frustration and restlessness. He listened as Dr Ritchie talked of bush hospitals, of river blindness and malaria, and he was for a moment transported out of the overfurnished, overheated drawing-room. After a while Ritchie added, 'Of course, there's need in Britain too. Though the National Health Service has made such a difference, don't you think?'

'I work in private practice.'

He saw the expression on the younger man's face alter, and he thought savagely, *Don't judge me, damn you, don't judge me.*

Ritchie made his excuses soon afterwards, and disappeared into the crowd. Guy, feeling increasingly unwell, left soon afterwards, alone. Eleanor chose to remain at the party. A friend had offered her a lift home, she explained.

It was raining, and in the darkness the wet roads gleamed like liquorice. As Guy drove through the London streets, the conversation with James Ritchie lingered in his memory, irritating like a fragment of sand in an oyster shell.

But the need, *Dr Neville . . . the need is so great . . .*

Preoccupied by thoughts of Africa, Guy caught only a glimpse of the cyclist who, lacking any lights, emerged without warning out of a side street. The van in front of Guy's car was going too fast to stop. A squeal of brakes, a jangle of metal and glass as the van, in a futile attempt to avoid the bicycle, swerved across the road. Guy himself yanked violently at his steering wheel and stabbed at his brakes. The wheels of the Rover mounted the kerb, and Guy's forehead slammed against the steering column.

After a few moments, when he could think again, he flung open the driver's door and ran forward. The cyclist, a young woman, lay motionless on the pavement. Beneath the amber glow of the street lamp Guy could see the van driver, slumped against the windscreen of his vehicle.

A small group of people had begun to gather. Guy threw his car keys to the lad who stood beside him, and said, 'There's a black bag in the boot of my Rover. Fetch it for me, won't you?' Then, as he knelt on the pavement beside the cyclist, he sent a woman in a floral quilted dressing gown back into her house to phone for an ambulance.

Though he seemed to have attended nothing more urgent than a grumbling appendix in ages, Guy found that as he knelt in the darkness, rain drumming onto his head and shoulders, all that his twenty years as a doctor had taught him came back to him. Check that the patient's breathing is unimpeded . . . staunch any arterial bleeding . . . try not to move the head and neck in case of spinal fractures. He forgot the rain, his head cold, the vague unfocused longing that increasingly these days troubled him, and he worked with calm, efficient speed, assessing his patient's condition. There was a deep gash to her upper arm, and he suspected that a broken rib or two had pierced one of her lungs. As Guy applied a tourniquet and adjusted the girl's position to ease her breathing, he sent one of the onlookers to check on the condition of the van driver. Shouting questions across the street, he realized that he was reminded of the excitement and danger of the Blitz: he had been perpetually exhausted, yes, but by God he had felt that he was contributing something. He had felt *alive*.

Then, in a flurry of bright lights and sirens, the ambulance arrived, and both the girl and the van driver were loaded onto stretchers. One of the attendants asked Guy if he needed treatment for the cut on his forehead, and he put his hand up to his brow and felt blood oozing from the gash the impact of the steering column had made. He had not, until now, noticed that he had been hurt. 'I'll sort it out myself,' he said, and went back to his car.

When the ambulance had gone, and the street was empty again, Guy sat for a while unmoving in the driver's seat of the Rover. In the aftermath of the incident, he felt drained and exhausted, shaky with reaction and adrenalin, his headache returned with magnified force. Yet the recollection of how he had felt, kneeling beside his patient in the rain, remained with him. He had forgotten that it was possible for the mind to be completely engaged; he had forgotten the heady pleasure of using all his skills, of losing himself in the practice of his art. That exhilaration lingered, and it was some time before Guy turned the key in the ignition and drove back to Holland Square.

The creeping chaos that Oliver had noticed at home on the first day of his Easter vacation persisted. The house was not exactly squalid, but it had become a little frayed around the edges. Balls of dust gathered on the stair-rods, and sometimes they ran out of things – important things like loo rolls and toothpaste and tea. A shirt put in the laundry basket might not reappear for a week. Oliver found it all vaguely disturbing. Home might be suffocating, but it was usually reliable.

The days melded into each other, formless, in no particular pattern. Oliver got up late, forgot to eat, slept badly. No-one seemed to notice. His father worked long hours; his mother seemed to be absorbed in her charity work. After a while, catching sight in the mirror of his unshaven chin, and the greyish shadows under his eyes, he made an effort to pull himself together. He tried to catch up with some of his college work, but fell asleep over it, and woke bug-eyed and dull-brained, face down in a diagram of the spleen. He offered to help his mother with her charity work, but she, rather to his surprise, refused him, so he was reduced to ambling off to the surgery with his father every now and then, to help with the routine paperwork. His father was delighted; Oliver despaired, but even working in the surgery was better than the stupefying disconnectedness that was becoming more and more his customary state of mind.

On Easter Monday, they waded through a vast lunch: soup, roast chicken, treacle tart, cheese and biscuits. Afterwards, Guy left for his club and Eleanor explained that she was going to a meeting. Oliver, feeling overstuffed, went for an aimless slope around the streets and then wandered back to the house. As he opened the back door he heard his mother's voice.

'. . . seems such a long time. How long must we go on pretending?'

He almost called out to her, but something stopped him. Instead, he paused halfway up the basement steps, listening.

'. . . too bad of you, darling. You know that's quite impossible.'

Her tone of voice did not match her words. She was coaxing, flirtatious. Sometimes, Oliver thought, she spoke to him like that: on their evenings out together, when his father was not there.

'Darling, how wicked. You mustn't say things like that!' A silvery laugh.

Oliver sat down. His heart was beating much too fast. He pressed the flat of his hand against his ribcage, and tried to remember whether one could die of a coronary at nineteen. There was a dull *ding* as Eleanor put the phone down, and then he half ran, half tumbled back down the stairs, through the kitchen, into the street.

He walked briskly, past the British Museum, across Oxford Street, down Shaftesbury Avenue, along Charing Cross Road. All the time he thought, *Darling*, she called him *darling*. He had no doubt whatsoever that his mother had been talking to a *him*.

She has a lover, he thought, as, turning down St Martin's Lane, he became caught up in the crowds heading for Trafalgar Square. *My mother has a lover*. The thought, tried out once or twice, rolled around in his head, did not become any more palatable. He knew that she had not been talking to his father. He had never, ever, heard his mother call his father 'darling'.

He could not at first work out why there were so many people in Trafalgar Square – a great sea of people, surging around the lions and up the steps of the National Gallery – but then he remembered the Aldermaston march. Oliver saw the banners and the placards, with their familiar circular symbol, and he remembered kneeling on the stone pavement behind Compton Deverall, painting that same symbol.

He let himself become caught up in the crowds. Within this great body of people, he no longer needed to think, to form opinions, to pretend. He was steered this way and that by the force of the crowd. The roars of applause that followed the speeches filled his head, temporarily expelling all other thoughts. He began to search for Elizabeth. He knew that to look for her in these crowds was ridiculous and futile, but it gave him something to do. It filled his mind, and blocked out the other, terrible thoughts. He looked for her methodically, mentally dividing the square into chunks. One section at a time. Every dark-haired, duffel-coated girl. There were rather a lot of dark-haired, duffel-coated girls, so, remembering Elizabeth at Compton Deverall, Oliver concentrated on the ones carrying banners. She would, he knew, be carrying a banner. She would have carried the bloody thing all the way from Aldermaston to London – forty-five exhausting miles – out of sheer tenacity and strength of purpose. Qualities, he thought, briefly amused, that he himself sorely lacked.

After half an hour or so, having surveyed the entire square twice, he knew that it was hopeless. He would have a drink instead, he thought. Adopt his father's solution to facing the unfaceable. It was too early for the pubs to open, but he might find an off-licence.

Pushing back through the crowds, not particularly caring whom he knocked into, he made his way to the perimeter of the square. Then he saw her.

She was sitting on the pavement, alone. She had no banner; a rucksack was slung beside her. She was fiddling with one of her shoes. Approaching her, he said her name.

She looked up at him. 'Oliver.' She did not smile. 'I thought you said you weren't going to come.'

Fleetingly, he considered lying, but discovered that he could not be bothered.

'I'd forgotten about the march, actually. I just ended up here by chance. I was trying to find you.' He studied her. 'You look a bit—'

'I look awful.' Her voice was sharp; she ran her fingers through her hair. 'I know I look awful.'

'I meant, you look tired.'

'I slept in a church hall the last couple of nights. And I had stomach-ache, and haven't eaten anything for ages.' She sounded, he thought, as miserable as he felt.

He said suddenly, 'I owe you a meal or two . . . Come on – let's find somewhere.'

When she hesitated, he said, 'Look, those things I said the other day—'

Her eyes were downcast, her fringe falling over them. 'It doesn't matter.'

'Yes, it does. We had a terrific day and I spoiled it. You must let me make it up to you.' He needed company, he thought. He needed someone – anyone – to take his mind off the conversation that he had overheard. He held out his hand. 'Come on.'

Her clear brown eyes focused warily on him, but she let him help her to her feet. 'I suppose . . . a cup of tea would be nice.'

They began to walk down St Martin's Lane. After only a step or two she began to lag behind him. He glanced at her.

'Are you hurt?'

Her face was white, and her teeth dug into her lip. She tried to smile. 'Blisters, Oliver. I have blisters growing on blisters. There was a nail in my shoe.'

'Here. Hold on to me.' He held out his arm, and steered her out of the square. He was glad of her weight at his side. It made him feel more solid, more real. As she hobbled, he put his arm round her, supporting her. He thought quickly, and remembered the key to his father's surgery, still in his pocket. Then he hailed a taxi.

Because it was a bank holiday, the surgery was empty. The smell of the place – disinfectant and floor polish – made him feel slightly sick, as usual. The windows were shut, the air close. Oliver adjusted the angle of the venetian blinds, and dust motes danced in the sunlight.

'Tea first, or feet?'

Elizabeth sat down heavily in a chair. 'You choose.'

He unlocked his father's desk and took the brandy bottle from the bottom drawer. 'Better than tea.' He poured large measures into two cups, and handed one to her. Then he knelt down in front of her, and unlaced her shoes. Brown, sensible schoolgirl shoes.

He heard her indrawn breath as he began to peel off her socks. He looked up. 'Sorry.'

'Not – your – fault.' Her face was white. 'I told you they were a mess.'

Her feet were bloody and raw. He did not, as he usually did when faced with human frailty, feel disgust, only an objective sort of pity. He said, 'Drink your brandy, Lizzie. I'll try not to hurt you.'

'You're not hurting me.' Each word was a gasp. 'You're very good. I suppose you learned first aid at medical school.'

He laughed, tearing off pieces of cotton wool. 'Not a bit of it. They don't teach us anything *useful* at medical school.'

There was a silence. Fragments of her sock had adhered to the worst blisters. He heard her say: 'You hate it, don't you?'

Surprised, he looked up at her. 'Hate what?'

'Training to be a doctor.'

'Yes.' It was the first time he had admitted it to anyone. 'Yes, I hate it.' He took the bowl to the sink, emptied it out, and filled it with clean water.

'Then why are you doing it?'

He knelt down in front of her again, and said, 'All the men in my family are doctors. My father . . . both grandfathers . . .'

'That doesn't mean *you* have to be a doctor. Have you told your parents how you feel?'

'Of course not.' He wished she would drop the subject.

'Why not?'

'Because they would—' His mother's voice echoed in his head. *Darling, how wicked.* He was aware of a searing, untypical pity for his father. 'Because they would be disappointed in me,' he said flatly, and stood up.

'I'm sure they'd understand. I'm sure they just want you to be happy.'

Her persistence, her naivety, angered him. He paused, closing his eyes, digging his nails into his palms.

'Oliver?' She sounded hesitant, frightened.

'You think they want me to be happy?' His voice shook. 'Actually, I believe that I stay at medical school because *I'd* like *them* to be happy.'

He turned away so that she would not see his face. He threw the soiled linen into the bin. He said, 'You see, having only one parent you can have absolutely no idea what it's like to have to live with two people who hate each other. Now, the obvious answer is to keep out of it, let them throttle each other if they wish, but the thing is that one becomes accustomed to a certain standard of living, a certain way of life, and, most of the time, it seems worth trying to keep the peace. Again, with Mummy and Daddy living in separate *continents* you can have no idea how much of a headache it sometimes gives one just to have to listen to the racket they make. In fact, you're a very lucky girl, aren't you, Elizabeth? Parents hardly ever there, fabulous house to come home to when you can't face roughing it any more, pots of money so that you don't have to—'

He stopped, silenced by the peculiar snuffling noise that she was making. He turned, and saw that she was crying.

'Oh, for God's sake,' he said wearily. She was trying to pull on her socks. 'Don't – I haven't put the sodding bandages on yet.' He crossed the room, seized her hand. Her face was blotched red; her nose dripped.

'Sorry,' he muttered. 'Look, Lizzie – Christ – I didn't mean it – it's been a lousy day.'

The snuffles changed to gulps. She sobbed, he thought, like a small child – uninhibited, thoughtless of her appearance. Because he could not bear the desolation of the sound that she made, or the sight of her struggling with bloodied toes and a holed sock, he pulled her to him, patting her back, stroking her hair, murmuring to her.

'I'm sorry. I'm a pig. I didn't mean it. You're a sweet girl, Lizzie, you really are, and I didn't mean to upset you.' He pressed his lips against the crown of her head. 'There. Don't cry. You mustn't take any notice of me – I'm in a foul mood – it's nothing to do with you.'

The sobs lessened slightly. After a while she looked up at him, and said, between hiccups, 'You think I'm stupid – you think that everything I do is stupid—'

'No, I don't,' he said soothingly. 'Honestly I don't.' A silvery snail-trail ran from her nostrils; he took his handkerchief from his pocket and held it to her nose. 'Blow.'

She blew, and then cried out, 'And you think that I'm just a silly little girl!'

He pulled her to him, patting her back again. Her breasts pressed against his chest. Not a little girl, he thought, suddenly aware of desire, coiling in the roots of his body. He had a sudden, disturbing vision of his mother, naked and in bed with some faceless, middle-aged adulterer, and the movement of his hand on Elizabeth's back altered almost imperceptibly, and became not the endearment of a friend, but the caress of the lover. He wanted her. He retained sufficient detachment to know that he might have wanted any woman, that sex had always worked better than alcohol for him, and that only in that sharp, intense pleasure could he hope to erase all the thoughts that he did not want to face.

'Elizabeth,' he whispered, and she looked up at him.

She said, 'I love you, Oliver. That's the thing – I love you,' and just for a moment, looking down at her dark trusting eyes, he knew that he should gently pull away, leave this room, not do what he knew he was about to do.

He began to kiss her. The thought crossed his mind that it did not matter what happened, that it did not matter what he and Elizabeth Kemp did together, because with Elizabeth Kemp went that house, that land, that future.

CHAPTER FIFTEEN

The holiday started going wrong from the very first day. Thinking to spare Ralph the exhaustion of train and ferry journeys, Faith had booked tickets on an aeroplane to Paris. Ralph grumbled incessantly. 'Hideous things. Like travelling in a sardine can. Blasted journey's over so quickly you don't feel you've been anywhere.'

In Paris, she had booked them – a special and extremely expensive treat – into the Crillon Hotel. Ralph loathed it. After two days, during which Ralph complained endlessly about both the staff ('fawning flunkies') and the food ('messed about with, Faith. I can't stand food that's been messed about with'), she was glad to leave. She helped Ralph search their room for a missing glove.

'I'll buy you a new pair of gloves, Pa.' She glanced yet again at her watch. 'We'll miss our train.'

'Perfectly good pair of gloves. Can't just throw away a perfectly good pair of gloves. Don't fuss, Faith. If we miss this train, there'll be others, won't there?'

She wailed, 'But I've booked seats! First class seats!'

'First class! What on earth did you do that for? Far more interesting conversation in second class, I've always told you that.' He glared at her. 'Where are we heading, anyway?'

'I told you, Pa, we're going to Bordeaux. And on Tuesday we'll travel to Nice and have three days there, and then on Wednesday we'll go to Marseilles. And then we are going to stay with Nicole for four nights, and then—'

'I don't want to go to Bordeaux. Had a thoroughly miserable time in Bordeaux – Poppy and I ran a bar there, do you remember, Faith? – back in the Twenties. I want to go to Brittany.' Ralph scrabbled down the back of an armchair, and emerged, triumphant, glove in hand. 'I've never seen the standing stones at Carnac. I've always wanted to see them.'

'Pa,' said Faith faintly. Her stomach was beginning to tie itself into a knot, as it often did in the course of conversations with her father. 'Pa, we can't go to Brittany. I've planned our journey, our hotels, everything—'

He roared, 'You can't plan everything! What pleasure is there in life if you plan everything?'

'Pa—'

'The best bits of life are always the surprising bits! Don't you know *that*, Faith?'

They went to Brittany. They travelled crushed in a crowded second-class carriage with a *curé* and a nun and farm labourers and schoolchildren. Ralph argued about religion with the *curé* and the nun, and explained to the farm labourers the irrigation system that he was using in his vegetable plot. Halfway through the journey he took a photograph out of his pocket, and showed it to everyone in the carriage. 'This is my son, Jake. Boy's travelling just now – wondered whether you'd come across him.' Spectacles were balanced on noses, the photograph studied, heads shaken. Faith bit her lip and stared out of the window.

At Huelgoat they walked beside the lake and ate *tarte aux prunes* in a pâtisserie in the town. At Roscoff they meandered along the sea front, watching the fishing-boats bob in a grey, stormy sea. In Carnac Ralph threaded between the long lines of dolmens, pausing to touch a stone every now and then with the flat of his hand, wonder in his eyes.

They stayed in small *pensions*, travelling by bus and train. Once, when the weather was fine, Ralph insisted on hiring bicycles. Her heart in her mouth, Faith pedalled furiously, struggling to keep up with her father as he hurled himself fearlessly into the traffic. She glanced at her watch less and less; she did not know what day of the week it was. In Quimper, she bought antique lace, and pottery patterned glorious reds and blues and greens, and in a junk shop she discovered lengths of old brocade, pairs of yellowing silk stockings, and old café posters, rolled up and tattered at the edges, of pre-war singers and dancers.

Someone told her about the medieval covered market in Vannes, so they ambled down the coast and wandered around the narrow old streets of the city. The stalls were like a treasure cave. Faith forgot Ralph, forgot Holly Blue, forgot even her mysterious, threatening caller. She searched through holed sweaters and ancient, fraying stays, and unearthed a plum-coloured evening dress with spaghetti straps, and a Victorian lace petticoat. As she delved deeper into the heap of old clothing, her heart began to hammer. She drew out her prize, and searched frantically for a label. Then she paid the stallkeeper and dashed out into the sunshine. She glimpsed Ralph sitting at a table on a café forecourt.

'Such a find, Pa!' Cars screeched to a halt as she

darted across the road. 'A Paul Poiret – influenced by Léon Bakst – for the ballet—' She could hardly speak for excitement.

Ralph screwed up his eyes. 'I saw *Schéhérazade* in Paris in 1910 . . . or was it '11 . . . ?'

She sat down and carefully and reverently unfolded the dress. 'Such wonderful colours, you see, Pa. Oh, I know that it doesn't look anything now, but that's because it's beneath layers and layers of dirt. After I've cleaned it – '

Ralph said smugly, 'Didn't I tell you, Faith, that we should enjoy ourselves in Brittany? And the *patron* has just told me that he may have seen Jake – it was some years ago, and his hair may have been different – longer, or whatever – and he looked older – and he may not have been quite so tall – but this isn't a good photograph, of course. It's very out of date. I can just imagine Jake heading through here, can't you? Wonderful news,' said Ralph, smiling as he heaped three spoonfuls of sugar into a very tiny cup of coffee. 'Wonderful news.'

He would stick it out until the end of the summer term, thought Oliver, and then he'd tell his parents that he was leaving medical school. He had not yet decided whether to fail his exams so spectacularly that there could be no question of Edinburgh's taking him back, however dreadful they made him feel, or whether to do his best and tell them that he was leaving anyway and spare himself the humiliation of having them think he just wasn't good enough.

Before he had gone back to Edinburgh, Elizabeth had suggested that he should just tell them the truth. Easier said than done, Oliver had thought later, sitting in the train, watching London slide away. He had never, ever told the truth to his parents; he had always told them what he thought they wanted to hear. Whatever he might resolve in private would dissolve, he feared, faced with his mother's hurt, his father's bewilderment. The usual bias of his emotions – his sympathies had always tended to lie with his mother rather than his father – had shifted since he had begun to wonder whether his mother was having an affair. Yet the certainty that he had felt that awful day in London had disappeared, and since then he had found himself questioning whether he had misinterpreted a perfectly innocent conversation.

Burdened by suspicions – *Darling, how wicked* – he had returned to college early, claiming that he needed to work. Back in Edinburgh, his problems seemed no less pressing. What on earth, he thought despairingly, was he to *do* having left medical school? The prospect of living at home appalled him, yet any decent career seemed to demand either capital or years of study or both. His grandfather's bequest was dependent upon his becoming a doctor; he had no other money of his own.

His own lack of resolution annoyed him; nineteen, for God's sake, Oliver said to himself, and still worrying about what Mummy and Daddy think of you. It crossed his mind to long for something dramatic, something cataclysmic, to happen, to make the decision for him. Walking from lecture theatre to lodging-house, lodging-house to hospital, he pictured an earthquake ripping up the genteel Edinburgh streets, a whirl-wind tearing through Holland Square's overstuffed rooms.

The cataclysm, when it came, was of a rather different nature. He was at his lodgings, lying on his bed, reading *On the Road*, and wishing he lived in America (or Canada or Australia – anywhere but bloody Edinburgh), when his landlady knocked on his door, and told him that there was a telephone call for him. Oliver hid the book under his pillow, and ambled downstairs.

The telephone was in the hall, the most uncomfortable part of the house, a place of wellingtons and wet duffel coats, and constant interruptions.

He picked up the receiver. 'Hello?'

'Oliver? It's Elizabeth.'

She had written to him several times since he had returned to college, long letters whose passionate content seemed at odds with her looping, schoolgirlish roundhand. His answering letters had been more restrained: he always imagined a critical eye looking over his shoulder as he wrote, a hangover from boarding school, perhaps.

'Lizzie.' He was surprised. 'I didn't know you knew my number.'

'I asked the operator.' There was a pause. 'The thing is, Oliver . . .'

Something in her tone of voice began to make him feel uneasy. His landlady was hovering in the passageway; Oliver turned his back on her.

'Lizzie? Are you all right?' He lowered his voice. 'Where are you?'

'I'm at home. Daddy's gone out for a walk, but I said I'd a headache.'

Another pause. The front door opened, letting in two fellow students, laughing and chattering. Oliver glared at them.

'Oliver? Are you still there?' Elizabeth sounded a

very long way away. 'Um,' she began again. 'The thing is, there's a bit of a problem . . .'

Mrs Phelps-Browne was the last of Guy's patients; bidding her farewell, shutting the door behind her, he checked his engagement diary – a free evening, thank heavens – and then headed home. He looked forward to cheese on toast in front of the fire (busy with her charity work, Eleanor rarely dined with him these days), a good book, and an early night. As he locked the surgery door behind him, he thought, *Good God, how middle-aged*, and walked down Cheviot Street, depression hovering over him like a great dark bird.

Reaching Holland Square, however, all thoughts of peace and quiet and an early night were dispelled by the discovery of both Oliver and Eleanor, sitting together in the drawing-room. Guy said, '*Oliver*,' and Oliver, his hands in the pockets of his sports jacket, rose and took a step or two towards him, and then retreated.

'Oliver. It's lovely to see you . . . but it's June . . . you should be in Edinburgh . . . your exams—'

'Tell him.' Eleanor's voice cut through Guy's confusion. Guy glanced at her. She sat bolt upright in her chair, her face pale, her lips tightly compressed. She repeated, 'Tell him, Oliver.'

'Tell me what?'

'I'm not going to sit my exams, Dad.'

Guy blinked. 'Have I the dates wrong? You said in your last letter . . .' But he could not recall what Oliver had said in his last letter. It had been weeks, months perhaps, since Oliver had written home.

'I'm not going back to Edinburgh.'

Seeing the white, set expression on Oliver's face, Guy

began to take in what his son was telling him. He had to sit down then; his heart was pounding uncomfortably.

'Such nonsense,' said Eleanor angrily. 'Tell him, Guy, that he's talking nonsense.'

Oliver avoided meeting his mother's eyes. 'It's not nonsense. I'm not going back to medical school. I told my tutor.'

Guy heard the words, but they would not immediately sink in. It was almost like being told of a sudden death. The death of his hopes: he had always assumed that Oliver would follow in his footsteps. That Oliver would become a doctor – like both his grandfathers, like Guy himself – had hardly ever been questioned. It had been the one thing about which he and Eleanor had consistently agreed. Guy, looking at Oliver, felt as though he was walking on eggshells: a single wrong word, and the future would be altered beyond recognition.

'Sit down, please, Oliver. Let's talk this through.'

Oliver, looking mulish, sat. 'I've chucked it, that's all. I hate it. I've always hated it.' The light detachment of his tone was, Guy suspected, calculated to annoy.

'You see?' cried Eleanor. 'Why are you just sitting there, Guy? Why don't you tell him how ridiculous he's being?' She turned to Oliver. 'You mustn't say such things, Oliver. You've always wanted to be a doctor.'

Oliver was staring into the middle distance. His blue eyes were wide. '*You* always wanted me to be a doctor. I told you, I hate it. The mess . . . the smells . . . the *misery*.'

Guy thought he understood. He too recalled feeling like that. He crossed the room, and sat on the sofa arm beside his son, and said gently, 'Every student doctor has doubts at one time or another, Oliver. I certainly did.'

'You make it sound like a bloody religion, Dad. Loss of faith.' Oliver's voice was sarcastic.

'I remember my first tonsillectomy – I nearly passed out.' Guy placed a tentative hand on Oliver's rigid shoulder. 'As for the human suffering – yes, that's the worst of it. But that's what it's all about, isn't it? That's the privilege you'll earn, if you stick it out. The opportunity to fulfil your ideals – to make things better, to alleviate suffering—'

'Like you, you mean?' Oliver, looking up at Guy, smiled unpleasantly; Guy's hand slid from his shoulder.

' "Make things better . . . alleviate suffering" – what sententious twaddle. And you talk of *ideals* – good God, such rubbish.' The supercilious smile lingered. 'Look at yourself, Dad. Where do ideals come into it? What's medicine to you other than an opportunity to build up a healthy bank balance?'

Guy had never smacked his son as a child, but he found himself wanting to do so now. With an effort at self-control, he said, 'Don't speak to me like that, Oliver. You have no right.' Yet even to him his voice sounded pompous and unconvincing.

Struggling to control his anger, he went to the window, and stared through the glass. The sky was still light; puffy lilac clouds blotted the horizon. *What's medicine to you other than an opportunity to build up a healthy bank balance?* Guy clenched his fists.

His back to Oliver, he said, 'And how will you manage for money? Your allowance is dependent on your remaining at medical school. Or are you expecting me to support you?'

'Not necessary, Dad. I'll be fine.'

Something in Oliver's tone made Guy turn back and look at him.

'You see, I'm going to get married,' Oliver said, and smiled.

Guy heard Eleanor's shocked gasp. He himself could only feebly repeat his son's last word. '*Married?*'

'Yes, Dad.'

'You can't possibly – it's quite out of the question – *married*—' Eleanor's protests shot across the room, incoherent bursts of machine-gun fire.

Guy's anger bubbled to the surface again. 'Is that what this is really all about? You've convinced yourself that you're in love with some girl, and you intend to throw up a promising career for *that*? Good God, Oliver, I thought you had more sense. *Think*, man! Be practical! It may be years before you're financially independent.'

'Lizzie's an heiress, so I won't need to worry about money. Good, isn't it?' Oliver's eyes glittered. 'I won't need you any more, Dad. I won't have to come crawling to you when I need a new suit, or when I fancy a week or two away from this dump. I'll be free.' He went to the sideboard, and took out a bottle of sherry. He filled three glasses, and placed one in front of Eleanor.

'Aren't you pleased? Aren't you going to congratulate me?'

'Congratulate you!' Eleanor pushed aside her glass. 'When you're planning to throw your life away because of some slut—'

Guy saw the sudden flare of anger in Oliver's eyes, and said quickly, 'Do you mean that you wish to become engaged?' He accepted the glass that Oliver held out to him, because to have done otherwise would have been histrionic and childish. 'Now that's a different matter – we've no objection to your becoming engaged, have we, Eleanor?' An early engagement – and the responsibility such a commitment involved – might tame Oliver, might be the making of him.

'Marriage, Dad,' said Oliver coldly. 'I'm getting married.'

Guy recognized in Oliver's expression the determination and stubbornness that had so often defeated him in Eleanor.

'How long have you known . . . what was her name . . . ?'

'Lizzie,' said Oliver. 'Lizzie Kemp.'

Oliver was still talking ('Elizabeth, actually. Elizabeth Anne Kemp – rather county, don't you think, Dad?'), but Guy hardly heard him. A persistent drumming noise filled the room. It took Guy a moment or two to realize that he was hearing the glass, still clutched in his hand, reverberating against the window sill. When he looked at Eleanor, he saw that the remaining colour had drained from her face. Her skin was bone white. Her mouth remained half open, as though Oliver's announcement had literally taken away from her the ability to speak. There had not been a single occasion, Guy thought wonderingly, in all the troubled years of their marriage, when he himself had been able to reduce her to such silence.

Oliver, partway through his monologue, faltered, and glanced from one parent to the other. 'What? What is it? What have I said?'

'Your . . . Oliver, your fiancée's name—'

'Lizzie. Yes.' Oliver looked bewildered.

Eleanor was staring at Guy, as if silently imploring

him to reassure her that this, her worst nightmare, was not taking place.

'Lizzie what, Oliver?'

'Lizzie Kemp.' Oliver added angrily, 'Why the hell are you looking at me like that?'

'Her father . . . ?'

'Something in the City. Perfectly respectable.' Oliver attempted to recover his bravado. 'Fabulous country house, Dad. Bloody enormous. And she's an only child.'

'*David* Kemp?'

Oliver nodded; Eleanor's wail almost drowned out Oliver's reply.

'Do you know him, Dad? Met him at the golf club or whatever? I haven't had the pleasure yet. I think he was given a K a year or two ago, so now he's *Sir* David Kemp, but—'

Eleanor had picked up her glass, and was gulping down the sherry. At first, her words were low, strangely timbred, almost inaudible. 'He wants to marry Nicole Mulgrave's daughter.' Then her voice soared in pitch. 'You can't marry *her*! You can't possibly marry *her*!'

Oliver, shocked, said furiously, 'I'll marry whom I damn well please!'

Eleanor seemed to recover herself a little. Slightly unsteady, she walked across the room to her son. 'You are nineteen, Oliver. And this girl – this girl is—'

'Seventeen.'

Guy, if his mind had not been frozen with shock, could have worked that out for himself.

Eleanor's eyes gleamed triumphantly. 'Until you are twenty-one, Oliver, you require our permission to marry. We will not give it.'

Oliver's face hardened. 'You will, Mother. You will. Believe me, you will. And you'll give me your blessing. And so will Lizzie's father.'

Guy, watching, sensed the coiled-up violence in his son, and his capacity for sheer, bloody-minded antagonism.

'Never,' whispered Eleanor. 'Never.'

'Oh, you will, Mother. Because, you understand, I *have* to marry Lizzie.' Oliver smiled. 'She's pregnant, you see.'

There was a silence. Then Eleanor turned to Guy. 'I suppose,' she said, 'I suppose you think this is funny?' Her voice trembled.

'Not in the least,' he replied, surprised, about to add, *I am as horrified as you, Eleanor*, or words to that effect. But he saw that she was not listening to him.

'I suppose you think that I deserve this because of Freddie—'

He could not think what she was talking about; he could not, just then, recall anyone called Freddie. Her eyes seemed to bulge out of their sockets. He said, 'Sit down, Eleanor, please. I'll get you a glass of water. I know this has been a terrible shock—' but she grabbed his jacket sleeve, staying him.

'It's all a mistake, isn't it, Guy? Tell me it's all a mistake.'

He could not speak; he just shook his head. Eleanor's fingers clawed at his sleeve.

'No,' she said loudly. 'No, I shall not allow it. I shall not allow my son to marry that woman's daughter.'

He said wearily, 'Eleanor, Elizabeth is expecting Oliver's child. It's too late. There's nothing we can do.'

The hatred in her eyes jolted him. Then she whispered, 'They've won, haven't they?' and into his

bewildered face she spat, 'The Mulgraves. After all this
time, they've won.'

'Eleanor—'

'After all I've done for you – after all I've done for
Oliver – the entertaining – this house – your career –
I've always done my duty – I've always done what's
right—' Her eyes glared; her voice had risen in pitch.

'And yet now we must live in *their* sort of world.
Their slovenly clothes . . . their lack of manners . . . I
had to stand up on the Underground today . . . not one
person offered me their seat. And the tradesmen . . . the
domestic servants' – Eleanor's breath came in thick,
clotted gulps – 'untidy and careless . . . without a please
or thank you . . . foul language—'

Her words blurred together, but out of the tangle he
heard her shriek, 'My son and *her* daughter! The bitch
– the conniving, cunning little bitch! Like her mother!
Like that bitch, Faith! Sluts all of them – opening their
legs for any man they like the look of – dear God! I
wish we'd never set eyes on them!' and he struck her
across the face, hard, with the flat of his hand.

Guy heard the door open, and the sound of Oliver's
fast footsteps on the stairs. Eleanor stared at him,
her mouth a wide, dark O. Then she slumped onto
the sofa, her white face blotched dark red around the
mouth, and began to weep. Guy ran out of the house in
search of his son.

He found Oliver sitting on a bench in the square of
dusty laurels opposite the house. Oliver's head was
bowed, his hands pressed against his forehead. When
Guy said his name, he looked up, and Guy saw how
pale his face was.

Guy said, with a conviction he himself did not feel,

'Your mother will be fine soon, Oliver. It was just the shock.'

Oliver, shoulders hunched, hands plunged into his jacket pockets, looked away. Guy sat down on the bench beside him.

'We have to talk, Oliver. We really do have to talk.'

'We've done enough talking, haven't we? Mother doesn't want me to marry Lizzie, and I'm damned well going to, and that's all there is to say.'

'I have to tell you about the Mulgraves.' He saw Oliver's restless defiance still slightly, and he knew that he had his attention. 'You see, your mother doesn't want you to marry Elizabeth Kemp, because, many years ago, I had an affair with her mother, Nicole Mulgrave.'

Yet it seemed improbable now. Telling Oliver about his younger self, he felt as though he was talking of another person, who had lived in a far-off country. Though he remembered clearly the details of their affair – seeing Nicole in London and mistaking her for Faith, and the snow that had disguised the wreckage of the Blitz – he found it hard to recall how he had felt.

There was a long silence. Then Oliver, a small smile playing around his lips, said, 'God. Rather extreme measures, Dad.'

'It's true. It was a long time ago, as I said. You were only two years old, and Elizabeth was a tiny baby.'

'Ah. Then at least we're not brother and sister. It's not *incestuous*—' Oliver blinked. 'That'd be one way of putting me off, wouldn't it? Rather *Duchess of Malfi*, but—'

'*Oliver*.' He wanted to touch him, but he sensed his son's brittleness, his barely contained emotions.

'How did you meet her, Oliver? How did you meet Lizzie Kemp?'

A pause. Then: 'Holly Blue,' said Oliver. 'Lizzie's aunt has a shop in Soho. That's where I met her.'

'Holly Blue,' whispered Guy. Dear God, Holly Blue. The crust of the past had indeed broken open.

Oliver, looking at him, was frowning. 'The card from the shop . . . ages ago, I found it in your wallet . . . I assumed you'd bought something there—' He broke off, and then he said suddenly, 'Faith. What Mother said—'

The Mulgraves . . . sluts all of them . . . I wish we'd never set eyes on them . . .

'You know Faith, too, don't you, Dad?'

There was a limit to how much truth could be told in one afternoon. *Actually, Oliver, I had an affair with Faith as well . . .*

Guy said, 'I knew all the Mulgraves. Ralph and Poppy – Poppy died in the war. And the children. Faith and Jake and Nicole.' He took a deep breath. 'Nicole Mulgrave – Nicole *Kemp* – and I had a love affair which began in the December of 1941. I could give you reasons, justifications, excuses, but I don't think you'd be interested. Nicole left her husband and baby daughter, and came to live with me. It didn't last long, and afterwards I went back to your mother. Nicole went abroad, I believe. I think that she's since married several times.' He added, trying to be fair, 'So you can see why your mother finds your engagement difficult to accept, Oliver.'

'Yes. Good God.' Oliver's laugh was humourless. 'Yes.'

The memory of Eleanor's hysteria, the words that anger and jealousy had torn from her mouth, sickened

Guy. The crack of his hand across her bleached white face: his palm still stung. He hated that Oliver had witnessed that.

'If you'd given us more warning, perhaps . . .' he said despairingly. 'If we'd had some idea that you'd met someone . . . that you'd fallen for someone . . .' He saw with horrible clarity the chasm that had widened between himself and his son over the past few years. He was aware of a deep shame and hurt.

'I didn't mean it to be like this,' muttered Oliver. 'I didn't plan it—'

'And medical school. Why didn't you tell me you weren't happy?'

Oliver shrugged. 'Don't know,' he mumbled. 'Didn't know how to, I s'pose.'

'You didn't feel able to confide in me?' Guy was unable to keep the pain from his voice.

He saw Oliver wince. Oliver said slowly, 'I got into a sort of habit, I suppose . . . I thought everything had to stay the same. Sometimes you forget that you can change things, make things better.'

Oliver had hidden from him the greater part of his life, thought Guy, just as he himself had hidden his most important memories, fears and dissatisfactions from Oliver.

He struggled to take in all these new realities. 'So you are a . . . a friend of Faith's?'

A nod.

He had to know. 'How is she? How's Faith?'

'She's fine. Very well, I think.'

'And Jake?' He was hungry for news. The Mulgraves had meant so much to him; he realized now that it was almost though he had, five and a half years earlier, deliberately cut off a part of himself.

'Jake was Lizzie's uncle, wasn't he? He's dead. She told me that he'd drowned.' Oliver, seeing Guy's expression alter, looked, for the first time, concerned. 'Sorry, Dad. I didn't mean to upset you. Were you very fond of him?'

'Very.' He could hardly speak.

Oliver said, 'I have to go – I'm late. Lizzie's expecting me.' He glanced at Guy again, and placed a tentative hand on his father's clenched fingers. 'Will you be all right, Dad?'

Guy made himself smile and nod, but he felt inside blank, empty, hopeless. He watched Oliver walk away, and knew that he had lost his son, just as he had also lost Faith and Jake and Nicole. If they had, in the conversation that had just taken place, made the beginnings of a reconciliation, it had nevertheless come too late. Soon Oliver would be a married man with a child of his own. He and Eleanor would no longer have first claim on Oliver's affections. Guy sat in the dusty little square until the sun had begun to go down, and then, because he could think of no alternative, he went back into the house.

Oliver headed, as planned, for the Black Cat café. He had always loathed the tube (the darkness, the rush of hot air), so he walked, hands in his pockets, his head lowered as he weaved through busy pavements.

She was waiting at her usual table downstairs. He knew that she had been waiting for a long time: a cheese roll, reduced to a mountain of crumbs, stood on the table in front of her, and the table was littered with cups of coffee, cold and with a nausea-inducing skin of milk. Her head jerked up as he crossed the room. She said, looking at him, 'Was it awful?' and he sat down in the chair opposite.

'Pretty bad.' He tried to smile, but his mouth felt stiff.

She reached out to touch his hand, but he shrank away. 'Cigarette,' he said. 'Have you a cigarette, Lizzie?'

She shook her head. Her eyes were huge and dark. 'I'll get you some.'

She left the table, and came back after a few moments with cigarettes and matches. Oliver fumbled with the cellophane, and the cigarettes tumbled like spillikins out of the box. He managed to get one between his lips; there followed a humiliating struggle as he tried to light the match. 'Shit,' he mumbled, as the first match broke unlit. 'Shit. Shit. *Shit*,' as a handful of matches showered onto his lap. He could hear his voice rising in pitch.

She said, 'Let me, Oliver,' but he stood up, his chair crashing to the floor. He knew that people were staring at him.

He muttered, 'Got to get out of this place,' and ran up the stairs. Outside, cars hooted at him as he crossed the road, heading for the river. Reaching the Embankment, he leaned against the wall, his forehead cradled on his elbows. When he felt her stroke his hair, he said: 'Sorry. I thought I was all right.'

She said gently, 'It doesn't matter what they think, Oliver. We've got each other, haven't we?'

He raised his head, and turned and looked at her. There were dark shadows round her eyes. Her face seemed thinner. He said, 'Mum wasn't too keen on the idea, actually. The thing is, there's an unexpected difficulty.'

She didn't say anything, but just looked at him.

'Bit of a spanner in the works.' He wanted to laugh. 'You see – your mother and my father—'

He heard her say, 'My mother and your father – what? What, Oliver?'

He said flatly, 'They had an affair.'

'Oh.'

After a while, when she did not say anything more, he turned round and looked at her.

'Is that all? *Oh?*'

'When? When did they have an affair?'

His mind, working with untypical slowness, could not at first find an answer. Then, recalling details of that appalling interview with his parents, he said, 'When you were a baby. December 1941. Yes, that was it – a few months – a wartime fling, I suppose.'

'Mummy left Daddy in November 1941.'

'You don't mind?'

She considered. 'No. No, not especially.' Her clear brown eyes met his. 'Mummy's had lots of husbands and lovers, you see. Daddy calls them the Lovesick Swains. I've met some of them. They're all awful, of course, and there's always a different Lovesick Swain the next time. Daddy really never talks about them, or about what happened between him and Mummy, but Auntie Faith has told me a little. Mummy wants to find someone perfect, you see.'

'Perfect?' repeated Oliver blankly.

'Perfect for Mummy. Terribly good-looking, of course, and dashing. Someone who likes the same music and the same books and—'

'How ridiculous,' said Oliver distantly. 'No-one's perfect.'

She looked at him. 'Aren't they? I suppose it depends

on your point of view. If you love someone enough, the things that you wouldn't necessarily have chosen about them become interesting and beautiful just because they are part of them. Anyway' – and Elizabeth looked sympathetically at Oliver – 'I suppose for me Mummy's always been like that, so I'm used to it. Whereas you – you thought of your parents in a particular way, and now you're having to get used to thinking of them in a different way.'

He felt suddenly years younger than she, rather than a year and a half older. 'Oh, Christ,' he said suddenly, despairingly, and sat down on a bench, looking out to the river. 'Don't you mind that it was *them*? Don't you mind that we – that they . . . ?'

She was standing behind him. She stroked his hair gently. 'It was a long time ago, Oliver.'

Her hands were soothing. He closed his eyes. He heard her say, 'It's nothing to do with us, is it? The only thing that I mind is that it's going to hurt Daddy.'

'I'm not sure I can face—'

'I'll speak to him first. You don't have to worry.'

'He'll probably kill me.'

She rested her cheek against the crown of his head. 'He'll probably *want* to kill you, but he won't, because I'll tell him how much I love you. And how happy we're going to be.'

He said suddenly, 'I wonder if that's why they quarrel? Because he . . . ?'

She slid round to the front of the bench, and sat on his lap, and linked her arms round his neck. 'If you fell in love with anyone else, I'd hate them, Oliver. And I'd be hideously angry with you.'

Behind the soft brown warmth of her eyes, he glimpsed steely determination. He stared at her, and rubbed his forehead, and said slowly, 'You see, it sort of lets me off the hook, doesn't it? I always thought they hated each other because of *me*. I thought it was my fault.'

'Oh, Oliver,' she said. 'Poor Oliver.' She began to kiss him. 'How could it be your fault? How could it be a child's fault?' She took his hand in hers. 'See,' she whispered. 'Feel it. Whatever happens to us, it can't be *her* fault, can it?' and she slid his hand under layers of shirt and vest and jeans, until his palm rested on her smooth skin.

Her belly was flat, unrounded by the growing child. She whispered, 'I'm reading a book about it. In a few weeks' time I'll be able to feel her move,' and, looking into her eyes, he recognized a deep, unquenchable joy.

Nicole had rented a house in the Marais Poitevin. A network of tiny rivers, thick with emerald-green pondweed and shadowed by willows, surrounded the house. There were two dogs, innumerable cats, a canary in a cage, a shaggy-coated donkey, and Stefan.

Nicole had found Stefan in Rome. 'He's half Polish and half Italian. Isn't he the most gorgeous man you've ever seen?'

Faith agreed that Stefan was very good-looking.

'And he plays the piano divinely, though he's a teeny bit over-generous with the pedal. I have to sing very loudly to make myself heard.' Nicole puffed up her chest, and gave an impression of herself, in a nightclub, singing '*Je ne regrette rien*' at full volume.

Before leaving for France, Faith had promised to telephone Annie, her assistant at Holly Blue, on each day of her fortnight's absence. But there was no phone at Nicole's house, and she found herself increasingly skipping a day or two, unwilling to make the journey to Niort, and a telephone box. She realized that she could not remember when she had last taken a holiday. She slept a great deal, ate a great deal, and drifted along the river with Nicole, dozing as the handsome Stefan punted. Her favourite occupation was to scour the nearby markets and antique shops.

When, one day, she found at the bottom of her suitcase a pile of papers from Holly Blue that she had meant to go through on holiday, she stared at them for a moment, and then thrust them back into the case, unable to bear to look at them. It shocked her to realize that she did not miss Holly Blue at all. She knew that she was lotus-eating, yet she found herself wondering whether the shop might survive without her for another week, or maybe two. The urge to travel on, to continue south, was surprisingly strong. She wondered whether her reluctance to return to London was due to her anonymous telephone caller. She admitted to herself that the incident with the rat had unnerved her, and that since then she had not slept soundly at night. She berated herself for her cowardice, and resolved to book return tickets the following day. She should go home, she told herself, and take up the reins of the shop once more. She should go home and buy a nice little house in London: somewhere sensible, somewhere practical. But, each morning, glimpsing the sunshine and the spring flowers, her resolve crumbled.

Then David's telegram arrived. It told them that Elizabeth was to marry Oliver Neville.

David and Elizabeth walked through the garden at Compton Deverall.

'In the church, Lizzie,' said David. 'On that I insist. You'll be married in church.'

'But we don't believe in any of that, Daddy,' Elizabeth explained. 'Oliver and I are both atheists.'

'I don't care if you worship the great Khan of China, Liz. Every Kemp since the Reformation has been married in the village church, and so will you.'

'But it'll take *weeks*! Reading banns . . . all that! We thought, a special licence—'

'No.' David's voice was firm. 'My daughter's wedding will not be a hole-in-the-corner affair. No, Lizzie. We'll do it properly, and if that means you have to wait a couple of months, then so be it.'

'But it'll be so awful, Dad! Oliver's parents . . . and Mummy . . .' She added, embarrassed, 'And it'll show.'

'You should have thought of that before you—' He broke off, seeing the expression on her face. 'I'm sorry, sweetheart. I shouldn't have said that.'

'It doesn't matter, Daddy.' She sighed, and linked her arm through his. 'In the church, then. Though you know how I hate frilly dresses and fuss.' She said tentatively, 'You do like him, don't you, Daddy?'

David, his hands in his pockets, stood at the perimeter of his property, and looked back at his house, his lands. He smiled, trying to disguise from her his sense of loss. 'To tell the truth, Lizzie, I loathe him. I thought that he was a personable, unprincipled scoundrel. But as you've chosen to marry a scoundrel, then I dare say I'll have to put up with him. And perhaps in time, and if he's good to you, I shall even learn to tolerate him.'

At Holland Square, Eleanor told Guy that she was leaving him.

'Freddie and I have been lovers for almost two years, Guy. I stayed with you because of Oliver, but now Oliver is lost to me, there's no point in remaining.' Seeing the incomprehension on his face, she cried, exasperated, 'Wilfred Clarke, Guy! Didn't you *know*?'

Dumbly, he shook his head.

'You will divorce me, Guy. You may cite adultery – I don't care. We'll marry as soon as the divorce comes through. You'll have to find somewhere else to live. This house is in my name, of course. I thought it only fair to warn you. Freddie and I are going to an hotel, but if you could arrange to have your belongings moved out within a fortnight.' She looked at him critically. 'You must pull yourself together, Guy. You've let yourself go.' She buttoned up her coat, gathered handbag and gloves.

He said, as she opened the door, 'The wedding . . . ?'

Eleanor did not even pause. 'What wedding? I know of no wedding.'

As the door slammed behind her, Guy caught sight of his reflection in the looking-glass over the fireplace. He knew that Eleanor was right, that he had let himself go. This morning he had, unable to find a clean shirt, put on yesterday's grubby one; rubbing his hand across his chin, he realized that he had forgotten to shave. He could not remember when he had last eaten.

He was haunted by his last conversation with Oliver. Phrases from it rang incessantly in his head, an insistent warning chime accompanying all that he did. *Fabulous country house, Dad. Bloody enormous. And she's an only child*. When he recalled the naked materialism in Oliver's voice, he shivered. Had he, in wanting the best for Oliver, too easily accepted Eleanor's version of what was best? Had the bargain that he had made with

Eleanor after his affair with Nicole Mulgrave been merely a continuation of folly, a sin greater than that which had provoked it?

Oliver had shown him how he had been at fault, pointing out to him the compromises that he had made. His summation to Oliver of the ideals he had once cherished had been meaningless, the unmotivated gibberings of a parrot. Passion, principle: he had mislaid both. Guy forced himself not to turn aside from that disturbing image in the mirror. Only by deliberately blurring his sight could he still make out the lineaments of his younger self. He could no longer, he thought, recall the young man who, travelling to the Continent for the first time, had had his money and passport stolen in Bordeaux. Neither could he recall his first meeting with Ralph, or his first glimpse of La Rouilly. Oh, he could visualize them, static and frozen in time like snapshots in an album, but he could not recall how he had *felt*.

Remember, he whispered to himself, remember. He wanted to shatter the glass on the mantelpiece, to press a shard to his flesh until he felt something, anything. But that – the dramatic, the flamboyant – had never been his way. He could only scratch away at the past, hoping that if he rubbed at the sore long enough, then it would begin to hurt.

Yet a kinder memory persisted. He recalled the warmth of Oliver's hand on his as they had sat side by side in the square. Oliver had said, *I thought everything had to stay the same. Sometimes you forget that you can change things, make things better.* Guy knew that he too had been stuck in a rut, caught on a treadmill. He remembered the young man he had met at Wilfred Clarke's – Eleanor's lover's – party. That evening he had come face to face with his younger, better self, but he had not until now acknowledged it. *I plan to work in Africa . . . the* need, *Dr Neville! The need is so great.* Guy's heart began to beat a little faster. He sat down at the table, his chin propped on his fists, and wondered whether one could, so late in one's life, claim a second chance.

Throughout the journey back from France, Faith thought, *It's my fault, it's my fault that Lizzie is to marry Oliver Neville.* She should, she told herself, after witnessing that first meeting between Oliver and Elizabeth, have sent Lizzie to the other end of the earth. And she should never, ever have allowed Oliver to visit her at Holly Blue.

In London they separated: Ralph to return to Norfolk, Nicole to travel to Compton Deverall, Faith herself to go home to Holly Blue. Yet it did not feel like a homecoming. Both the shop and the flat seemed cold, unfamiliar, unwelcoming. Though she began immediately to sort through the chaos created by the weeks of her absence, she could summon up little enthusiasm for her task.

A week after her return home, she was woken in the middle of the night by a loud crash. Tiptoeing cautiously downstairs, she discovered that a brick had been thrown through the shop window. Shards of glass were scattered over the floor and the stock. The light from the street lamp made the fragments glitter, so that the dresses seemed to be beaded with diamonds. A cold breeze blew through the broken window. Faith telephoned the police, cleaned up the mess as best she could, and checked the locks and bolts that divided the shop from the flat. Though she went back to bed she could not sleep. Propped against the pillows, wrapped in her eiderdown, it seemed to her that the ordered, settled existence she had created for herself was falling apart. And much, much worse, she was no longer sure whether she wanted it anyway.

In August, Faith and Ralph were to travel together from Heronsmead to Compton Deverall. Faith planned their journey with meticulous detail. If she could have organized all the betraying, vagabond feelings that assaulted her in the hours before dawn, then she would have done so. But at the last moment her plans went awry: though it was early August it poured with rain, and Ralph mislaid both his umbrella and his wedding present, and only discovered them after half an hour's searching, stowed in the potting shed.

Because of the delay, they missed their train from Holt, and consequently also missed their connection from Waterloo. When the train paused at Reading station, Ralph insisted on getting out of the carriage and buying tea and sandwiches from the platform buffet ('No *breakfast*, Faith, I cannot endure this ridiculous farrago without any breakfast') leaving her waiting in the carriage, dreading that the guard would wave his green flag before her father had returned to the train. Arriving at Salisbury station, Faith discovered that whichever wedding guest had been detailed to meet them had given up, and that there was not a taxi to be found, and that they were stranded, rain soaking their finery, as the hands of the clock turned.

'Damnable country,' swore Ralph. 'Damnable weather. Don't *fuss*, Faith.'

They walked the first half-mile to Compton Deverall, waved down a bus which took them most of the remainder of the journey, and then they ran down the green lane to the church. The churchyard was empty. Through the ancient fabric of its walls Faith could hear singing. Ralph was already striding into the porch. Squeezing into the back of the church, he joined in the hymn, very loudly and tunelessly, 'Love divine, all loves excelling . . .'

She had caught her breath, Faith thought, by the time Oliver and Elizabeth walked back down the aisle. She thought how lovely Lizzie looked, and how handsome Oliver, and searched through her pockets for the rice she was sure she had put there, and wondered where on earth Ralph had got to. One of her heels had broken, climbing over a stile; she discarded both ruined shoes beneath the pew. Her wet hair clung in rat's tails to the back of her neck. Her dress, hand-dyed by Con, was not waterproof: jade seeped into turquoise, tattooing her skin. A crush of hatted and morning-suited wedding guests began to head out of the church. Someone stood on her toes, and an elbow jabbed her ribs. Familiar faces smiled at her, old friends called to her in greeting. And then she turned, and found herself face to face with Guy Neville.

He was a ghost at the feast, Guy thought. Far too many ghosts, Mulgrave, Kemp and Neville, crammed into that tiny church. Just then, he was glad that he had arranged things so that he would not have to inflict the embarrassment of his presence on the Kemps for too long.

Behind Oliver were ranks of empty pews: such a barren, passionless lot, thought Guy, that he and Eleanor had once been part of. He had wondered whether Eleanor would change her mind and, partway through the ceremony, when the porch door had opened, letting in a skirl of rain, he had glanced round, half expecting her. But he had seen, squeezing into the pews at the back, not Eleanor, but Ralph and Faith.

It had all fallen into place then. In one sudden, unexpected, drowning moment, he had remembered walking for the first time into the kitchen at La Rouilly. No longer a snapshot, but a moving film, perfectly recalled, with sound, sight, smell. The bunch of wild flowers that he had given to Poppy. Poppy's beautiful, delicate, tired face. Somewhere in the distance a piano had played, and someone had sung, stripping the covering from his soul. He remembered the huge, dusty kitchen, the cobwebs strung between the empty wine bottles beneath the sink, the cat curled in the pool of sunlight flooding through the window.

He understood that all those years ago he had fallen in love. Blindingly, irretrievably, for the first time in his life. He understood too that he had loved all of them, in such different ways. Ralph, Poppy, Faith, Jake, Nicole. And La Rouilly itself, of course. Though his passion had changed in character over the years, it had never quite left him. They had given him something that he had lacked, something that he had only just begun to glimpse again.

When the service was over, he congratulated Oliver and Elizabeth, and then, as they were swallowed up in crowds of Kemp friends and relations, he began to shoulder his way towards the Mulgraves. All the guests were funnelling into the porch; momentarily Guy lost sight of Faith and Ralph. Anxiously he glanced at his watch, and then, looking up, he glimpsed once more a fair head, a blue-green sleeve. Weaving between weeping great-aunts and restless infants, he drew level with her.

When he spoke to her, she shook her head, cupping her ear: 'Pardon, Guy?'

'I said,' he yelled, 'you look marvellous!'

Other guests jostled him; she was speaking to him, but he could not hear what she said, her mouth opening and shutting as in a silent movie. He shouted, 'Shall we go outside?' and took her elbow and helped her through the crowds.

Outside, in the peace and shelter of the lich-gate, he found himself for a moment unable to speak. There were a thousand things he wanted to say to her, yet he knew that every one of them would be both arrogant and presumptuous. How could he tell her that he loved her, when he had let her down over and over again? How could he tell her that just to see her repaired his soul, when he recalled, too well, the expression on her face when they had last parted?

Instead, he said, 'I was so sorry to hear about Jake. Oliver told me. It's so hard to believe that he's gone.'

In the churchyard, photographers were setting up cameras, and wedding guests were lining up to have their pictures taken. Someone called over to them, gesturing for them to join the group.

Faith said, 'Jake drowned himself. They never found the body.' Her words were cold and clipped. 'He just walked into the sea off Cornwall, near the school where he taught.' For a moment, then, her guard seemed to slip a little. 'He left his clothes in a neat pile on a rock. That wasn't like Jake, was it?'

He wanted to take her in his arms, to attempt to assuage the pain which he glimpsed naked in her eyes, but a voice called out his name and, turning, he saw Ralph heading towards them.

Faith said quickly, 'Pa persists in believing that Jake is still alive. We don't talk about it much.'

Ralph shouted, 'Guy! Guy Neville! How splendid!' and Guy was smothered in acres of wet overcoat. He heard Ralph begin to talk about the sermon ('Mealy-mouthed, hypocritical rantings. I can't stand bloody priests') and Guy glanced once more at his watch and saw that the hands had moved on with indecent haste.

Ralph added, 'You must walk with us to Compton Deverall, Guy, for the reception.'

'I thought I'd skip the reception. Bit awkward and all that.'

'Having sat through that appalling religious mumbo-jumbo, I should have thought that we could both do with something to drink.'

'I'm trying to cut down, to be honest. And besides, attending the reception would be pushing it a bit, don't you agree?'

'I can't think what on earth you are talking about.'

'Nicole,' said Guy.

'Oh, that,' said Ralph dismissively. 'Everyone's forgotten *that*.'

He looked away from Ralph, towards Faith. He felt as though he were being torn in two. 'The thing is,' he explained, 'that I've a journey to make.'

Her smile faded. He said desperately, 'If I don't go now, I'll miss my plane.'

'A journey?' Ralph was envious. 'Where are you going?'

'To Africa,' said Guy.

*　　*　　*

'*Africa*, Nicole! For two years! You can't get much further away than that, can you?' Faith looked out of the window. The lawns behind Compton Deverall were scattered with tables, chairs and discarded umbrellas. They had endured the dinner and the speeches in the Great Hall, and had since escaped to a window seat, drawing the curtains, shutting themselves away. 'Not that it matters, anyway. It was all finished with ages ago.'

Nicole put down her champagne glass. 'But what will you do?'

'Do? Why should I *do* anything?'

'But . . . Guy. You've always wanted Guy.'

'I suppose it's just been too long.' She thought back, yet again, to the conversation she and Guy had had in the churchyard. She frowned. 'Do you remember that restaurant we used to go to in Aix? Pa used to say they cooked the best cassoulet in Provence. Whenever we went there we'd wait hours and hours, and Pa wouldn't mind because he'd get roaring drunk, and Ma wouldn't mind because at least she could sit down and someone else was doing the cooking. But we used to hate it.'

Nicole nodded, remembering. 'Jake used to be *sick* from hunger.'

'And by the time dinner was served none of us could eat a thing. Pa used to be furious with us, and Ma always thought we were sickening for something. But we weren't, there was nothing wrong with us, we'd just waited too long.'

Faith remembered the last time she had seen Guy, in the little café with the juke box and the leather-jacketed youths and the man with the cloth cap. She had told Guy never to speak to her again. And now, when she longed to talk to him, when every atom of her being wanted to share with him the successes and disappointments of the years since their parting, he was going to Africa.

She looked at Nicole. 'I suppose it's like that with Guy and me. We've just waited too long.'

'That's nonsense, Faith. It's not the same at all. You don't just get tired of loving someone. Love doesn't go off, like a bottle of milk you've left out in the sun.'

'And besides, I expect that Guy thinks it's all my fault.'

'What's your fault?'

'All this.' She gestured to the lawn. They could hear, from somewhere in the bowels of the house, Ralph singing 'Mademoiselle from Armentières'. 'If I hadn't let Oliver visit me at Holly Blue—'

'Oh, do shut up about that, Faith.' Nicole dunked a biscuit into her champagne, and said through a mouthful of crumbs, 'Oliver might be the best thing in the world for Lizzie. Elizabeth is a Mulgrave. She might take after David in appearance, but underneath she's like us. It's taken me years to realize that, but I know that I'm right. She is passionate. If it wasn't for Oliver, she'd probably end up in prison after some wretched Ban the Bomb march. At least with him – and the baby – she'll have something worth being passionate about. And after all, we both fell in love with Guy, didn't we? So it's not surprising that Elizabeth has fallen in love with his son.' Nicole beamed. 'Such a gorgeous dress, Faith. I was afraid she'd insist on her dreadful sweater and jeans.'

'Con designed it and I made it. And the veil is David's grandmother's.'

Nicole looked sentimental. 'I was married in that veil, do you remember?' Her expression altered. 'Don't look so miserable, Faith. It's a *wedding*. You're supposed to be enjoying yourself.'

'The thing is,' said Faith, after a short silence, 'that I can't imagine that they'll be happy.'

Nicole did not, as Faith had half expected, immediately dismiss her fears.

'They're very young, of course.' Nicole flicked a blond curl out of her eyes. 'I suppose that Lizzie might find it all unbearable, as I did. Though she has a more constant nature, don't you think?'

Faith said drily, 'It would be hard to imagine a less constant nature than yours, Nicole.'

Nicole was not offended. 'Odd, isn't it? I never intended to be like that. Quite the opposite, in fact.' She frowned. 'It *might* work. It's best to be optimistic. Lizzie might be a one-man woman, like you, Faith. One really can't tell.'

Faith glanced at Nicole. 'How's Stefan?'

Nicole sighed. 'He won't do, I'm afraid, darling.'

'Really? Why not?'

'He eats noisily. Well, that's quite impossible, isn't it?'

'You could train him—'

'I have tried, darling. Believe me. He'd be perfect if he wasn't so hopeless with soup.' Nicole giggled. 'Don't you sometimes think it's funny . . . you and me . . . you are so practical, Faith, and I've always been such a hopeless romantic.' Her blue eyes bright with laughter, she looked at Faith. 'And yet you have been in love with the same man for *aeons*, whereas I—'

'Searching for The One, you have fallen for Dozens.' Faith, too, began to laugh.

'And some have been so dreadful. Do you remember Miguel?'

'He played the guitar . . . very badly—'

'And Simon. *Sonnets*.' Nicole clutched her arms to her shaking sides. 'And Rupert – terribly handsome, darling, but I don't think he really liked women—'

'That dreadful Russian . . .' Tears were running down Faith's cheeks.

Helpless with laughter, they struggled for breath, and then Nicole said: 'And anyway, I found The One years ago, but I was too stupid to realize it.'

Faith wiped her eyes. 'David?'

'Of course. You see, I'm a drifter, like Ralph. I was never anything much else. All the things I thought I wanted – a handsome lover, a beautiful house, and to be a famous singer – I found out quite quickly that I didn't really want them at all. Oh, I'd want them for a while, but then I'd get bored with them. I sing in the most awful dives, you know, Faith. Dreadful little clubs where the only place one can change is in the ladies' lavatory. Down-at-heel theatres with rickety stages. Sometimes the audience is drunk, and sometimes they're playing pool or cards, and sometimes there isn't an audience.'

They ate in companionable silence for a while, and then Nicole said, 'You do know that Guy and Eleanor are getting divorced, don't you, Faith?'

Lizzie had told her during a fitting. Faith had almost swallowed a mouthful of pins. She whispered, 'Eleanor has been having an affair.'

Nicole began to giggle again. 'Can you imagine? Stripping off her tweeds as she bounds into the arms of her lover . . .'

When they had both stopped laughing, Nicole said

suddenly, 'Oh, I do wish that Jake was here! Nothing is the same without him. He would have argued with Pa and danced with Lizzie and made all those spotty girls fall in love with him, and we would all have had so much more *fun*.'

Tears prickled behind Faith's lids. Too much champagne, she supposed. 'Do you suppose . . . ?' She looked at Nicole. 'Pa's still convinced—'

'I don't know.' Nicole sounded sad. 'I really don't know, Faith.'

Elizabeth was taking off her wedding dress. Her mother was supposed to be helping her, but her mother was nowhere to be found, so Oliver was helping instead.

He undid the zip, and slid his hands round her waist. She said, suddenly apprehensive, 'Does it bother you?'

'What?'

'This.' Elizabeth patted her stomach. She had had to carry a rather large bouquet.

He did not reply, but instead eased the dress from her shoulders, and cupped her breasts, sighing with pleasure as he buried his face between them.

She said, '*Oliver*. Someone might come.'

He came up for air just long enough to say, 'Does it matter? We're allowed to now.'

She supposed that they were. It would take her a while to get used to that: it still felt forbidden.

She said doubtfully, 'I have to change into that awful suit. So hot and sticky.'

'In fact,' he continued, as though she hadn't spoken, 'I'm *obliged* to do this.'

'Really?' The wedding dress had slipped to the floor; it circled her heels like a vast cream-coloured omelette.

'Really. We aren't legally married until we've been to bed.'

When he said *been to bed* her mouth went dry. She had been incarcerated at Compton Deverall for the last two months. She had not realized how much she would miss what he did to her. She said suddenly, 'I do think your father's wonderful, going to work in a hospital in Africa. You must be awfully proud of him.'

Oliver paused in the task of peeling off Elizabeth's slip. 'I suppose I am.' He looked surprised.

She said, 'Have you enjoyed today?'

'The wedding? Ghastly. Utterly ghastly.'

'Wasn't it?' she agreed fervently. 'The longest, most tiresome day of my whole life.'

'Such *undercurrents*.'

He was caressing her navel with his tongue. He looked up. 'Do you think they still lust after each other – your mother and my father – in a middle-aged sort of way, of course?'

Elizabeth made a face, and then shivered as Oliver kissed her gently rounded belly. 'They're all much too old for that sort of thing,' she said firmly. She closed her eyes. His golden hair brushed against her thighs. 'Oh, Oliver,' she said. 'We don't have to wait until the hotel tonight, do we?'

Ralph, extremely drunk, was sitting on the stairs, talking very loudly to half a dozen of Elizabeth's CND friends. In the Great Hall, a gramophone was playing rock and roll, and people were dancing. Elizabeth and Oliver had left for their honeymoon in Cornwall. The clatter of tin cans and boots and uncurling paper streamers had disrupted the dignified tranquillity of

Compton Deverall. It had stopped raining, and on the terrace someone was strumming a guitar. Other guests wandered around the garden, discarding their wineglasses in planters and parterres. A great many young men, whom Nicole supposed to be college friends of Oliver's, were making cocktails in the kitchen from leftover sherry and champagne, garnishing the glasses with cherries and pineapple scooped out of the bottom of the trifle bowl. It had become, Nicole thought, in spite of David's best efforts, a Mulgrave sort of wedding.

Guests had begun to drift away, car lights to diminish as they faded into the beech avenue. Nicole walked through the house. Strange how it seemed now like home. Strange how sometimes, lying on a Mediterranean beach, or making up her face in a dingy little room in a club in Los Angeles, she would long for haunted, echoing corridors, and the scent of beechmast in the rain.

She found him in the gallery, studying the paintings. 'I used to think,' she said, as she walked towards him, 'that they disapproved of me.'

'My ancestors?' David turned to her and smiled. 'Not at all. They would have adored you, and thought me incomparably dull.'

He had paused beside a Jacobean Kemp. Studying it, she said, 'I can't imagine you with an earring and a lovelock, David.'

'Which,' he said, as she looped her hand round his arm, 'is just what I meant.' He looked at her. 'I'm taking sanctuary. Why are you here, Nicole?'

'I was searching for you, of course.' She laid the back of her hand against his face. 'Poor David. You've hated it, haven't you?'

'Seven hours,' he said. 'This dreadful celebration has so far lasted almost seven hours.'

'You mustn't worry,' she said gently. 'Elizabeth will be happy, I know that she will.'

'She's so *young*! A schoolgirl.' He shook his head. 'And that boy—'

'Faith likes Oliver tremendously. And she's good at people. Much better than me.' Nicole looked at him fondly. 'I'd never much of a talent for knowing the ones to hold on to, and the ones to let go.'

He bent and kissed her. She said, after a while, 'Please try not to mind too much, David. For Lizzie's sake. And for mine too, perhaps. I don't regret much, but I do regret what Guy and I did, a little.'

CHAPTER SIXTEEN

The wheels of the Land Rover bounced on the hard, dry road. It was January, and the sun had baked the red dirt tracks into rigid folds, like a gigantic ribbon of corrugated cardboard. Ten minutes after driving away from the mission hospital, Guy had been covered from head to toe in red dust. 'Put your foot down, old chap,' the old Africa hands at the club had advised him on a previous visit to Dar es Salaam. 'Then you won't feel the bumps.' Guy pressed hard on the accelerator and thought, *If my Cheviot Street patients could see me now* . . . The same thought had occurred to him countless times during the five months of his stay in Tanganyika.

He could not get used to the scale, the extreme nature of the place. He could not get used to the flash floods in the rainy season that transformed roads to rivers, rivers to torrents. He could not get used to the heat which, in the dry season, seemed to possess a solidity, something to be physically wrestled with.

He drove to Dar es Salaam once a month, to pick up supplies and post. It was, Guy thought, a necessary respite. When he had first applied to work at the Anglican mission hospital, he had envisaged a life of relentless asceticism. By embracing work and poverty, he would excoriate a soul that had been dulled by age

566

and experience, and in doing so discover whether anything true and good lingered beneath the surface. Tanganyika was indeed peeling away the layers; just as the tropical sun burned his skin, and just as fevers stripped excess flesh from his bones, so was his time in Africa also robbing him of self-delusion. So much of the knowledge that he had acquired over the past thirty years was useless here. He had encountered new enemies. Malaria and sleeping sickness: he had become as familiar with the symptoms of these as he had once been with the symptoms of gastric ulcers and heart disease. He had become a student again; late at night, when his body was aching for rest, he pored over textbooks. *Malaria is caused by single-celled protozoans of the genus Plasmodeum, transmitted by the Anopheles mosquito. There are several different strains of malaria, the most serious being falciparum malaria, which is responsible for cerebral malaria . . .*

Each day, he was confronted by his limitations. His skills seemed puny and inadequate. There were never enough beds, never enough drugs, and there was never enough time. Throughout his first few weeks in Tanganyika Guy had felt as though he were holding back floodgates pressed by a weight of misery and pain. After a while he had realized his arrogance: how could he possibly hope to contain the immense need and energy that was Africa?

As Guy drove into the red-roofed suburbs of Dar es Salaam, he acknowledged that it had taken him still less time to discover that at forty-six you did not possess the same resilience that you had had at twenty-six. An iron bed and a lumpy mattress left him stiff and aching all day, and he could not, as he had once been able to, eat anything put in front of him. Now, his head pounded – the result, he thought, of the endless jolting in the heat.

At his club, one white-gowned servant took his bag, and another fetched his post. Guy took the heap of letters and parcels up to his room. Sitting on the bed, his hands shook slightly as a mixture of hope, anticipation and fear curled in his stomach. The telegram was halfway down the pile. Guy tore open the envelope. He read, CHRISTABEL LAURA POPPY BORN 18 DEC STOP BOTH WELL STOP HAPPY NEW YEAR STOP LOVE OLIVER.

After he had bathed, Guy walked to the sea front. Palms and mangroves were motionless in the still air. Dhows, each one with a painted eye affixed to its bow, bobbed in the harbour, waiting for a more favourable wind to ply the route to the island of Zanzibar. The telegram clutched in Guy's hand shivered like the lateen sails of the dhows. Christabel Laura Poppy, he thought. Tears trailed down his face. *My granddaughter*.

'Didn't you know?' Peggy Macdonald inhaled the smoke from her cigarette. 'I heard it from Dick Farnborough, and he heard it from Millie Peckham, who heard it from One-eyed Jack.'

It was evening, and they were in the bar of the Gymkhana Club. An Indian band was playing European dance tunes in the adjacent room; couples were moving slowly around the floor.

'One-eyed Jack?' said Guy, feigning interest. He had already forgotten the titbit of gossip that Mrs Macdonald had told him.

'Don't you know him?' She flicked her lids. 'I thought everyone in Dar knew One-eyed Jack. He comes here occasionally, but' – she glanced quickly around the room – 'I can't see him tonight. He teaches,

I believe – at a school for the native children, not the International School. Millie runs some peculiar charity for him. Collects second-hand schoolbooks from home. *Janet and John Go Shopping*.' She gave a croak of laughter. 'One can't help wondering what the poor little creatures make of them.'

Guy smiled politely, and wondered whether it was too early to leave. The heat seemed particularly unbearable. His shirt clung to his back, and it was an effort to raise his glass to his lips, an effort to make conversation. An effort, he acknowledged grimly, to think.

He realized that Peggy Macdonald was still speaking to him, and he looked up apologetically. 'Sorry. I was miles away.'

'I said, you must come to lunch tomorrow.'

'I can't, I'm afraid.'

'Robert's away, you see.' Her hand rested on his arm. 'So we could have the whole day to ourselves.'

The invitation was unmistakable. Though she was attractive, well dressed, in her late thirties, he guessed, he felt not a flicker of interest, only a mixture of embarrassment and impatience.

'I have to go shopping,' he explained.

'Shopping?'

'I have to buy a christening present for my granddaughter.'

'Your *granddaughter*.' Her eyebrows rose. 'Oh, well.' She was philosophical. 'What are you going to buy her?'

He shook his head. 'I haven't a clue.'

Mrs Macdonald said helpfully, 'One usually buys a christening mug, Guy, or a silver spoon.'

'She'll have dozens of those. I'd like to get her something different. Something African, I thought. Something special.'

'Then we'll go shopping. I'll meet you at your club at . . . let me see, nine o'clock tomorrow morning.' She looked at him, and said kindly, 'You should go to bed, Guy. You don't look awfully well.'

His guts performed an unpleasant twist. 'I do seem,' he said ruefully, 'to be taking rather a long time to get acclimatized.'

'Some people never do, darling,' she said. She patted his hand again, but this time her touch was maternal rather than seductive. 'Some people never do.'

In the morning, Guy met Peggy Macdonald in the hotel foyer.

She kissed his cheek. 'You look frightful, darling. Are you sure you're up to this?'

Guy said, 'Perfectly sure,' with a certainty he was far from feeling. He rattled with quinine and aspirin. They stepped out into the sunshine.

She led him through the street markets of Samora Avenue, and along the bustling maze of Kariakoo Market. The scents, sights and sounds of Dar es Salaam assaulted him: the hoots of buses and taxis, the golds and russets of the sacks of spices on the stalls, and the heady, salty tang of the Indian Ocean, never far away. Peggy Macdonald inspected rugs, brassware and carvings with brisk efficiency.

In the midday heat they escaped to the Gymkhana Club for lunch. In spite of the blinds and the fans, Guy felt no cooler. In the privacy of the club bathroom he pressed a hot hand against an equally hot forehead, and tried to guess how high his fever was.

'I'll tell you what I'll do,' said Mrs Macdonald when he came back to the table. 'I'll ask Jack.'

'Jack?'

'You remember, I told you about him last night. I'll ask him to find you a lovely piece of makonde. You liked that, didn't you?'

Makonde was a type of traditional ebony carving. In the market, Guy had admired the dark, sinuous shapes; Peggy had considered them of inferior quality.

Guy said dubiously, 'It seems an imposition.'

'Jack won't mind. He found me a lovely piece last year for my sister-in-law. Jack and I are good friends. And he once taught at my sons' prep school in England. Isn't that a coincidence?'

'Bit of a change – from an English prep school to Dar es Salaam.'

'Oh, Jack's done everything!' Peggy raised her glass of rum and coke. 'He's travelled everywhere, and has traded in just about anything you can think of – legal and illegal, darling – and he claims to have crewed a pirate ship in the China Seas, though I've my doubts about that. The eyepatch – it's too convenient. And Bobby Hope-Johnstone says that he remembers him from France, in the war. SOE, darling,' she explained, lowering her voice a little, 'but Jack won't talk about that.'

The food arrived, curry and rice. Sauce from the curry solidified in a gelatinous pool. Guy looked away.

Peggy said, 'I'll find something lovely for you by the next time you come to Dar. You visit once a month, don't you?' She looked at him. 'And don't feel obliged to stay on my account, Guy. You look quite green. You're putting me off my lunch.'

She had Elizabeth's dark eyes, and his own fair hair. When his daughter was two weeks old Oliver wrapped her up in layers of shawls and blankets and showed her the house and estate. This is the gallery, he said, and these are portraits of your great-great-great-grandparents. Their blood is your blood. This is the Great Hall, and painted on the ceiling are your emblems and escutcheons. These are your lands, as far as the stream in the south, and to the border of the beech wood in the north. I shall sell this meadow and that copse, and in doing so I shall keep your inheritance safe.

Snow began to fall, floating like feathers through the windless air, so he carried her back to the warmest part of the house. He opened the door to their bedroom very quietly; Elizabeth was asleep on the bed, curled up in a nest of blankets and eiderdowns. The room was cluttered with crib and baby clothes, and the talcum powder scattered on the polished wooden floor echoed the bleached sky outside. Journals and leaflets were heaped on a chest of drawers. The headline on the topmost one said, INTO THE SIXTIES: DECADE OF DISARMAMENT OR NUCLEAR DISASTER?

Oliver shivered and looked down at his sleeping daughter, still cradled in his arms. Other, unwanted images intruded on her already familiar features. An obscene mushroom cloud; photographs of small Japanese children, their skin flayed from their backs. The fear that seemed always to accompany the intensity of his love for his daughter threatened to overwhelm him. He felt helpless and impotent, and he drew his child to him as though in the warmth and shelter of his body she might find sanctuary from all the horrors of the world.

The estate agent grumbled as they drove out of Holt's rain-drenched streets. 'Should've auctioned the place years ago. Told them they'd never get a good price for it. People want modern conveniences, don't they? Inside bathroom, central heating . . .'

Faith hardly listened. They had left the town, and were heading through open countryside where water dripped from black, naked branches, and puddles spread half the width of the roads. The clumps of trees, the high hedgerows and narrow lanes, became familiar. She felt unexpectedly nervous, and her mouth was dry. When the estate agent slowed the car, muttering, 'Must look at the map . . . damned confusing . . .' she had to clear her throat before saying: 'Just keep driving down this road, Mr Bolsover, and turn left at that avenue of trees ahead.'

He glanced at her, surprised. 'I thought you hadn't seen the house yet.'

'Not for years,' she said, and smiled. 'Not for many, many years.'

As they turned up the track, the car lurched and jolted on the rutted ground. 'My suspension,' Mr Bolsover groaned.

Faith climbed out of the car and looked up at the house. The extent of its decay shocked her. One of the shutters hung drunkenly from a single hinge, and there were tiles missing from the roof. Momentarily her resolution faltered. Shopping with Ralph in Holt the previous month she had glimpsed the advertisement for the house, once more for sale, in the estate agent's window. Later, an impulse had led her to telephone the estate agent and arrange a viewing. She was, she thought, behaving in a typical Mulgrave way. She was planning to throw away an existence that was both safe and secure – and for what? For a dream? A fantasy?

Mr Bolsover's voice followed her as she walked

along the path. 'Your umbrella, Miss Mulgrave!' Drops of rain, like pearls, cascaded down the long runners of the dog roses. The papery seeds of honesty shivered in the downpour.

Mr Bolsover, catching up with her, said dubiously, 'Someone comes in twice a year and hacks this lot back, I believe. Could be nice . . .' When he opened the front door, a flurry of dead leaves fanned out onto the porch. He glanced at the flysheet.

'The hall.' He flicked the light switch, but the bare bulb remained unlit. 'I asked them to put the electricity on,' he said irritably. 'There's a private supply from the estate at Deanridge. This house was originally part of the estate. Fortunately' – he smiled, pleased with himself – 'I've brought a torch.'

Light illuminated the narrow passageway. Faith opened a door.

'The living-room.' They both blinked in the dim, dusty light. 'A wealth of original features. You're fortunate, Miss Mulgrave, that the previous owners didn't make too many alterations. Fashions change, don't they? The panelled doors and the fireplace,' said Mr Bolsover heartily, 'make up for other deficiencies, don't you agree?'

A bird's nest had fallen down the chimney, scattering the grate with twigs and straw. Wallpaper bulged and peeled. Mr Bolsover said, 'Shall we look at the bedrooms before we attempt the kitchen?' and they went upstairs.

'You could convert one of the bedrooms to a bathroom, of course, Miss Mulgrave. If you intend to live in the house alone . . .' His voice trailed away, as though embarrassed by her childlessness, her spinsterhood.

She explained, 'My father will be sharing the house with me, Mr Bolsover.'

They wandered from room to room. Dark patches on the wall showed where damp had come through, and in the smallest bedroom a flurry of plaster had fallen. Opening the kitchen door, she recalled clearly, a sharp sudden visual image, Guy tracing his fingertip across the dusty kitchen shelf.

What are you writing?

Guy loves Faith. What else?

She crossed the kitchen and looked down at the shelf. Nothing to see, of course, except a thick felting of dust. Since Guy had left England she had found herself wondering whether, in going to Africa, he had meant not to leave things behind, but to rediscover something.

The estate agent was speaking. '. . . must apologize for the state of the house, Miss Mulgrave. Perhaps you'd let me show you round some other properties? I have a well-appointed detached bungalow in Norwich.'

Faith thought of Poppy, eloping with Ralph, and Jake, running away to fight in the Spanish Civil War. To hell with the consequences, she thought. To hell with being sensible.

'That's very kind of you, Mr Bolsover,' she said, 'but I intend to make an offer for this house.' She walked back to the car.

He had never, Guy acknowledged, fully regained his strength after the attack of malaria he had suffered in Dar es Salaam. *No anti-malarial drug is completely efficacious* – he was a living proof of the medical textbooks. In the hospital, his stomach would cramp and twist, pointing out to him that he was in for another bad night. Sitting on the veranda of his hut, seeing the elegant, red-robed Masai and their skinny cattle silhouetted against the sinking tropical sun, he would feel sweat gather on his brow. When he lay in bed at night, listening to the drone of the mosquitoes and watching the geckos' curious dance across the ceiling, sleep, which should have offered him a respite, was exhausting and dream-laden. Once he cried out, and an Anglican nun, returning to her living quarters from night duty at the hospital, tapped on his door and asked him if he was all right. Once he went to the chapel, which was mud-walled and roofed in corrugated iron, like most of the other buildings in the compound, and sat there, hoping for – he was not sure what. The heat gathered and multiplied in the confined space, but after a while he began to feel better.

One night, he dreamed that he was walking along Blakeney Point. The shingle was shifting beneath his feet, and an icy wind was blowing off the North Sea. He was looking for Faith, but he could not find her. He knew she was there – that she was round that headland, or standing in the shadow of that dune – but no matter how he forced his aching legs to persevere, he caught only a glimpse of pale hair, or a flicker of a bluish-purple dress. From the sea, the eyes painted on the wooden prows of the boats watched him. Waves rose up, lashing the beach, soaking him. The sky was lead grey, and in the place where water licked the shingle spit, ice was forming, tying the sea to the land. When Guy looked down at himself, he saw that the frost had touched him, forming a gleaming, impenetrable skin. The wooden eyes glared at him, wide open, judging him. Though his shivering intensified, the covering of ice did not break. As each saltwater wave washed over him, it solidified.

Guy woke up. Cold sweat was running off him in rivulets. Rigors possessed him, grating bone against bone. He rubbed his fisted hands against his eye sockets. The dream, peculiarly vivid, lingered. The nagging suspicion that there was something important waiting just round the corner, if only he had eyes to see it, persisted. When he closed his eyes brightly coloured images flickered through his head, disconnected scenes from a constantly turning magic lantern.

Then, as if she were standing beside him, he heard Mrs Macdonald say: *Jack taught at my sons' prep school . . . Hope-Johnstone remembers him from France, in the war . . . SOE, darling.* His eyes suddenly wide and staring, Guy thought, *Jake.*

He sat up, and with trembling hands poured himself a glass of water from the flask beside the bed. As he drank, he told himself not to be silly. That was what fevers did: they muddled up fantasy and memory and reality. Yet the conjecture could not be rubbed away. Jake had taught in a boys' prep school; Jake had worked undercover in France during the war. As he sank back into the sheets, Guy tried to work out whether Jake Mulgrave, who had six years ago walked into the sea from a Cornish beach, could possibly have washed up on the shores of the Indian Ocean.

The following week he went back to Dar es Salaam. In the dining-room of the Gymkhana Club, he looked for Peggy Macdonald and glimpsed her standing beside an open window, glass in hand. A younger man, fair-haired and thickset, stood next to her. As Guy approached, Mrs Macdonald turned and waved to him.

'Guy.' She smiled and pecked him on the cheek. 'Let

me introduce you to Larry Raven. Larry's a new friend of mine.'

They shook hands. Guy said urgently, 'Peggy, I need to talk to you about that chap you mentioned the last time we met. One-eyed Jack . . . ?'

Her hand flew to her mouth; she looked slightly abashed. 'I said I'd ask Jack to get you a piece of makonde, didn't I, darling? I'm most frightfully sorry, but it just hasn't worked out. Jack hasn't been to the club, you see. Sometimes he does, and sometimes he doesn't. It was to be a present for your granddaughter, wasn't it? Have I landed you in the most frightful pickle?'

'That doesn't matter. Could you tell me his sur-name?'

'His surname? Whose surname? Jack's?' She looked blank. 'Haven't a clue, darling. He's just One-eyed Jack.'

'What does he look like?'

'Oh.' The corners of her mouth turned down. 'Fair-haired . . . the eyepatch, of course . . . frightfully handsome, if one could ignore that. Though' – and she smiled – 'I do think there's something rather *dashing* about it.'

'Blue-eyed?'

'The most gorgeous blue eyes . . . blue *eye*, I mean. I've always,' she added, looking at her escort, 'been attracted to blue-eyed men.'

'How old is he?'

'Jack?' Peggy shook her head. 'My sort of age, I suppose. And now you really must excuse me, Guy. My feet are just *aching* to dance.'

As she wove through the crowds, he called after her, 'Tell me where to find him!' and she turned briefly, and said: 'In some frightful bar, I expect. Though he may have left Dar. He likes to travel, you know.'

Guy knew why he was pursuing what could so easily be a futile and pointless quest. It was because he remembered the expression in Faith's eyes when she had said to him, *Jake drowned himself*. He recalled that she had also said, *They never found the body*. That memory gave him hope. This was for Faith. His gift to her. What better gift than her brother, back from the dead?

Yet his confidence diminished as he began to search the city. Every enquiry was met with a shake of the head or a shrug of the shoulders. He might never know whether One-eyed Jack was indeed Jake Mulgrave, because the wretched man was nowhere to be found.

He concentrated upon the African quarter of the city. Laughter and conversation faded as he walked into tiny bars lit by single electric light bulbs. No women, and no white faces but his own. Air that was thick with the sweet scent of bhang. Past midnight, his eyelids heavy with exhaustion, Guy walked down a dark, narrow alleyway. A bead curtain rattled as he ducked inside an ill-lit tin shack. In halting Swahili he asked the question he had asked already twenty times that evening, and the barman cocked a thumb towards a corner of the room.

Among the dark faces there was one pale one. Looking at the man sitting at the table, Guy felt a dull pang of disappointment. Then he looked again. The eyepatch was distracting, and so were the thin channels of scar tissue that accompanied it. Only the fair hair, the graceful posture, reminded him of Jake Mulgrave. But if he blinked, if he let his vision blur so that the years peeled back, then it was possible, just possible—

'You are thinking, Guy, how bloody awful I look. I have to tell you that I was thinking much the same thing about you.'

Jake smiled and stood up. Guy held out his hand. Jake ignored it, throwing his arms around him, crushing Guy's aching bones in an embrace.

Later, Jake said, 'I have to admit that I did think of drowning myself. Rather histrionic, wasn't it? I really can't remember exactly what happened. I think I fancied a swim and I went in out of my depth, and then I realized that the current was stronger than I'd expected. And then I thought – well, why the hell not? I'd made such a bloody mess of everything – women, family, work – it hardly seemed worth going on.' He smiled. 'But the thing was, Guy, that I just couldn't seem to drown. I kept bobbing up and down like a cork. It was quite farcical.'

They were in Jake's flat. Two small, bare rooms, a chair and a heap of cushions on which Jake sat cross-legged. A battered suitcase in one corner of the room and a tower of books in another. It occurred to Guy that Jake lived, literally, out of a suitcase.

Guy prompted Jake. 'So you were out of your depth—'

'Adrift, I should say. Yes, that's the word. Adrift.' Jake laughed. 'Anyway, eventually I washed up further along the Cornish coast. I'm not sure where, I never knew the name of the place. But I was stark naked and unbelievably bloody cold. I wasn't sure whether I'd get arrested first or catch frostbite.'

'What did you do?'

Jake refilled their glasses. 'Stole some togs from someone's washing line and walked to the next village.

There was a fishing-boat bound for the Scillies – they were short of hands so I asked for a job. I was a couple of weeks on Tresco – pretty, but as dull as hell – and then I hitched a ride on another boat, to Brest. They were selling onions or something.' He shrugged. 'And then . . . then I went all over the place. I've forgotten a lot of it.' His single eye narrowed. 'Some of it's best forgotten.'

'Your eye,' said Guy curiously. 'What happened to your eye?'

'I usually tell men that I was clawed by a leopard, and women that I was knifed by a whore in Macao. But I'll tell you the truth, Guy, which was that I'd had far too much to drink, and had smoked God knows what else besides, and I blacked out and when I woke up someone was picking my pocket. I argued, and he had a knife and I didn't, and anyway I was drunk, so he had the best of it.' Jake's fingertips went to the patch, touched it, and came away again. 'I had a glass eye, but the damn thing kept falling out, and this is easier, really.'

'Jesus,' said Guy, under his breath.

'I ended up in some wretched hell-hole of a hospital for two months – in Tangiers, for God's sake – so I had to sober up. It made me look at myself. I didn't much care for what I saw. And to have attempted suicide again would have been absurd, wouldn't it?' Jake focused on Guy. 'And you, Guy. What on earth are you doing here?'

'Healing the sick, supposedly.' He grimaced. 'I'm working in a mission hospital in the bush. Only I've managed to contract both malaria and amoebic dysentery, so they're talking about sending me home. Early discharge on grounds of ill health.'

Jake said, 'Why come here, Guy? Last time we met you seemed very settled in London.'

Guy shrugged. 'It just wasn't enough. I felt more and more restless. I was on a treadmill and I hated it, but I couldn't see what to do, and then, when Oliver told me that he was marrying Elizabeth—'

'Oliver? Your Oliver?'

Guy looked at Jake. 'He married Elizabeth Kemp last August.'

At first, Jake looked blank. Then the blankness changed to hilarity and his shoulders began to shake. He wheezed, 'Oliver and Elizabeth? Your Oliver . . . and Nicole's Elizabeth?'

Guy felt irritated. 'I can't see what's so funny. It's not what any of us would have chosen.'

'Things rarely are, are they?' Jake tried to stop laughing.

'Elizabeth was pregnant, you see.'

Jake's single eye widened.

'I've a granddaughter,' said Guy proudly. 'She's called Christabel.'

Jake blinked. 'Congratulations.' His voice was only slightly unsteady. 'And Eleanor? *Not* a doting grandmother, I assume?'

'I've no idea. We don't correspond.'

Jake said thoughtfully, 'I almost – *almost*, mind – feel sorry for her.' He glanced sharply at Guy. 'You don't correspond? She isn't in Africa, then?'

'Good God, no. We're getting divorced.' Guy frowned again. 'Not only because of Oliver and Elizabeth. That was just a catalyst.' He felt suddenly enormously depressed. 'The whole damn thing – Eleanor and I – was a mistake. Can you imagine what it's like, Jake, to realize that twenty years of your life have been a mistake?' His voice was savage.

Jake's lips twitched. 'Of course I can, Guy. My life has been nothing but a series of mistakes. A good deal of them self-inflicted, of course, but then mistakes so often are, aren't they?'

There was a silence, broken only by the sound of footsteps running in the street outside, and a swirl of small, white, papery moths, their wings fluttering against the oil lamp.

'And now I find myself thinking,' Guy said slowly, 'how *pompous* of me, to think that I could make a difference. To think that I could save the world – or save myself. My voyage of self-discovery has left me with only two conclusions – that I have a weak liver, and that at the age of forty-six I'm still naive.'

Jake said gently, 'You're an idealist, Guy. You always have been.'

A generous interpretation, thought Guy. The line between idealism and self-delusion seemed to him just then to be very, very fine.

'So you and Eleanor have split up. Faith . . . what about Faith?'

'She was at the wedding. She looked well.'

'That was not,' said Jake, eyeing Guy severely, 'what I meant.'

'I left early. Well, I could hardly go to the reception, could I?'

Jake looked as though he was trying not to laugh again. 'I almost regret it. Not being there, I mean. I suppose you might have felt rather de trop.'

'Absolutely,' said Guy feelingly.

'So you just . . . went?'

He said defensively, 'I had a plane to catch.'

'So you saw Faith, told her that you were buggering

off to Africa, and disappeared out of her life yet again?'

'It wasn't like that. Or if it was, I didn't intend it to be.' Yet he remembered how Faith's expression had altered after he had told Ralph that he was going to Africa. The small dying of the light in her eyes.

Jake said, 'Faith loves you, Guy. She has always loved you, and always will love you.'

Looking at Jake, Guy began to feel for the first time in months a flickering of hope. 'Do you think so?'

'I *know* so.' Jake sounded exasperated. 'Oh, for God's sake, Guy – you don't mean that you haven't told Faith how you feel about her? Assuming, that is, you do still love her.'

'Oh, I love her,' he said quietly. He tried to explain. 'It would have been rather ridiculous and arrogant of me, don't you think, to have assumed after all that's happened that Faith should still want me. Even I couldn't manage quite that level of conceit.'

'You must put things right.' Jake's fist struck his palm. 'You must speak to her.'

'Just as you, Jake, have told Faith that you're alive and well?'

'Touché,' muttered Jake and, rising, flung open the shutters. A haze of insects rushed into the room.

'Why didn't you write to her? Just a letter . . . a postcard . . . ? Good God, man – you must have known what she'd think!'

It was Jake's turn to look guilty. 'I didn't really think about it much at all, to begin with. I was too busy racketing around the world, getting angry with everyone. And then, when I was in hospital, I thought – a heap of clothes dumped on a beach, a letter left in a knapsack – and yes, I knew what they'd assume.

584

Although I did wonder whether the man whose clothes I took . . . or the fishermen . . . ?'

'No. Apparently not.'

'Anyway, I thought of writing, but then I thought – why bother? They'd be better off without me. Faith was right. After Ma died, we dumped everything on her.'

'Ralph is convinced that you're still alive.'

Jake smiled. 'Pa always had an amazing ability to believe what he wanted to believe.' His tone was affectionate. He looked at Guy. 'Has it occurred to you Guy, that we've done quite well just to survive?' Darkness pooled in the visible eye. 'Remember what we've lived through. And remember what we've lost. Spain . . . and France—'

'La Rouilly,' said Guy.

'And the people . . . that girl that Faith worked with . . . Nicole's RAF friend . . . Genya and Sarah—'

'Five years of Oliver's life,' muttered Guy.

'Ma,' said Jake. His back to Guy, he said, 'I remember someone once saying to me that the war was shuffling us up like a pack of cards. She was right, wasn't she? Only we've never managed to get back into the right order. And just think – just think what we have seen. What we *know*. Our generation – we've witnessed the unbearable. Auschwitz . . . and Hiroshima. How do you live with that?' He touched the eyepatch. 'Some people manage to remain blind, of course, but I don't think that either you or I are capable of that.'

The wash of night air had cooled the room a little. Guy said tentatively, 'If they send me back to England . . . if you were to write a letter, Jake, I could post it. I could make sure that Faith knew that you were safe and well.'

'No,' said Jake.

'For pity's sake—'

'Not a letter.' Jake pressed his knuckles against his teeth. He looked up at Guy. 'You're to go to her. You're to go and see Faith – yourself, Guy, not a letter or a phone call. You're to promise me.' He stared fiercely at Guy. 'Promise, Guy.'

There was a silence. Guy thought of seeing Faith again, and his heart swelled with longing.

He stood up. 'And if I go to Faith,' he said, 'what shall I tell her?'

Jake smiled. 'Tell her that I'm happy. Tell her that I have everything I want.'

Guy glanced at the small, bare room, with its chair and cushions and battered suitcase. Then he shook Jake's hand, and walked back through the night to his club.

Ralph had taken to writing himself notes, because otherwise he forgot important things like eating and putting out the dustbins and meeting Harry and Ted at the Woolpack. He tended to lose the notes, though. Forgetfulness seemed to be an irritating and embarrassing concomitant of old age. Standing at the bus stop one morning he looked down at himself and realized that beneath his overcoat he was still wearing his pyjamas; he walked back to Heronsmead, thankful that no-one had seen him.

Faith, telephoning in the evenings, reminded him of things. Because she had a tendency to fuss, Ralph pretended to have remembered whatever she reminded him of, telling her, for instance, that he had eaten the ham she had cooked for him at the weekend, and not that it was greenly mouldering in the back of the larder.

She, too, left him lists: lists of telephone numbers of doctors and tradesmen, lists of the washed and ironed clothes she had left stacked in the airing cupboard, lists of the cakes and pies and preserves in the larder. Ralph threw away the telephone numbers – he had plenty of friends if he needed them, and he had always loathed doctors – and he lost all the other lists, rediscovering them with some surprise on the floor of the hen-hut, blotched with guano.

When the cold that he had caught eased off, Ralph decided to go on an expedition. He would go to Cromer, he thought. Though his destinations were not as far-flung as they once had been, he nevertheless still needed the adventure of the occasional journey. And besides, he had to buy a present for the baby. Faith had told him that there was to be a party at Compton Deverall in a few weeks' time, so Ralph had scrawled BABY'S PRESENT in very large letters on a piece of paper, and pinned it to the back door, so he could not possibly forget.

He put on his favourite old black overcoat (Faith had bought him a new one, but his old coat was like a dear familiar friend), wrapped his red muffler round his neck, and covered his head with his black hat. Then he walked along the track that led beside the salt marsh to the main road. The weather was cold but fine, and only a gentle breeze feathered the fronds of the reeds. Ralph thought, as he always did when he looked at the marsh, of Poppy. His forgetfulness touched only the present day, not the past. He remembered hearing the German aeroplane, and the crack of gunfire, and knowing. He remembered carrying her home, cradled in his arms. He remembered that the following day he had walked to the salt marsh, and tried to trace her footsteps along the path. He had needed to know whether, when the Messerschmitt had shot her, she had been coming home. He had needed to know whether, before her death, she had forgiven him. But the ground had been frost-hardened, as it was today, and had not kept the shape of her footprints, and after a while tears had prevented him seeing clearly.

In Cromer, Ralph bought tea and kippers and a pot of jam. He had forgotten his list, but he could live happily for the remainder of the week on tea and kippers and jam. He remembered that he must buy a present for the baby (Christabel Laura Poppy – quite charming), so he spent a happy half-hour peering into shop windows. At the back of a musty old junk shop he found a conch shell, pink and white and perfectly curling. When he held it against his ear he could hear the sea. The assistant wrapped it in tissue paper for him, and then he walked to the sea front. A few fishing-boats bobbed on the waves, but the beach huts, the whelk stalls and amusement halls were all closed for the winter. When, after half an hour's brisk walking, he decided that it was time for a cup of tea, Ralph discovered that the sea-front cafés were also closed. The cold had begun to bite; the blue of sea and sky was illusory. Ralph pressed on. He would treat himself to fish and chips, he decided. Fish and chips were one of this country's few decent culinary inventions. But the chip shops, too, were closed.

He caught sight of a group of youths on the far side of the promenade, and crossed the road to speak to them. 'I beg your pardon,' he said politely, raising his hat, 'but I wonder whether you could direct me to a café? All these establishments seem to be closed.'

They all wore shabby leather jackets and thin, close-fitting jeans. They reminded him, oddly, of the ranks of recruits he had seen outside the Gare du Nord in Paris, in 1914. Their hair was slicked back and shiny, and their thin faces were pinched with cold. One said, 'Half-closing, innit, Granddad,' but another began, in tones of extreme and unconvincing grandeur, to imitate Ralph ('I beg your *pahdon* . . . such a frightful place . . . all the blahsted servants . . .'), and then, turning to him, said, 'Nice hat, old chap,' and in a sudden darting movement, lifted Ralph's hat from his head.

'I say,' said Ralph. Though he tried to retrieve his hat, he was too slow, and it was kicked halfway across the road, like a football.

'I say, lads,' he said again, trying to smile, trying to reason with them, 'I know you're just having fun, but really, it's damnably cold.'

They did not seem to hear him. There was a roar of laughter, and a shout of, 'Come on, Jonesy – goal!' and his hat soared up into the air and landed on the shore. As he started across the road, Ralph thought he might tell them about the game of football he had once played in the Mexican desert, with a dried-out gourd for a ball, and the skulls of wild dogs for goalposts, but then one of the boys, lurching backwards, whooping with laughter, cannoned into him, and he found himself in the gutter, the contents of his string bag strewn halfway across the pavement.

A passer-by called out, and the boys scattered, running away down the promenade. A woman helped him to his feet and gathered up the remains of his shopping. The packet of tea had torn, scattering its contents like ash on the paving stones, and the jam pot oozed gorily into the gutter. The shell, which had travelled all the way from the Indian Ocean to this cold coast, was unmarked, though. The woman looked at Ralph anxiously and asked him if he was all right, and suggested a cup of tea to warm him up, but Ralph, who wanted suddenly and intensely to be back home, assured her that he was perfectly fine.

He fetched his hat from the beach, and brushed the sand from the brim, and walked to the bus stop. His legs were shaky, and the bus was late; waiting for it, he became cold. Throughout the journey, he felt exhausted and drained. The bus rattled and jolted, and Ralph cradled the conch shell on his lap. He would go home and light a fire, he thought, and listen to the wireless. And not go on another expedition for a long time.

Disembarking from the bus, he began to walk down the narrow road that led to the village. He had to walk slowly because his legs were still trembling. The day had chilled, and the blue skies of the morning had paled to pearly white. The sun was a small, gleaming disc of glass. There was not now a scrap of wind, and the gorse and the reeds and even the small birds that inhabited them were as still as if they had been frozen in a photograph.

Halfway home, he paused, gathering his breath. He did not feel ill, exactly, but he did feel rather peculiar. There was a sort of pressure in his chest, as though something was about to burst. His hands and his feet were terribly cold. He would have liked to put down his shopping bag, which seemed to have become very heavy, but his fingers, curled round the string handle, would not open. When he tried to walk on, the tightness in his chest worsened. Pain flowered in tight bands round his ribcage, and seared the length of his left arm. He sat down on the verge, gasping.

Ralph looked up. He could see the cottage, perched on the edge of the marsh. The sun had become very bright, like the sun at La Rouilly. Ralph stared at the sky. His nanny scolded him. 'Don't look at the sun, Ralph, it's bad for your eyes.' '*Bloody* woman,' muttered Ralph. 'Bloody bossy damnable woman,' he said out loud, and then he closed his eyes.

Faith started in the kitchen, sweeping away the thick grey ropes of spiders' webs, tearing out rotten cupboards and rusty pots and pans. Beneath the dirty linoleum she discovered encaustic tiles, small perfect squares of terracotta, cream and black. When the room was clean and empty, she painted the ceiling white and the walls turquoise. Though some of the other rooms were not yet habitable, though rainwater seeped in places through the patchy roof, she had nevertheless brought with her a few treasures of her own: a pair of celadon-green vases, a floral bone-china teaset. They matched perfectly the green and brown of the house. In her mind's eye she recalled belongings that she had owned years ago. A bracelet that she had bought in Marrakesh, a Spanish shawl that Poppy had given her. She could not remember when or where she had lost them. Mulgrave possessions scattered the Continent, she supposed, dimly retained in her memory like the oscillating tracks a snake made in the sand.

After lunch, she lit a bonfire in the garden, and watched the sparks soar, orange specks against a wintry sky. She decided that in the evening she would talk to Ralph about her house. He would be unenthusiastic at first but, she told herself, when he saw the house, he would love it. It was near enough to Heronsmead to visit both the churchyard and the beach every weekend, if he so wished. Ralph could have the large back bedroom that overlooked the garden, and she would clear out the small front room and use it to store her dresses. The Vionnet, the Schiaparelli, the Paul Poiret that she had discovered in France . . .

At five o'clock, Faith washed her hands and face in a bucket of water, locked up and drove away. She felt pleasantly exhausted; bouncing along the rutted track, she made lists in her head. She must find a plasterer and a chimney sweep, and someone to replace the missing roof tiles. She must search out the local tradesmen. They would need coal and groceries. She would engage a carpenter to make bookshelves, and explore junk shops, looking for suitable furniture.

She parked the van on the roadside, and walked down the grassy track that led to Heronsmead. She thought, and I must find someone to look at the drains, and I must ask Paddy if I've enough money in the bank to have a proper bathroom put in, and I must—

Opening the gate, she knew immediately that something was wrong. The unfamiliar bicycle parked against the wall; the front door, which Ralph never unlocked, gaping wide open. She began to run.

When they told her that Ralph was dead, that he had collapsed and died of a heart attack on the road beside the salt marsh, she said, 'Then there's just me now, isn't there? Everyone else has gone.' The village policeman, who had been waiting for her at Heronsmead, placed a glass of brandy into her cold hands and made her sit by the fire. She realized that she was shaking visibly, so she tried to still herself by forcing her knees together and pressing the soles of her feet into the floor.

The following day she spoke to the vicar, the undertaker, and the doctor. She made telephone calls and wrote letters, and seemed to drive endlessly between the village and Holt and Norwich, where she registered the death. She thought how ridiculous it was that you had months to organize a nice thing like a wedding, yet only a week or two for a funeral. And that you had to think about catering and hymns and filling in all sorts of dreadful forms when your mind was a soup of dislocated thoughts, and you forgot things as soon as people told them to you.

Heronsmead itself defeated her. As she opened drawers, their contents spilled to the floor. When she searched through cupboards, musty, moth-eaten clothes slipped from their hangers, smothering her. She tried to make a list of mourners to ask to the funeral. She could not remember the names of all Ralph's friends; she could not remember which were alive and which were dead. The telephone rang incessantly. 'There is a lovely passage by Gurdjieff, Faith dear' – an ancient, quavering Lodger – 'that you might feel is suitable for the service. I know Ralph wasn't a *disciple*, but I always sensed that he had *sympathies*.' After she put the phone down, Faith looked for her list. She thought that she had left it on the table, but it was not there now. She tried to remember what she had been doing before she had answered the telephone. She had been searching for Ralph's address book – if he possessed such a thing, which seemed, she acknowledged, rather unlikely. Or she had, perhaps, been making a cup of tea. She had made a great many cups of tea in the four days since Ralph's death, and had forgotten to drink most of them.

She went into the kitchen, which was strewn with dirty cups and broken biscuits from the packet with which she had sought earlier that afternoon to appease the vicar. Her list was neither in the washing basket nor the larder. The telephone rang once more: Annie, from Holly Blue, panic in her voice, telling her that the stock they had ordered had not yet arrived. Shut up the shop, close it down, Faith said, and fleetingly enjoyed the shocked silence. She put the phone down, and collapsed on the sofa. The tiny living-room was strewn with papers, cardboard boxes, raincoats and wellingtons. She had once been so *organized*, she thought despairingly. When she covered her face with her hands, she did not know whether she was weeping because of the mess, or because of Ralph. All the contents of the room, once so much a part of him, now alarmed her. The battered armchairs and old-fashioned sideboards seemed to suck her remaining vitality from her.

There was a knock on the door. She was too tired to move, and remained seated in the armchair, her feet curled beneath her, an old jersey of Ralph's wrapped round her shoulders. If I don't answer it, she thought, whoever it is will go away. She closed her eyes. She would take a nap, she thought, and when she woke up she would be able to find her list, or she would start a new one.

The knocking stopped. She was drifting off to sleep when she heard footsteps crunching on the cinder path at the side of the house. She thought *Ralph*, and then woke up properly, and wanted to weep again.

From the back door, Nicole called out, 'Faith! Are you there? It's me!'

Ralph's funeral took place at the end of the following week. Nicole organized everything. Nicole convinced the vicar that Ralph, though not a conventional believer, was fit to be buried beside his wife in the village churchyard. Nicole chose the hymns (' "Fight the good fight with all thy might" – that'll do for Pa'); Nicole spoke to the undertaker. If Ralph had ever noted the address of a friend on the back of a sweet wrapping, or scrawled a telephone number onto the flyleaf of a book, then Nicole discovered it, copied it down, and wrote or telephoned. Mourners packed the tiny village church for the funeral. Afterwards, Nicole shepherded the congregation back to Heronsmead, where Elizabeth was putting the finishing touches to a buffet lunch.

The Lodgers were consuming vast quantities of sandwiches, cakes and beer when Elizabeth bent and whispered: 'She's awake now, Auntie Faith. Come and say hello to her.'

Faith followed Elizabeth upstairs to where Christabel lay in her carrycot in Ralph's bedroom, eyes wide, mesmerized by the sprigged wallpaper. Elizabeth stooped and picked up her daughter.

'Let me introduce you to your Great-aunt Faith, darling.' Carefully, she placed the baby in Faith's arms. 'I must go downstairs for a while if you don't mind keeping an eye on her, Auntie Faith. Last time I saw him poor Daddy was being buttonholed about agricultural subsidies by a simply terrifying Italian count.'

Faith sat down in an armchair, the baby cradled in her arms. She heard the door close behind Elizabeth. She suspected that Lizzie was trying to be tactful, that Lizzie had seen the tears shining in her eyes. She did not know why she was crying – for Ralph's loss or for the almost forgotten delight of holding a very young baby – but she did know that she was glad of this small oasis of calm in a succession of days that had been both harrowing and exhausting.

She wiped her eyes on her sleeve and looked down at Christabel, gazing with wonder at the curled fingers, with their miraculously small shell-like nails, and the scalloped upper lip, with its tiny sucking blister. Such pale, miniature perfection. Dark blue eyes met hers, paused for a moment, and then drifted away. Still sometimes she dreamed of having a child of her own. The longing persisted, bubbling to the surface every now and then however ruthlessly she fought it down.

The door opened and Oliver came into the room. 'I brought another shawl. I thought she might be cold.'

Faith laid the back of her hand against Christabel's cheek. 'I think she's fine, Oliver.'

'Still.' He knelt beside his daughter. 'Lizzie said she sneezed. Perhaps she's getting a cold.' He looked anxious. 'Or a fever.' Oliver gathered Christabel up in his arms and took her to the window. 'She's quite pink. Do you think she looks pink, Faith?'

'She's fine, honestly, Oliver.' And then, to take his mind off his paternal concerns, she asked: 'Have you thought any more about what I said to you?'

He grinned fleetingly. 'Actually, I've set the ball rolling, so I hope you're not going to tell me you've changed your mind.'

He was such a curious mixture, she thought, of the vulnerable and the practical, the generous and the acquisitive. Though not so curious, she supposed, if one thought of Guy and Eleanor. The success of Oliver and Elizabeth's marriage had allayed her previous fears. Early days yet, Faith reminded herself, yet it seemed to her that his ambition and her idealism, which might so easily have fought against each other, had found common purpose in the preservation of the Compton Deverall estate, in their protectiveness towards their daughter, and in their obvious mutual desire.

He added, 'I've got a solicitor on to it. Says he'll get the paperwork done double quick.' He looked at her. 'You are sure, aren't you? I mean – it must be a wrench for you—'

She said firmly, 'I'm quite sure, Oliver. One needs to shake up one's life every now and then, don't you think?'

'Yes,' he said fervently. 'Oh yes.' He planted a kiss on Christabel's forehead, and then said, 'Oh, I almost forgot. I had a letter from Dad. Well – not a letter. A telegram. It arrived just before we left Compton Deverall.' The baby cradled in the crook of his arm, Oliver fumbled in his pocket. 'There was a message for you.'

Faith's heart beat a little faster. 'For me? Are you sure?'

He drew from his pocket a handkerchief, a dummy, a pen, a tiny knitted pink bonnet. Like a conjuror, she thought impatiently. He said, 'Bit of a muddle, really. We wanted to tell Dad about Ralph – they knew each other quite well once, didn't they? – but Dad seems to be in hospital somewhere, so I think the letters must have crossed, or got lost. Post's lousy there, anyway.'

'Your father's ill?' she said. This time, she thought, her tone of voice must have given her away.

But he did not seem to notice. When you are young, she remembered, the world orbits only round your own concerns.

'Nothing too awful, by the sound of it,' said Oliver.

Then, 'Found it!' he cried triumphantly, waving a scrap of paper. 'Here we are. It's a bit crumpled. Shall I read it to you, Faith?'

Nicole said, 'Taxis, David. Do you think you could phone for taxis?' It was four o'clock in the afternoon. Her feet ached.

'I could run them to the station, if you like. In relays.'

She shook her head. 'I need you here.'

He studied her, concerned. 'You look worn out. What can I do?'

She made herself smile. 'Just *organize* them, please, darling David. I'd forgotten how exhausting they are.'

Within half an hour, all the Lodgers had been despatched from Heronsmead. Elizabeth and Oliver had disappeared together upstairs (for a rest, Oliver had said, but Nicole doubted that), and Faith was asleep on the front-room sofa, which pleased Nicole, because it had seemed to her that Faith had slept hardly at all during the previous ten days.

Which left David and Nicole to sort through the wreckage in the kitchen. 'I'll wash up,' said David. He slung his black jacket over the back of a chair. 'And you talk to me.' He patted the cushioned chair by the stove.

'Dear David,' said Nicole. 'Always so commanding. So masterful.' She sat down.

David snorted, and began to fill the sink. After a while he said, 'What are your plans, Nicole?'

'Plans? After today, you mean?' She shook her head. 'I haven't a clue. You know I never plan.'

There was a silence. Then she said slowly, 'To tell the truth, David, I've no idea what I'll do. We have to clear the cottage, of course, but Faith and I have done a lot of that already.'

'What'll happen to it?'

'Aunt Iris is going to sell it. It'll be odd, won't it, to think of Heronsmead belonging to someone else. To think of it belonging to a stranger.' She looked at him, silhouetted by the window. 'The thing is, David, that I haven't been able to imagine further than today. The funeral, I mean. It seems such an ending. Such an enormous full stop.'

He put a last plate on the draining board and dried his hands on a tea towel, and went to sit on the chair arm beside her. She wept into his shirt. It was the first time she had cried since she had received from Faith the letter telling her that her father was dead.

She heard him say, 'I'm going to be masterful again, I'm afraid. I'm going to say that you should come back to Compton Deverall with me, Nicole.'

She blew her nose and looked up at him. 'For a holiday, you mean?'

'If that's what you want. Or—' He closed his eyes for a moment. 'Nicole, I have never, in all the years since you left me, asked you to come back to me. When you first went away, during the war . . . When you moved to America, or later, when you lived in France . . . I never asked you, did I?'

She shook her head.

'But I'm asking you now,' he said gently. 'Soon I'm going to take Oliver and Elizabeth and the baby back to our hotel, so that you and Faith can have some peace. But tomorrow I would like you to come back to Compton Deverall with me. To stay there, Nicole. To live with me once more.'

*   *   *

Nicole held out her hand. 'Look what I've found.'

Faith, sitting up and rubbing her eyes, looked at the photograph. The three Vanburgh girls, each with her pretty Victorian flower name, stared solemnly at the camera lens, remnants of a more ordered age.

'Ma,' said Faith, smiling. She still felt pleasantly drowsy. 'Ma and Aunt Iris and Aunt Rose.'

'They look . . . hopeful.'

'Ma looks very young. It must have been taken before the war. The first war, I mean. I wonder . . . if they'd known what was going to happen to them, what they would have thought.'

'Poor old Aunt Rose went mad. Iris told me. Apparently it's a dreadful family secret. As for Ma' – Nicole made a face – 'I can't imagine. She had Pa, and she travelled round the world, and she had three children—'

'Four,' said Faith. 'Don't you remember the baby in Spain?'

'Of course. Four.'

David, Elizabeth, Oliver and the baby had driven away to their hotel in Holt, leaving Nicole and Faith alone in the cottage. Faith glanced at her watch. She had slept, she realized, for almost four hours.

Nicole placed the photograph in a cardboard box. 'David has asked me to go home with him.'

'Will you?'

'I might do. I might *try*. I don't know whether it would work. It's rather frightening, really.' She looked up at Faith. 'But what about you?'

'I'll be fine. As soon as we've finished here I'll go to my house.'

Nicole looked doubtful. 'I don't like to think of you alone.'

Strange how hard it was to voice even to her sister her newly discovered hopes. Strange how hard it was to believe that in the middle of despair one could find joy.

Nicole was still looking at her. 'What is it?' She narrowed her eyes. 'What's happened, Faith? You look—'

'I've something to tell you, Nicole.' The easy bit first, she thought. 'I've sold Holly Blue. I've sold it to Oliver.'

Nicole's eyes widened. She opened her mouth to speak, but Faith said quickly, 'The thing is, I haven't enjoyed it for ages. I thought it was what I wanted, but it wasn't. And the rat . . . the broken window . . . I didn't want to be driven out, you see. But then I realized at last that I'd had enough, and I thought of Oliver.'

'But the shop . . . I can't imagine Oliver running a shop.'

Faith laughed. 'He won't. He'll sell the lease and make a fortune by building something dreadful on the land. Soho is full of dreadful things nowadays. It's changed so much since Con and I began. And David has told me that Oliver is awfully good at making money out of land.'

'But what will you do, Faith?'

She said calmly, 'I shall do what I love doing. What I should have gone back to doing years ago. I'll buy and sell second-hand clothes. Only nowadays they call them *antique* clothes. I shan't have a shop. I don't want another shop. I'll travel for part of the year. You can find such wonderful things in North Africa, for instance – djellabas and kaftans and marvellous jewellery.' She smiled. 'I'm taking a risk. I don't know whether it'll work out, but it'll be an adventure, won't it?'

'Everyone needs adventures.' Nicole patted Faith's knee. 'Is that why you look happy again? Because you're not tied to the shop any more?'

Faith stood up and went to the window. On the sill lay a box of old jewellery. She let a strand of Venetian glass beads, which she could remember strung round Poppy's neck, trail through her fingers. She said, 'It's not just that. Oliver had a telegram from Guy, you see. He's coming home.'

'When?'

'He didn't say exactly. But soon. He won't be going back to Africa because he's been unwell. He's coming home to stay, Nicole.'

'And . . . ?' whispered Nicole.

'And he's coming to see me.' Her smile felt rusty with disuse. 'He asked Oliver to tell me that he's coming to see me. He says that he has a present for me.'

'What sort of a present?'

'I can't imagine. I've no idea.' It would be enough, Faith thought, just to see Guy again. She hugged her arms round herself and looked out to where the dying sun cast rainbow colours on the wet grass.

'Will he know where you are?'

'Oh, I think so.' Faith remembered the room in which she and Guy had made love, their bodies dappled with dust and sunlight. 'Yes, I think so. Guy was always good at finding his way, wasn't he, Nicole?'

That evening, they made a bonfire. They had intended to build it in the back garden, but then Nicole said, 'The beach, Faith, the beach. I know it isn't Pa's birthday, but we must go to the beach.'

They made a fire of driftwood on the shingles, and heaped upon it old letters, clothes, broken sticks of furniture, threadbare blankets. Each spark, dancing up into the sky, seemed to Faith to contain a memory. That chair, with its rickety leg, was the one on which Poppy had sat in the kitchen, peeling vegetables; that tie, fraying at both ends, she herself had bought for Ralph in Bordeaux. The flames consumed the memories and soared, fiery jewels, into the inky sky. Nicole, wearing her moth-eaten mink, stood beside her, and the sea lapped the shore. Nicole's arm threaded through Faith's, and Faith thought, *Mulgrave Rules: stick together whatever the cost*. The tears that trailed down both their faces glittered like gold.

Leaving the aeroplane, walking across the tarmac at London Airport, Guy, in spite of the cold of an English spring, was aware of an utter delight. The early morning mist washed over the roofs of the houses, painting them with silver; above, the pale disc of the sun was obscured by clouds. Guy dug his hands into the pockets of his overcoat, filled his lungs with chill air, and felt almost drunk with the relief of coming home.

A taxi deposited him in the centre of London. Guy booked into an hotel, dumped his baggage, and then caught the tube to Soho. Turning the corner into Tate Street, his heart lifted as he walked past the betting shop, the dubious bookshop, the jazz club. As he reached Holly Blue, cars roared by and pedestrians jostled him. Yet for Guy, history seemed to twist in on itself, a disturbing Moebius strip of time, plunging him back to the year of 1940, and the Blitz. The roof of the house in which Faith had once lived had disappeared. The building was naked, empty, open to the elements.

There was no glass in the windows, and the curtains, grey with grime, flapped in the wind. Roof tiles and bricks were heaped on the derelict land beside the house. He could almost imagine that he heard bombers overhead.

Guy walked round to the back of the shop. The noise was deafening. Hammers thudded against beams, tiles crashed two storeys to the ground. He had to shout his question to a labourer who was perched on a jagged lip of brickwork.

'Haven't a clue, mate!' the man yelled down. 'Started demolishing the place a week ago – none too soon, by the state of it.'

As he headed back to the street, Guy's mind was oddly blank. Since he had discovered Jake Mulgrave in Dar es Salaam, he had pictured this moment: returning to London, making his way to the shop, seeing Faith. He would tell her that her brother was alive – his gift to her – and then somehow, miraculously, everything would be all right. And yet it was not all right. Holly Blue no longer existed. Faith no longer lived in the flat above the shop. He did not know where to find her.

In spite of the chilly weather, he felt suddenly hot. His hands shook; there was sweat on his forehead. Not *now*, Guy said to himself angrily, and went into the first café he could find. There he ordered tea and something to eat, and shovelled down half a dozen pills. He was unsure whether the food or the medicine had done the trick, but after a while the determination and certainty that had sustained him during his weeks of illness, and for the length of the exhausting journey from Africa, began to return. He thought of Ralph. Ralph would know what had happened, where she was. After he had left the café, Guy headed for

Liverpool Street station. On the train journey he dozed, waking at Norwich in time to change to the branch line to Holt. It had begun to drizzle, a fine silky rain. Disembarking at Holt, Guy searched for a taxi, but found none. He saw a bus and dashed across the road, calling up to the conductor.

The bus lurched and jolted for half an hour, and then Guy disembarked at the triangle of grass where, years ago, he had once met Faith. Walking up the narrow road beside the salt marsh, he was reminded, incongruously, of Africa. The whispering of the reeds brought back to him the whispering of the tall grass; in the distance a seabird shrieked, and the hair on the back of his neck prickled.

He had never before visited Ralph's cottage. He almost missed the path that led from the road through a narrow gap in the thicket of willow. Brambles clawed at him, and his shoes slithered in the mud. Soaking grass wrapped around his ankles. Reaching a five-bar gate, Guy saw the name, *Heronsmead*, painted on the uppermost strut. Yet, before he had even opened the gate, he suspected that this journey, too, had brought him to a dead end. The untended garden, the empty washing line, and the absence of smoke issuing from the chimney all made him wonder whether the cottage, too, had been deserted.

He hammered on the front door with his fist, his ears strained for the sound of footsteps. Ralph's hearing may have dulled, Guy reminded himself, or he may be arthritic. He tried to work out how old Ralph was, and estimated, with a sense of shock, that he must be in his mid-seventies. After a while, he wandered round to the back of the house. An intermittent tapping noise told him that the back door was unlocked, banging against the jamb. He pushed it open. The kitchen stove was cold, and there were no jars on the shelves, no plates on the draining board. The rooms were bare of furniture, and the chill dampness of the small building suggested that the house had been uninhabited for some time.

He thought once more of Holly Blue: the peeling away of the layers – roof, walls, windows – as though someone was trying to erase or alter the passage of a life. Holly Blue and Heronsmead, both empty, both deserted. What had prompted Faith to undergo such an upheaval? The elation that had accompanied his return to England had disappeared, and he thought, with a sudden chill of fear, that they had perhaps gone abroad again, that father and daughter had chosen to return to the gypsy way of life of Faith's childhood. Jake had been mistaken, Guy thought. I have left it too late. I expected everything to remain the same in my absence, but it has not, of course, everything has changed, and I have left it too late.

Yet, as he walked away from the deserted cottage, a different explanation occurred to him. When he emerged from the narrow track and regained the main road, he looked around, trying to recover his bearings. Glimpsing the thin needlepoint of a spire, he headed for the church.

In the graveyard he found them, Ralph and Poppy, together again. He sat down on a bench and pressed the palms of his hands against his face as tears trickled through his fingers. He remembered standing at the roadside near Bordeaux, thumb outstretched, full of alarm at being penniless and passportless in a foreign country. He remembered Ralph drawing up beside him in a battered old Citroën van, and offering him a lift. In no time at all Ralph had extracted from him both his present impasse and much of his life story as well. Ralph had insisted Guy accompany him to La Rouilly, and at La Rouilly he had met Poppy, and he had met Faith.

He remembered, too, losing his own father. His sense of being all at sea, a little boat lost in a featureless ocean. *Adrift*, Jake had said. He could only begin to imagine what Ralph's death must mean to Faith. As the shock of his discovery began to retreat a little, leaving him able to think again, Guy's determination to find her redoubled. She should not have to bear this alone. And, even if he could not return Ralph to her, the news of Jake's survival must lighten the darkness. Whatever solace she would accept, he would offer. But, dear God, where *was* she? It occurred to Guy to do what he should perhaps have done before leaving London: telephone Oliver at Compton Deverall and discover the whereabouts of Lizzie's Aunt Faith.

But he seemed to hear her voice then, whispering through the years. *It's a quest . . . Something I have to do alone for the good of my soul.* And he remembered the house in the woods.

Guy walked back to the main road. No bus appeared, so he stuck out his thumb and hitched a lift in a lorry back to Holt. There, he hired a car. He drove south at first, parallel to the coast, the glittering sea to one side of him. And then inland, through narrow lanes banked with high hedgerows. He thanked Providence that he had always had a good sense of direction, a good memory.

It was dusk when he reached the avenue of beech trees that led to the house. He parked the car at the opening of the track, and walked the rest of the way on foot. It seemed more appropriate, somehow. One should make such a quest on foot. If he had been younger and healthier, he might have travelled the last few yards of his pilgrimage on his knees. Just for a moment, as the dim shape of the building pierced the bright green of the tightly furled leaves, his courage faltered. But then, as he emerged from the shadow of the trees, and saw the upstairs window, and the woman moving behind the glass, he knew that he had found his way at last, that he had come home.

The small, whitewashed room was filled with dresses. Their colours – deep emeralds, glimmering sapphires and gorgeous crimsons – surrounded her. She reached out a hand and touched a velvet sleeve, a fold of silk.

When she looked out of the window, she saw him. A small, dark figure heading up the avenue of trees towards the house. A long time ago she had waited for him; this time, Faith thought, she had not waited, she had continued to live her life, and still he had come. They had moved endlessly across oceans, she and Guy, their journeys sometimes coinciding, their paths crossing and then drifting apart. Storms had divided them, and tempests had shaken them from their set course. Yet she had followed through the years the compass of her heart, keeping to the path that the stars had ordained.

She trusted that they had found, at last, a favourable wind. Flinging open the window, she leaned out, and called his name.

THE END